COULD IT BE POSSIBLE
SHE WANTED TO BE KISSED?

By a notorious rake like the marquess no less? No, that was preposterous. Unthinkable. Lady Pamela Hancock could not, would not sink that low.

"Stop this at once," she heard herself say in a small, unconvincing voice. But she made no move to struggle, and the marquess merely laughed. The sound of it washed over her, caressing her skin, making her body tingle in odd places.

And suddenly he was doing it. His lips touched hers, gently at first until she felt the resistance go out of her, and then he opened his mouth, and Pamela was unprepared for the rush of heat that enveloped her. The brush of his tongue against her teeth, the gentle probing, the warm, wet sensation as he explored her mouth. All of it left her dizzy and light-headed.

An
Inconvenient
Wife

Patricia Oliver

A SIGNET BOOK

SIGNET
Published by the Penguin Group
Penguin Putnam Inc., 375 Hudson Street,
New York, New York 10014, U.S.A.
Penguin Books Ltd, 27 Wrights Lane,
London W8 5TZ, England
Penguin Books Australia Ltd, Ringwood,
Victoria, Australia
Penguin Books Canada Ltd, 10 Alcorn Avenue,
Toronto, Ontario, Canada M4V 3B2
Penguin Books (N.Z.) Ltd, 182–190 Wairau Road,
Auckland 10, New Zealand

Penguin Books Ltd, Registered Offices:
Harmondsworth, Middlesex, England

First published by Signet, an imprint of Dutton NAL,
a division of Penguin Putnam Inc.

First Printing, May, 1998
10 9 8 7 6 5 4 3 2 1

PROLOGUE

The Wager

London, May 1817

"I say, old man, no need to look so glum," a slightly thick voice called from the end of the dinner table. "Marriage ain't the end of the world, you know."

This sally was greeted by hoots of ribald laughter and a number of bawdy comments from the other guests.

Robert Stilton, Marquess of Monroyal, cast a jaundiced eye at the speaker, a man he had always considered to be full of excellent good sense. Until recently, he had even counted Lord Gresham among his closest friends.

"Right you are, Robert," Ned Hart cut in with his boyish grin. "Can't say I regret a moment of my own marriage to Sophy. And I have yet to hear my esteemed brother-in-law complaining about his lovely Cassandra." Hart winked suggestively at the Earl of Mansfield, who gave the young man a dismissive glance and motioned to the servant to fill his glass.

As he allowed his gaze to wander over his boisterous dinner companions, the marquess felt his spirits sink. For the first time in his six-and-thirty years he felt the weight of his advancing age. Gresham's careless words seemed to ring the knell of doom on the life he had thought to enjoy until the day—far off in the distant future—when he stuck his well-worn spoon in the wall. To listen to Gresham declaring in favor of marriage made the marquess feel positively nauseated.

Of the group of gentlemen—most of whom belonged to that loose fraternity of friends known as the Corinthians—gathered round the table at White's that evening. Robert Heathercott, Lord Gresham, was perhaps the only one who had ever seriously rivaled Monroyal's reputation for unrestrained womanizing and debauchery. They had been two of a kind, the two Roberts. A pair of bored hedonists, blessed with classical good looks, rank, and fortune, who made it their life's goal to wring the last ounce of pleasure from London's glittering *beau monde*.

A faint smile twitched at Monroyal's thin lips as he remembered how he and the Marquess of Gresham had, over the years, indulged in every outrageous wager, lost and won vast sums of money in every gambling hell in Town, and cut a seemingly endless swath through the boudoirs of married ladies as bored and immoral as they were themselves.

They had become masters in the fine art of dissolution, envied and aped by every moonling fresh down from Oxford. But Gresham's unexpected marriage to Lady Sarah Stanton, a vividly beautiful widow from Devon, had put paid to that idyllic existence. Monroyal was still reeling from the shock of it.

And now young Hawkhurst was about to get himself riveted to an obscure baronet's daughter from Yorkshire. It did not bear thinking about.

Monroyal had not wanted to attend the impromptu dinner at White's to celebrate this new disaster. He had counted Major Hawkhurst, the Duke of Wolverton, as one of the more promising rakes among the young men whose company he found stimulating. But now Hawk, too, had fallen prey to Cupid's arrow.

The marquess glanced down the table to where the duke sat nursing his first glass of wine of the evening. Guy Hawkhurst had thrown himself into a frenzy of debauchery when he returned from the Peninsula several years ago. But now the younger man appeared cold sober, the marquess thought disgustedly.

Impatiently, he motioned to one of the hovering servants, who hastened to refill his glass. Like Wolverton, he had not done justice to the Club's excellent French Burgundy, and failed to appreciate the raucous repartee de rigueur at these bachelor celebrations. He raised his glass and drank deeply. But even as the fragrant wine slipped smoothly down his throat, Monroyal experienced a sinking sensation in the pit of his stomach. No amount of spirits, he realized with a maudlin certainty, would cure the growing sense of loneliness that threatened to engulf him.

Unlike Hawkhurst, Monroyal had no innocent bride to wean him from his frivolous pastimes. He had no use for innocents in any case, he reminded himself. The endless parade of simpering misses thrust into his notice by marriage-minded mamas during each successive Season had disgusted him long ago. He no longer wasted a glance on any of them. No virgin bride would play a role in his future, he thought cynically.

"You should try it, Robert."

Monroyal raised his eyes from his glass as the softly spoken words intruded upon his musings. The Earl of Mansfield was gazing at him steadily from across the table. There was a world of understanding in that dark gaze that touched areas of his heart the marquess had thought buried and forgotten.

"Seriously, old man," the earl continued in his rich, deep voice, "it is time you stopped sulking and joined the rest of us in the rites of Aphrodite. Admit it, Robert, that was a damned stupid wager you made ten years ago, but there is nothing holding you to it except pride. And five thousand pounds, of course, which you can well afford to lose."

Sulking? The marquess bristled and glared at his friend. The earl's reproach opened a flood of memories he would rather forget. It was unfair of Mansfield to remind him of sweet Cassandra Drayton, now Countess of Mansfield, the only innocent who had actually tempted the marquess to break the vow that had been recorded in the books at White's as one of the more bizarre wagers of that long ago Season.

"What wager is this, Raven?" Lord Hart demanded loudly of his brother-in-law, causing a lull in the conversation.

"You were still in lead-strings, Ned," Mansfield replied shortly, obviously reluctant to discuss the issue.

But the other diners refused to let the subject die.

"True enough, Raven," an elegantly dressed gentleman with a rotund, jolly face took up the topic. "And Ned was certainly in his infancy. What was it, Robert? Ten . . . twelve years ago at least. Perhaps more. What age are you now? Forty, is it?"

"I am six-and-thirty," Monroyal corrected him sharply.

"Is that *all*? My dear chap, I had quite thought you to be more advanced towards . . . But be that as it may," the Honorable Willoughby Hampton continued merrily, "our dear Robert was particularly averse to marriage in his heyday, and vowed that no virgin would trample his heart in the dust."

"Tiresome things, females," a slurred voice contributed from the end of the table. All heads turned towards the speaker, and the Earl of Kimbalton raised his glass in a mock salute.

"That did not stop you seeking one out in a hurry when the dowager insisted you offer for one of those whey-faced Benington sisters," cut in Hampton with a sly grin. "Now that would have been a disaster of the first order, old boy. I barely escaped getting leg-shackled to one of them myself."

"You have barely escaped parson's mousetrap half a dozen

times since I came down from Oxford, Willy," Ned Hart pointed out in an amused voice.

"Yes," agreed Lord Gresham. "We have all ceased counting the broken hearts you leave scattered behind you, Hampton."

"Look who is talking of broken hearts," Hampton scoffed. "The ground around Gresham House is littered with them."

"Ah, but none of them were innocents, my dear Willy, and hence far less dangerous to a man's freedom."

"Unlike Monroyal here, our Willy attracts innocents like bees to honey," Mansfield remarked, flicking an amused glance at the marquess. "Undoubtedly it is his innate charm that makes him appear harmless."

"Who says I am harmless?" Hampton spluttered, his cheerful face creased with a frown.

"They do not call you Sweet Willy for nothing, old man," Hart exclaimed in high good humor. "Monroyal could learn a thing or two from you."

The marquess made a moue of distaste. "I have no wish to further my acquaintance with anything that smacks of innocence," he said coldly. He was getting bored with the subject, and wondered how soon he might reasonably take his congé.

"You will soon be the only one of us left unwed, Robert," Mansfield said gently, his eyes full of dark shadows.

The marquess had the uncomfortable impression that his friend pitied him. Mansfield could well afford to, of course, since he was married to Cassandra. The thought of her could still twist Robert's insides into knots. Not for the first time, he wondered how much Raven knew or guessed about his friend's feelings for his wife. How much had Cassandra confided to him about that aborted encounter at Seven Oaks in Kent? Had she told her new husband that the notorious Marquess of Monroyal had practically begged her to run away to Paris with him?

"Are you forgetting me, Raven?" Hampton cut in abruptly. "The last time I checked, I was still unwed, as is David Laughton." He waved at the tall, sardonic-looking gentleman of military bearing who sat beside the guest of honor.

Lord Gresham gave a crack of laughter. "Laughton is a widower and does not count. But your turn will come sooner than you imagine, Willy. Any day now we shall be sitting around this very table, celebrating your nuptials, old man."

Hampton gave a snort of disgust. "I would not waste any blunt on it, Gresham," he said huffily. "Monroyal is more likely to be snared by one of his despised virgins before anyone will see me walking down the aisle."

"And since that will never happen," the marquess remarked in a bored voice, "you can count on remaining a bachelor for the rest of your natural days, Hampton."

"Are you telling us that your wager is still in force, Monroyal?"

The marquess glanced at the speaker, and the skin on his neck pricked with apprehension. Simon Weatherby, the Duke of Ashford, had a devilish glitter in his dark eyes and a challenging grin on his face. Monroyal had known Beau Weatherby for years before the duke's recent accession to his uncle's title, and the Beau's well-earned reputation as a dyed-in-the-wool gambler was no secret to the *ton.* But Monroyal had heard rumors that marriage to his cousin's beautiful widow and the birth of his first son had settled Weatherby down until he was a mere shadow of his former flamboyant self.

The marquess shuddered. This revolting fate would not catch up with him. No, he vowed under his breath, not if he had any say in the matter. That wager of so long ago was *definitely* still in force. Perhaps he had been in his cups at the time—he did not recall the exact circumstances—but it expressed one of the basic principles upon which he had founded his life. The aversion to innocence in all its forms had become second nature to him, and the marquess used it as a shield to keep marriageable females at bay.

"Well?" Weatherby insisted, seconded by several others whose interest had been piqued by the mention of a challenge.

"Never doubt it for a moment, Beau," the marquess drawled with a slight smile. "You may double the stakes, too, if you wish. It is all the same to me. This is one wager I cannot lose."

"Ten thousand pounds?" Lord Hart's voice was hushed with awe.

"You are tempting fate, Robert," Mansfield warned from across the table, his gaze troubled.

The marquess shrugged. He had tempted fate before and usually emerged victorious. He did not doubt his ability to do so once again.

There was a sudden hush around the table.

Beau Weatherby cleared his throat audibly. "A wager you cannot lose, eh? A rash challenge to the gods if ever I heard one, Robert. If the wager concerned a horse, I could understand your confidence, old man. You have some prime bits of blood in your stables. But we are dealing with females here. Or should I say one particular female who is destined to leg-shackle you one of these days?"

"Too many of us at this table know the power of Cupid's dart," the Earl of Kimbalton remarked somberly. "It is high time he struck you down, too."

"Speak for yourself, Giles," the marquess retorted, beginning to enjoy the repartee. "Just because you have allowed Lady Kimbalton to talk you into digging up your ancestral Park to plant rose-trees does not mean that we should all be so faint-hearted."

"Harriet has plans for rose-gardens in the front prospect, too," Kimbalton said in a dreamy voice. "And I object to being called faint-hearted for trying to please my wife, Robert. You should try it yourself one day. There is an odd satisfaction to it, believe me."

Monroyal gave a derisive snort of laughter. "You are besotted, Giles," he chided. "Can you honestly say that your Harriet does not lead you around by the nose?"

"There is not a shred of truth to that blasphemy," Kimbalton retorted, not noticeably put out. "And were we not celebrating Hawk's recent betrothal to an unexceptional young lady, I would call you out for that, Robert. Too cynical by half, you are. And one day you will regret it, believe me. Which reminds me," he added abruptly, "I must be off before it gets too late. Harriet wishes to return to Hampshire tomorrow. Something about a new shipment of roses."

"Why not forget all about this ridiculous wager and look about for a wife of your own, Robert?" Mansfield's voice cut through the laughter that greeted Kimbalton's revealing comment, and the marquess saw real concern in his eyes. "You will find that marriage can be remarkably comfortable, you know."

"I do not welsh on my wagers," Monroyal said shortly. He wondered briefly what marriage to Cassandra Drayton might have been like, but the thought brought too much pain with it, so he thrust it quickly aside.

"Well, if the wager still stands," he heard Weatherby drawl in an amused voice, "I suggest we make it our business to discover that fortunate female who will make our friend Robert eat his words."

"I second that," Lord Gresham agreed with alacrity, causing the marquess to cast him a reproachful glance.

"An excellent idea, Gresham." Hawkhurst added his voice to the clamor that had erupted at Weatherby's suggestion. "Robert has played Cupid to many of us in the past, I say it is time we returned the favor. And with ten thousand pounds to sweeten the pot, I am confident we shall come up with a suitable candidate."

The marquess allowed himself to relax as he glanced around at the flushed, expectant faces of his friends. "Very well. But only innocent females qualify," he reminded them. "No widows allowed." He grinned. The prospect of pitting his wits and survival instincts against the ingenious plots these gentlemen were bound to devise to trick him went a long way towards lifting the mood of melancholy that had plagued him all evening.

"I say, what a splendid idea," Willy Hampton chortled in high good humor. "What time limit are we talking about?"

The marquess smiled as several faces turned in his direction. Here was a heaven-sent opportunity to escape getting caught in the snare in which his friends intended to trap him.

"A year should be sufficient to prove to all the world that there is no female alive clever enough to bring me to heel, gentlemen," he drawled, conscious that he was boasting again. "If by this day next year I am still a single man, then I will be declared the winner, and you will owe me ten thousand pounds."

"Which you will—in that unlikely event—donate to the London Asylum for Unwed Mothers," Lord Gresham suggested. "A fitting tribute to the perversity of men of your ilk who shirk their responsibilities to womankind," he added with a derisive smirk.

The marquess regarded his friend in silence for a moment. Then he nodded. "Whatever you say, Robert."

After all, it would not be his ten thousand pounds the unfortunate women would enjoy, he reminded himself later, as his carriage conveyed him through the silent streets and set him down before Stilton House on St. James's Square.

Monroyal smiled cynically as he mounted the steps and handed his hat and gloves to the night porter.

Those ten thousand would be the easiest he had ever won. He looked forward to it.

CHAPTER ONE

Love Strikes

Hampshire, June 1817

Lady Pamela heard her father's heavy step in the hall long before the door to the music room swung open with a crash, and the Earl of Melrose stood silhouetted in the threshold.

"Pamela, I want you to reconsider removing to Brighton for the summer," he said, his familiar autocratic tone grating on her nerves as it often did.

She sighed, and paused in the middle of the difficult passage of the new *étude* she had been working on for several days. The piece was beginning to take shape, and Lady Pamela had hoped to complete this particular passage before nuncheon. Her father's appearance precluded any such hope.

A glance at her sole remaining parent convinced Lady Pamela that Lord Melrose was in one of his argumentative moods. She flexed her fingers and laid them in her lap, closing her mind to the barrage of words. It was usually best to abandon all creative activity when her father launched into one of his long-winded, often arbitrary perorations upon actions he had already decided to adopt.

Pamela sighed again, and looked down at the ivory keys of the elegant pianoforte that had once been her mother's. She had inherited her love of music from Lady Melrose, and the long hours of practice she had endured as a girl had forged a bond between mother and daughter that was as strong today, five years after her mother's death, as it had ever been. The *étude* had been conceived as a tribute to that memory, and Lady Pamela's only regret was that her beloved mother was not there to help her over the difficult passages.

"Pamela!" Her father's voice cut into her thoughts. "I am talking to you, child. I want you to remove to Brighton with me next week."

She wished he would not refer to her as a child. Her five-and-twentieth birthday had come and gone. She was definitely at her last prayers, as her father never failed to point out to her. Her one and only Season in London five years ago had failed to attract the kind of husband Lord Melrose considered acceptable, and she had used her mother's sudden death as an excuse to eschew any further sorties into the Marriage Mart.

"I thought we had agreed to spend the summer here at Melrose Park this year, Father," she said patiently. "Remember how impossible Brighton was last year when Aunt Rose descended upon us with all those dreadful grandchildren of hers. You said yourself that you would not tolerate another invasion of rambunctious schoolchildren and screaming toddlers, and Aunt Rose has been angling for another invitation since March."

She had not been able to write a single note of music during that nightmarish two months, Lady Pamela recalled, but she refrained from using this as an argument. Her father disapproved of her passion for music. An unhealthy obsession he called it. Musical ability was desirable in a young lady, of course, as was competence with watercolors and embroidery, but composing was another thing entirely. Besides, Lord Melrose had pointed out in his autocratic way, there were altogether too many male composers in the world already.

"It is precisely your Aunt Rose who has convinced me to change my mind, my dear." Lord Melrose ceased his striding up and down the narrow room and came to a halt beside the pianoforte.

Lady Pamela met his gaze calmly. "Now you have intrigued me, Father," she murmured with a slight smile. "I never would have thought poor Aunt Rose could have achieved such a feat."

Oblivious of his daughter's gentle sarcasm, Lord Melrose clasped both hands behind his back and rocked back on his heels. Lady Pamela recognized the signs all too well. Her father had devised a plan that required her cooperation, and woe betide her peace of mind if she opposed him.

"Tell me all about it, Father," she suggested, relinquishing any notion of completing her *étude* that morning.

"I received a letter from Rose this morning," her father began, "and you are quite right, my dear; your aunt is anxious to spend another summer with us in Brighton. Luckily, it appears that both her daughters will be in Scotland with the children, so we shall not be forced to endure that infernal hubbub again. I have sent off a note inviting her to join us, but she particularly wishes for your company, Pamela, so I have told her you will accompany me."

He paused, and Lady Pamela felt a prickle of apprehension. There was something her father was not telling her. She gazed at him reproachfully.

"I see you have already made up your mind, Father, so I shall, of course, obey your wishes. But pray do not ask me to spend all my mornings at the modiste with my aunt, being fitted for frivolous gowns I shall never have occasion to wear. I have quite a dozen of them hanging in my clothespress from last summer that I have never worn. You know I detest such frippery, and the expense of getting rigged out in the first stare of fashion makes me shudder."

Lord Melrose waved a hand impatiently. "I would not begrudge a single penny of it were it to do any good, my dear. If you would only make up your mind to behave like a normal young lady of your station, Pamela, and cultivate a taste for fashionable pursuits, you might still acquire a suitable husband. But you have become a veritable recluse and bluestocking. Men do not offer for bluestockings, as I have warned you many times. They look for beauty, rank, and social graces. No man wants a wife with too much intelligence, child, believe me."

Lady Pamela believed him only too well. She had long suspected that her mother was not the only female forced to hide her light under the proverbial bushel in order to keep her husband content. Only with her daughter had Lady Melrose allowed her lively mind to blossom forth uninhibited. Unconsciously, Pamela had followed her mother's lead and masked her intellectual curiosity in her father's presence.

Lord Melrose's petulant complaint—one she had heard all too often—triggered a familiar warning signal. During the past year, Lady Pamela had dared to hope that her father had given up his ambition to see her married off and raising a family—as all her friends had done long since, he was fond of reminding her. But here he was raising the dreaded subject yet again. She eyed him anxiously.

"What else did Aunt Rose say?" she inquired, suspecting that her aunt was on one of her matchmaking rampages again.

Lord Melrose shot her a sharp glance. "You know your aunt," he said evasively, "she natters on about every last thing. She did mention, however, that Lord Summerset has taken a house in Brighton for the summer. Summerset is related to Rose from her husband's side of the family, you remember. It seems he lost his wife last year to influenza."

Lady Pamela smiled grimly. It was just as she thought.

"So dear Aunt Rose believes this Lord Summerset might be in need of a second wife to care for his children, does she?" she murmured wryly. "How many does he have now? Four at last count, I believe?"

"Rose says he has five," Lord Melrose remarked, falling innocently into his daughter's trap. "The last is a mere infant, of course. But that should not signify. He employs two nurses and a governess for the eldest boys."

Her father's unusual interest in Viscount Summerset's domestic arrangements told Lady Pamela all she needed to know. She sighed.

"I presume Lord Summerset's rank and fortune make him an eligible *parti*?" she remarked brightly. "No doubt he will select a chit just out of the schoolroom, although I suspect he must have passed his fiftieth year."

"Summerset is barely six-and-forty," her father declared with such authority that Lady Pamela knew instantly that he had made it his business to find out all that he needed to know about the widowed viscount. She waited for Lord Melrose to remark on the coincidence of Lord Summerset's presence in Brighton that summer and his fortuitous need for a second wife.

"A fine, strapping man," he remarked. "Your Aunt Rose suggested that it might be well worth our while to invite Summerset to dinner occasionally," her father added offhandedly. "Rose assures me that he makes a pleasant escort, and she has promised to help you select a new wardrobe so that you may appear to advantage, my dear."

Lady Pamela groaned inwardly and took the bit between her teeth. "Are you suggesting that I set my cap at this paragon, Father?" she inquired sweetly.

Lord Melrose bristled. "I am suggesting nothing quite so vulgar, child," he snapped. "All I ask is that you make a push to be agreeable to a gentleman who is eminently eligible, and who might be induced to overlook the unfortunate fact that you are not in the first flush of youth."

"Neither is Lord Summerset," she ventured to point out. "And then there are those five children. I suspect that being saddled with five of them would be enough to deter a female even more firmly on the shelf than I, Father."

"That is patently absurd, child," her father huffed. "You are still a fine-looking girl, and if you would stop mooning over that upstart Morton, who had the effrontery to approach me last year for permission to pay his addresses—"

"Sir Rodney happens to be the only gentleman who has ever done so, Father," Lady Pamela reminded him.

"Morton is no gentleman," came the sharp reply. "His great-grandfather married a mere tavern wench, and his mother is a vicar's daughter. How you came to encourage such a pretentious mushroom is beyond my comprehension."

"We run into the Mortons at every social event in the neighborhood," Lady Pamela pointed out patiently. "And I have never given Sir Rodney the least encouragement."

"Then perhaps you can explain to me why that rudesby has made you the focus of his impertinent attention," Lord Melrose demanded truculently.

"Perhaps Sir Rodney finds my conversation stimulating," Lady Pamela remarked with an edge to her voice. "He is very fond of music, you know."

Lord Melrose snorted in disgust. "The rogue finds your *dowry* stimulating, Pamela, as even you must admit. The Mortons have teetered on the edge of financial ruin for years. An advantageous marriage is the quickest way to pull the family out of that hole, but I refuse to allow *my* daughter to be the sacrificial lamb, and so I told that jackstraw when he dared to bring up the subject."

"I sincerely trust you said nothing so uncivil, Father," Lady Pamela said calmly. Her friendship with the dashing Sir Rodney had been the cause of many a heated argument with her irate sire. Years ago, when she was young and giddy, Pamela had flirted with the idea of an alliance with her handsome neighbor. She still remembered her disappointment when she discovered that Rodney was considerably less than the shining knight she had imagined him. She was glad they had remained friends, however, for she truly enjoyed his company. But when the baronet attempted, more recently, to convince her that she would be happier as his wife, Pamela found his argument seriously flawed.

It was indeed lowering to discover that her father had been right after all. Rodney needed money more than he needed a wife, but he was apparently willing to take one if she came with eighty thousand pounds. This disillusionment, coming on the heels of that disastrous first Season in London, convinced Lady Pamela that her world of music was infinitely preferable to the grand passion she had read about in romantical novels from the Minerva Press.

Only rarely did Lady Pamela regret her decision to eschew marriage. She had worked stubbornly to persuade her father to accept this decision and she had no desire to relinquish her freedom for one gentleman who merely wished to replenish his family fortunes or another who needed a mother for his five offspring. As far as she was concerned, Pamela thought, listening in silence to Lord Melrose's description of the amusements in store for her in Brighton, Lord Summerset might look elsewhere for a wife.

Warming to his subject, Lord Melrose continued his discourse on the benefits of matrimony all through nuncheon. Lady Pamela had begun to despair of being allowed to escape upstairs to her music, when the door to the small dining room swung open and a young gentleman strode in, looking for all the world as though he had stepped out of a fashion plate.

"Freddy!" she exclaimed, half in relief at the interruption to her father's disquisition, half in joy at the sight of her favorite cousin. "How good to see you again. We looked for you last month, my dear. Whatever kept you in London so far into June?"

She jumped to her feet and moved towards the exquisitely dressed young man, who opened his arms to receive her in an affectionate hug.

"Pamela, love, you look blooming as usual," Mr. Frederick Hancock announced in his easy, bantering manner. "But do be careful with my cravat, my dear," he added, glancing nervously at the gargantuan creation he wore round his neck. "It took poor Boodle over an hour to achieve that particular effect. Rather modish, what? I trust I find you well, Uncle," he said, moving forward to shake hands with Lord Melrose as the butler set another place at the table.

"No need for that, Bowles," Freddy said jovially, "I stopped off for a bite at the Golden Hind in Guildford."

Lady Pamela laughed and regarded her cousin affectionately. "If I know you, Freddy," she said gaily, "you are probably ready for another bite right about now."

Freddy cast a speculative glance at the dishes set out on the sideboard and grinned. "That ham does look rather good, Bowles," he remarked lazily. "Perhaps I will have a nibble or two. It's a long time before tea."

"Do sit down, Freddy, and let Bowles pour you a glass of claret," Lady Pamela said with a warm smile. She was extremely fond of her young cousin, and his frequent visits to Melrose Park never failed to raise her spirits. Luckily, Lord Melrose also had a soft spot for his eldest nephew and heir, and Pamela had often suspected that her father would not have minded changing places with his brother, who had produced a healthy number of boys over the years.

"Glad to see you, m'boy," the earl was saying, his tone jovial. "Had you come next week, you would have found the Park empty. Pamela and I have agreed to spend a month or two in Brighton."

Freddy regarded his cousin, one eyebrow cocked. "I understood you to say that you would be fixed at the Park for the summer, Pamela."

Lady Pamela shot him a speaking glance. "We have since changed our minds," she murmured. "Aunt Rose is pining for the seaside again, and Father has agreed to humor her. We leave on Tuesday, and I do hope you can accompany us."

"Yes, I am counting on you to join us, lad," the earl remarked between forkfuls of Yorkshire ham. Well versed in the ways her father's mind worked, Lady Pamela realized that his seemingly casual comment was more in the nature of a command. Her cousin evidently thought so, too, for he winked at her.

"That is an excellent idea, Uncle," he exclaimed. "In fact, the main purpose of my visit today was to persuade you both to accompany me to Brighton." He paused, grinning self-consciously when his uncle and cousin stared at him in surprise. "There is someone residing there I am anxious for you to meet."

"Ah, Freddy," Lady Pamela teased, "do not tell me you wish to drag us to another of those barbaric pugilistic affairs you are so addicted to. I shall not easily forget the spectacle of two grown men battering each other senseless. Father enjoys these sporting events, but I must beg to be excused, dear. One such bloody encounter is quite enough for me, thank you."

"Nothing of the sort, Cousin," Freddy assured her. "Although there is a rumor that Jackson has agreed to referee a rematch between the champion and that challenger from the colonies he trounced last year at Guildford."

"In Brighton?" the earl inquired, an eager gleam in his eyes. "If it is not too late in the Season, we shall certainly attend, Freddy. I shall insist upon it."

"Delighted, Uncle," Freddy responded with alacrity. "I hear the champion is in fine fettle, and—"

"Freddy!" Lady Pamela interrupted ruthlessly. "You were about to tell us why you want us to accompany you to Brighton. What folly are you up to now?"

"No such thing, Pamela," her cousin exclaimed. "Why do you always assume I am involved in some childish prank or other?

Need I remind you that I reached my majority two months ago
and am prepared to settle down in earnest."

Lady Pamela could not resist laughing at her cousin's expression of offended dignity. "Oh, I know your age well enough,
Freddy, since your birthday falls so close to my own, but you cannot deny that you are always involved in such flights of fancy,
dear," she pointed out. "Like the time you drove down from
Guildford in that donkey cart, dressed in the suit of armor you
borrowed from the Duke of Wexley's castle. You were lucky that
Father is a friend of the duke's; otherwise that caper might have
cost you a public thrashing."

"That is all behind me now," Freddy announced in an oddly serious voice. "I have reformed my ways and . . ." He hesitated, and
Lady Pamela noticed a fatuous gleam in his brown eyes.

"And what?" she demanded, sensing that her cousin was not
about to confess to one of his usual pranks. Unless she were much
mistaken, her dear Freddy was in an entirely different kind of
tangle.

"As I said," he repeated, "I am a changed man. I have decided
it is high time I settled down—"

"Settled down?" Lady Pamela echoed, in growing astonishment. "You are not referring by any chance to settling down in
the sense of getting married and setting up your nursery, are you,
Freddy?"

Mr. Hancock's boyish face turned a bright pink, and Lady
Pamela knew she had hit upon the truth of the matter.

"As a m-matter of f-fact, I do," he stammered. "That is exactly
w-what I do m-mean." He glared at her as though daring her to
contradict him.

"But Freddy, you are far too young to be thinking of marriage,"
Lady Pamela exclaimed. "Father, did you hear that? Freddy is
contemplating marriage again."

"Not everyone is so set against the wedded state as you are,
Cousin," Freddy said stiffly. "And this time is not like the others,
Pamela. It so happens that I met an absolute Paragon of Beauty at
Lady Berkford's alfresco concert a month ago," he added, his
voice softening noticeably.

Lady Pamela heard the reverence with which her cousin spoke
of this mystery female, and she stifled a smile. Poor Freddy was
in love again. He had done so with alarming regularity since he
had come down from Oxford, but she could not recall any of
these past conquests being described in such glowing terms.

"Plenty of time to think of getting riveted when you are older, my dear boy," Lord Melrose remarked, motioning to Bowles to serve him another slice of ham. While the butler was busy at the sideboard, the earl regarded his nephew affectionately. "Did not get shackled myself until I was over thirty," he remarked. "And then only took the plunge because Lady Melrose showed alarming signs of accepting Wexley's offer."

Lady Pamela swung around and stared at her father. He chuckled. "Never knew your mother might have been a duchess, now did you, m'love?" he said, looking highly pleased with his startling revelation.

"You cannot mean Regina Heathercott's father?"

"What other Wexley do we know?" he responded, evidently enjoying his daughter's discomfiture. "Gresham he was then, of course, and as handsome and rakish in his day as that son of his. But your mother chose me," he added unnecessarily. "Gresham was too rakish for her taste, she told me later. Her parents favored an heir to a dukedom, naturally, but your mother prevailed, and Gresham withdrew his offer."

Lord Melrose applied himself to his nuncheon with renewed vigor, apparently unaware that he had shaken his daughter to the marrow.

In the silence that followed her father's disclosure, Lady Pamela wondered why Lady Melrose had never confided this romantic episode in her past to her daughter. She must have loved her father very much to reject an offer from the dashing Marquess of Gresham, now the Duke of Wexley.

Why were there no handsome suitors vying for her daughter's hand? she wondered, vaguely aggrieved that no dark and dangerously attractive nobleman had yet come forward to sweep Lady Pamela Hancock off her feet. She would never be the Beauty her mother had been, of course. Pamela had long ago accepted that fact, but in light of her father's latest revelations, she wondered if her distaste for marriage might not have been far different had she been courted by truly eligible noblemen as her mother had been. Of course, now it was getting too late for such daydreams, but still . . .

Freddy's petulant voice cut into her reverie.

"I do not wish to wait until I am older, Uncle. I am quite sure in my own mind that this is the only female I will ever wish to carry my name. But naturally, I have not spoken my mind to the young lady before obtaining your approval, sir."

"Glad to hear you showed some sense there, Freddy m'lad," the earl remarked gruffly. "London is full of fortune hunters these

days, you know, and you are a prime candidate for some scheming hussy who has her heart set on being a countess. No small responsibility being a Melrose, believe me. Why even your cousin
has had some experience with fortune hunters, have you not,
m'love?"

"If you mean Rodney Morton, Uncle," Freddy broke in before
Lady Pamela could respond to her father's unpleasant reminder of
their recent argument, "you may rest easy on that score. Cousin
Pamela has more sense than to throw herself away on that jackstraw."

Lady Pamela gave her cousin a thin smile. "I am relieved to
hear you say so, Cousin," she said acidly.

"You were always full of good sense, Pamela," he responded,
evidently missing the sarcasm in her tone. "Unfortunately, not all
young ladies have your strength of character, my dear. That is
why I was obliged to remain in London until now."

"Dancing attendance on some chit, no doubt," Lord Melrose
mumbled from the head of the table. He regarded his nephew
from beneath shaggy brows, but his eyes belied his threatening
demeanor.

"She is no *ordinary* chit, Uncle," Freddy protested heatedly.
"She is the most beautiful and innocent of creatures. So trusting,
indeed, that I am anxious for her safety."

"And does this Paragon have a name, lad?" the earl inquired.

"Miss Prudence Erskin-Jones," Freddy responded reverently,
as though the very sound of the Beauty's name had thrown him
into a trance. "And I know you will agree, sir, when you meet her,
that she is a jewel worthy of the Melrose crown."

This extraordinary pronouncement was followed by a tense silence around the dining-room table. Lady Pamela stared at her
cousin in consternation. She had seen Freddy in love many times,
but never before had she heard him spout such utter rubbish about
any of the young ladies who had—to borrow his own expression—stolen his heart away.

She glanced at her father. The earl was also staring at his
nephew, his expression frankly skeptical.

"I do not seem to recall anyone by that name," Lady Pamela
began cautiously.

"Oh, that is understandable," Freddy said defensively. "Miss
Erskin-Jones does not move in the highest circles. The family is
not too plump in the pocket, I gather. They make no bones about
the fact that her father was the son of a minor baronet in
Northumberland. Near the coast somewhere, I believe."

"What brings them to London?" the earl demanded. "Or perhaps that is too obvious a question?"

Freddy glanced accusingly at his uncle. "Miss Erskin-Jones's beauty was quite wasted on the local swains, I imagine," he said severely. "Naturally her mother wishes to establish her only daughter creditably, so London seemed the obvious place to launch her into Society. Prudence has attracted a flattering amount of attention."

"That I can well believe," Lady Pamela remarked dryly. "But tell me, Freddy, are you the only gentleman she has dangling after her?"

Her cousin glanced at her suspiciously, but he answered readily enough. "Why, no. As a matter of fact, I had the devil of a time convincing her mother that most of Prudence's admirers did not have serious intentions in mind. The only really serious rival I have at the moment is a marquess, and unfortunately both Mrs. Erskin-Jones and her daughter are dazzled by his title and fortune."

"And this marquess, are his intentions honest?" Lady Pamela wanted to know.

Freddy looked uncomfortable. "Prudence swears they are, but I confess to doubts myself. He is a notorious rake, you see, but I have never seen such a charming fellow. Prudence fairly melts when he addresses her. Luckily, I have convinced her mother to remove her daughter out of his way."

"Where is she now, this Paragon?" Lady Pamela inquired, an uncomfortable suspicion taking root in her mind. "No, wait! Let me guess. Miss Erskin-Jones has removed to Brighton. Am I not correct, Freddy?"

Her cousin gave her a brilliant smile. "As a matter of fact, you are, Pamela. I thought that if I could persuade you to spend the summer there, too, you might take Prudence under your wing sort of thing. Keep that rake at bay if he should decide to pursue his interest with her."

Lady Pamela grimaced. "You are asking me to play the dragon, in other words, Freddy. Is that correct?"

Freddy had the grace to blush. "Only for the shortest possible time, Pamela," he pleaded. "As soon as Uncle James gives his approval to the match, I shall announce our betrothal, and that will keep the rogue away."

"I cannot say I like what I hear about this female, Freddy," Lord Melrose said. "Her breeding definitely leaves much to be desired if she is allowed to encourage London rakes to dangle after her."

"Miss Erskin-Jones is such an innocent," Freddy exclaimed in besotted tones. "She finds it almost impossible to believe that not every gentleman has her best interests at heart as I do."

"Indeed?" Lady Pamela remarked, unconvinced. "She sounds perilously like a brainless little widgeon to me, Freddy. And whatever is her mother thinking of to allow a notorious rake anywhere near her daughter? What do you think, Father?"

"Something havey-cavey about the whole affair," Lord Melrose muttered dismissively. "If you ask me, I would say let the marquess fellow have her. She appears to be far beneath your touch, Freddy."

"She is an absolute angel!" Freddy exclaimed. "All I ask is that you meet her, Uncle; then you would see how perfect she is."

"Very well," the earl agreed, evidently swayed by his favorite nephew's earnest entreaties. "We shall be in Brighton in any event. No harm in taking a look at the gel. You could arrange that, could you not, Pamela?"

Lady Pamela sighed. She had just been commissioned to play gooseberry to her cousin and his brainless little flirt. If her instinct served her well, she thought, Miss Prudence Erskin-Jones would turn out to be nothing but another of Freddy's flawed angels, all golden loveliness and charm on the outside, a dark, rapacious heart on the inside.

"Of course, Father," she said meekly, knowing it would be fruitless to argue. "But I have one question for Freddy before I step into this romantic tangle."

"Ask away, my love."

Her cousin was evidently under the naive impression that all obstacles to his future nuptials were about to melt miraculously away. Lady Pamela was not nearly so convinced.

"What is the name of the marquess who has set himself up as your rival for the lady's hand, Freddy?"

"Oh, I would hardly call him a serious rival, Pamela," Freddy responded blithely. "He is quite old, for one thing. Gray hairs and that sort of thing. All the crack, of course, but must be at least forty. Besides, I doubt he has serious intentions. The thing is he is so dashed charming and witty. Handsome too, in a patrician sort of way. Prudence is quite bedazzled with his address, and I fear she might be drawn into something foolish."

His boyish face lost its merry expression for a moment, and Lady Pamela wondered if her cousin realized that the man he had described sounded like a very serious rival indeed—especially for the attention of an impressionable girl from a small coastal village in the north of England.

"Well?" she prodded. "What is his name?"

"Oh, did I not say? He is the Marquess of Monroyal," Freddy blurted out, unaware of the effect that forbidden name had on his listeners.

Lady Pamela felt herself go pale. She glanced at her father. The earl's face had assumed his gargoyle expression, and Pamela knew that he was remembering the present marquess's father and the duel they had fought many years ago over Lady Monroyal's honor. She knew little of the encounter, since her father never spoke of it, but rumor had it that the late marchioness had been wildly indiscreet with Lord Melrose both before and after her arranged marriage to the marquess. The scandal which had— again according to rumor—rocked the *ton* to its foundations, had occurred long before the dashing earl had married Pamela's mother.

"I forbid you to have anything to do with that man, Pamela." The earl's handsome expression was harsh and forbidding as he glared at his daughter. "And if he is expected to be in Brighton, we shall cancel our own visit there."

Freddy stared from his cousin to his uncle in comical dismay. "Oh, there is no fear of that, Uncle," he blurted out impulsively— and with no great assurance, Lady Pamela suspected. "Monroyal is not the kind of man to put himself out for anyone, even a Paragon like my lovely Prudence."

Lady Pamela lowered her eyes, her heart bleeding for her ingenuous cousin. Summer in Brighton promised to be full of melodrama. A lovesick swain in the throes of a grand passion, a naive Beauty fancied by a dark, lecherous rogue, and of course, that Drury Lane villain himself. Lady Pamela shuddered involuntarily when she thought of the villain. Was he the sort of man to let the willing Beauty slip through his fingers? From the scandalous rumors about this particular marquess that had found their way into rural Hampshire, she doubted it. He would play out his part as all such men did.

In spite of her father's disapproval, Lady Pamela quite looked forward to the performance.

CHAPTER TWO

Prospective Bride

Brighton, July 1817

"Are you sure this is not some wild-goose chase, Willy?"

The Honorable Willoughby Hampton cast his friend a reproving glance. "Not getting cold feet are you, Robert? I have it on the best possible authority that the chit removed to Brighton a sennight ago."

"How can you be so sure?" the marquess demanded, perhaps for the fifth time since he had agreed to this ridiculous wager. "Believe me, I have better things to do with my time than go haring off to the seaside on a fool's errand."

"My second footman is walking out with the chit's abigail," Hampton responded calmly, his cherubic face breaking into a grin. "So I have it from the horse's mouth, so to speak."

The marquess merely grunted. The escapade that a week ago had appeared to be rather a good lark had lost much of its allure in the cold light of day. He had been suffering from a familiar onslaught of ennui, as he did every year as the London Season came to a close, and the wager—thrown out casually by Lord Gresham—had offered an amusing alternative to removing to his family seat for the summer and its interminable round of houseguests.

If truth be told, it had sounded suspiciously easy for a man of his expertise with the petticoat company to seduce the latest Beauty to dazzle London's *beau monde*.

Five hundred pounds if he mounted the filly within a month, his friend had suggested in the middle of a card game at Boodles a week ago. A paltry sum, the marquess thought, considering the amount he had wagered at Hawkhurst's celebration dinner at White's last month. But he had been bored, and there was no denying the girl was delicious.

And she was no virgin, Gresham had assured him, with obvious reference to the previous wager. The marquess had suspected as much after his first encounter with the chit. The latest Incomparable was a practiced flirt, but had resisted all attempts to draw her into an amorous liaison. She had even refused a chaste kiss from one of Gresham's younger brothers. Rumor was that her mother, who never left her side, had brought her daughter to Town to beguile a titled husband into overlooking the Beauty's past peccadilloes and elevating her to respectability in the peerage.

"Why Brighton?" he demanded abruptly. "Has that old dragon got some unfortunate blighter in her sights at last?"

"That was the *on dit* around Town last week," Hampton responded. "I could not tell you the victim's name, but you may be sure that he is plump in the pocket and moonstruck. I can almost find it in my heart to pity the poor fellow. The Beauty is bound to lead him a merry dance."

"Not until after I have won Gresham's wager, I trust," the marquess remarked lazily.

"I see no serious impediment to that endeavor," Hampton responded, his leprechaun grin reappearing.

"You are not betting against me, I gather?"

"Not on your life. In truth, I confess to a small side wager with Mansfield that you will finish the business and be back in London within the week."

"Raven is betting against me?" This piece of news surprised the marquess. "I shall have to call him out on this."

"Raven claims you are losing your edge, old man," Hampton explained with a laugh. "Although he did not actually say so, I got the impression Raven considers you past the age of seducing an experienced fortune hunter like our lovely Incomparable."

"And you, Willy?" the marquess inquired with deceptive mildness. "Do you agree with him?"

"Never!" Hampton exclaimed, throwing up his hands in mock horror. "No such sacrilegious notion crossed my mind, Robert. Perhaps you are rather more selective than you were as a raw youth, but far be it from me to suggest that you have slipped into your dotage, old chap. No such thing. Word of a gentleman."

It occurred to Monroyal, in the silence that followed this outburst, that his friend protested rather too much. The thought disturbed him. Was he truly in danger of becoming one of those lecherous old philanderers who haunted London's fashionable gatherings to prey on the young and innocent?

To dispel the unpleasant thought, the marquess flicked his whip expertly over the ears of his lead horses and guided them round an elegant traveling chaise that was making slow progress up a hill. As his curricle and four dashed past in a flurry of speed, Monroyal caught a glimpse of the crest on the highly varnished door of the chaise. Something about it jogged his memory, but he could not immediately identify it, and the chaise was forgotten as he crested the hill and came down the other side at a smart pace. Pulling down to a more sedate trot, he entered the small hamlet of Balcombe and turned into the yard of the Horse and Hound.

"What do you say to a tankard of ale to celebrate your confidence in me, Willy," he drawled, amused in spite of himself. "Then we had best get to Brighton and discover where the Beauty is staying." He tossed the ribbons to a young stable-lad who had appeared beside the curricle.

"She has an aunt here, or so my footman tells me," Hampton volunteered as the two men entered the taproom and set the innkeeper in a flurry of activity.

"And what about your own aunt, Willy? As I remember from the last time Raven and I came down with you, Lady Emmaline Stevens knew everybody here. Perhaps she can help us find the elusive Beauty."

Hampton grinned and took a long swallow of ale. "You can be sure that the advent of the Beauty will not go unnoticed, Robert. And if I know anything about that mother of hers, the chit will be flaunted at the Assembly Halls and along the Marine Parade as soon as she has changed her bonnet."

The marquess merely grunted and finished his ale, setting the pewter tankard down with a satisfied thump. He would finish this business in Brighton as quickly as possible and join his stepmother and his lively brood of halfsiblings at Stilton Grange without further delay. Last Christmas he had rashly promised to teach the boys to play cricket, and he suddenly felt an unfamiliar urge to play big brother again. He must be getting old, he thought cynically, if he preferred the company of four boisterous young lads to that of the female who had been unofficially recognized as this Season's reigning Beauty.

The thought nagged at him, but he brushed it aside and climbed into the curricle. As he guided his rested team under the stone arch and out onto the main thoroughfare, he glimpsed the chaise he had passed earlier waiting to enter the narrow passage into the inn yard. His practiced glance noted that the four horses were prime stock and showed little sign of having come far.

"I wonder whose carriage that is," he remarked idly, holding his team down to a sedate pace as they made their way through the busy streets. "I seem to have seen that crest before."

Hampton looked at him in silence for a moment. "Melrose, I believe, old man," he said with studied casualness. "Noticed it as we passed the carriage back on the hill." He paused for a moment, then continued with an embarrassed chuckle. "Not a crest I would forget had I been in your shoes, Robert."

Monroyal suppressed the angry retort that rose to his lips. He had not thought of those painful old memories in a long time. He did not want to remember them now.

"All that is in the past, Willy," he said coolly, wishing more than ever that he was on his way to Stilton Grange and not Brighton.

Now he had yet another reason for bedding the Beauty as quickly as possible and shaking the dust of Brighton from his boots. An encounter with Melrose or any of his family was an experience the marquess devoutly wished to avoid.

"I say we stop for a bite to eat at the Horse and Hounds," Freddy exclaimed as the Melrose chaise clattered into the small village of Balcombe. "Old Mrs. Tobin makes a scrumptious apple pie. And besides, I could use a mug of ale to whet my whistle. What do you say, Uncle?"

At her cousin's jovial suggestion, seconded by Lord Melrose, Lady Pamela shook off the sense of foreboding that had settled upon her as soon as they left the calm haven of Melrose Park. She was being missish, she told herself firmly. This sojourn in the seaside town was no different from the many others she had made over the years. Normally, she enjoyed the sea air and the informality that prevailed in the holiday setting. But this time she was not looking forward to it with any degree of pleasure.

Her attention was caught by an elegant equipage making its way out of the inn yard as they approached. The yellow-wheeled curricle was flamboyant, as was the team of glossy bays hitched to the sporting vehicle. Their coats gleamed in the sunshine, and their ears twitched nervously as they came abreast of the Melrose coach.

The driver was a tall gentleman whose broad shoulders, enhanced by a many-caped driving coat, made him look rather threatening. He would have made an excellent highwayman, Lady Pamela thought, amused at her own whimsy.

His companion, who glanced briefly in her direction, had an open, jovial face and wore a monstrous nosegay in his buttonhole.

She recognized him immediately as the gentleman who had danced with her at the first ball of her one and only Season in London. She had felt the veriest wallflower and must have looked like one, for none of the young bucks had approached her. She had been condemned to stand up with friends of her father's, pressed into service by the earl, she did not doubt. And then Mr. Hampton had suddenly materialized beside her, warm brown eyes twinkling in his round, Puck-like face. He had appeared genuinely interested in dancing with her, Pamela remembered, and she had never forgotten that one kind gesture in an evening of painful memories.

Hampton had not seen her, of course, and even if he had, Lady Pamela doubted he would remember that lonely young girl he had danced with five years ago. How could he? No doubt he had extended similar small kindnesses to countless other wallflowers in his time. He appeared to have a kind heart, a rare enough feature in a London gentleman, she thought with more than a little cynicism.

She knew instinctively that Hampton's broad-shouldered companion was not the sort to put himself out for anyone, much less a young girl at her first ball. And even though he had not turned to stare, as so many bucks did nowadays on the public roads, Lady Pamela caught a fleeting impression of aristocratic aloofness in his chiseled profile, a cold disinterest that brought a brief chill to her heart.

She brushed the irrational feeling aside and turned to her cousin, an amused comment about the outrageous size of Mr. Hampton's fashionable nosegay on her lips. The expression on Freddy's face chased the frivolous remark from her mind.

"What is it, Freddy?" she inquired solicitously. "You look as though you have seen a ghost."

Her cousin gave her a warning glance as he descended from the carriage and held out his hand to assist her. He cast a nervous glance at the departing curricle as they followed Lord Melrose into the inn.

"That's him," he mumbled enigmatically out of the side of his mouth.

Lady Pamela felt a prickle of apprehension. "Whom do you mean, Freddy?"

"In that fancy yellow curricle," her cousin whispered. "Did you not see the licentious rogue?"

"I saw Mr. Hampton, if that is whom you mean, Cousin. But I

hardly think he deserves the name of rogue. He was one of the few gentleman—"

"Not *him*," Freddy interrupted brusquely. "Willy Hampton is a top-of-the-trees sort of fellow. It is the other one who is the devil incarnate."

"Oh!" Lady Pamela stared at her cousin as the significance of his cryptic words sank in. "Are you telling me that we have just encountered the fiendish marquess himself?" she whispered under her breath, glancing apprehensively at her father.

Luckily, the earl was absorbed in a jovial exchange with Mr. Tobin and seemed unaware of the close brush he had just had with his sworn enemy.

"Precisely," Freddy whispered hoarsely. "And there is only one reason I can think of for his odious presence in Brighton." He drew Lady Pamela towards the private parlor and lowered his voice still further. "He is resolved to add my lovely Prudence to his list of conquests. But he will have me to reckon with, Pamela," he added with tight-lipped determination. "Promise you will help me save the poor innocent from this lecherous monster, Cousin. Tell me I can count on your support."

Although privately Lady Pamela considered her cousin's plea to be melodramatic in the extreme—after all what harm could come to a young girl constantly surrounded by company?—she had not the heart to refuse him. Besides, the notion of thwarting the evil designs of her father's enemy appealed to her spirit of justice. It also promised to imbue her stay in Brighton with a dash of intrigue that she found oddly stimulating.

"You may certainly count on me to thwart the marquess's nefarious plans for seducing your lady-love, Freddy," she replied soothingly.

"You are a great gun, Pamela," her cousin said happily, his face losing its worried expression. "And I hope you will consent to be the godmother to my first-born, when the happy event occurs."

"I suggest you focus your energies on the present, Freddy," the earl remarked sternly, entering the parlor in time to hear his heir's impulsive speech. "There will be time enough to talk of godparents once we are convinced that Miss Erskin-Jones lives up to the Melrose standards."

This dampening remark seemed to have no visible effect on Mr. Hancock, who spent the entire meal rhapsodizing over the many extraordinary virtues and accomplishments of his chosen bride.

By the time she resumed her place in the chaise, Lady Pamela was beginning to be heartily sick of listening to her cousin sing the praises of Miss Erskin-Jones. No female of her acquaintance could possibly embody such perfection, she argued to herself. And if by one of those flukes of nature, Prudence turned out to be as perfect as Freddy painted her, Lady Pamela had little doubt that she would be insufferably tiresome.

Her patience with the honorable Freddy was wearing very thin indeed by the time the chaise pulled up before Number 8 Adelaide Crescent, and she was able to escape in the bustle of unpacking.

After a restless night punctuated by dreams of dark, unidentifiable forces closing in upon her, Lady Pamela rose early and enjoyed her breakfast in her private sitting room. Knowing that the two gentleman would not come downstairs much before eleven, she made her way to the small music room her mother had insisted upon when Lord Melrose brought her as a bride to Brighton the summer of their marriage.

Lady Pamela had heard the story many times, and as she sat down at the rosewood pianoforte, she ran her fingers over the gold leaf inscription that identified the instrument as one of John Broadwood's, dating from 1790, the year of her mother's marriage. She wondered, as she had many times during the past five years, what her life might have been like had Lady Melrose not contracted smallpox while visiting the rector's wife on her deathbed.

Idly, her fingers skimmed the polished surface of the instrument and settled on the ivory keyboard. Almost of their own accord, she slipped into the *étude* she was composing for her mother. It was a haunting melody, expressing both the gaiety of Lady Melrose's presence and the nostalgia of her absence. When she came to the difficult passage she had been struggling with at Melrose Park, the phrasing suddenly fell into place, as if her mother's spirit had guided her fingers. She played the passage over again, reveling at the magic of the intricate melody.

So absorbed was Lady Pamela in this bittersweet exercise that she jumped when the door opened to admit her cousin, dressed to the nines and with a conspiratorial grin on his face.

"My, you are up early this morning, Freddy," she said, her mind still entranced with her music. "I had not expected to see you before noon."

"I plan to call on Prudence and warn her that Monroyal is in

Brighton," her cousin said calmly, "I thought you might like to accompany me, Cousin."

Although Lady Pamela would much rather have spent her morning at the keyboard, she smiled up into her cousin's eager face. "How kind of you, Freddy," she replied, deliberately stretching the truth. "The morning is so fine, I would enjoy a drive. And besides," she added, her smile widening, "I am all agog to meet this Incomparable you have been puffing up to us since yesterday."

This was the wrong thing to say, she soon discovered. Freddy needed no other encouragement to launch into another tedious panegyric on the superlative attributes of his lady-love. By the time his curricle pulled up before the modest residence on East Street, Lady Pamela was heartily sick of the whole affair and would have given anything to be able to turn about and return home. Since this course of action was patently impossible, she resigned herself to the encounter, hoping that perhaps the Beauty might not be as insipid as she feared.

Insipid the Beauty certainly was not. The vision in palest pink sarcenet, who rose from the shabby settee and flew across the room to greet them as they entered the morning room, erred from an excess of liveliness.

"Oh, Freddy!" Miss Erskin-Jones squealed delightedly, offering both delicately white hands to that besotted gentleman in a charming gesture, "how very happy I am to see you! You have no idea how bored I have been since you ran off and left me in London."

"Prudence!" The sharp reprimand startled Lady Pamela, whose attention had been riveted on the Beauty's ingenuous performance. Her gaze flew to a wing chair beside the fire, where she encountered the probing stare of a lady whose beauty must, at one time, have rivaled that of her daughter's.

"How many times must I remind you, dearest," the lady continued in an unpleasantly strident voice, "that gentlemen deplore such hoydenish starts in a young lady. Whatever will our dear Mr. Hancock think of you, Prudence, if you throw yourself at him in a fashion more appropriate to a fishwife than to the Toast of London."

Miss Erskin-Jones cast an impatient glance over her shoulder, but she did not withdraw her hands from her "dear Mr. Hancock's" clasp. Lady Pamela noticed that the Beauty affected a charming pout when she returned her gaze to Freddy's face, which was wreathed in a fatuous grin.

"Oh, Freddy would never dream of mistaking me for a fish-wife, Mama," the Beauty remarked with paralyzing frankness. "He is my hero, my knight on a white horse, my savior, who has vowed to love me forever. Is that not so, Freddy?" she added guilelessly.

Lady Pamela saw that her cousin appeared to be reduced to a witless wonder by the coy smile that accompanied this artless speech. He opened his mouth several times, but no sound came out. He turned various shades of red before he managed to stutter, "That is a-absolutely t-true, Pru . . . that is, Miss Erskin-Jones. I c-cannot say I ride a white horse at the moment, b-but I do not doubt that one might be procured without too much trouble if it would please you, my dear."

"Oh, yes, indeed," the Beauty gushed, leaning forward so alarmingly that Lady Pamela was certain her cousin had an unimpaired view down the chit's bodice from neck to navel.

Tired of being ignored by this ill-mannered minx, Lady Pamela gently cleared her throat. But it was her cousin who turned, glassy-eyed, to stare at her as if he had never seen her before. When recognition dawned, Freddy shook his head presumably to clear the mists from his brain and made the introductions.

"Oh, Lady Pamela," the Beauty gushed, evidently bound by some inner compulsion to begin every sentence with an exclamation of delight, "you have no notion how anxious I have been to make your acquaintance. Freddy has told me so much about you, I am convinced we shall deal admirably together."

Her cousin's blank stare confirmed Lady Pamela's suspicion that this pronouncement was a bouncer of the first water, but she smiled graciously. If she was committed to playing gooseberry to the vivacious and quite shameless Beauty—a task that was bound to stretch her patience to the utmost—she decided, she had better put a good face on the matter.

CHAPTER THREE

Rival Suitor

"And what might your business be with that shameless Jones hussy, Willoughby?" Lady Emmaline Stevens demanded in her foghorn voice that must have echoed, Lord Monroyal imagined, clear down in the kitchens. "I daresay you are quite old enough to be her father."

"It is Miss *Erskin*-Jones, Aunt Emma." Willy's smile began to show signs of strain as he corrected his aged relative for the fifth time since the topic had come up at the breakfast table. "And Miss Prudence is the Season's reigning Beauty, Aunt, in case you had not heard."

"Pooh! of course I had heard that piece of nonsense," the old lady snapped, "just as I hear everything that happens in the *ton*, my boy. Which only goes to show how pitiful the standards have become since my own days in the Metropolis. Appalling, I call it. Any mushroom with a pretty face and a simpering smile is accounted a Beauty now. In my day, one had to be well born and impeccably bred, in short, a lady of quality, to—pass the marmalade, Willoughby, will you?"

Lord Monroyal paused in the act of raising a forkful of York ham to his mouth and glanced across the table at his friend. His amusement at the old lady's startling pronouncement that only ladies of quality could pass the marmalade in her day must have been apparent, for Willy's brown eyes resumed their natural twinkle as he passed the cut-glass dish to his aunt.

"I will agree with you, Aunt, that Prudence's family is perhaps not top drawer by your standards, but—"

"Balderdash!" Lady Stevens cut in vehemently. "Her grandfather on her mother's side was in *Trade.*" She pronounced the condemning word with a moue of distaste, her large aristocratic nose jerking ceilingward a full two inches, as though the very sound of the word had offended her sensibilities. "And her father was plain Sir Henry Jones, as his father before him. An obscure baronet in Northumberland with no pretense at refinement to speak of. A mere pig-farmer by all accounts." She snorted and scooped a dollop of marmalade onto her toast, her crimped curls quivering with the force of her scorn.

"My father—your own brother, Aunt Em—raised pigs," Willy pointed out soothingly. "In fact, we still raise them in Devon. Mighty profitable they are, too."

"That's as may be," Lady Stevens boomed stridently. "But I presume you do not know each individual pig by its name, do you, lad?"

Monroyal relished the look of consternation that flitted across his friend's pleasantly round face. Willy's powers of recovery were such, however, that after a reproachful glance across the table, he was able to reply with his usual sangfroid.

"I am not in the habit of naming my pigs at all, Aunt," he said with hardly a flicker of a smile, "so the question is moot. In point of fact, I cannot even recall how many such animals are kept at my various estates. I daresay there are a healthy number—"

"Well, Sir Henry did," his aunt interrupted, almost gleefully, Monroyal thought.

"Did what, Aunt?" Willy murmured, his attention having moved from the live animal to the smoked variety that the butler was carving expertly on the sideboard. "I'll take a couple of slices of that, Jenkins," he said, addressing the butler.

"Knew their names, of course," Lady Stevens snapped with a dry chuckle. "Which merely goes to emphasize his lack of breeding. No gentleman I know would go about calling pigs by name, or allowing animals to run tame in the gardens, which I have it on the best authority he was in the habit of doing."

The marquess listened to this barrage of trivial gossip with no little admiration. Hampton had warned him that his Aunt Em was a fountain of information on every member of the *ton* in the entire length and breadth of the land. She had bosom-bows and childhood cronies on every conceivable level of society, and kept a secretary whose sole task it was to answer the stacks of letters that arrived at No. 10 Brunswick Square every morning of the year. Monroyal wondered idly how the old lady remembered it all.

"Are we to assume that you do not know where Miss Erskin-Jones is staying in Brighton, Aunt?" Willy ventured, after stuffing a large piece of ham into his mouth and chewing contentedly for several moments.

The marquess surmised that his friend was deliberately baiting his irascible relative, and his suspicion proved to be correct. No sooner had the words been uttered than Lady Stevens set down her cup with a clatter and glared at her nephew, her ample eyebrows clustering contentiously above the bridge of her patrician nose.

The sight was not a pretty one, Monroyal thought, and reminded him vividly of his own outspoken Aunt Honoria, banished long ago to one of his lesser estates on the coast of Dorset for her role as a go-between and chief instigator of family scandal. At least at Holly Lodge the peppery Lady Honoria Stilton, contemporary and bosom-bow to her brother's wayward wife, could not cause the family any major embarrassment. He wondered if Hampton's redoubtable Aunt Emma had been banished to Brighton for similar reasons.

"Of course, I know where the little trollop is staying, you silly twit," Lady Stevens thundered, so loudly that Monroyal barely restrained himself from clapping his hands to his ears in protest. Such an action, he knew from experience, would bring the old harridan's wrath down upon his head. He returned his attention to his breakfast.

Willy glanced apologetically at his aunt. "We had complete confidence in you, Aunt Em," he said soothingly. "But I fear you malign the young lady. Miss Prudence may not be top-drawer, but neither has she sunk to the depths of ignominy you are suggesting."

"Fiddle!" Lady Stevens burst out impatiently. "Much you know about the matter, my lad. Only last week I received another letter from poor Violet Boodle, the vicar of Littlefield's wife, confirming the rumors I had already heard last spring from Lady Rothanbriar, whose son has a largish estate in Northumberland. Both ladies swear that the Jones chit made such a spectacle of herself when the 49th Dragoons were stationed in Newcastle last summer that her father had to intervene to prevent her eloping with some half-pay officer. He packed her off to London to see if he could pass the little doxy off as undamaged goods. And more power to him, I say," she added with one of her dry chuckles. "If a man ain't got the gumption to check a filly's teeth before he mounts her, he deserves to find himself in the briars, I always say."

The incongruity of the old lady's comparison caused the marquess to choke on a piece of ham and fall into a fit of coughing. He imagined she had meant pedigree rather than teeth, but he preferred the bawdy implications of the latter. Visions of his latest *inamorata* submitting to such an examination triggered a wave of laughter that he was barely able to stifle.

Lady Stevens glared at him. "Have I said something to amuse you, my lord?" she demanded icily.

Lord Monroyal could do little more than mumble an apology. He dared not look across the table at his friend, but he sensed that Hampton was enjoying the spectacle he was making of himself.

"Personally," the old lady continued coldly, "I find it discouraging that too many gentlemen, even those of the highest rank and fortune, all too often allow their duty to family and name to be trampled beneath the muddy feet of their animal passions." She paused, as if hit by an unpleasant thought, then turned to her nephew. "Tell me that you are not one of those despicable creatures, Willoughby," she exclaimed in ringing tones, her eyebrows again clashing above her nose as if in mortal combat. "Tell me that you are not dangling after this mindless little chit."

Monroyal glanced at Willy and grinned, relieved that the harridan's wrath had found a new victim. It was Hampton's turn to choke and stammer.

"If you are asking whether I intend to make Miss Erskin-Jones an offer of marriage, Aunt Emma," he said stiffly, "allow me to put your fears to rest. No such outlandish notion ever entered my head. I thought I had made it abundantly clear to my family that I have no intention of bending my neck to the yoke of matrimony until I am in my dotage. And perhaps not even then," he added, his Puckish face creasing into a smile. "I have no title to preserve, after all, and there are plenty of nephews to inherit my estates. I am that increasingly rare phenomenon, a happy man."

"Here, here," the marquess remarked laconically, passing his cup to be refilled by Jenkins. "You may count me among those privileged creatures, Willy. Men who have no need to risk life and limb in parson's mousetrap."

Lady Stevens turned to him, astonishment on her face. "But you *do* have a title to preserve, Monroyal," she chided, her double chin quivering indignantly. "A very prestigious one at that."

"I also have a brother and four halfbrothers to carry on the line for me," he drawled. "I am entirely at liberty to eschew the blessed bonds of matrimony, which is precisely what I intend to do." He chuckled at his own cynicism and at the thunderous frown his hostess threw in his direction. "Your nephew and I will keep each other company when we are old and gray," he added with a grin and a wink at Hampton.

"You are gray already, Monroyal," Lady Stevens snapped, a

malicious glint in her sharp blue eyes. "And getting along in years, too, I can see. What are you? Two-and-forty if I am not mistaken. Your mother married Stilton in . . . what was it? Seventy-two? Seventy-three?"

"I am six-and-thirty," growled the marquess, inexplicably annoyed at this constant reminder of the passing years. "My parents wed in 1778, and I was born in 1780."

Hampton shifted impatiently in his chair. "Well, Aunt Em," he prodded. "Are you going to tell us where to find the Beauty, or shall we be obliged to apply to Lady Grifford?"

"That hussy could not tell you where her feet are when she falls out of bed in the morning." Lady Stevens sniffed contemptuously. "And as soon as you answer my original question, Willy, I shall be happy to tell you where to find the Jones chit."

"What question is that, Aunt?" Willy demanded.

The marquess decided that it was high time he took a hand in the proceedings. If it were left to Hampton, they would spend all day trying to pry a simple piece of information from the cantankerous old biddy. "It is something in the nature of a wager, Lady Stevens," he murmured, coughing discreetly and ignoring the horrified glance Willy threw him from across the table.

The sharp blue gaze swung round to skewer him. "A wager, eh? What kind of wager?"

"I fear it is not appropriate for me to say, my lady," Monroyal murmured with feigned regret.

"But it has nothing to do with my nephew, I trust?"

The marquess conjured up his most charming smile. "That I can guarantee, my lady. Willy is as innocent as the driven snow."

Lady Stevens snorted at this piece of nonsense. "What absolute drivel," she barked. "If the wager concerns you, Monroyal, I do not wish to know about it. But if you embroil my nephew in your petticoat escapades, I shall hold you responsible, let me tell you, sir."

With this withering comment, Lady Stevens rose majestically and swept out of the breakfast room, followed by a bouncing, scrambling, yapping cluster of pugs, streaming out from under the table in a veritable avalanche of pigmy gargoyles.

"Which gown would ye be wanting me to press for this evening, milady?"

The abigail's question reminded Lady Pamela with a start that last night over dinner she had allowed her cousin to cajole her into attending one of the many assemblies offered in Brighton during the summer months. Miss Erskin-Jones had promised to be present, Freddy had informed them with great gusto, and the dear girl was anxious to renew her acquaintance with Lady Pamela.

Suppressing a sigh at this unlikely event, Lady Pamela put down her half-finished cup of chocolate on the little rosewood table beside the bed. Suddenly, the thick, fragrant liquid had lost its appeal.

Privately, Freddy had confessed to his cousin that his *in-amorata* rather dreaded her first encounter with Lord Melrose and was counting on Lady Pamela to support her in this ordeal. Although she considered this to be another fanciful exaggeration on Freddy's part, Lady Pamela had taken pity on him and forfeited a good night's rest in the cause of true love.

"The blue silk, I believe," she replied distractedly. Her eye had been caught by the green muslin walking gown Betty was laying out on the bed, evidence of yet another rash promise she had made to her cousin. Freddy had insisted that she drive out with him that morning, assuring her that her company was de rigueur if he hoped to convince Prudence's mother to allow him to take the Beauty up in his curricle.

"And just what do you expect me to do in the meanwhile?" she had demanded, a hint of tartness on her tongue, as the red-wheeled curricle bowled along the Marine Parade and turned into Queen's Park Road. "Sit in the shade and pacify the dragon, I suppose."

"Oh, Pamela, you are such a brick," Freddy had gushed, missing the irony entirely. "The very finest friend a man could ever wish for, I swear it. And besides, you are the best hand at pacifying dragons I have yet to meet. Only consider how my uncle eats out of your hand, my dear. I am counting on you to sing Prudence's praises to him tonight. My whole life depends upon it, I can tell you."

Lady Pamela had not the heart to tell him that the chances of her father accepting Miss Prudence Erskin-Jones as the future Countess of Melrose were only slightly higher than his agreeing to marry the chit himself. She held her tongue, however, and concentrated her energy on praying that the Beauty had chosen this morning to lie abed.

The huge chestnut trees were in their full glory, she noticed as they entered the Park, and the flower beds glowed with brilliant summer color. Freddy drew his team down to a snail's pace and cast his gaze about anxiously. By his side, his cousin clasped her hands tightly in silent supplication.

To Lady Pamela's vast relief, the sole occupants of the Park at this early hour appeared to be nursemaids with their rambunctious charges. By the time the curricle rounded the curve at the far end to complete the circular drive, Lady Pamela began to hope in earnest that the Beauty was safely at home in bed. Her initial encounter with the chit the previous afternoon had sorely tried her patience, and a second exposure to fluttering eyelashes and simpering pouts might well undo her entirely.

She had opened her mouth to suggest to Freddy that they return to Melrose House to join her father in a second breakfast when a bright yellow racing curricle drawn by four flashy bays whipped into the Park from Queen's Park Road and raced along the opposite side of the promenade at a spanking pace.

Mouth still agape, Lady Pamela stared in open approval at the spectacle. More than a competent whip herself, she had always shared the love of sleek, well-fed creatures that took up so much of her father's energy. This magnificent equipage must have set its owner back more than a thousand pounds, she calculated. The high-stepping bays were perfectly matched, their coats brushed to a high gloss, their elegant ears alert, heads arrogantly poised, legs moving in perfect rhythm as if pulled by invisible strings.

An unpleasant thought suddenly jerked her out of her bemused reverie. She had seen this curricle before—quite recently, too. When her startled gaze took in the driver of the vehicle, Lady Pamela recalled where and when she had seen it—and who owned the extravagant equipage.

Not until that moment did it register in her befuddled brain that the infamous marquess was not alone. A bright profusion of pink—beribboned gown, rose-encrusted bonnet, and lace-trimmed parasol—blazoned the identity of the young lady who sat beside him, clutching his arm in apparent fright. The little shrieks of laughter that reached them clearly across the wide expanse of lawn and flower beds as the yellow curricle approached gave the lie to the chit's Cheltenham performance, and Lady Pamela had little doubt that Miss Prudence Erskin-Jones was enjoying this highly improper adventure hugely.

Lady Pamela paled and turned to her cousin. "Freddy," she began, "that is . . ."

"So I see," came the terse reply. Freddy's expression was grim as he jerked his team to a standstill and sawed at the reins to turn the curricle around.

Lady Pamela heartily disapproved of such cow-handed methods and told her cousin so, only to be greeted with a grunt and the admonition to keep out of his way.

"Surely you do not intend to start a mill with that villain single-handedly, Freddy?" Lady Pamela queried in an alarmed voice. Even from that distance, she had ample opportunity to note that the marquess was taller, broader, heavier, and doubtless far more experienced in casual street brawls than her young cousin. And furthermore, she thought ruefully, Lord Melrose would certainly find a way to blame her if anything harmful befell his heir.

"I aim to impress upon the rogue that no gentleman with a shred of honor would expose an innocent young girl's reputation to public censure as he is doing this very instant," Freddy growled, flicking his long whip over his team to send the frightened creatures bolting back the way they had come.

Clinging on for dear life, Lady Pamela's alarm abruptly turned to anger. "I suggest you reconsider, Cousin, before you make a spectacle of yourself," she cried out, clutching wildly at her bonnet that showed signs of wishing to take flight with the flock of pigeons that rose at their passing. "That innocent young girl's mother appears to find nothing wrong with her daughter's hoydenish behavior."

Risking life and limb, Lady Pamela released her grip on the rail to gesture at the yellow curricle that had come to rest beside a bench on the other side of the Park. The driver descended in one fluid movement, showing no sign—she noted irrelevantly—of the advancing age Freddy had made so much of in his dismissive account of his rival. With equal agility, the marquess swung his passenger, who uttered unmistakable little squeals of delight, down from the high seat of the vehicle. As Lady Pamela watched, the scoundrel placed one pink-gloved hand in the crook of his arm, with what she considered deplorable familiarity, and escorted the chit to the bench where Mrs. Erskin-Jones sat smirking like a Cheshire cat.

Her cousin had slowed his wild pace at the sight of the Beauty's mother, and Lady Pamela took the opportunity to press home an argument she had, in the excitement of the moment, entirely overlooked.

"If you have no objection, Freddy," she said acidly, "I would really rather not have to acknowledge Monroyal. And I dare not hazard a guess at Father's fury should he discover that his heir stooped to bandy words with his sworn enemy in the public thoroughfare."

Freddy pulled his team to a halt and stared at her. "You would not tell him, would you, Pamela?" he asked, an anxious frown marring his normally cheerful expression.

Settling her bonnet more firmly on her head, Lady Pamela smiled thinly. "You are not suggesting, are you, Freddy, that we conceal from his lordship the unpleasant discovery that his heir's chosen bride is making a spectacle of herself over the son of a man he considers his worst enemy."

Her cousin's hangdog look made her regret her harsh words, and she relented slightly. "Of course, the chit's extreme youth . . ."

"And innocence," Freddy chimed in, brightening visibly.

"Yes, mm, and her innocence," she conceded with no great conviction, "make her an easy target for men of Monroyal's ilk. On the other hand, one cannot condone impropriety even in the young and innocent. Particularly one who may well be chosen for an exalted position in the *haut monde.*"

"Oh, she already *has* been chosen, Pamela," Freddy protested vehemently. "I thought I had made that perfectly clear to you. Prudence is the only female I can ever think of as my countess."

"If my father approves of her, my dear," Lady Pamela reminded him gently. "And I warn you, Freddy, if Prudence does not learn to curb this hoydenish streak, my father will wash his hands of the whole business."

"I will take her to Gretna Green," Freddy said mulishly.

"Oh, I am sure she would think that a great lark," Lady Pamela said with heavy sarcasm that once again was lost on her cousin.

"I am sure she would," he said ingenuously. "But of course I would never suggest such a havey-cavey way of doing things. There must be nothing but the best for the future Countess of Melrose," he added with a fatuous grin. "Would you not agree, Cousin?"

Lady Pamela sighed and made no reply.

A clatter of hooves from the other side of the Park interrupted this uncomfortable exchange, and Lady Pamela saw with relief that the marquess had turned his vehicle and was disappearing back the way he had come with characteristic recklessness.

A few minutes later, having resumed their progress at a more respectable pace, Freddy drew the curricle to a standstill before the Erskin-Jones ladies and tipped his beaver.

The reaction of the younger lady was predictable. "Why, Freddy!" Prudence exclaimed in a high falsetto that echoed—or so Lady Pamela imagined—throughout the length and breadth of the Park, "what a wonderful coincidence that you should have

brought Lady Pamela to the Park this morning." Not waiting for
Freddy to assist his cousin from the vehicle, Prudence tripped
happily over and attached herself to his sleeve, smiling up at him
with wide-eyed adulation.

Realizing that her cousin had forgotten her existence, Lady
Pamela settled back in her seat, prepared to enjoy the farce being
played out before her. She was not disappointed.

"Oh, Freddy!" the Beauty exclaimed again, pressing her pink-
clad bosom against the gentleman's arm with a charming display
of spontaneity. "You will never guess who took me up in his carriage just now."

Lady Pamela marveled at her cousin's restraint. "I can indeed,
Prudence," he answered shortly. "And I thought I warned you
not to have anything to do with that old roué. He is notorious . . .
for . . ." His voice trailed off as he hesitated, apparently reluctant
to enter into details of the cause of his rival's notoriety. He
coughed nervously.

"Notorious for what, Freddy?" Obviously the Beauty had no
such scruples, and Lady Pamela could have sworn she saw a
glimmer of devilry in those pansy-blue eyes.

Freddy seemed to have difficulty swallowing. "Monroyal is a
fiend of the worst kind, my dear. No female who values her reputation would dream of driving out with him. Alone!" he added, a
definite note of reproach in his voice.

Prudence opened her eyes in surprise—feigned, Lady Pamela
suspected. "But he is a *marquess,* Freddy," she said, awe radiat-
ing from every pore. "Surely you are mistaken about him."

From her perch in the curricle, Lady Pamela heard her cousin's
long-suffering sigh.

"That is no guarantee that he is not a vile lecher, Prudence," he
said tersely. "You must take my word for it, my dear. Or ask my
cousin, and she will tell you the same thing. Is that not correct,
Pamela?" He threw her such a desperate glance that Lady Pamela
found herself nodding sagely.

"My cousin is absolutely right, Miss Erskin-Jones," she con-
curred blithely. "The Marquess of Monroyal is a depraved and
heartless scoundrel." She paused, then added with a touch of
irony, "No fit escort for a young lady who aspires to be accepted
by the *ton,* you may trust me."

The Beauty swung her pansy gaze round and fixed it on Lady
Pamela, who found it oddly calculating. "You speak with so
much authority, my lady," she murmured, veiling her eyes. "Were

you perchance one of his victims, then?" she asked, her tone all innocence.

Lady Pamela felt herself go pale and clearly heard Freddy's gasp of dismay. "Miss Erskin-Jones!" he exclaimed in shocked tones, his expression sterner than Lady Pamela had ever seen it. "My cousin is a lady without the slightest blemish on her character. She would die rather than be seen in the company of a man like that." He swallowed with some difficulty and lowered his voice. "I must ask you never, ever, to cast such aspersions on any member of my family again."

Coming from mild-mannered Freddy, this was strong stuff, and predictably, the Beauty burst into tears.

It took Freddy nearly twenty minutes to convince the girl that no, he was not really angry with her, and that yes, he still loved her. To prove to her that his devotion had not faltered, he prevailed upon Mrs. Erskin-Jones to allow her daughter to take a turn round the Park in Freddy's curricle.

At the mention of this treat, the Beauty's tears miraculously disappeared, and she uttered one of her artificially bright trills of laughter that set Lady Pamela's teeth on edge. Nevertheless, she obligingly ceded her seat in the vehicle to the Beauty and accepted Mrs. Erskin-Jones's invitation to join her on the bench.

She lived to regret this display of civility, and by the time Freddy returned with his precious cargo—as Lady Pamela distinctly heard him refer to the contentious little chit—she had grown utterly weary of evading impertinent questions on the size and luxury of the establishment destined to become her little girl's home in the near future.

On the drive back to Adelaide Crescent, Lady Pamela was strangely silent. It had begun to dawn on her that if Freddy insisted on this outrageous mésalliance with the Jones chit, her own future at Melrose Park would be bleak indeed. The prospect of residing under the same roof as Mrs. Erskin-Jones was bad enough, but to be dependent on the good will of a hussy like Prudence was not to be borne.

CHAPTER FOUR

Amorous Rendezvous

"I gather from that smug grin on your phiz that the ladybird took the bait, Robert," Willy remarked with a lewd wink as Lord Monroyal sauntered into the breakfast room later that morning.

He gave his friend a lopsided smirk and drew out a chair. Forgoing his early morning cup of coffee had been a small price to pay for the reward he anticipated in the near future. But now that the preliminaries were out of the way, his interest shifted from seduction to sustenance. He was starving and allowed Jenkins to fill his plate with large helpings from the sideboard.

"Well?" Willy murmured impatiently after the marquess had chewed steadily for several minutes, "ain't you going to share your success with a friend and fellow conspirator?"

Lord Monroyal glanced up and grinned. "It was just as we anticipated, Willy. Our Prudence did not live up to her name, and that mother of hers is a scheming harridan if ever I saw one. Fairly drooled all over my new coat in her ecstasy at being noticed by a bloody marquess." His sensuous mouth turned down in a moue of distaste. "It was really too easy to persuade her to allow me to drive her precious daughter down to the Marine Parade and back. More than enough time, let me tell you," he added with a wink, "to present the chit with the gewgaw I bought for her yesterday, and promise more substantial tokens of my regard if she would drive with me again tomorrow."

Willy beamed and dismissed the butler before posing his next question. "When and where is the actual seduction going to take place, laddie?" he asked, his eyes twinkling with devilry.

"There's the rub. I can hardly bring the chit here," Monroyal remarked with a crooked grin at the startled look on his friend's face. "I doubt your Auntie Em would take kindly to that sort of carrying on under her roof. And not having a pied-à-terre in Brighton myself, I wondered if you might know of a secluded nook where one might be undisturbed for an hour or two."

Willy frowned. "Are you certain that the Beauty knows the

game she is getting herself into, old man?" His brown eyes regarded the marquess uncertainly. "She is only seventeen, after all."

Lord Monroyal laughed cynically. "If I did not know any better, Willy, I would think you have never seduced a female before," he remarked, putting a large piece of ham into his mouth and sighing contentedly. "Of course, the chit knows the game. She has undoubtedly played it before and will again when this is all over, and I am safely back in Devon. Which reminds me, Willy," he said, changing the subject abruptly, "as always, Lady Monroyal is expecting to see you at Stilton Grange again this summer. You are one of her favorite guests, though I could never understand what she sees in you."

His friend chose not to take umbrage at this unkind remark and rose to serve himself a dish of coddled eggs. "I daresay it never occurred to you, Robert, that some females prefer a sunny disposition and even temper to titled arrogance and brooding good looks. Arrogance is not my style, old man, as well you know, and besides, I have not the nose for it." He grinned across the table at the marquess. "Nor the stomach," he added, his amiable expression giving the proof to his words.

Lord Monroyal grimaced. "Let us leave your nose and stomach out of the conversation for the moment, Willy," he drawled. "I need you to come up with an appropriate trysting place before tomorrow afternoon. I doubt our Incomparable Prudence would agree to enter a common posting inn in my company. And even if she were innocent enough to compromise herself so blatantly, I am far too leery to be caught in such a trap," he added with a cynical smile. "Unscrupulous chits have been known to set up an unwary pigeon to be plucked red-handed; but I am not a besotted moonling to be caught with such an old trick."

Hampton glanced up in surprise. "You suspect the Beauty has designs on your worn-out hide? The rumor is that she has the heir to an earldom in her pocket already. Why should she set her sights on you and jeopardize a sure mark?"

The marquess let out a crack of cynical laughter. "Who can say why females do anything, my friend? I have long since ceased to bother my head over such imponderables. My sole concern is to make sure that the little darlings fall into my bed willingly with enough regularity to ward off boredom."

"Raven was right," Hampton muttered, returning to his food. "Not only are you a jaded hedonist, but amoral into the bargain."

"Spare me the lectures, Willy, and set your mind to finding a convenient love nest for our imprudent Beauty."

Lord Monroyal watched his friend chew methodically for a few minutes, his ruddy face pensive. The marquess was confident that Hampton would solve his dilemma. The Hamptons were a large, clannish family, and Willy had relatives scattered all over the south of England. No doubt one of them would be able to provide an appropriate place to take the Beauty during their drive tomorrow.

He was not disappointed. Willy abruptly raised his eyes from his plate, a forkful of ham poised in midair. "I have just the thing, old man," he said cheerily. "I happened to learn last night from Aunt Em that old George Hampton, a cousin of hers, is up in Scotland with his daughter and her family. Trout fishing or something of that nature." He paused to carry the fork to his mouth.

"And how does dear old George enter the picture?" Monroyal queried gently. "I am all agog to hear the rest of this story."

"Well, Cousin George is a fanatic fisherman and owns a small cottage about six miles west along the coast. He spends most of his time there now that his wife is dead. I have been there several times, but since my tastes run more to mutton than to fish," he said with a salacious grin, "I have never taken up George's open invitation to take my friends there to fish."

"Open invitation?" the marquess repeated, his gray eyes lighting up. "Do you mean to tell me you have a key to the cottage?"

Willy smirked. "Precisely, old man," he said. "If you care to, we can drive out there this afternoon to take a gander at the place. But I think it might be just the thing for an amorous rendezvous."

The marquess smiled softly. Everything was falling into place with predictable ease. Never for a moment had he expected otherwise, of course. He was not accustomed to insurmountable obstacles in his pursuit of females and did not foresee any hitch in bedding the Incomparable. She was, in his considered opinion, more than willing to be bedded. His tastes ran to rather more sophisticated *amourettes,* and he would have preferred a more experienced target for his efforts, but he had accepted the wager and was determined to see it through. In truth, he considered the seduction of the Beauty a *fait accompli,* and looked forward to collecting Gresham's blunt.

He glanced across the table at his friend with a faint smile. "Two days from now we can be on our way to Stilton Grange," he remarked, suddenly anxious to put the amorous encounter behind him and get back to his Devon estate—And to his rambunctious half-brothers.

"I intend to teach the boys to play cricket this summer," he added impulsively, his amusement now genuine. "And I am counting on you to support me in this grueling endeavor, Willy."

Lady Pamela had a premonition of disaster long before the Melrose carriage drew up before the imposing doors of the Assembly Hall on Edward Street. Had it not been that Freddy was counting on her to see the evening through, she would have pleaded a megrim and returned to Adelaide Crescent. Her father would undoubtedly be put out by such missishness and would insist that she spend at least part of the evening in the company of Miss Erskin-Jones. She owed it to her cousin, he would say in that autocratic voice of his.

Lady Pamela grimaced at the thought of the earl's reaction when he actually came face-to-face with her cousin's hoydenish *inamorata*. Perhaps it would help Freddy's cause that their first encounter was to occur in such a public place, Pamela reasoned, as she allowed her father to hand her down from the carriage. The Beauty—no doubt under strict instructions from her mother—had prettily declined Lady Pamela's invitation to take tea at Adelaide Crescent that afternoon. Her mother, shrewd as she could hold together, obviously preferred to thrust her daughter into the earl's notice in all her finery in the formal setting in which Prudence was accustomed to shine. Small tea-parties did not bring out the best in the Beauty, as Lady Pamela had discovered yesterday to her great dismay.

Neither did improper drives in the Park, she recalled with a shudder of distaste. While the Earl of Melrose might be counted upon never to take the Beauty up in any of his vehicles for a clandestine outing, it was inevitable that, sooner or later, he would encounter the unpredictable chit over tea at Melrose House. And then the cat would be out of the bag.

The orchestra was warming up for a waltz as Lady Pamela trod up the shallow steps on her father's arm. She glanced hastily around the imposing hall, but saw no flurry of masculine interest that would signal the Beauty's presence. She had delayed their departure from Adelaide Crescent until the last possible moment, secretly reluctant, she supposed—although she would never admit to such a shameful weakness—to witness poor innocent Freddy making a cake of himself in public.

Disregarding the speculative stares from a group of matrons across the room, Lord Melrose escorted her to a seat and procured her a glass of lemonade. Lady Pamela sensed that her father was anxious to retire to the card room, and his eyes were fixed impatiently on the entrance as if willing his nephew to appear with his charges.

Suddenly, he tensed. "What in Hades is that insolent jackstraw doing here?" he muttered under his breath.

For a heart-stopping moment, Lady Pamela had visions of her father and the notorious marquess engaged in a vulgar brawl in plain sight of Brighton gossips. But it was not Lord Monroyal who had entered the hall and stood regarding the couples assembling for the next dance. She sighed in relief.

"That is no jackstraw, Father," she said soothingly. "That is only Sir Rodney Morton, and I would hardly call him insolent either."

"What do you call it when a penniless rogue has the gall to ask me for my daughter?" the earl muttered, loud enough to attract the curious glances of nearby couples.

"The Mortons have been our neighbors for generations, Father," she chided gently. "It behooves us to be civil."

Ignoring the earl's grunt of derision, Lady Pamela smiled at the baronet when their eyes met across the hall. She was oddly gratified when the handsome Sir Rodney immediately made his way to her side. After respectfully greeting the earl, who pointedly ignored him, Morton bowed elegantly over her hand.

"Sir Rodney, what a pleasant surprise to find you in Brighton," she exclaimed. "I understood from your mother that you had planned to visit your aunt in Bath this summer."

"Hampshire was dashed dull without your charming presence, Lady Pamela," he murmured with practiced gallantry, his blue eyes twinkling flirtatiously. "And poor Aunt Gretchen came down with one of her interminable congestions, so I sent Mother off to nurse her and decided to try my luck in Brighton. As it turns out, my dear Pamela," he added with a wicked grin, "I am glad I did, since you are here."

Ignoring the low growl of warning that issued from the earl's throat at this unseemly familiarity, Sir Rodney invited Lady Pamela to join him on the dance floor.

Much to her relief, her father offered no resistance beyond a glowering frown. "I shall be in the card room, Pamela," he snapped as she rose from her chair. "Send for me when that cousin of yours deigns to put in an appearance."

"Aha!" the baronet remarked as they watched Lord Melrose disappear into the crowd. "So our Fearless Freddy is with you, Pamela. And which particular lovely has caught his eye this summer? Last year, if I remember correctly, it was the Galloway chit who had him jumping through hoops. Not a chance in a million, of course, but he bled all over me for more than a month before the chit became betrothed to Wentworth's heir. I understand they are expecting their first child in August."

The music struck up at that point, and Morton placed an arm about her waist and guided her expertly round the floor. Lady Pamela found the seductive rhythm of the waltz particularly pleasing, and Sir Rodney was, as she well knew, an excellent dancer. Having eschewed the London Season for the past few years, she had little opportunity to indulge her passion for dancing, and suddenly she felt a glow of pleasure to find herself once again caught up in the wonder of the music in the arms of her childhood friend and erstwhile suitor.

"Well, who is she?"

Sir Rodney's gentle prodding brought her back from the romantic haze of the music.

"Freddy's new *inamorata*?"

"Who else?" he said with a wide grin.

"You are a sad gossip, Rodney," she remarked, knowing that she spoke nothing but the truth. The baronet was a fountain of information about all the various peccadilloes and scandals that bubbled beneath the serene surface of the *haut monde*.

"I fear that poor Freddy is completely smitten with Miss Prudence Erskin-Jones," she said in a neutral voice. "So much so, in fact, that he is talking marriage again. Father has yet to meet the chit."

The baronet's reaction was not exactly the one Lady Pamela had expected. First he looked startled, and a flash of something perilously close to a leer crossed his handsome face. Then he laughed, throwing his head back with uninhibited amusement and drawing not a few censorial glances from the couples around them.

"The Incomparable? Surely you are jesting, my dear Pamela. Even Fearless Freddy cannot be quite as naive as that."

"I am afraid he is, Rodney," Lady Pamela replied, wondering just what her friend knew about Prudence that warranted his caustic remark.

Sir Rodney regarded her speculatively. "I gather you have met the little Beauty," he said, raising one elegant eyebrow questioningly.

"Indeed I have," she said shortly. She was not anxious to blurt out her misgivings about her cousin's latest flirt, but she was well aware that if anyone would know every last bit of scandal about the Beauty, it would be Sir Rodney.

The baronet grinned, seeming to read her thoughts. "And do you approve of Freddy's choice of bride, my dear?" he demanded, amusement clearly visible in his eyes.

Lady Pamela felt a stab of pity for the Beauty, whose reputation Sir Rodney was evidently eager to shred. "She is so very young . . ." she began hesitantly.

Sir Rodney laughed again, and this time Pamela was sure he leered. "Oh, yes indeed, the darling girl is that all right, but she makes up for lack of years with surfeit of experience, my dear Pamela." Suddenly, his expression became serious. "I will not sully your ears with tales out of school, but I will say that Miss Prudence is not the kind of female I would welcome into my family, which has, let us face it, harbored its own black sheep over the years."

Lady Pamela gazed up at him in dismay. The baronet had done no more than confirm the suspicions that had flitted through her own head ever since meeting the Beauty. She had hoped that she might be wrong in her judgment of the younger girl, but now it appeared that her worst fears were confirmed. Freddy was about to fall victim to a scheme as old as the world itself.

"I do not want to believe what you are telling me, Rodney. But if you are quite sure it is so, perhaps you could warn Freddy. He will not listen to me."

The baronet's face showed sudden alarm. "I would do anything to please you, Pamela," he said quickly. "You know that. But do not ask me to meddle in another man's *affaires de coeur*. I daresay Freddy will wake up sooner or later to the sad truth that females are rarely what they appear to be. A man places life and limb, not to mention his heart, in jeopardy when he chooses a wife."

Lady Pamela bristled. "How cynical you have grown, Rodney," she said acidly. "It is news to me that you have a heart. And if all gentlemen endorsed your philosophy, none of them would ever marry."

"Most of us wish we did not have to, my dear—"

"Now that is arrant nonsense," she interrupted crossly. "Do you wish to see poor Freddy suffer another disaster like last year's fiasco with Miss Galloway?''

"It is nothing to me what your cousin does, Pamela. You refine too much on the matter. His eyes will soon be opened, believe me. The Beauty makes little attempt to hide her preference for titles and deep pockets, and Freddy lacks both at present."

"You are callous beyond bearing," Lady Pamela snapped, thoroughly put out by the baronet's nonchalant attitude. "After all, you claim to have proof of the Beauty's . . ." She hesitated, not comfortable with the word that she had been about to utter. "Proof of Prudence's lack of . . ." she began again, only to pause for want of a proper word. "Her want of propriety," she finished lamely, wishing that Rodney would cease grinning at her.

"You are much too kind, my dear," he remarked. "And anything I might say must surely pale before the scandal I suspect is about to unfold when our flirtatious Beauty hits her stride tonight. Already she has all the bucks in the room ogling her."

From across the room, Lady Pamela clearly detected the unmistakable tinkling laughter of Miss Prudence Erskin-Jones. Slowly she turned towards the entrance and was struck once again by the perfect beauty of the girl standing at the entrance smiling charmingly at the gentlemen who began to crowd around her. She was flanked on one side by her mother, whose sharp face reflected a triumphant expression, and on the other by a bemused-looking Freddy, who was getting edged out by the more seasoned gentlemen demanding to sign the Beauty's dance card.

To her chagrin, Sir Rodney took her arm and started across the room. "I trust I will not be too late to get my name on that card," he murmured as they made their way through the couples who were taking their places for the next set.

"I take it you know Prudence," she remarked coldly, unaccountably put out at the notion.

Sir Rodney laughed easily, his eyes brushing hers briefly. "I have never been known as a slow-top," he answered lightly. "I make it my business to know all the latest lovelies."

This was more than Lady Pamela could endure. Resolutely, she came to a halt and withdrew her hand from Sir Rodney's arm. "Then I suggest you run along and secure your dance, Rodney," she remarked coolly. "I shall inform my father that Freddy and his party have arrived."

Without waiting to see the baronet's reaction, she turned on her heel and directed her steps towards the card room, hoping that her father was not in the middle of a game.

*   *   *

When Lord Melrose finally emerged from the card room, Lady Pamela felt her premonition of calamity increase considerably. Her father was accompanied by none other than her Aunt Rose's cousin by marriage, Archibald West, Viscount Summerset. She sighed and pasted a cordial smile on her face.

"Ah, Pamela," her father exclaimed jovially as soon as he saw her, "you remember Lord Summerset from last summer do you not, my dear? Aunt Rose's cousin. As luck would have it, we were at the same faro table, and I have invited him to dine with us tomorrow night. Summerset tells me he has taken a house for the summer," he added, quite as though he did not already know this fact, "so we shall be seeing him frequently, I trust."

Lady Pamela forced her smile to widen. "Yes, indeed," she murmured, wishing her father were not quite so transparent in his efforts to snare the viscount for his daughter. "Aunt Rose should be here by then, and I am sure she will be happy to see you, my lord."

"There you are mistaken, my dear," her father cut in. "It appears that Rose has been called up to Scotland after all. The children have come down with mumps, or something of that nature. So she will not be joining us after all."

Pamela thought nostalgically of her pianoforte languishing back at Melrose Park.

Lord Summerset bowed, but said nothing, and Lady Pamela recalled that scintillating conversation had not been one of his lordship's captivating qualities. She tried again.

"Are the children with you, my lord?" she asked innocently, conscious of her father's sudden frown.

"Yes," the viscount replied shortly.

"All five of them?" she inquired sweetly, disregarding her father's warning scowl. "How vastly entertaining!" she added, deciding at the last minute that the viscount might take umbrage at her impertinence.

Lord Summerset stared at her briefly, and for an agonizing moment Lady Pamela thought he might give her the set-down she deserved. His eyes were inscrutable, however, and he surprised her by deflecting her curiosity with a question of his own.

"Am I to understand that you like children, Lady Pamela?"

Nonplussed, Lady Pamela wondered whether the widower was more astute than she had given him credit for. She met his brown gaze frankly, and wondered what would happen if she confessed a disinclination to raise another woman's brood. Her father would doubtless have a fit of apoplexy were she to admit such an unnatural predilection, and too much honesty at this point would put an end to his expectations of securing the viscount as a son-in-law. So she lowered her eyes modestly and murmured something deliberately incoherent. Anything, she reasoned, was preferable to an outright lie.

Lord Summerset cleared his throat and tactfully changed the subject. "Dare I hope that you will honor me with a dance later this evening, Lady Pamela?"

With a feeling of relief, Lady Pamela raised her eyes to his face and smiled. Was she perhaps whistling an eligible suitor down the wind? she wondered, holding out her card and watching the viscount covertly as he scrawled his bold signature opposite a cotillion.

The viscount was an imposing figure of a man, Lady Pamela had to admit. Rather too stern and humorless for her taste, but tall and impressive in a donnish sort of way. He was well known at Oxford for his lectures on Anglo-Saxon archeology, and was presently engaged in exploring an ancient barrow recently discovered along the coast west of Brighton. Idly, she wondered if the viscount would expect his wife to take an interest in his old bones and rusty swords. The notion held no appeal for her.

Further exchange was interrupted by Cousin Freddy, who appeared by her side, looking anything but pleased with himself. Lady Pamela could see at a glance the cause of his frustration. He was accompanied, not by the glittering Beauty he had hoped to present to his uncle, but by a smug-faced Mrs. Erskin-Jones, who lost no time in gushing volubly, first over Lady Pamela and then, after Freddy's curt introductions, over Lord Melrose and the viscount.

"My darling Prudence is dying to make your acquaintance, my lord," the purple-gowned matron declared in a voice that was a shade too strident to be pleasing. "She is all atwitter at the honor you bestow upon her, my lord." She turned her shrewd gaze to the viscount and beamed ingratiatingly. "And what a grand surprise she will have when she discovers that she is about to add, not only an earl, but also a viscount to her list of acquaintances. She will be ecstatic, my lord, I assure you."

Some imp of mischief within Lady Pamela refused to let this pass unchallenged. "Surely you do not mean to imply that your daughter spent the entire London Season as the Toast of the Town without running afoul of those notorious titled rakes who seem to be accepted everywhere?"

Mrs. Erskin-Jones looked at her sharply. "Prudence has strict
orders not to encourage such rogues, Lady Pamela," she said, her
mouth primly pursed as though she had bitten into a green damson.

"I applaud your sentiments, madam," Lord Summerset remarked dryly, his gaze resting briefly on Lady Pamela's face.

Could it be that the starched-up viscount meant his comment as
a mild reproach? she wondered, amused at the notion. No doubt
the man considered females vastly silly creatures who needed
constant guidance from a father or husband to keep their dainty
feet on the straight and narrow. And from falling into the clutches
of rakes and libertines like that abominable marquess in Queen's
Road Park this morning. Lady Pamela wondered whether she
dared remind the Beauty's mother of that clandestine meeting. A
glance at Freddy's worried face warned her to keep that piece of
scandal for another time.

"You are very gracious, my lord," the matron simpered. "Gentlemen do not often understand how difficult it is to raise a delicate flower like my daughter and keep her innocence pure and
unsullied in a world that holds virtues lightly. Luckily, I have
been blessed with a modest and obedient daughter, and I shall be
loath to part with her, my lord. But the time has come to find a
gentleman of honor and impeccable reputation to accept the responsibility of guiding my sweet little girl through the vicissi-
tudes of life with a gentle and loving hand."

In the leaden silence that followed this extraordinary speech,
Lady Pamela felt her unruly inner imp dying to ask Mrs. Erskin-
Jones if her precious daughter liked children. She resisted the
temptation however, when she noticed the gentlemen's shocked
expressions. Her father looked predictably revolted by the lady's
intemperate display of sentiment, his brushy eyebrows bridging
his nose threateningly. Lord Summerset's face was frozen into an
expression of intense distaste, and his lips drawn into a thin, forbidding line. Freddy, however, appeared torn between embarrassment and gratification. Apparently convinced that he was that
fortunate gentleman who would lead the Beauty through life with
love and tenderness, he fairly beamed with pride.

Lady Pamela wished her cousin were less naive.

The awkward moment, which seemed to stretch out inter-
minably, was interrupted by the unmistakable tinkle of girlish
laughter—a shade too piercing for propriety—and Lady Pamela
saw her father wince. She dared not cross glances with the viscount.

"Why, here is the dear girl now," the Beauty's mother ex-claimed in a doting voice, turning to scan the dance floor, where couples were clustered at the close of a country dance.

Lady Pamela followed the matron's gaze and was not surprised to see the blond Beauty clinging with unbecoming familiarity to the arm of Sir Rodney Morton, while bandying words with an ad-miring group of young bucks. She caught the baronet's amused glance and frowned a warning. Sir Rodney recalled his manners and adroitly steered the giggling partner towards the Melrose party, while Lady Pamela watched with cynical amusement as the Beauty's limpid blue eyes fixed themselves speculatively on Lord Summerset.

Would the icy formality of the stiff-rumped viscount melt under the onslaught of beauty he was about to experience? she wondered. Frost versus fire. She had a sneaking suspicion that the viscount would find himself ensnared and that poor Freddy's nose would be sadly out of joint before much longer.

CHAPTER FIVE

Beauty Versus Beast

The two gentlemen arriving at a ridiculously late hour—more fashionable in the Metropolis than in the semi-informal setting of a Brighton Assembly Hall—caused heads to turn and tongues to wag. A lively country dance was in full swing, but that did not prevent the young ladies on the floor to cast their eyes longingly over the impeccably dressed gentlemen lounging at the entrance. The matrons gathered on the settees at the far end of the hall eyed the newcomers avidly, speculating in hushed voices on the names of their tailors—the shorter gentleman obviously favored Scott, while the tall one's coat could have come from none other than Weston—their breeding, rank, and fortune, and, perhaps of more immediate interest to the gossips, whether one or the other of them stood in need of a wife.

"That looks like Emmaline Stevens's nephew."

The high stage whisper reached them from across the room as the music came to a sudden halt, and prompted the taller of the two gentlemen to raise his jeweled quizzing glass and fix his enlarged eye on the culprit until that flustered lady took refuge behind her fan.

"I wonder who the arrogant-looking gent is," a less refined voice remarked above the rising hubbub of voices. "Looks like one of your London dandies, to be sure. I wager he is up to no good, Abigail. Best keep your Flossy away from the likes of him."

"Dandy?" Lord Monroyal murmured under his breath to his companion, his fine upper lip curling contemptuously. "I knew I should not have come here, Willy. Let us retire instantly before these rural Tabbies hurl worse insults at me."

"My dear Robert," Hampton said soothingly, his brown eyes twinkling with genuine amusement, "if you wish to sample a plump pullet, old man, you must step into the hen house. No two ways about it." He waved a manicured hand in the general direction of the gossips. "This is a small price to pay for the delights in store for you tomorrow if our lovely Prudence proves to be as willing as you say she is."

"Oh, she is willing, all right," the marquess replied testily, "but I am beginning to wonder if this fiasco is worth the five hundred guineas that Gresham wagered. I must have been beyond anything bored to have taken him up on it. Either that or in my cups."

He stared around the hall morosely for a moment, wishing he could back out of the wager without losing face. The precocious Beauty had lost her appeal; the thrill of the chase, which as a young man had driven him to feats of recklessness, had turned sour in his mouth, and the need to prove to the Earl of Ravenville that he could still seduce any female he set his mind to now seemed a puerile and pathetic endeavor. The entire scheme was unworthy of him, and for perhaps the first time in his life, the marquess despised himself for accepting such a childish challenge.

But a gentleman did not refuse a wager, he thought wryly.

Suddenly, a thought that had been floating around the edges of his consciousness took on a tangible shape. He turned to Hampton, fixing his friend with a hard stare. "Unless, of course," he murmured softly in a dangerous voice, "in spite of all reports to the contrary, the chit is a virgin." He paused for a moment, wondering if the guileless Willy had been induced to lead him like a bear to the slaughter. "If such were the case," he continued, his voice suddenly icy, "tomorrow's little rendezvous could cost me ten thousand pounds."

Willy Hampton's mouth opened, but no sound came out. Then he shook his head vigorously. "You are all about in the head, lad," he blurted in a voice unsteady with emotion, "if you believe I could play you such a scurvy trick, Robert. Or Raven either, for that matter. And if you still doubt me, I will cover the damned wager myself. My word on it."

His friend's surprise and outrage were genuine; the marquess was sure of it. He smiled ruefully. "No offense meant, old man." He glanced around the hall, oblivious of the curious stares of the dancers gathering for the next set. "If you want the truth, Willy," he said reluctantly, "I am bloody bored with the whole thing. Chits of seventeen are not my style anyway. More hair than wit, most of them. Cannot wait to put all this behind me, old chap, and that is gospel truth."

Hampton stared at him for a long moment, his brown eyes worried. Then his face split into a grin, and he slapped the marquess on the shoulder. "I gather you are serious, Robert. Never heard you talk of the gospel before. I suggest we get this affair over with and shake the dust from our boots, old man. Day after tomorrow we can leave at the crack of dawn and be at Stilton Grange by tea-time. What do you say, sport?"

"And founder my team in the attempt, I assume?" the marquess replied, some of his humor returning. "But you are right, Willy, as usual. Let us seek out the lovely Prudence and dazzle her with our famous charm."

"You have an unusual amount of competition tonight, Robert," Hampton twitted him. "Mostly moonlings and gapeseeds by the look of it, but I spy a more substantial rival among them. Summerset, is it not? Wonder what that dry old stick expects to gain by dancing attendance on the Beauty.

"What we all expect to gain, no doubt," the marquess replied bluntly. "Except that I intend to be the one to take the prize."

Without further ado he stepped down onto the dance floor and strode over to where Miss Prudence held court in the center of a group of young bucks vying for a dance. Shouldering his way to her side, the marquess lifted her small gloved hand to his lips in an elegant gesture and gazed into her eyes with a lazy smile he knew was lethal to females of all ages.

"My *dear* Miss Erskin-Jones," he murmured seductively, "what a delight to see you again. I think this waltz is mine, is it not?" He twitched the card out of her slack grasp and perused it with a half smile on his lips. There was not a single dance unclaimed, but this did not faze a man of his experience. "Ah, here we are," he murmured, scrawling his name above the signature already claiming the dance in question.

"I say, Monroyal," a voice protested at his elbow, "Miss Erskin-Jones has promised the waltz to me. Fair is fair."

Lord Monroyal turned very slowly and glared icily down at the young man who had ventured to thwart him. "Fair?" he repeated softly, as though the word was foreign to him.

The young man blenched and seemed to shrink to size.

The Beauty giggled. "Oh, do not be such a spoil sport, Freddy," she gushed in a shrill, girlish voice that grated on the marquess's ears. "I shall save you a dance later." After that ingenuous speech, she seemed to forget the young man's existence. Placing her hand in Monroyal's, she allowed herself to be led onto the floor.

From the other side of the hall, where she sat with Mrs. Erskin-Jones, Lady Pamela had seen the two elegantly dressed gentlemen enter the dance hall. She turned her face away to avoid meeting their gaze and concentrated on describing to the garrulous matron the time she had spent in Bath at a private academy for young girls. The matron claimed to know several ladies of distinction who made their homes in that spa resort, but Lady Pamela was acquainted with none of them. She envied her father, who had once again escaped to the card room.

The telltale tinkle of the Beauty's laughter tempted her to cast a glance in that direction. The set had ended, and Prudence stood bandying words with a ragtag group of young men who were ogling the chit shamelessly. As she watched, Lady Pamela saw the marquess stride purposefully across the dance floor and shoulder his way into the rowdy group. From where she sat, the gentleman's salute to the Beauty seemed too intimate by half, but the chit's only response was another exaggerated tinkle of delight.

Where on earth was Freddy? Lady Pamela fumed. And why had he not claimed the Beauty after her dance with Lord Summerset and escorted her back to her mother as propriety demanded? A girl as young as Prudence had no business standing up for the waltz, in any case, she thought crossly. From a catty remark by the Beauty's mama, Lady Pamela had discovered that, in spite of her astonishing beauty, Prudence had never received one of those coveted vouchers for Almack's that had been known to make or break a young lady's first Season. This in itself spoke volumes about the Beauty's real standing in London's *beau monde*. If the patronesses of Almack's—known by mothers of girls who had been slighted as the Gorgons—had made it their business to ignore the Beauty, then Lady Pamela's suspicions had been right on the mark. Miss Erskin-Jones was not top-drawer, or anywhere near it.

Glancing at the young lady in question, Lady Pamela was in time to see the marquess lead the Beauty onto the dance floor. She considered intervening in the name of propriety, but was unsure of her ability to impress upon the chit's mother that well-bred young ladies of seventeen did not dance the waltz, just as they did not wear silk ball gowns in deep pink tones, cut to reveal the vast majority of the chit's abundant charms. Nor did they wear diamonds, and in such quantities, too. In such *vulgar* quantities she added, with a surge of waspishness that shocked her.

It would be equally useless to inform the smirking matron at her side that Prudence should not be dancing with the Marquess of Monroyal at all. To encourage a notorious rake and libertine was tantamount to announcing one's lack of morals to the entire world. Even as she watched, the Beauty glided by in a haze of pink silk, sparkling diamonds, and tantalizing laughter. Lady Pamela gritted her teeth in frustration. A fine chaperone she had turned out to be.

Whatever his faults, one had to admit the rogue was a splendid dancer.

Reluctantly, Lady Pamela's eyes lingered on the gentleman's lithe form, mesmerized by the hypnotic sway of his body, the ripple of muscle beneath the dove-gray knee breeches, the possessive curve of his arm firmly encircling the Beauty's tiny waist. It would be enchanting to dance with such a man, she thought dreamily. The notion captivated her imagination, and without conscious effort her vivid mind transported her to the dance floor and put her into the arms of the gentleman in gray. She distinctly felt the pressure of his palm on her back, the magnetic pull of his chest only inches—surely less than the required twelve—from her own, the tingle of excitement every time his knee accidentally—or was that deliberately?—brushed her thigh in the turns.

And then he smiled, a cynical, predatory, wolfish smile, and Lady Pamela's dream faded, leaving her oddly breathless and vaguely unsatisfied. That smile had held the promise of forbidden pleasures of which she knew less than nothing. And it had not been for her in any case, she reminded herself bluntly. The Beauty did not appear to share her fear of that predatory smile, for she laughed up into the gentleman's lean face and fluttered her eyelashes furiously.

Lady Pamela looked away abruptly, disgusted at the shameless spectacle. *Disgusted?* She paused suddenly as an unpleasant thought stuck her. Was it really disgust she felt? Could it not be a less noble sentiment?

Always scrupulously honest with herself, Lady Pamela forced her gaze to seek out the couple who had caused her such distress. The marquess was still smiling, that contented, cat-like smile that told her more clearly than words that the villain was intent on seducing Miss Prudence Erskin-Jones. Had already seduced her, in all probability, and that lewd smile a prelude to his enjoyment of the prize.

Shocked at the direction of her thoughts, Lady Pamela nevertheless had to admit that no man had ever smiled at her like that. Not even Rodney at his most desperate. Nor did she wish for it, she told herself sternly, almost convincing herself that this was true. And in any event, she compromised, she would never welcome such impertinence from a man as depraved as the marquess.

Suddenly overcome by confusing and contradictory emotions,

Lady Pamela stood up, interrupting Mrs. Erskin-Jones in the middle of a scandalous story about the young and giddy Duchess of Ridgeway, and trod purposefully in the direction of the card room. Ten minutes later, her father joined her, a frown of annoyance on his face.

"What ails you, child?" he demanded. "Surely it is not time to go home already?"

"Yes, Father, it is," she responded firmly. When Lord Melrose was winning, he was never eager to leave, but Lady Pamela was adamant. "I simply cannot stand another minute in that female's company."

"I thought Summerset was with you, Pamela. What have you done to scare him off?"

"Lord Summerset made his excuses after that vulgar Tabby started to quiz him about the amenities and staff at Summerset Hall. She had the gall to tell the poor man that his servants were probably cheating him, and that his children needed the loving hand of a mother."

"And where is that chit Freddy is so taken with?" Lord Melrose demanded after a moment's pause. "I gather you are none too impressed with her either?"

Instead of answering, Lady Pamela gestured towards the dance floor, where the marquess, clearly visible above the crowd, and the Beauty, the focus of everyone's eyes, still waltzed together as though they were alone.

Lord Melrose observed the pair for a long moment, his face turning an angry purple. Then he escorted his daughter out of the hall, muttering under his breath about rogues and hussies.

Lady Pamela was glad of the heavy silence on the drive home. It gave her more than enough time to admit that her premonition had been correct. The evening had been a total disaster. Besides which, she had developed a real megrim.

After a restless night, Lady Pamela opened one jaundiced eye when Betty tapped at her door the next morning, drank half a cup of her morning chocolate, and went back to bed. She was not to be disturbed, she instructed the abigail. Not even for her cousin, she emphasized, knowing that Freddy had a way with servants, especially the females, who were all following the romantic saga of his courtship with bated breath.

It had never been her custom to dawdle in bed, even after a late night, so Pamela was not surprised that sleep would not come. In any case it would not have mattered, for barely an hour later,

Betty appeared by her bedside and coughed apologetically. Pamela considered pretending oblivion. Lord Melrose was unlikely to disturb her at that hour, so the culprit must be Freddy, and her cousin was one man she had no desire to see in her present state. On second thought, she changed her mind. She had an alarming number of things she wished to say to Freddy, and perhaps the sooner they were said and done with, the sooner she could get back to her piano and unfinished *étude*.

She opened her eyes and sat up.

"Oh, I am sorry to disturb you, milady," Betty stammered, twisting her apron strings nervously, "but Mr. Hancock assured me it was a matter of life and death."

"Everything is a matter of life and death for Mr. Hancock," she responded shortly. "Did he happen to mention whose life and whose death is at stake this time?"

"Oh, I am sure Mr. Hancock was talking about himself, milady," Betty said innocently, failing to catch the irony of her mistress's question.

"I am sure he was," Lady Pamela agreed, mentally adding hyperbole to Freddy's list of sins.

Thirty minutes later, when she entered the morning room to find an overwrought Freddy pacing up and down before the empty hearth, her suspicions were confirmed: her cousin was indeed in what her mother had always referred to as a state.

He swung round as soon as she opened the door, his face a picture of anguish. "Oh, Pamela!" he exclaimed, striding forward to take both her hands in his. "I am in a terrible pickle. Please say you will help me."

"Would I be correct to assume that this pickle, as you call it, involves Miss Erskin-Jones?" Pamela shook off her cousin's damp hands and sat down in a wing chair before the open window.

"Why, yes, naturally it concerns Prudence," he blurted impatiently. "Who else could it possibly concern?"

"There is no need to shout at me, Freddy," she remarked coldly. "Do sit down and get hold of yourself."

"I did not shout at you, Pamela," he countered, momentarily diverted.

"Well, sit down and tell me what has sent you up into the boughs, dear," she said more kindly, pointing at the green leather settee.

Freddy did as he was bid, and had Pamela not seen her cousin in a similar state the summer before, when his infatuation with

Miss Lucilla Galloway had run its course, she might have sent for the doctor immediately.

"The most terrible thing has happened, Pamela," he began, his youthful face clouded with gloom. "Uncle is being beastly about Prudence, and I need your help to straighten things out."

"What exactly did Father say?" she asked, having a pretty good idea of the earl's sentiments on the subject.

"He took violent exception to Prudence dancing with Monroyal last night. As if I could have done anything about it." His voice rose into a whine of despair. "I did mention to him—in a civil way you understand—that the waltz was promised to me, but do you know what that scoundrel did?"

"No, but do tell me, Freddy. I am all agog to hear how rakes overcome such conventional obstacles."

Her cousin looked aggrieved. "It is no laughing matter, Pamela. The bully merely scratched my name out and wrote in his own."

"Did he, indeed?" Pamela could easily imagine the marquess doing something this outrageous. It was definitely his style, and she was sure that nobody, including the Beauty herself, dared to gainsay the rogue. Prudence probably relished the attention, she thought uncharitably. It was just the kind of arrogant display by the aristocracy that would appeal to a mushroom like the Beauty. She should wash her hands of the whole affair and send Freddy off with a bee in his bonnet about his execrable taste in females. Instead, she was startled to hear herself say: "And what would you like me to do, Freddy?"

Her cousin brightened miraculously. "Oh, you are a brick, Pamela. I knew I could count on you. I beg you will call on Prudence immediately and lay the whole before her. I admit she is high-spirited and often careless in her ways—"

"High-spirited?" Pamela interrupted incredulously. "My dear Freddy, that girl is the most headstrong chit I have seen in a long time."

"How unkind you are, Cousin," Freddy said stiffly. "She is so young and innocent, and she can be the sweetest little darling when she chooses."

Lady Pamela agreed that this was so, particularly when the young lady was intent on getting her own way, although she did not say so to her infatuated cousin. "But she is rather forward, Freddy," she added, "even you will admit that. And her taste in gowns is too daring for her years."

Freddy looked nonplussed. "Everyone at the Assembly last

night seemed to think she looked enchanting," he argued in defense of his beloved.

"All the gentlemen did so, that I will grant you," Pamela said dryly. "But she should not wear that shade of pink."

Her cousin waved this remark aside. "I need you to make the darling see that if our betrothal is to go forward, she must forget about that rake Monroyal—"

"I agree entirely," Pamela broke in with no little relish. "However, I foresee some difficulty there, Freddy."

"What difficulty could there possibly be?"

Lady Pamela shook her head in exasperation. "Not to put too fine a point on the matter, Cousin, it seems obvious to me that the marquess has set his sights on the Beauty."

Freddy looked surprised. "Set his sights . . . ? Do you mean he is about to make my Prudence an offer?" His voice took on a tinge of indignation. "Monroyal does not strike me as the kind of man to fall into parson's mousetrap so easily."

"Precisely," Pamela said shortly. "I doubt a marriage offer is the kind he has in mind," she added bluntly. "And if you are honest with yourself, Freddy, you must see that such an . . . an informal arrangement might hold a certain allure for a girl like Prudence."

"I see nothing of the sort," he retorted angrily. "Are you trying to tell me that you think my Prudence is a lightskirt?"

Lady Pamela sighed. She did not have the heart to confess that unpalatable truth to Freddy in his present state. If he lacked the wit to see that, even without marriage, the dashing marquess outshone plain Freddy Hancock as patently as one of the many chandeliers hanging in the Regent's Pavilion outshone a simple wall sconce in Melrose House, then she was wasting her time arguing with him.

"Of course not, Freddy," she said patiently. "Now, tell me what you wish me to say to Miss Erskin-Jones."

As a result of that rash promise, Pamela soon found herself dressing for a drive in the Park. According to her cousin, Prudence had refused to drive out with him that afternoon, pleading a monstrous megrim—the Beauty's exact words, Freddy had assured her. Armed with a special tisane her mother had always prepared for her father on similar occasions, Pamela ordered the tilbury—declining John Coachman's reluctant offer to drive that humble conveyance over to Number 14 East Street—and set out to make the best of an impossible situation.

So engrossed was she in considering the best way to broach the

topic of ladylike behavior and to impress upon the Beauty the
need to embrace good manners with gusto and total dedication,
that she had turned into East Street and was halfway to the Erskin-
Jones residence when it dawned upon her that there was a vehicle
drawn up before Number 14. Instinctively, she drew her horse
down to a walk. There was something familiar about that curricle.

At that moment a gentleman came down the steps of Number
14 and Pamela recognized the marquess instantly. There was a
lady with him. A lady dressed in a light gown of pink muslin, entirely inappropriate for driving. But Miss Erskin-Jones appeared
oblivious to this sartorial faux pas. She was clinging limpet-like
to the gentleman's arm and laughing up into his face as though
they shared some naughty secret. Which no doubt they did,
Pamela thought enviously.

Her horse came to a stop of its own accord, and Pamela let it
stand while she watched with morbid fascination the playful flir-
tation in progress a scant fifty yards away.

The marquess tenderly deposited the pink bundle into his curricle and swung up himself with a lithe grace that Pamela found
hard not to admire.

And then with a sharp slap of the reins on the backs of his
glossy bay horses, the marquess shot out into the sparse traffic
and rattled away down East Street as if he owned it.

For several moments Pamela sat petrified, her mind in a whirl.
The Beauty had obviously recovered miraculously from her *monstrous* megrim; but why was she driving out without even a maid
to lend some appearance of propriety to the affair? And with that
notorious rake again? She could not be so naive as to believe that
the *haut monde* could turn a blind eye to such blatant transgressions of its rigid code?

No, Pamela told herself reluctantly. The Beauty was neither
naive nor stupid. The only other alternative was that she had
thrown her lot in with the marquess. Perhaps they were running
off to be married, she mused, unwilling to look squarely at the
facts. No, there were no trunks, and Pamela strongly doubted the
Beauty would leave without her colorful gowns and jewels. Besides, one usually engaged a closed traveling chaise to elope. At
least that was what she had heard Lord Humphries's daughter did
when she ran off to Gretna Green two years ago with that half-
pay soldier. Luckily, the runaway couple had been caught within
a few hours, but the rumors still persisted that poor Margery
would die a spinster.

The picture of poor Freddy eating his heart out with worry at

Melrose House made her suddenly furious. Who did this chit
think she was to dally with a gentleman's affections so callously?
And what did that wretch think he was doing with a chit young
enough to be his daughter? It was simply not fair, and it was up to
Lady Pamela to do something about it. She owed it to Freddy.
This silly chit needed a keeper, and Freddy had given her the job.
She would do it, regardless of the consequences.

    Her face set in determined lines, Lady Pamela slapped the reins
across the rump of a very surprised horse and set him trotting
smartly in the direction taken by the curricle, which even now
swung round a corner and disappeared from sight.

CHAPTER SIX

Caught in the Act

The drive along the coastal road to the west of Brighton was pleasantly picturesque, and the weather warm and sunny. In truth, the marquess thought as he steadied his eager team through a flock of grazing geeze, the outing would have been close to perfect had not the lady sitting beside him in the curricle chattered without pause, quite putting to shame the blackbirds that rose in flocks from the hedgerows as they passed.

The countryside was similar enough to his own boyhood home in Devon to remind him that tomorrow at first light he would be on his way to Stilton Grange, even if he had to drag Willy from his bed long before his friend's usual hour.

An increased pressure on the vise-like grip Miss Erskin-Jones had clamped on his arm since they departed East Street also reminded him that certain things would be expected of him before he could be free again. Not for the first time, Lord Monroyal cursed himself for becoming embroiled with a chit hardly out of the schoolroom.

"Why will you not show me what you have bought for me, my lord?" the Beauty murmured, her rosy lips pouting prettily.

"After our picnic you may open it, my dear," the marquess replied lazily, patting the jeweler's box in his coat pocket. He glanced down at her upturned face and smiled teasingly. The chit really was a tasty armful of pink delight, he mused, his eyes taking in the tempting roundness of her bosom, spilling invitingly out of her bodice. Why then did she make him feel so ancient?

The thought startled him, and he brushed it hastily aside. He was *not* old, he reminded himself sharply, only experienced. The main reason for accepting this absurd wager was to prove to Raven that he had lost none of that experience, that *savoir faire* when it came to the art of seduction. He had always been the master, the envy of other men. He still was. The jarring thought that still festered at the back of his mind was patently ridiculous. Why should he feel the need to prove himself?

He felt another tug on his arm and glanced down ruefully at the sleeve of his new coat, mangled almost beyond recognition.

"I insist you give it to me *now.*" The dulcet voice threatened to turn shrill, and the marquess gritted his teeth. He glanced up ahead and was relieved to see the little cottage belonging to Willy's uncle rise above the hedgerow.

"We are nearly there, my pet," he said soothingly. "Over there." He pointed towards the cliffs. "Do you see it? The cottage with the thatched roof and hollyhocks by the front door."

"A cottage? Oh, how pretty it is," the Beauty cried, her annoyance evaporating. "And so many flowers! I would so love to have a little cottage like that. Does it belong to you, my lord?"

The marquess winced at the girl's lack of sublety. "No," he answered shortly. "I have only borrowed it for the afternoon so we may enjoy our picnic in comfort."

"How sweet of you," she simpered, all smiles again. "But do hurry up, my lord. I cannot wait to see what you have bought for me."

He pulled the curricle to a halt near a small copse of hazelnut bushes and jumped down to secure the horses. Then he reached up to the Beauty, who leaned out to him eagerly, clutching at him and squealing with mock fright as he swung her down. Had chits this age always been so tiresome, he wondered idly, or was he only now beginning to notice it?

He lifted down the picnic basket, prepared by Lady Stevens's cook, and led the Beauty, still clinging to his arm, into the cottage. Luckily, she was instantly captivated by the cozy interior, consisting of an ample parlor furnished with stuffed chairs and large, sprawling sofas. Through an archway, he could see a small dining room and a door into what must be the kitchen. A narrow, dark staircase circled up to the first floor and, he supposed, the two bedrooms Willy had spoken of when they visited the place the day before.

On the whole, the marquess thought, the little cottage made an ideal site for an amorous rendezvous. Perhaps he should give some thought to acquiring a hideaway of his own on the Devon coast for just such tender assignations. As the secluded nature of the setting began to work its magic, he felt the familiar stirrings of desire. When the Beauty moved, with a practiced expertise that belied her innocence, into his arms, he found himself holding her as he had held more women in his day than he cared to remember.

This one was not only young and beautiful, she was also delightfully eager, and some of his misgivings dissipated. It was not long before the marquess was thoroughly absorbed in peeling the Beauty's bodice and chemise down to her waist and savoring the warmth of her perfumed skin with his mouth and hands.

Somewhere along the path to complete intimacy, he had shed his coat and encouraged the slim fingers of his latest conquest to loosen his neatly tied cravat and eventually, as the lady became more demanding, to pull it carelessly from his neck and unbutton his shirt. He had reached the crucial point in the game and was ready to lay the seductive creature down on one of the comfortable-looking sofas, when he thought he heard a noise in the kitchen.

He paused for a moment, but when the Beauty's mouth moaned softly against his bare chest, any thought of investigating fled his heated brain. As he reached for the closing of his breeches, the noise came again, this time much closer.

And then he clearly heard a female gasp.

The sound brought his head up abruptly, and the marquess found himself staring into a pair of horrified hazel eyes.

"Prudence!" Lady Pamela exclaimed in shocked tones, "whatever do you think you are doing, child?"

Even before the words left her mouth, Pamela realized how ridiculous they must seem to the two occupants of the parlor. It was as plain as the nose of her face what the chit was doing, and she noted a flicker of cynical amusement in the gentleman's hooded gray eyes. The rogue was laughing at her. She felt herself blushing furiously.

Averting her offended gaze from the sight of the Beauty's bare pink bosom nestling intimately against the gentleman's chest, Pamela took a deep breath and tried to control her racing heart. Never in her entire life had she been privy to such a shockingly immodest spectacle, and for a moment words failed her.

Since neither of the culprits seemed inclined to answer her, Pamela swallowed hard and tried again. "What a disgraceful spectacle," she began, realizing too late that her choice of words came nowhere near describing the lewd nature of the sin Miss Erskin-Jones had been caught in the act of committing. "Cover yourself instantly, girl. And tidy your hair. You look like a common tart."

Prudence looked mutinous, and her face puckered as if she meant to burst into tears.

"And no Cheltenham melodramas if you please," Lady Pamela added coldly. She tried unsuccessfully to keep from staring at Lord Monroyal's naked throat and the slice of muscular chest she could see through the open shirt. He was standing, one hand on a

lean hip, the other still loosely clasping the girl to his side, his
eyes alight with unholy amusement.

He looked magnificent—lithe, and lethal, and all too masculine
for her comfort. Pamela felt an uncontrollable urge to touch the
curly black hairs that escaped through the shirt with the tips of her
fingers. She had no idea where these sinful desires sprang from,
but she quashed them ruthlessly.

"We are only having a picnic," Prudence muttered with an attempt at flippancy that did not quite come off. "Now you have
spoiled everything," she added, her voice full of resentment.

Lady Pamela could not beleive her ears.

"You will do as you are told this instant," she said through gritted teeth. "And then you will leave by the back door and get into
the tilbury. I intend to deliver you to your mother and suggest that
she take you back to Northumberland immediately. You are not to
be trusted here."

"But I do not *want* to leave," the Beauty whined, her lovely
face screwed up in an ugly moue. "I want to stay for the picnic."
She paused for a second, and then, with a calculating gleam in her
eyes, she added in a wheedling voice, "Would you like to join us?
I am sure his lordship would not mind. Would you, Robert?"

Lady Pamela felt her cheeks burn. Not only did the chit have
the impertinence to pretend that the picnic was the main reason
for this disgraceful assignation, but she was inviting her, Lady
Pamela Hancock, to participate in the festivities. The visions of
what this invitation entailed gave her serious palpitations, and she
closed her mind resolutely to the disturbing pictures that danced
before her eyes.

She dared not glance at the marquess, but felt his eyes apprais-
ing her and heard his chuckle of amusement.

"*Au contraire,* my pet," he drawled. "I wholeheartedly endorse
your intriguing idea. Perhaps we can teach your . . . your guardian
angel is she?—a thing or two about—"

She had wanted to avoid addressing the licentious rogue, but
his suggestion was the outside of enough. "Are you so lost to all
sense of decency that you can insult a lady with impunity?" she
demanded hotly. "You are beyond anything vulgar and depraved.
Prudence"—she turned to the Beauty who had, she was thankful
to note, pulled her bodice up into place—"go out to the tilbury
immediately. I shall join you in a moment."

With a flounce and a pout, Prudence flung out of the room, and
Pamela heard the back door slam with a resounding crack.

In the silence that followed, she fixed the marquess with an indignant stare. "And as for you, sirrah," she said icily, trembling a little at her own temerity, "I trust that at least you will have the decency not to bruit this incident about among your friends. A young girl's reputation may not have any significance to one such as you," she added, her lip curling in disgust, "but believe me that if this scandal gets out, poor Prudence will be ruined for life."

He was beginning to look annoyed, and Pamela felt a tremor of fear. When he spoke, his gray eyes were hard, and they regarded her insolently.

"Am I to understand, madam, that you believe poor Prudence, as you call her, is an innocent?"

"Of course she is," Pamela retorted angrily, quelling the ugly doubt that his words had stirred in her fevered brain.

He laughed then, and Pamela found herself mesmerized by the movement of his bare throat. There was something about this handsome scoundrel that touched some inner core that Pamela refused to acknowledge. Ruthlessly, she fixed her face in a frown.

"I see nothing amusing in the ruin of a young girl's life."

His lazy smile implied that they shared a delicious secret and made Pamela's mouth suddenly dry.

"Neither do I," he drawled in that warm voice of his that made her toes tingle. "I am not in the habit of debauching innocents. You will perhaps find that hard to believe, but I assure you that innocence holds no appeal for me. I never touch virgins."

Ths bald statement brought another flush to Pamela's face. She should have felt relief knowing that her own innocence put her beyond the scope of this man's interest. She *did* feel relieved, she told herself firmly, quickly suppressing a flash of disappointment that he had excluded her.

"You are mistaken about Prudence, my lord," she said stiffly, her eyes roving aimlessly about the room to avoid meeting his knowing gaze.

He sighed audibly. "I fear it is you who are mistaken, my dear girl," he said. "I can guarantee that your Beauty has about as much prudence in her as a cat in heat. Take my word for it; I am an expert in females."

Shocked beyond measure at his coarse comment, Pamela spat out the first thing that came into her head. "I am not your dear anything, sir, so I must ask you to mind your language."

"Ah, I see it is you who are the prude, madam," he said with a sensuous grin. "By the way, what is your name, my dear?"

Outrage at this cavalier treatment momentarily stunned her. "That is none of your concern, sir," she responded icily. "Now I

demand your word of honor . . ." Her voice trailed off as the
sound of a galloping horse was heard in the driveway. Her startled gaze flew to the window only to see her worst fears realized.
Her tilbury was racing away, rocking and jolting on the rough
road, the horse apparently bolting. The Beauty, hair flying wildly
behind her, pink skirt billowing in the wind, flapped the reins
recklessly and cracked the long whip over the horse's flattened
ears. Stepping across to the window, Pamela was in time to see
her conveyance sway out of the driveway onto the main road back
to Brighton and disappear in a cloud of dust.

"Well, there goes five hundred guineas up in smoke."

The caressing voice spoke so close behind her that Pamela
jumped. She could feel the marquess's warm breath on her neck.
The effect was disconcerting. When the import of his words sank
in, she whirled about, finding herself so close to him that she
could clearly see the flecks of darker gray in his eyes. He was
smiling down at her in a strange way, and Pamela felt a pang of
apprehension.

"Five hundred guineas?" she repeated stupidly. "Do you mean
to tell me," she demanded in a voice that was not quite steady,
"that this whole sordid affair was the result of a wager? A silly,
meaningless game?"

His grin widened, and Pamela's heart fluttered. "Females are
always a game to me, my dear. A delightful game to be sure, but a
game nevertheless."

"You are abominable," she hissed between clenched teeth. She
wished most fervently that she could think up a worse name to
call him, but she was not in the habit of insulting gentlemen to
their faces. His eyes slid down to her mouth, and Pamela experienced an odd mixture of fear and expectation. She tried to step
back, but the window ledge prevented her escape. She was
trapped, she thought, panic rising in her throat.

The marquess seemed amused at her plight, as though he knew
every one of her thoughts. He raised a hand and gently traced her
cheek and chin with one finger, while she stood petrified with
fear. But was it only fear that kept her rooted to the floor? she
wondered, incapable of turning her head or protesting this unseemly behavior.

Suddenly, he smiled, and Pamela had never seen such a seductive yet thoroughly dangerous smile on any man. She could not
suppress a shudder, whether of revulsion or anticipation she could
not say.

"Aye," he said softly, his breath warm on her face, "perhaps the day is not a total loss after all. The gaudy pheasant has flown, but perhaps this shy little dove might be persuaded to take her place."

Shy little dove? Although not exactly how Pamela thought of herself, it was supremely gratifying to hear a man refer to her so tenderly. He looked at her mouth again, and Pamela knew in her bones this rogue was going to kiss her.

But she was a *virgin,* she reminded herself, finding some comfort in the thought. Did he not say that innocence did not interest him? She remembered hearing him quite clearly. He did not touch virgins, he had said. Then why was he touching her now? Was it possible that he could not tell? Somewhere among her scattered bits of knowledge about gentlemen she had heard that they could always identify a virgin. How else would they know which one to choose as a wife? She was a little fuzzy on the subject, but she was sure that gentlemen, particularly those with a title to protect, always married virgins. So surely she was safe from this libertine?

Perhaps not, she thought in growing panic. Even now the marquess was moving closer, slipping a hand round her waist, pulling her against that fascinating bare chest. He *was* going to kiss her.

All she had to do was tell him, she reminded herself angrily, tell him she was one of those innocents he never touched. Why could she not seem to open her mouth to save herself? The smell of him enveloped her—shaving soap, tobacco, a faint whiff of brandy. They were all distinctively masculine smells, and they appeared to have deprived her of mobility and good sense.

Could it be possible that she wanted to be kissed? By a notorious rake like the marquess no less? No, that was preposterous. Unthinkable. Lady Pamela Hancock could not, *would* not sink that low.

"Stop this at once," she heard herself say in a small, unconvincing voice. But she made no move to struggle, and the marquess merely laughed. The sound of it washed over her, caressing her skin, making her body tingle in odd places.

And then suddenly he was doing it. His lips touched hers, gently at first until she felt the resistance go out of her, and then he opened his mouth, and Pamela was unprepared for the rush of heat that enveloped her. The brush of his tongue against her teeth, the gentle probing until she let him inside, the warm, wet sensation of his tongue exploring her mouth. All of it left her dizzy and light-headed.

In a haze of desire, Pamela became aware of his hands, warm

on her back, her hips, her neck, her hair. Her bonnet thrown aside, she felt her hair being unpinned, falling in waves over her shoulders. He buried his face in it and moaned in pleasure, before claiming her lips again in a kiss deeper and more demanding than the first.

She made only a token resistance when he molded her to his body until she felt every hard angle of him. The heat from his chest burned through her thin bodice, setting her breasts on fire. It no longer seemed to matter that no decent female should allow a gentleman to hold her so close and take such liberties with her. How many times had her mother warned her not to trust a gentleman who tried to cross the invisible line between propriety and licence. Such gentlemen did not respect females, Mother had said, and Pamela wondered what her mother would say if she could see her daughter now, locked in an embrace far more sensuous than she had ever dreamed possible.

It was this last thought that gave her the strength to break away. The marquess obviously did not respect her. The sweet wildness of his kisses could only be a prelude to intimacies Pamela had merely speculated about. They were not a subject her mother had felt the need to expand upon.

Grimly telling herself that this man was a notorious seducer who had taken advantage of her inexperience to work his magic upon her, Pamela stiffened her resolve. Of course she was partly to blame, she admitted, pushing against his chest with little effect. She would have spoken up the minute she realized his intent. If she had confessed her innocence, none of this would have happened.

She squirmed and struggled until the marquess lifted his head and gazed at her in surprise, his face flushed with passion.

"Let me go," she whispered, watching his eyes turn dark and flinty. "Please let me go."

His arms relaxed fractionally, and then he pulled her roughly against him again. "So," he growled in a mocking voice that filled her heart with dread, "you are a tease as well as a prude, are you? Well, let me tell you, sweetheart, you shall not escape so easily. I refuse to be cheated out of my pleasure twice in one afternoon."

These ominous words—their import clearer than anything her mother had ever told her—made Pamela quake; but in spite of her fear, she felt the sensuous warmth from his body invading her limbs, turning her knees to jelly, sapping her resistance. Desperately, she forced herself out of her dangerous lethargy. If she did not act at once, she thought in rising panic, she would be lost. Ruined. The hideous reality of this danger impelled her into action, and she raised her eyes to his face.

The marquess was still smiling, but his smile had lost some of its warmth. There was a cynical twist to his lips that Pamela felt the insane urge to kiss away. She suppressed this sinful thought before it could take root and took a deep breath.

"I am sorry to disappoint you, sir," she began. "but you see . . ."

"Oh, you will not disappoint me, my dear," he said softly. "I intend to have my little picnic, and you will join me. I promise you will not regret it. Come now, my sweet, coyness does not suit you." He bent his head and in a flash of intuition, Pamela saw that if he kissed her again, she would indeed be lost.

"No!" she exclaimed, more forcefully this time. "You really cannot do this. You see I am a . . ." Her protest faltered. She had never imagined it would be so difficult to confess her innocence. She tried again. "I have to tell you that I am . . ." Again her voice died away before she could pronounce the word that would save her—the word that would throw up a barrier between them that he would not cross. Something perverse prevented her from taking that step, as if she did not want that barrier between them, did not want to be saved.

The sudden realization of just how far this rogue had undermined her natural defenses frightened Pamela into blurting out the truth. "I am an innocent, my lord," she said, as if confessing to some unnatural flaw.

He stared at her a moment without moving. Then he let out a crack of laughter that had no amusement in it. "I do not believe you."

"I trust you will reconsider, my lord," she insisted. "Only think how awkward it would be to discover I am right after it is too late."

This argument appeared to carry some weight because he released her and started pacing up and down the cramped parlor, pausing every now and then to scowl at her. Still scandalized at what she had dared to say, Pamela prayed the floor would open and swallow her. No such miracle occurred, and when the marquess came to a halt before her, his expression was thunderous.

"Who put you up to this?" he demanded, his voice chilling her to the bone.

Pamela flinched. "Put me up to w-what?"

"Do not play the simpleton with me," he snarled. "Which of

my so-called *friends* put you up to this Canterbury trick? How much are they paying you to snare me into forfeiting the wager?"

"Another wager?" Pamela whispered helplessly.

"Yes," he barked, glowering at her. "And had it not been for your last-minute scruples, my dear, I would have been poorer by ten thousand pounds. I suppose I should thank you," he added sarcastically, "for deciding that your virginity is worth more than they offered you."

As the implications of this fantastic story began to sink in, Pamela felt her anger simmer.

"Tell me who sent you here to trick me, and I will make it worth your while. I will even double what they offered."

"No one sent me here, nor did anybody offer me anything," she stated emphatically. "My cousin asked me, as a favor, to keep an eye on Prudence. That is the only reason I am here, to prevent her from doing anything she will regret later."

"I do not believe that either," the marquess said, his gray eyes boring into hers. "Why would your cousin want you to protect a little tart like that? Has designs on her himself, is that it?"

Pamela's anger bubbled to the surface. "Must you always think the worst of people? If you must know, my cousin wants to *marry* Prudence. Not that it is any of your business," she added waspishly.

"Marry her? I can see that you really are an innocent, my dear." The marquess burst out laughing, and Pamela noticed that some of the humor was back in his voice. "What kind of a slow-top is this cousin of yours? I trust you will give him a full account of what you witnessed here today. That should open his eyes for him."

"You are insufferably arrogant and ill-mannered," Pamela exclaimed hotly. "And I think it is high time you escorted me back to Brighton."

"If you are quite sure you will not picnic with me, my dear," he remarked with a knowing smile that made Pamela's heart skip a beat. "And by the way, there is something that belongs to that little Beauty of yours, although she did not earn it." He took a black jeweler's box from his coat pocket and handed it to Pamela, who gazed at it in horror.

"Unless, of course, *you* would like to have it," he added with a faint smirk. "After all I do owe you something for saving me a considerable amount of money."

In a fit of fury, Pamela threw the box away from her. It landed on one of the sofas, and a ruby bracelet spilled out of the satin nest. "You owe me nothing, sir," she said in a choked voice. The thought of accepting anything from this man revolted her, particularly a bauble intended for another female in payment for unspeakable debauchery. She felt a sudden wave of nausea and closed her eyes to stop the room from swaying.

The pressure of a comforting arm about her shoulders and a lavender-scented handkerchief applied to her forehead felt good. Too good, she thought, knowing she could not afford to fall under the spell of this seductive rogue again. Instead of repulsing the marquess, Pamela found her head resting on his warm chest, his curly hair tickling her nose.

"You are overwrought, my dear," he murmured in her ear. "Perhaps you should rest a while before we leave."

Did this rogue never give up? she wondered, fighting off the dizziness that threatened to claim her. She dared not faint. Heaven alone knew what he would do to her if she lost consciousness. She raised her head, grasping his arms to steady herself.

"No," she whispered. "I am better now," she lied, aware that without his support she would sink to the floor and make a spectacle of herself.

"I think we should g-go," she stammered, "before—"

The slam of the front door opening violently interrupted her. She remembered hearing the marquess utter an oath, and then she turned to stare at the intruders.

Painfully conscious of the marquess's arm around her, her hands still clasping him for support, her hair loose about her shoulders, Lady Pamela felt the floor sway sickeningly under her feet.

"What is the meaning of this outrage?" she heard her father shout in a thunderous voice. Pamela gave a little moan and crumpled against that warm, inviting chest.

CHAPTER SEVEN

Desperate Measures

Robert Stilton, the sixth Marquess of Monroyal, had been in any number of tight corners in his long career as London's premier rake. Until today he had not regretted a single one of them, regarding these hair-raising experiences as part of the sport of chasing beautiful women, the thrill of trespassing successfully on other men's preserves.

Of course, until today he had never been caught.

The marquess glanced down at the unconscious woman in his arms. Although her face was unremarkable, he noted with odd detachment, her long lashes curved in a silky curtain against her pale cheeks. Thick chestnut hair framed the small face with a riot of curls whose charming disarray hinted at intimacies they had not enjoyed together. The irony of the situation was not lost on him. He was to be castigated for a crime he had not committed.

"What the devil are you doing with my daughter, sir?"

The harsh voice thrust itself relentlessly into Lord Monroyal's reverie, and the words—when they sank into his befuddled brain—caused a tremor of apprehension to shake his habitual sang-froid.

He raised his eyes and surveyed the angry red face of the gentleman who had addressed him. *His daughter?* If this were the case, and the chit was the innocent she claimed to be, he was facing a ticklish situation indeed. One that would require all his aristocratic aplomb and celebrated charm to escape unscathed. One which—an annoying little voice in a secluded part of his brain whispered with malicious glee—he might not escape at all.

"Well?" that relentless voice insisted. "What have you got to say for yourself, Monroyal?"

So, the marquess mused ruefully, his identity was known to the enraged gentleman standing in the doorway. And if the gentleman knew his name, he would undoubtedly be aware of his reputation. For a brief moment Monroyal regretted the misspent life that had brought him the notoriety he had, until that moment, cherished with a certain degree of perverse pride.

"You have the advantage of me, sir," he said coldly, delaying the moment when he would be forced to invent a plausible explanation for his presence in this lonely cottage, clutching a damsel in his arms who might well turn out to be his nemesis.

The broad-shouldered gentleman's face took on an ugly mottled hue, and he stepped menacingly into the room. "I am Melrose," he said harshly, "and that is my daughter you are mauling about. I trust you have a satisfactory explanation for this highly irregular behavior, my lord."

This thinly veiled threat brought an icy chill to the cozy room, and the marquess felt his blood congeal in his veins. *Melrose!* The man who had sliced his father's left arm to ribbons nearly thirty years ago and brought him close to death. Robert had been a lad at the time, but old enough to know that all was not well at Stilton Grange and to sense his mother's unhappiness. He had loved her unconditionally, disregarding his father's brusque advice to leave flowers and music to females, and concern himself with becoming more like his father. But Robert did not want to be like the late marquess, although everyone said he was the spitting image of his father. He wanted most desperately to comfort his mother, to bring back the smile that occasionally brightened her face when the marquess was away in London. Which was far too often, he had overheard the Stilton butler remark in his sententious way to the housekeeper when they thought he was up in the nursery with his tutor.

Believing, in his innocence, that his father's prolonged absences caused his mother's grief, Robert had run down to the stables one morning as the marquess waited for his team to be poled up. He still remembered vividly his father's cynical laugh when his son had begged him not to make his mother sad again.

" 'Tis not my leaving that makes her sad, Robert," Lord Monroyal had said bluntly, "but my staying." And then, as if suddenly aware that he had said too much, the marquess turned to chide the grooms for dallying. "Besides, it is out of the question to postpone my journey," he added after he had stepped into the curricle and taken the ribbons in his gloved hands. "I have important business in Town." He grinned then, but there was no humor in his eyes. "When you are older, Robert, you will understand exactly what I mean."

Years later, Robert had indeed understood. His father's business in Town had been a string of mistresses and the hedonistic life of a wastrel. Had he not grown up to follow precisely in his father's footsteps? the marquess reminded himself grimly, returning Lord Melrose's contemptuous stare unblinkingly. And that careless, self-indulgent career was about to land him—unless he was either very, very convincing or extremely lucky—in a situation from which he would be unable, with any degree of honor, to extricate himself.

"Answer my uncle, you filthy lecher!" exclaimed the young man who had remained half hidden behind the earl. "And what the devil have you done with Prudence?"

"Hush, Frederick," Lord Melrose snapped, without taking his eyes from the marquess. "No doubt this scoundrel has her upstairs awaiting his pleasure. Now, unhand my daughter instantly, unless you wish to answer to me for your temerity in laying a hand on my innocent child."

Monroyal felt an insane urge to laugh. The scene was turning into a Cheltenham melodrama played by an undistinguished company of second-rate actors. The stage was set for a farcical denouement: the outraged father, the ineffectual young suitor, the ravished maiden, lured to this secluded spot for a nefarious attack on her virtue by the lecherous villain—his own definitive role, Robert thought cynically. But what would that final scene entail? he wondered, strangely aloof from the imminent disaster he could feel gathering over his head. A theatrical duel perhance? A crowd-pleaser indeed, but hardly appropriate between that puny gapeseed cowering behind his uncle and a villain whose skill with the foils was common knowledge in London.

An uneasy thought struck him. Was it possible that history was about to repeat itself? he wondered, half intrigued, half appalled by the notion of crossing foils with his father's almost fatal opponent. But that was nearly thirty years ago, he reminded himself sharply. The Earl of Melrose—or plain Mr. Brown, the name Robert had known him by in those days—was thirty years older, thirty years slower than on that scandalous day he had faced Robert's father and bested him, one of the best swordsmen in England—a distinction Robert had inherited along with his father's lands and title and other less honorable pursuits.

The marquess glanced down again at the unconscious woman in his arms and felt an unfamiliar stab of pity for this unsuspecting innocent who had walked into the lair of the beast, so to speak. She would soon wake up to the unpleasant consequences of her rash action. Unless, of course . . .

His momentary pity dissipated as a new thought began to form insidiously in his mind. Unless between them, father and daughter, they had planned it this way. Why had he not though of it before? It was not as if this was the first time the marquess had been lured, cajoled, manipulated, or coerced towards the fatal jaws of parson's mousetrap—not by a long shot. He had grown wise in the little hypocrisies and deceits practiced by desperate mothers, eager to land one of the most coveted prizes on the Marriage Mart. In the past few years, of course, his aversion to matrimony had become so well established in the *haut monde* that he had ceased to be the target of serious-minded females. He had thought himself safe. That had been his mistake. He had grown overconfident, careless.

And now, here he was with one foot in the very trap he had spent twenty years avoiding.

With cold deliberation the marquess stepped over to the comfortable sofa he had intended for quite another purpose and gently laid his burden down. He settled a cushion under her head and brushed a wayward curl from her pale cheek. Then he turned to face the lady's father, a dangerous half smile on his face.

The sound of her father's angry voice intruded into the comfortable depths of her subconscious. Lady Pamela willed herself to ignore his bitter, strident tones, but she could not overcome the years of playing the dutiful daughter, and the safe haven of blackness gradually slipped away. She listened reluctantly as the jumble of angry words began to take shape around her. He was beyond reason outraged over something, and Pamela wondered what could possibly have provoked such a vitriolic outburst.

And then it all came back to her in agonizing detail. The wild chase after Prudence to the lonely cottage on the cliff. The silly chit's ingratitude at being saved from a lifetime of shame. Her running off with the tilbury. Lady Pamela herself abandoned in the company of a lecher and debaucher of young girls. And the devastating kiss that unscrupulous rogue had forced upon her. Had her father and Freddy not arrived in the nick of time, she thought, she might well have been ruined for life herself.

Freddy! Whatever was she going to tell poor Freddy about the unforgivable behavior of the girl he had planned to marry? She moaned softly and opened her eyes.

The sound of angry voices came to an abrupt halt, and Pamela found herself looking up into the faces of three gentlemen, all of them glaring at her quite hideously.

"Pamela," wailed Freddy in evident distress, "what have you done with my darling Prudence? You were supposed to look after her, or had you forgotten?"

Pamela struggled to sit up, stung by her cousin's unfair accusation into speaking her mind. "Your precious Prudence is a hoyden of the worst sort, I'll have you know, Freddy," she responded hotly. "Quite by chance I caught her driving out with this . . ." She paused to glance censorially at the marquess, who seemd to have turned into an inscrutable sphinx. "This libertine," she continued. "I followed them in my tilbury all the way out to this isolated cottage. The wretched girl had the effrontery to tell me they had planned a picnic," she added, her voice heavy with sarcasm. "Naturally I did not believe such a Banbury tale—"

"Then she is *here*?" Freddy interrupted eagerly, seemingly oblivious of his cousin's plight. He glanced around the small room as if expecting to see Prudence hiding under the furniture.

"You have not heard a word I said, Freddy," Pamela said disgustedly. "The silly chit ran away with the tilbury, and left me here to fend for myself."

After the words were spoken, Pamela wished she had chosen a less inflammatory turn of phrase. She glanced at the marquess and was chilled by the thin smile on his face and the ferocious glitter in his eyes.

Her father had remained ominously silent during this exchange. When he spoke, his tone brooked no argument. "You are a blithering idiot, Frederick," he said harsly. "Instead of wasting your breath on a little tart who is no better than she should be, as you would have realized had you listened to me earlier, you should concern yourself with your cousin's reputation."

"Prudence is *not* a tart," Freddy exclaimed, defying his uncle for perhaps the first time in his life. "I dare anyone to say she is," he added belligerently, avoiding Lord Melrose's ferocious scowl.

"I can guarantee that his lordship is absolutely correct."

This softly spoken observation contrasted oddly with the nervous tension in the room. All eyes swiveled towards the marquess, and Pamela clearly saw those cynical lips curl up at one corner. She also noted that he had not bothered to button his shirt or retrieve his cravat. With an effort she wrenched her gaze away from the bare chest, willing herself to forget the warmth of his skin against her cheek.

"That is quite enough, boy," the earl interjected sharply as his nephew took a threatening step towards the marquess. "Be thankful that you have escaped becoming the laughingstock of the *ton*.

And as for you, my girl," he added, glaring at Pamela, "all I can say is that I am heartily glad your sainted mother is not here to witness your shame."

Pamela felt as though the breath had been knocked out of her. "Shame?" she repeated faintly. "Whatever are you talking about, Father?"

No one answered her, and as Pamela glanced at each gentleman in turn, her eye was caught by the reflection of a female in a small mirror hanging over an ancient sideboard. The familiar face, framed by a tangle of chestnut curls, stared back at her. It was a face she saw every morning in her bedroom glass. It looked out of place, provocatively so, in the small parlor surrounded by three gentlemen. With a small gasp of mortification, she raised both hands to tidy the rebellious tendrils, but all her pins were gone. Finally, she twisted it into an untidy knot at the back of her head and glanced around desperately for her bonnet.

"Exactly, my dear," her father said dryly.

"I can explain everything, Father," she began, mortified at the tremor in her voice.

"There is nothing to explain, Pamela," the earl said with a finality that chilled her bones. "Lord Monroyal has agreed to wait upon us tomorrow morning—"

"Lord Monroyal? Wait upon us?" Pamela looked from her father to the marquess in astonishment. "Whatever for? This has nothing to do with him, Father."

"I rather think it has everything to do with him, my child. Here, put on your bonnet and go out to the carriage with your cousin. I wish a final word with his lordship." In his hand he held her new chipped straw bonnet, which looked every bit as though it had been trampled by a herd of runaway horses.

Pamela glanced imploringly at the marquess, but he appeared to be staring with fierce concentration at a particularly unpleasant painting of a dead rabbit on the far wall.

"My lord—"

"Go along now, child," her father interrupted brusquely, "Freddy will see you to the carriage."

"But, Father—"

"Do as you are bid, Pamela," Lord Melrose said harshly, pointing inexorably towards the door.

The picture of the dead rabbit stayed with Lady Pamela all the way back to Adelaide Crescent.

* * *

Lady Pamela spent the rest of the day closeted in her chamber, ignoring the urgent messages from a distraught Freddy, who had yet to acknowledge that his infatuation with the fickle Miss Erskin-Jones had died on the vine. Her appetite had fled, so she excused herself from dinner, and when a footman brought up her dinner tray, the sight of the braised sole floating in thick white sauce nauseated her. Her abigail's nervous strictures that she must keep up her strength for the morrow, which—according to Betty, who was quite beside herself with suppressed excitement— promised to be a momentous day.

By some unexplained quirk of fate, all the servants in the house appeared to be in possession of the quite preposterous notion that Lady Pamela was about to receive an offer from one of the most elusive bachelors in England. Upon learning of this astonishing piece of news from an awed Betty, when the abigail brought up her morning chocolate, Pamela was frankly appalled and contemplated staying in bed all day.

"I do not know, and I am quite sure I do not care what time his lordship is to arrive, or even if he is to arrive at all," she snapped crossly after Betty had hinted for the fourth time that her ladyship should rise and begin preparations for the grand event. "It is all a hum in any event, and I do not wish to hear another word about it."

The summons from her father came before she was fully dressed, and as a result Lady Pamela was somewhat flustered when she was ushered into the earl's study by a beaming Bowles, quite as though she were a visitor of some no little importance.

Her father was standing at the window, his hands clasped behind him. Pamela instantly recognized the rigid set of his shoulders and grimaced. He was evidently in one of his intransigent moods, and she wished she had stayed in bed. When he turned to face her, Pamela quaked at the stern expression in his eyes.

"Sit down, child," the earl said without preamble.

As Pamela settled herself in one of the big leather chairs, she noticed the empty glass on the little rosewood table beside her. The sight of a matching glass on her father's cluttered desk shook her out of her torpor and sent a cold chill snaking down her spine.

Had the marquess been here already? Had he allowed Lord Melrose to bully him into . . . ? The thought remained inchoate, too horrible to examine seriously. He had not struck her as a man given to taking orders from others, she reasoned, trying to convince herself that she was safe from that quarter. But gentlemen, she knew from experience, were given to odd starts, and followed a rigid code of behavior that often made no sense to females.

Lord Melrose cleared his throat.

Lady Pamela returned her father's piercing blue gaze with growing apprehension. Her intuition warned her that this was no ordinary clashing of wills over one of her minor transgressions. This had the feel of a conflict she was not destined to win. But she *must* prevail, she told herself firmly. Father must be brought to see that all this fuss and pother was quite unnecessary. The conviction that she was right calmed her.

"Lord Monroyal will be calling shortly," her father said, glancing at the clock on the mantel. "I trust I do not have to explain your duty to you, Pamela."

Her heart suddenly fluttering like a trapped bird, Pamela heard herself say with a calm she did not feel, "I am at a loss to understand what you can mean, Father. Have I not always done my duty towards you?"

Lord Melrose snorted in frustration. "I know you too well, my girl," he retorted. "But let me tell you plainly that I will tolerate none of your infernal defiance. For once in your life, child, you will do as you are told."

Pamela's heart settled into a cold lump in her stomach. "Of course I will, Father. But what has Lord Monroyal to say to anything? I doubt the rogue might be induced to set foot in this house."

"Do not play the simpleton with me, Pamela," her father warned, his face purpling dangerously. "His lordship comes to restore what he so nefariously stole from you."

Pamela forced herself to relax. "His lordship stole nothing from me, Father," she lied, resolutely suppressing all memory of that kiss that had shaken her very soul. "I am as innocent today as ever I was before I had the misfortune to meet Lord Monroyal. So you may rest easy on that account."

"Rest easy, indeed," her father bellowed, discarding all attempts at moderation. "So I am to rest easy, am I? Rest easy while that scurvy rakehell boasts of seducing my daughter? I trust I am no such spineless weakling. He will pay for this, he will," he muttered, pacing the length of the study, his countenance set in a thunderous frown. "And pay dearly."

Appalled at her father's sudden fury, Pamela rose to her feet. "I am sure that you are mistaken about his lordship, Father. Say what you will, he is a gentleman, and gentlemen do not drag a lady's name in the mud. Particularly when nothing of an improper nature took place," she added quickly.

"That does not signify in the slightest," her father snapped angrily. "And besides, the villain did not deny it."

Lady Pamela stared at her parent as the implications of his words sunk in. "Are you suggesting that he admitted . . . that he admitted he . . ." Words failed her. "There is no truth in it whatsoever," she burst out indignantly. "I cannot believe that he would make such a claim."

"That does not signify either, child," her father retorted. "The fact of the matter is that Monroyal will shortly make you an offer of marriage, which you will naturally accept. Like it or not, you will accept. Do you understand me, Pamela? It is the only honorable way to resolve this matter."

Lady Pamela choked. Her father's blunt announcement disconcerted her, and before she could stop it, a hysterical giggle escaped her. "Honorable?" she managed to gasp after a while. "Ridiculous, I think you mean, Father. I never heard such a Banbury tale in all my life. Lord Monroyal is probably at this very moment enjoying his breakfast in his London residence, lamenting that he has forfeited five hundred pounds." She paused to wipe her streaming eyes. "Were you aware, Father, that he wagered that paltry sum—his very words, I swear it—that he could seduce poor Prudence in under a week. And this is the man," she spat out, her humor dissipating as the enormity of what her father proposed dawned upon her, "this is the lecherous rogue you wish me to accept in marriage? I will *die* first!"

Lord Melrose looked rather shaken, but he did not relent. "You will do as I say, Pamela, or else—"

Pamela never heard what dire threat her father had in mind, for at that moment the study door burst open, and a disheveled Freddy stood on the threshold, his mangled cravat signaling his distress more eloquently than any words.

"Well," his uncle demanded shortly, "what has happened to warrant this deplorable behavior, Frederick?"

Lady Pamela felt a premonition of disaster even before her cousin opened his mouth, which he did several times before any words emerged.

"They are s-saying . . ." he stammered, glancing from his uncle to Pamela with eyes starting out of his head.

"Yes, lad, what are they saying?" his uncle prompted impatiently. "And who are *they*?"

Freddy swallowed visibly. "Perhaps I should speak with you when you are alone, Uncle," he mumbled nervously.

"If it concerns your cousin, you may speak freely, Freddy," the earl said. "What have you heard?"

"I was driving on the Marine Parade this morning, and I wondered why some old Tabbies were eyeing me strangely. Then Tommy Steadman, a particular friend of mine, warned me that the word is out about Lady Pamela." He stopped and glanced at his cousin.

"Out with it, lad," his uncle growled.

"Yes, what have I done to attract the gossip?"

"You were seen with Lord Monroyal at the cottage," Freddy blurted out. "It is being bruited about that you kept a secret assignation with him."

Lady Pamela felt a chill wind envelop her heart. "That is quite impossible," she protested weakly. "The only ones who saw us there were you and Father."

"And your precious little tart, Frederick," Lord Melrose said heavily. "It is clear that the silly chit is a mischief maker as well as a tart. 'Tis a good thing that Monroyal will soon put a stop to such malicious gabble-mongering."

"He w-will not c-come, Father," Pamela insisted, her voice trembling. Not that she wished the immoral rogue to come, of course, but the alternative loomed like thunderclouds over her head. What would it be like to live the rest of her life ostracized as a fallen woman? she wondered distractedly—condemned for a sin she had not even committed.

"You know nothing of the man, Pamela," her father said angrily. "I fully expect him to appear at any minute." They all glanced at the clock on the mantel.

As if by prearrangement, the door of the study opened, and Bowles appeared, his face rigidly blank—except for his eyes, Pamela noticed, which flickered briefly in her direction.

"The Marquess of Monroyal to see you, milord."

CHAPTER EIGHT

Clash of Wills

"What the devil do you mean, Robert?" Willy Hampton exclaimed, astonishment replacing his usual placid expression. "I thought you were all hot to leave Brighton behind you. Now you tell me we must wait another day. Cannot tear yourself away from our Prudence, is that it?"

Lord Monroyal cut another piece of ham and carried it to his mouth. He was not hungry, but felt the need for sustenance in the trial that lay ahead of him. He chewed methodically, but he might have been eating straw for all the pleasure he derived from the savory ham. He raised his mug and took a long swallow of Lady Stevens's excellent ale. Only then did he raise his eyes to meet his friend's quizzical glance across the breakfast table.

He sighed. "You are not going to believe this, Willy. I hardly believe it myself. But the truth of the matter is that I find myself in somewhat of a pickle."

Monroyal grinned wryly at the understatement. His present predicament was far and away more serious than a pickle. He had spent much of the night wrestling with the various alternatives open to him. In the end he had come to the unpleasant realization that the solution expected of him by the lady's father was the only one that he would be able to accept with a clear conscience.

The devil fly away with the woman, he thought bitterly. With all women, for that matter. Much as he enjoyed their company and the pleasures they offered, Robert could not for the life of him remember a single one with whom he would have been content to spend the rest of his life. He was hard put to remember even the names of any but the most recent of his *amourettes*. Although he would remember that baggage Prudence for a long time to come, he thought cynically. Thanks to that feckless chit, he had fallen into one of the oldest traps in history.

"And what is it I will not believe, old man?" Willy inquired, a smile of anticipation on his jovial face. "Out with it. I gather it has something to do with our dear Prudence?"

The marquess carefully cut another piece of ham and speared it with his fork. "Oh, yes indeed," he responded with a forced smile, "it most certainly has to do with that perverse chit." He brought the fork up to his lips, but at the last minute the smell of the ham made him feel sick. He returned it to the plate and sat back, staring morosely at his friend.

"If you want the unvarnished truth, Willy, we must delay our departure for Stilton Grange because I have an offer to make."

Willy's mouth fell open, and he blinked rapidly several times. Then he chortled merrily and applied himself to the mountain of food on his plate. "Damn it, Robert, you gave me a nasty start there. I take it you are buying another horse? Be glad to offer my services, of course. Considered something of an expert on horses, as you know."

"I wish it were that simple," the marquess said heavily. "But it is not a horse, Willy." He paused, as if by delaying the revelation of his plight, he could make it disappear. "It is a woman."

"Ah!" Willy exclaimed, as if the matter were suddenly made clear. "The lass was so good you are going to offer her *carte blanche* is that it?" He looked up expectantly.

Monroyal shook his head. "No such luck, my friend. I am talking of a marriage offer."

"To Prudence?" The horrified expression on Hampton's face made the marquess laugh shortly.

"Not in a million years; I have not lost my senses completely."

Willy looked puzzled. "Then who is this mysterious female who has succeeded where dozens of hopefuls have failed, Robert? Only yesterday you were avowing your firm intention to drift into a comfortable bachelorhood with me. I cannot believe that in such a short time you have fallen under the spell of some charmer." When the marquess made no response, he added quietly, "Tell me it is not true, Robert."

The marquess nodded glumly. "All too true, Willy. And there was nothing charming about it," he began, but the memory of soft lips and a surprisingly tender mouth made him pause. He brushed the thought away impatiently. "I was caught, my friend. Caught when I least expected it. Which only goes to show that none of us is safe."

"I take it this is not a love match then?"

The marquess's mouth curled cynically into a sneer. "Hardly, old man."

"Are you not going to tell me her name?"

"Pamela Hancock," Monroyal said bluntly.

Once again Hampton's face registered surprise. "Melrose's daughter? You cannot be serious, Robert. After that old scandal with your father, surely Melrose would never accept you for his daughter."

"The wench is definitely on the shelf, if you recall, Willy. I imagine that in such cases any man is better than none," he added with studied cynicism, reluctant to add that the Marquess of Monroyal was not exactly any man. "I am expected at Melrose House this morning, and if I cannot escape this noose, I am counting on you to support me in this ordeal, Willy."

"Of course, I will, old man, but perhaps it will not come to that. Tell me the whole, Robert. Perhaps you have mistaken the matter."

After some reluctance, the marquess gave his friend an abbreviated account of that fatal picnic at the cottage. As he recounted the details of his foiled seduction of the elusive Prudence, Robert became more firmly convinced that his choices were limited to the one he was most reluctant to take.

When he finally fell silent, he was not surprised to see Willy shake his head. "It does not look good, Robert, that I have to admit. There is little doubt that the lady's reputation has been tarnished. And even if she did set out to entrap you, which I will not believe, you cannot deny that you were alone in the cottage together."

"Does it not strike you as peculiar that the father and cousin knew where to find us?" the marquess demanded. "I cannot get it out of my mind that Melrose may have been behind this. What a fiendishly clever way of getting in the last word in that old quarrel."

"From what you say, they expected to find Prudence with you, Robert. I suspect it was an unfortunate coincidence that you were caught with the wrong female."

Monroyal shook his head dubiously. "Too much of a coincidence if you ask me. I tell you plainly, Willy, I do not like the smell of this whole affair. It smacks of a carefully laid plan. Why did that silly chit rush off and leave me alone with the Hancock wench? Particularly since she knew I had a bauble for her, which she did not earn, of course. And why did the Hancock girl come after us in the first place? And how did Prudence get back to town without meeting Melrose's carriage?"

"Perhaps she did," Willy said slowly. "That would explain how Lord Melrose knew where his daughter was. And with whom," he added softly.

The marquess stared hard at his friend, his mouth a grim line. "If it was a plot to trap me, I shall get to the bottom of it, Willy. You can count on it. Even if I have to wring that girl's neck."

His friend remained silent until the marquess guided his team along the elegant tree-lined Adelaide Crescent and pulled up before Number 8. "If the worst does happen, old man," he mumbled apologetically, "that is to say, if you h-have to . . ." He paused, and Monroyal glanced at him with a baleful smile.

"If I have to *marry* the wench, I suppose you mean," he finished harshly.

"Well, yes. That is the point, exactly, Robert. I do not wish to be in the way or anything like that. I can bolt back to London in a trice."

"Oh, no, you will not," the marquess said sharply, throwing the ribbons to a groom who had materialized beside the curricle. "You promised to support me through this, remember?"

Willy looked perplexed. "And I intend to keep that promise, old man. But after the ceremony—"

"After the ceremony—if we do come to that unfortunate impasse—I will need your support more than ever, Willy."

"What about the wedding trip?" Hampton stammered.

Lord Monroyal stared into his friend's blank face and let out a crack of humorless laughter. "There will be no wedding trip," he explained dryly. "At least not in the usual sense. And I shall need your presence to witness that this marriage was never consummated. We will accompany the new bride to Holly Lodge and leave her with Aunt Honoria. His devious lordship will get no grandchildren out of me, on my oath he will not."

"What about that poor girl?" Hampton asked. "That is a scurvy trick to play on a new bride."

"If this whole affair is a plot, as I suspect it is, then she will get no more than she deserves, would you not say?"

His friend was silent while they trod up the shallow steps to the front door that was flung open by the Melrose butler.

"And what if there is no plot?" Hampton murmured.

The marquess considered the possibility briefly as the butler relieved them of hats and gloves. There was little doubt in his mind that he had been duped by a man who had held a grudge against his father for thirty years. His recollections of that long-ago scandal were hazy, but he had always known the duel had been fought over his mother.

Neither of his parents had ever confirmed or denied his mother's guilty actions, but the aura of adultery had colored his fantasy for years. He had never seen the mysterious Mr. Brown in the neighborhood again, and after his brother Geoffrey was born, the tensions at Stilton Grange had disappeared and a tenuous harmony restored.

But Robert had not forgotten that intruder.

He owed it to his father not to allow his old antagonist to win this latest encounter. Robert might be obliged, for the sake of his own honor, to wed Lady Pamela Hancock, but no daughter of Melrose's, innocent or not, would ever be mistress of Stilton Grange.

The atmosphere in the morning room was uncomfortably tense. Lady Pamela could not remain seated more than two minutes at a time. The urge to escape caused her to pace nervously up and down the room like a caged animal. Indeed, she felt very like an animal, forced to obey, with a helpless, simmering rage that made her quite ill, the arbitrary commands of her father, who had commissioned her cousin quite twenty minutes since to escort her to the morning room to await his pleasure.

She wished she could escape up to her chamber as she had after that first disastrous interview in her father's study. But flinging herself on her bed and bursting into angry tears had not erased the vision of Lord Melrose's face, mottled with fury at Cousin Freddy's unsavory news. Had Freddy not realized that his revelations would eliminate any hope Pamela had of slipping out of the net she felt closing around her?

How was it possible, she asked herself for the tenth time since that harrowing encounter, that the whole of Brighton appeared to know of her scandalous rendezvous with the marquess? Who had seen them at the cottage except her own father and cousin? And Prudence, of course. But it hardly seemed possible that the silly chit would reveal anything about that clandestine assignation that would naturally implicate her as well.

Or would she?

Pamela glanced at her cousin, who had been sent, she suspected, to make sure she stayed in the morning room awaiting her fate.

"Do you suppose, Freddy, that Prudence is behind all this malicious gossip?"

Her cousin jumped like a startled rabbit, rustling the newspaper he had been reading. His eyes were suspiciously red, and Pamela silently cursed the capricious female who had brought grief and possibly ruin down on all of them.

"It is highly possible, Cousin," Freddy said in a subdued voice. "But I would much rather not talk about it if you please."

He went back to his reading, which was merely a pretense, Pamela suspected, to avoid discussing the betrayal of his precious Prudence. She, on the other hand, was anxious to know how her father would emerge from the clash of wills that must inevitably be taking place in his study. She devoutly hoped that Lord Monroyal would enlighten her father as to what exactly happened, or did not happen, at the cottage, and persuade the earl that no drastic action was necessary to salvage her good name.

Perhaps Monroyal would flatly refuse to wed her. He was certainly odious enough to do so, she thought. For some odd reason that possibility did not appeal to her, and Pamela had to remind herself that his refusal to bow to her father's demands was precisely what she herself most wished for. Her own pride would be sadly bruised, but she could bear that mortification calmly enough. And it was not as though Pamela had deliberately wounded the gentleman for showing himself vulnerable to her charms.

Of course, that was not the case here, she reminded herself sharply. The arrogant marquess must detest her almost as much as she detested him. If indeed he had formed any opinion on her at all, which she doubted, accustomed as he was to frequent the most beautiful women in London. He must be extremely put out by Lord Melrose's demands, and she prayed that his disgust at the notion of an alliance with her might provoke him into defying her father.

"Do you think Lord Monroyal will feel obligated to accept father's terms?" she asked after a long pause, the threat of such an eventuality disrupting her usual serenity.

"Of course, he will," her cousin answered impatiently from behind the sporting pages of the *Morning Post*. "What kind of a ninny are you, Pamela, to think he has any alternative?"

"Surely, a man of his rank and fortune can refuse to be forced into such an arrangement, Freddy."

Her cousin looked up at that. "He will see it as a matter of honor, Pamela. There are two things a man of honor does not do," he explained heavily. "The first is to welch on his gambling debts, the other is to compromise a lady's good name."

Lady Pamela came to halt before her cousin, her eyes glittering angrily. "Am I to suppose the gambling debts to be more important?" she asked icily. "It would not surprise me in the least. I trust that his lordship has discharged the five-hundred-pound wager regarding the conquest of Miss Erskin-Jones. At least he did not succeed in that vile endeavor."

Even before these rash words had left her mouth, Pamela was appalled at her own insensitivity. Her cousin's face lost what little color it had, and he rose to his feet, fists clenched, the *Post* falling unheeded to the carpet. "Oh, Freddy," she cried, rushing over to lay a hand of his sleeve, "I did not mean that. He was probably boasting, anyway."

"Monroyal told you this?"

"No. Er, yes. That is to say, no, not precisely."

"Did he or did he not?"

"Well, he hinted at it," Pamela lied gamely. "But he was more concerned about the ten thousand he stands to lose if he weds me. That is why I have high hopes of his refusal to accommodate Father."

Freddy looked puzzled, but no less incensed. "What are you blathering about, Pamela? Are you telling me the wretch made you the object of a wager, too?"

"Not me, precisely, Cousin," she exclaimed, eager to divert his attention from the attempted seduction of Prudence. "I understand it is a long-standing wager, well known to all the gentlemen in London, I should imagine."

"And what wager might this be?"

"I imagine you were at Oxford when it was recorded at White's," Pamela began, wishing she had left the subject untouched. "As I understand it, the marquess made a very public denouncement of virgins. Apparently, he abhors innocence in all its forms. That is why I fully expected him not to show his face at Adelaide Crescent. I confess I was surprised to hear that he condescended to attend my father's summons. But disabuse yourself, Cousin; his lordship will not wish to throw away ten thousand pounds on me."

"Then you are off the mark, my dear," a chilly voice murmured from the open doorway. "It appears I shall be obliged to do precisely that."

Lady Pamela whirled to meet the glacial stare of her nemesis, the Marquess of Monroyal.

The marquess had spent an exceedingly disagreeable hour with Lord Melrose in his study. The earl had been barely civil to him, and Lord Monroyal had no difficulty in sensing the older man's satisfaction in holding the trump card over his enemy's son and heir.

It was as Robert has suspected all along. His father's old adversary was enjoying his momentary triumph. By forcing Robert to do the honorable thing, Melrose undoubtedly thought to gain a double victory. On one hand he would settle his only daughter—plain and spinsterish as she undeniably was—in the enviable position of acquiring a title and fortune far beyond what she might have hoped for. On the other hand, the earl must relish the irony of seeing a Hancock admitted into the family of the very man who had—according to what little Robert had learned about his mother—outbid him years ago for the hand of one of London's most glittering Beauties.

He was still seething with resentment when the butler escorted him up to the morning room, where—the earl had informed him with a barely concealed smile—the Lady Pamela awaited the formality of his offer. Mr. Hampton, who had awaited him in the hall below, trailed behind him. Willy had wisely refused to be present during the interview with Lord Melrose, and Robert could not really blame him.

"I am counting on you to stand firm, Willy," he said between his teeth as the butler opened the door and they stepped softly into the room.

The first words the marquess heard were not destined to improve his foul humor. The lady's reference to his unfortunate wager—the satisfaction of which he had small hopes of postponing much longer—only served to remind him of his misfortune. So, he thought cynically, Lady Pamela had not expected her father to bring him up to scratch. She had been wrong. He would do his duty, but there was nothing to prevent him from making it as disagreeable as possible.

"Then you are off the mark, my dear," he drawled in his haughtiest, most offensive tone. "It appears I shall be obliged to do precisely that."

Her eyes were wide with apprehension when she turned at the sound of his voice.

"My l-lord," she stammered, her eyes lowered after that first startled glance. "And Mr. Hampton, is it not? Bowles," she said quickly, addressing the butler, "send up refreshments, if you please."

"That will not be necessary, my lady." The sharpness of his tone brought her eyes once more to his face. There was fear in them, he saw with some satisfaction. Fear and mortification. He

examined her critically, letting his gaze rake her from head to toe
with studied insolence. It was as he remembered; there was nothing here to recommend her to a man of his fastidious taste in females. Or to any other man with a modicum of good taste, he
thought bitterly. And this woman was to be his *wife*. The notion
was noxious to the extreme.

Beside him, Willy coughed nervously.

"My business with you, my lady, may be concluded very
briefly," he began as the butler closed the door behind him. "Very
briefly indeed," he added dryly. "It appears I have your esteemed
parent's permission . . ." He paused to stare at her until she
dropped her eyes again. "Nay, that is too tame a word, would you
not agree, Hampton? Perhaps I should say, his command, expressed in the strongest terms, to present myself to you as a favored candidate—"

"Pray do not continue, my lord."

The sharp words took him by surprise. He had thought her to
be another spineless female, aging and anxious for a suitable
match. By his estimation Lady Pamela should be overwhelmed at
the honor he was, however reluctantly, about to bestow upon her.
He could think of a score of women, far and away more beautiful
and better endowed than this mouse of a girl, who would give
their most treasured possession to be the object of the offer he
was about to make. Many of them had given it, he thought cynically, to no avail.

"I beg your pardon?" he said coldly.

To his consternation, Lady Pamela smiled, and her face lost
some of its sharpness. "I must beg you to save your breath, my
lord," she said bluntly. "The notion of a match between us"—and
here she had the grace to blush—"is absurd. So let us not proceed
any further with this farce."

Farce? Robert could hardly believe he had heard aright. An
offer of marriage, however unwilling made, from the Marquess of
Monroyal was being called a farce? He glared at her, his brows
coming together over his patrician nose.

"I must inform you, my lady," he said stiffly, "that you have no
say in the matter. The settlements are signed and—"

"Then you may unsign them," she said brightly. "For I must inform *you*, my lord, that I have no intention of accepting your so
gracious offer."

Although he stood at least a foot taller than the lady, the marquess had the distinct impression that she was looking down her
nose at him. He was not accustomed to people looking down their

noses at him, particularly not a female. In recent memory he could not recall a single one who had dared. Furthermore, her comment had contained a hint of sarcasm he could not like.

"You will forgive me for saying so, my lady," he said in his most arrogant tone, "but you really have no—"

"Well, I do not forgive you, sir," she snapped, her eyes glittering with what looked perilously like contempt. "I had thought you a man of courage and fortitude. One who did not tamely take orders from another. But I see you are no better than other gentlemen of my acquaintance, all bluster and no bottom."

"Pamela!" exclaimed her cousin in horrified tones. "You cannot put aside his lordship's offer so cavalierly. Your father will be livid."

The marquess detected a smothered chuckle from Mr. Hampton, which the latter suppressed with difficulty when Robert cast him a withering glance.

"His lordship has yet to make me an offer I can, with a clear conscience, consider in the least acceptable." She actually tossed her head, Robert noted, astonished at such disregard for his rank and consequence.

"You will give his lordship a disgust for you, Pamela," young Hancock hissed in her ear.

"Oh, you may be sure his lordship already has a hearty disgust of me, Freddy," the lady retorted, closer to the truth than she imagined, Robert thought. "And if I can add to that disgust, so much the better. Perhaps he will take the hint that his suit is not welcome here."

The marquess distinctly heard Willy gasp at this plain speaking. He wished that he might stalk out of this bedlam and depart Brighton within the hour. Rarely had he been so insulted, and it made little difference to him that the lady spoke nothing but what he himself was feeling. It was as if she could read his mind.

Lord Monroyal drew himself to his full height and glared down at the culprit, but before he could devise a suitably crushing reply to this piece of impertinence, Lady Pamela continued in a more reasonable tone.

"You cannot, in all honesty, deny that I am the last female in England—perhaps in the entire world—whom you wish to wed, my lord," she announced with what Robert considered quite unbecoming frankness. "I am convinced of it. Such an arrangement can bring only misery to us both, and why would you willingly seek to be miserable? You do not strike me as lacking reason, my lord, although I have heard that you are often wild to a fault. Unbecoming in one of your years, I might add."

Of all the lady's insulting comments, this last snide—or so it appeared to Robert—remark about his age goaded him as nothing else could. With no small effort he repressed the scathing remark that trembled on his lips.

"All this is very much beside the point," he said icily. "The match is a *fait accompli*. There remains only your acceptance, which I assure you is merely a formality, for the event to go forward."

That would show the saucy wench where her place was, the marquess mused with some satisfaction. He had been alarmed at Lady Pamela's unexpected display of waywardness. He had thought her a mousy creature, obedient in all things to her father's will; expected her fawning gratitude for saving her from a lifetime of spinsterish boredom playing aunt to her cousin's offspring. Lord Melrose had promised as much. His daughter was in all things mild and accommodating, he had said with no little pride. She was a good girl who would make an ideal, if unobtrusive, wife.

The lady was anything but unobtrusive at the moment, Robert thought, noting the rebellious glitter in her hazel eyes and the contemptuous quirk of her lips. Her voice, when she spoke, was anything but mild.

"And pray, whatever gave you the notion that you would make a good husband, my lord?" she said coolly. "Have you ever assessed your worth in terms other than rank and fortune? Take those away—and believe me I value neither of them—what is left? An aging roué who spends his life in the pursuit of dissipation and debauchery in all their most disgusting forms. A libertine who would seduce a brainless chit of seventeen for a paltry wager of five hundred pounds. What sensible female would consider such a man an eligible match? What have you to say to *that*, my lord?"

In the deathly silence that followed this extraordinary speech, the marquess clearly heard Hampton's dismayed gasp. Mr. Hancock's mouth hung open, and his face was turning an unhealthy shade of red. Robert himself felt as though one of Gentleman Jackson's punishing rights had driven every ounce of air from his body.

Before he could find words harsh enough to crush this female who had insulted him as no gentleman would have dared and lived, the morning-room door opened behind them, and Lord

Melrose came into the room. The satisfied smirk on his face faded when he beheld the silent tableau.

"Well?" he demanded with forced joviality, "have you concluded matters to everyone's satisfaction, my lord?"

The marquess turned slowly, his mind still grappling with the enormity of Lady Pamela's effrontery.

"I fear not, my lord," he said in a clear, cold voice. "Your daughter considers me a dissipated roué unworthy of her hand."

CHAPTER NINE

Reluctant Bride

One glance at her father's thunderous face and Lady Pamela fervently wished the floor would open and swallow her. Her glance slid to Lord Monroyal's face, and the chill of his stony gaze expressed his disapproval more clearly than words.

"Is this true, Pamela?" Lord Melrose's voice cut through the heavy silence like a thunderclap. "Am I to believe that a daughter of mine had the temerity and ill breeding to insult his lordship under my roof?"

Lady Pamela felt her courage dissipate. Her father was going to insist on this monstrous arrangement. She was to be condemned to a joyless marriage with a man who would rather be dead, she suspected.

Her gaze dropped to the marquess's highly polished boots, whose white hunting tops proclaimed them to be Hoby's much sought-after handiwork. Whimsically, she imagined them trampling all over her, leaving the imprint of the wearer's heels in her soft flesh. She shuddered and withdrew her gaze quickly, focusing on Mr. Hampton's footwear. To her heightened senses that gentleman's well-worn yet impeccably polished Hessians appeared less threatening. She already knew from experience that Mr. Hampton had a kind heart. Would he make a kind husband? she wondered. Had he been her father's choice, would she have been so set against him? Pamela did not think so.

"Well?" her father's harsh voice interrupted her ruminations. "What have you to say for yourself, child?"

She drew a deep breath. "It is true that I was rather . . ." She paused and raised her eyes to her father's stern face. "Rather too f-forthcoming with his lordship," she admitted, ignoring the snort of derision from the marquess. "But since his lordship was barely civil to me, I saw no point in toadying to him. He admits to a disgust for me—"

"I admitted no such thing, my lord," the marquess interjected

sharply. "If my memory serves, your daughter laid those sentiments at my door."

"And can you deny that you find this proposed union abhorrent, my lord?" If he would only admit this basic truth, Pamela
thought, she might retire to Melrose Park and spend the rest of her
days at her beloved pianoforte.

"Whether I do or not is quite beside the point, madam," the
marquess retorted, his temper visibly fraying. "My lord"—he
turned to the earl—"I have done my part. It remains for you to
convince your daughter of her own best interests. With your permission, I shall procure a special license and a preacher, and return in the morning to conclude this matter."

"Pamela!" Lord Melrose roared, beside himself with frustration. "You will accept his lordship's gracious offer without further roundaboutation. Do I make myself clear? And I will hear
your apology to his lordship, too, my girl. This mulishness is not
to be tolerated. I will not be gainsaid."

Pamela regarded her father in silence. She could think of no
possible arguments that might move him, but she would resist to
the bitter end, she thought stubbornly. They would have to drag
her to the altar, a step she did not put past these men, so entrenched in the belief of their own righteousness.

Mr. Hampton cleared his throat. "Begging your pardon, Lord
Melrose," he began soothingly, "but perhaps if we gave the couple some privacy, your daughter might feel less constrained to
quarrel with his lordship on this matter."

After a moment's hesitation, her father nodded. "Perhaps you
are right, Hampton. Come, gentlemen. We shall await you in the
library, my lord." He bowed stiffly, shooting a warning glance at
Pamela before leading the way out of the room.

In the silence that followed, Pamela took a deep breath and
tried to marshal her thoughts. She must make this man see the disastrous consequences of his proposed action. A daunting feat indeed, she thought gloomily, her gaze roving his harsh, angular
countenance. But rather than protest her disinclination for the
marriage, perhaps she should concentrate on representing to this
odious man the inconvenience of such a step to his own comfort.
That argument might carry more weight.

"Am I to understand that you wish me to renew my offer, Lady
Pamela?" the marquess drawled, his cold voice chilling her to the
bone.

The man had no sense of humor at all, she thought wryly,
flinching at the disdain in his tone. She wondered if he was so un-

yielding with his family and friends. With his numerous mistresses. Did he ever crack a smile, for instance? Suddenly, the memory of their unforeseen encounter in the seaside cottage rushed back, and she recalled that he did indeed know how to smile. A cynical, insinuating smile, of course, but a smile nevertheless. Pamela blushed at the recollection of the circumstances which provoked that predatory smile.

"Not at all, my lord," she said, unable to suppress a faint smile at her predicament. If indeed, the necessity of refusing an offer of marriage from England's premier bachelor might be so termed. "I was unpardonably rude to you just now," she began frankly, with all the calmness she could muster, "for which breach of good manners I sincerely beg your forgiveness."

He bowed wordlessly, and Pamela continued before she lost her nerve. "I must confess you surprised me, my lord. I had not for a moment imagined the Marquess of Monroyal would allow himself to be maneuvered into this kind of situation." She raised a hand when he would speak. "Allow me to finish, my lord. My cousin tells me that you are an avowed enemy of the married state. I do not blame you. Too many couples are thrown together for reasons that do not bear too close an examination. Only consider our own case. It is clear to me that you have no wish to wed, and if you had, I would not be your choice."

"I cannot argue that point," he said shortly.

Pamela's sense of humor bubbled up at this unflattering concession, and she laughed. "See, my lord? We can agree on something at least. But it may not be so clear to you, accustomed as you must be to women falling all over themselves for your attention, that you would not be my choice either." She paused, put off by the gleam of cynical amusement in his gray eyes.

"I sincerely trust you will not subject me to a repetition of all my faults, my dear. I doubt my self-consequence could weather another barrage of such unbridled censure."

"I *was* rather rough on you, I admit," Pamela said with another laugh. "And I have apologized for it, sir. But the truth is—since we are being so frank—that you are the last man I would ever wish to wed. Barring, naturally, the navvies on the London docks, the inmates of Newgate, and other unsavory characters abroad on London's streets."

He bowed again, his lips curled in a cynical smile. "You flatter me, my dear."

Pamela began to relax. "You choose to jest, my lord, but it is the truth. I am not a chit fresh from the schoolroom who dreams of the ideal husband. There is no such animal, of course. Neither am I an accredited Beauty whose sole ambition in life is to make a brilliant match and shine in the *beau monde* of London. I am, as you may have already guessed, a shrewish spinster, with an uncertain temper, who has been on the shelf these five years or more. I am also one of those quite dreadful managing females, one who will find fault with everything you do, my lord. My health has always been indifferent, and I suffer from constant megrims. Only ask my poor father how often I have been at death's door. Besides which," she concluded, "I must confess, on the condition that you do not mention it to my father, that I am a pianist and composer of some talent and an inveterate bluestocking." She paused, quite breathless after this recitation of fact and fiction, confident that she had made her point abundantly clear.

The marquess had sauntered over to the window during this extraordinary declaration and stood looking down into the street, his quizzing-glass swinging idly in one hand. He turned and smiled, clearly amused. Pamela noticed with a start that when he smiled just so, he looked younger, less intimidating, and actually quite attractive in a dark, disturbing way.

"I am glad to hear it, my dear," he drawled softly. "You have taken a great load off my mind." He raised the quizzing-glass and surveyed her languorously from head to toe.

Pamela felt as though her new green twilled silk, which she had thought so modest this morning, had suddenly become utterly transparent. She blushed, but could not wrench her eyes from that probing, glass stare.

"You will be able to entertain me in my dotage when the gout confines me to my fireside," the marquess continued in a low, caressing voice that suggested that the entertainment he had in mind had nothing to do with gout or dotage.

"You mock me, my lord," Pamela said crossly, moving to stand before him and glaring up into his amused face. "And deliberately misunderstand me. I wish to make you see how very ill suited we are, and all you can do is make a jest of it. Do you *wish* to be miserable for the rest of your life? Do you dislike me so much you wish to make me miserable, too?"

She watched his smile fade slowly and his eyes turn flinty again.

"Explain to me, if you will, my dear, how becoming a marchioness will make you miserable. I had, in my ignorance perhaps, considered it to be the prime ambition of every unattached female in Town. A cause for celebration rather than long faces."

Pamela felt her heart sink. What was the use? she thought. The man was just like her father, refusing to see what he did not wish to—insisting that the world was arranged solely for his convenience; that his word was law; that marriage was an unpleasant duty to be avoided if possible; that a wife was naught but an inconvenience to be tolerated with indifference.

She turned to gaze out on the cloudless summer sky. What would the future hold for her as this odious creature's wife? she wondered. Startled at the insidious notion, she suppressed the thought before it took root in her imagination. She would have to appeal to his better nature, if he had one. She would beg if necessary—go down on her knees. She felt a definite lump in her throat and blinked back tears of frustration.

"My lord," she began, turning to gaze up into those implacable gray eyes that seemed to see right through her, "I b-beg of you . . ." Her voice suddenly faltered, and Pamela felt the wetness on her cheeks before she realized that the tears had spilled over. Impatiently, she brushed at them, furious that her emotions had betrayed her into making a cake of herself.

"My lord," she began again, fighting the weakness she despised, "*please* do not do this. There must be some other way to repair my good name. Perhaps . . ." She hesitated as a brilliant notion suddenly occurred to her. "Perhaps if some other gentleman were to come forward—" She stopped abruptly at the flash of empathy in his eyes.

"Am I to understand that your heart is set on another?"

Pamela flinched at the derision in his tone. Did this arrogant man imagine that she had received no other offers for her hand at all? She wished she might say truthfully that her heart was indeed given irrevocably to another, but she dared not indulge in so blatant an untruth.

"My heart's inclinations are no concern of yours, my lord," she said stiffly. "But it did occur to me that were I to accept another offer, you might be free to wash your hands of me and go back to your . . . er, your . . . o-other pursuits."

"Who is he?"

The flatness of the question made Pamela flinch. For some odd reason the marquess's eyes had turned to bleak gray slate, and his sensuous mouth was drawn into a thin, angry line. Lady Pamela experienced an unexpected and perverse thrill of amusement. The grand Lord Monroyal was put out at the thought of being supplanted. She could not repress a smile.

"I doubt he is known to you, my lord," she replied sweetly. "He does not move in your exalted circles."

"Who is he?" he repeated sharply.

She looked up at him, enjoying the discovery of an unsuspected vulnerability in this pompous lord's ego.

"A childhood friend, my lord. Sir Rodney Morton. His estate lies next to Melrose Park. Rodney is a charming gentleman, close to my own age," she added with a hint of malice, "who has shown a flattering degree of interest." This last was certainly true, she reflected, although Rodney's motives were hardly disinterested.

"Ah, an affair of the heart after all," the marquess said dismissively.

"No, hardly that, my lord," she replied calmly. "My father refused his permission. Poor Rodney's pockets are always to let, and I have a respectable portion."

"What makes you think Lord Melrose would accept Morton now?"

Pamela regarded him a moment before venturing a reply. This was the crux of the matter, she thought. Without Lord Monroyal's support, she had no hope of persuading her father to agree to the substitution.

"I was counting on your support, my lord. I gather you are not exactly overjoyed at being saddled with a wife, particularly one with so little to recommend her."

She was unprepared for the crack of cynical laughter that greeted this remark.

"Are you so bird-witted, my dear child, as to expect Lord Melrose to relinquish a marquess in favor of a penniless baronet?" The bitterness in his laughter touched Pamela deeply. What he said was undeniably true, of course, but she refused to lose heart.

"If you were to impress upon him, my lord, that my *happiness* is at stake, perhaps—"

"You are indeed an innocent, my girl," he replied harshly, turning to stare out of the window. "Happiness has no place in this bargain, neither yours nor mine. We are condemned to this course. There is no other choice, believe me. If there were, do you think I would not have taken it?"

Pamela felt the tears of rage and frustration well up and threaten to spill over again. "Then you w-will not support me?" she blurted out.

"No, indeed not," came the cold response from the man at the window.

She had lost, Pamela thought, no longer caring that hot tears ran down her cheeks. She would have to learn to love misery, for the Marquess of Monroyal would surely bring her more than her fair share of it.

Without another word, she turned on her heel and ran out of the room.

"I still cannot quite believe that the elusive Robert Stilton, bane of every hopeful mama in England with marriageable daughters, has been caught at last!" exclaimed Lady Stevens for perhaps the fifth time since their small party sat down to dinner.

Monroyal winced at this unfortunate choice of words. He had taken his friend's advice and broken the news to her ladyship moments before Jenkins announced dinner that evening. He would have preferred to forget about the whole ordeal, or, failing that, delay the announcement of his imminent nuptials as long as decently possible. Given the smirks, impertinent salutes, and sly nods his passage through the streets occasioned in even the most casual acquaintances, however, the marquess discarded any thought of secrecy. Young Hancock had been right; the news of his indiscretion was common knowledge. His appearance at Melrose House must have confirmed the rumors, and the outcome was inevitable.

"If my aunt discovers that you have kept such important news from her, she will never speak to me again, Robert," Hampton had urged as they drove back to Number 10 Brunswick Square after procuring a special license from the bishop. "Besides, you would not wish the news to get back to Lady Monroyal at Stilton Grange before you have informed her yourself, would you, old man? I imagine that might distress her greatly."

Hampton was right, as he usually was, Robert thought, but the mention of his stepmother caused him a moment of distress himself. His father's second wife had become—after an initial period of furious rejection of this female who dared to usurp his mother's place—a source of comfort and unstinting affection for the young heir and his baby brother Geoffrey. In truth, Geoffrey remembered no other mother but Lady Sophia, the second Marchioness of Monroyal, and when his two half-sisters had arrived, followed a few years later by four healthy boys, the Stiltons had become a family again. Robert had been able to bury his nightmares about that old scandal and the summer evening he had seen his mother kissing the stranger—who called himself Mr. Brown—in the gazebo.

It was the thought of distressing Lady Sophia that drove him to make the dreaded announcement to Lady Stevens before he was fully reconciled to the betrothal himself. But before he came down to dinner that evening, he had sent off a carefully worded note to Stilton Grange with one of his grooms, advising his stepmother, from whom he never hid any but the most reprehensible of his escapades, of the true nature of his sudden nuptials.

Robert had also confided his determination to install his new wife—he resisted thinking of Lady Pamela as the Marchioness of Monroyal—at Holly Lodge in Dorset rather than conveying her directly to Stilton Grange to occupy her rightful place in his life. The truth was, he thought grimly, this particular female had no rightful place in his life. Never would have a place if he had anything to say in the matter. But the inevitability of their marriage had become clear to him as his interview with the lady progressed. Her attempts to fob him off had amused him, once he had recovered from the shock of having his offer thrown in his face.

The marquess had never considered the possibility of rejection, certainly not from a female. He had never before made an offer of marriage; had never intended to, of course. The whole of London knew he had long ago sworn off the coils of wedlock. And now, as Lady Stevens so elegantly put it, he had been caught at his own game. Well and truly caught, he thought grimly. And he had only his own carelessness to blame. His original conviction that the whole cottage episode had been an elaborate plan to steer him into parson's mousetrap became ridiculous in the face of the lady's tears. Lady Pamela had actually begged him to support her in *avoiding* a match between them.

His emotions still in turmoil from the shock of this novel revelation, Robert blankly regarded his hostess at the head of the table. Lady Stevens was staring at him expectantly.

"I do beg your pardon, madam," he murmured distractedly, "my thoughts seem to be wandering."

No sooner were the words spoken then he regretted them. Lady Stevens gave a huge gargle of laughter that reminded Robert of the turkeys in the poultry yard at Stilton Grange. "Nervous as a filly at her first steeplechase, ain't you, m'lad," she chortled, delighted at her own jest. "Well, you never can tell which nag will win the race, as my dear husband used to say. And Lady Pamela had us all fooled, I can tell you. Such a mild, mousy sort of creature, there is no denying. Breeding aplenty, but no style to speak of, but one should not judge a horse by its color, as they say. Who would ever have thought she had it in her to run away with the trophy of the Season? Sure to set the Tabbies all a twitter, would you not agree, nevvy?"

Robert gazed at his hostess blankly, struggling to untangle the web of metaphors that spewed out of her ladyship's mouth. He turned to Hampton for support, but his friend only winked broadly. "I would except any impending bridegroom to be thrown into high fidgets at the prospect of getting riveted, Aunt Em," he said facetiously, "but I would hardly call Robert a filly. Might find that offensive, you know."

"Nonsense!" her ladyship exclaimed, dismissing her nephew's remark with a wave of her bejeweled hand. "I am all agog to hear how this event came to a head so suddenly, Monroyal, when only yesterday I heard you vowing to end your days as a bachelor." She glared at him expectantly, her pale blue eyes dancing with excitement. "Out with it, lad. And no Banbury tales, mind you."

Robert cleared his throat. "It is a long-standing arrangement, my lady," he began diffidently, hoping to deflect the old lady's curiosity.

"Fiddle!" she scoffed disdainfully. "What kind of cabbage-head do you take me for, boy? I cut my eyeteeth before you were born, I will have you know. And I can tell a prime plumper when I hear one. Long-standing arrangement, indeed! Not very likely. At least not between your father and Lord Melrose at any rate."

The marquess tensed and stared at his hostess. Was it possible that Lady Stevens, a gabble-grinder of the first stare, knew the truth about his father's duel so many years ago?

"Why is it so unlikely, my lady?" he inquired in a flat voice.

"Bad blood there, my lad," Lady Stevens answered without hesitation. Disregarding a futile gesture from her nephew, the old lady insisted upon having her say. "I cannot see any way James Hancock would give his only daughter to the son of a man he had sliced to pieces in a duel thirty years ago," she continued, seeming unaware of the sudden silence that had fallen over the dinner table. "The very man he had offended so villainously, if the rumors of the day may be believed."

"And exactly what did the rumors say, madam?"

Something in the marquess's tone must have alerted her, for Lady Stevens glanced at her nephew's stricken expression and changed the subject abruptly.

"I trust I will receive an invitation, Monroyal," she remarked, waving the butler to bring in the next course. "I knew your father rather well, you know. He showed a flattering interest at one time, which my father discouraged, of course. The late marquess being the devil he was. Quite notorious in his day; somewhat like yourself, my dear boy. Handsome and quite charming, but not the match a sensible female would wish for." She smiled to take the sting from her words.

"You are saying that my mother was not sensible?" the marquess inquired softly.

"Oh, goodness gracious no!" his hostess exclaimed in a flustered voice. "The first marchioness was that rare combination of sense and sensibility. And what a beauty she was, too. Your father appeared quite besotted with her. However, rumors put it about that the match—splendid as it undoubtedly was—did not please her. I had it on good authority that her heart was set on another." Lady Stevens paused and uttered a deep sigh. "Unfortunately, females are not supposed to follow their hearts in such matters. I often wonder that gentlemen allow us to admit to that piece of anatomy at all."

Robert felt oddly uncomfortable. Lady Stevens had given him a glimpse of his mother he had not seen before.

"But my mother accepted him," he pointed out, wondering how much the old dragon knew of that old scandal.

"Oh, yes." Lady Stevens's voice held a hint of sarcasm. "Lady Pamela—what a coincidence that she carried the same name as your own betrothed—bowed to her father's wishes and became a marchioness. I have always wondered if she ever regretted it. I danced at their wedding, you know," she added abruptly, changing the somber tone of this recital. "I do not regret that, for it was there I met . . ." Her voice tapered off, and when she again spoke, it was to chide one of her dogs, clustered, as usual, around her chair.

"I shall have to order something to wear, of course," she remarked in her ordinary tone after a lengthy pause. "The wedding of a marquess is no ordinary affair, as I know from experience. Have you set a date yet, my lord?"

"Tomorrow morning, my lady," Robert said stiffly.

The tone of Lady Stevens's conversation had affected him oddly, and the reminder that his mother had been another Pamela disturbed him. Or perhaps he should admit that what really bothered him was that Lord Melrose had dared to name his daughter after the woman he had wronged. Not that there could be any connection between the two Pamelas, he reasoned. Why should there be? His imagination was overwrought—that must be it.

"But my dear boy, that is impossible," his hostess exclaimed in amazement. "My modiste simply cannot have a new gown ready in time. Tell me that you jest, my lord."

Before the marquess would reply to this remark, a footman slipped into the room and whispered something to Jenkins. The butler's eyebrows lifted fractionally, but he trod across the carpet and bent to whisper in the ear of his mistress.

"Let him come in, Jenkins," she ordered after this consultation. "He may have urgent news to impart to his lordship."

Moments later, a pale-faced Freddy Hancock stumbled into the room, coming to an abrupt halt when he perceived the guests still at dinner.

"I earnestly beg your pardon, Lady Stevens," he stammered, glancing wildly at the marquess. "But my uncle sends me to accompany his lordship to Adelaide Crescent immediately."

Her curiosity thoroughly aroused, Lady Stevens urged the visitor to accept a glass of claret and disgorge his news without further loss of time.

Freddy seemed not to hear her ladyship's invitation. He fixed his eyes on the marquess and tried several times to say something, but without success.

"Out with it, Freddy," Robert commanded impatiently, rising to his feet and looming over the shorter man menacingly. "Why does your uncle summon me to Melrose House?"

"She is g-gone," Freddy blurted out, his eyes starting from his head. "Pamela has run off, and Uncle fears the worst."

After a moment of heavy silence, the marquess took the unfortunate visitor by his shoulders and shook him vigorously.

"What exactly is it Lord Melrose fears?" he asked icily.

"He fears she has run off with that Morton fellow. At least two hours ago, my lord. Pamela is nowhere to be found. We have searched the house, and she is not in bed with the megrim as she claimed. You must hurry if we are to catch up with them."

Robert swore under his breath. Then he made his apologies to his hostess and, accompanied by the other two gentleman, strode out of the room.

CHAPTER TEN

The Great Chase

The summer twilight brought with it a hint of rain, and Lady Pamela wished she had thought to bring a warmer cloak. She pulled the carriage rug more snugly over her knees and wondered, with no little exasperation, what fresh disaster would arise to delay their journey. One of Sir Rodney's prized cattle had cast a shoe before they reached Albourne, so they had stopped at the Turk's Head posting inn to change the team Sir Rodney had boasted would easily see them as far as Red Hill. So much for horses, Pamela thought dourly; they were almost as unreliable as gentlemen; one simply could not count on them at all.

Outside Handcross, when Pamela was beginning to entertain hopes of arriving in London in time for dinner, the coach had floundered in a particularly insidious hole, jolted Pamela's bonnet off her head, and broken a wheel with a resounding crack. Luckily, they had been within walking distance of the King's Arms Inn, and Pamela had sat drinking weak tea for over an hour in a private parlor while Sir Rodney sought out the wheelwright and arranged the repairs.

Sir Rodney had apologized profusely, of course, but by the time they set out again, twilight was falling, and the coastal breeze from the south had become cool enough to be uncomfortable.

"I trust we shall reach London before dark, Rodney," Pamela said to the baronet as they stood beside the chaise. She looked anxiously over her shoulder. "I expect Father has discovered my note by this time and will have informed the marquess."

Sir Rodney chuckled. "If I know anything about Monroyal, my dear, he is hardly cast into transports at the notion of being leg-shackled. More than likely, he will wash his hands of the whole affair."

Oddly, this comforting remark did nothing to soothe Pamela's nerves. "He is firmly set on the match, Rodney," she replied crossly. "He told me so quite adamantly."

"No need to fly into the boughs, m'dear," the baronet said easily. "You have yet to tell me how Lord Melrose brought that plump pigeon up to scratch, Pamela. Seems rather havey-cavey to me that a matrimonial catch of that magnitude would . . ." He stopped abruptly, evidently realizing what he had been about to say.

Pamela was not nearly so mealy-mouthed. Furthermore, she was furious that Rodney would have so little consideration for her feelings. "Would choose a female with nothing but a fortune to recommend her? Is that what you were about to say, sir? Have you stopped to consider that perhaps his lordship has had a run of bad luck at the tables or at Newcastle? You are not the only gentleman with pockets to let who considers marriage to an heiress the simplest way of coming about."

Sir Rodney bridled at this rebuke. "No need to get into a pucker, Pamela," he retorted. "And it is not just the money with me, you know. I have always been fond of you. Ever since you were a gawky beanstick of fifteen."

"Very flattering indeed," Pamela snapped, and turned with an angry flounce to climb into the carriage. She could not imagine the marquess calling a lady a beanstick to her face. The comparison gave Pamela pause for thought. Had she made the right decision, she wondered, in sending that wildly emotional note to her childhood friend, begging him to save her from a monster? She brushed the doubt aside. If she must marry, surely life with Sir Rodney, whose faults she knew all too well, would be less onerous than being the unwanted wife of the cold, arrogant Lord Monroyal?

The team that was poled up in Redhill proved to be veritable slugs, and Sir Rodney's repeated orders to his coachman to spring them increased their speed not a whit. After what seemed to Pamela hours of jog-trotting at a snail's pace, the chaise pulled into the Two-Headed Boar in Purley. She lowered the window and motioned to Sir Rodney, who had chosen, for propriety's sake, to ride alongside. It was now almost dark, and Pamela could barely distinguish Rodney's expression when he pulled his skittish roan up beside the chaise.

"Why are we stopping *again*?" Pamela inquired impatiently. "You promised we would be in London hours ago. Perhaps you wish the marquess to catch up with us. Is that it?" Fatigue had made her pettish, she thought, and it would not do to come to points with Rodney. He was quite capable of turning short about and taking her back to Adelaide Crescent.

"If you must be forever nagging at me, perhaps it would be better for me if he did," the baronet answered crossly. "There is little point in going on with these job horses if we expect to get to London before midnight. I suggest we bespeak a fresh team for the morning and rack up here for the night. I hear the hostler's wife is famous for her braised duck, and I am famished, let me tell you."

Before Pamela could protest, the baronet had swung off his horse and flung open the coach door. Accustomed to traveling in the well-sprung Melrose carriage, Pamela felt as though every bone in her body had been subjected to the rack, so she was only too glad to enter the cozy parlor and listen to the host list the delicacies he could set before her at her convenience.

Lulled by the warmth and bustle of the inn, and tempted by the delicious smells that wafted up from the kitchens, Pamela decided to overlook the impropriety of staying at an inn with a man as yet unrelated to her. She discovered, as soon as the covers were set and the generous platters of pigeon pie, a haunch of venison, and the famous braised duckling carried in by the host himself, that she had a healthy appetite. Unlike the baronet, who called for two extra flagons as the meal progressed, Pamela partook sparingly of the excellent claret. Rodney insisted upon filling her glass several times and was in such an excellent humor that she drank more than usual. By the time the damson tartlets and custard were set before her, Pamela felt at peace with the world. By tomorrow morning she would be Lady Morton, and all connections with the top-lofty marquess would be severed.

She smiled fondly across the table at the white knight who had saved her from a lifetime of misery, as she chose to see the timely intervention of her childhood hero. She really had harbored a tendre for Rodney even before he had noticed that she was a skinny beanstick, she remembered. His endless teasing had left her heartsick and often in tears. But the day he had complimented her on her hair, Pamela had seen stars in the middle of a gray afternoon. When it became apparent that the baronet no longer considered her a gawky beanstick, his favorite name for her, Pamela's first reaction had been unmitigated joy. Only when she noticed that his most extravagant flattery was invariably accompanied by a request for a small loan, did Pamela's feet settle back on solid ground. And when she could no longer pretend not to see the connection between herself and her fortune in Rodney's mind, Pamela's infatuation had died a slow and painful death.

"Was it not a brilliant idea to stop for dinner, my love?" Sir Rodney asked in the softly cajoling tones Pamela had heard before. She wondered idly if her white knight had enough of the ready to pay the shot. Instantly, she chided herself for this unworthy thought and returned his smile with more enthusiasm than was her wont.

"Yes, indeed," she responded warmly, basking in the affectionate glow she saw in his eyes. Rodney reached across the table and took her hand in both of his, raising it to his lips for a languorous kiss. He really was quite handsome, she mused, and when he looked at her just so, she could forget that he was here solely on account of the eighty thousand pounds she would bring him when they wed.

When they wed? The idea rattled insistently around in her mind, jarring her out of her comfortable haze. Exactly when were they to be wed?

"Rodney," she said, resolutely pulling her hand from his grasp, "do you suppose the local vicar would consent to marry us tonight?" The sudden flare of passion in Rodney's eyes told her that she had given entirely the wrong impression. But it was too late to remedy that, and her heart pounded wildly at the triumph in his laugh.

The baronet sprang to his feet and came around the table, clasping her hands in his and going down on one knee, confirming what Pamela had read in countless romantical novels without believing a word of such fustian.

"My darling girl," he murmured throatily, while Pamela regarded him in disbelief. "I am delighted to know that we are of the same mind. I, too, am impatient to make you mine. Doubtless the vicar of Purley will be delighted to oblige us." He followed this speech, which was not as reassuring as Pamela could have wished, with a shower of kisses on her fingers, palms, and wrists.

"Oh, do get up, Rodney," Pamela exclaimed, torn between derision and amusement. "You are being quite absurd." She tugged ineffectually, but his grip only tightened on her wrists. "And release me this instant!" she cried, trying not to give in to her growing anxiety.

The baronet rose unsteadily to his feet, but rather than release her, he threw an arm about her waist and drew her roughly against him. Before Pamela could react, she found herself in the throes of a torrid embrace. She had known that sooner or later she would be subjected to whatever intimacies her new husband chose to inflict upon her. Pamela had been resigned to that. But they were as yet unwed, and Rodney appeared to have overlooked that vital fact.

Trying not to panic, Pamela wriggled free of the baronet's

mouth, which appeared to be intent on claiming every inch of her face and neck. Rodney grunted in protest and jerked her against him with such force that Pamela felt every curve of his lean frame imprinted against her own. It became instantly clear to her that her white knight had much more than kisses on his mind.

Shocked, but not surprised at Rodney's hot-headed lack of control, Pamela was again reminded of horses. Let the brutes once get the bit between their teeth, and there was no diverting them from their course. She had found this out to her sorrow the day she defied her father and took his Satan out for a gallop. She experienced the same helpless fury now as she had then, carried along against her will in a whirlwind of pure force that had excited yet terrified her, too.

"Rodney," she managed to gasp when the baronet began to nuzzle her bosom, which he had partially exposed during their struggles. "What about the vicar?" she gasped. "Surely, you should seek him out before the hour is too advanced?" The scene had so many elements of Italian melodrama about it that Pamela had a sudden urge to laugh. Was she about to be ravished on the parlor table? she wondered hysterically. How had her white knight turned so abruptly into the dragon? "Rodney," she repeated more forcefully, "did you hear what I said?"

"Leave the vicar to me, sweetheart," the baronet murmured warmly against her throat, one hand fumbling with the opening of her gown. "I promise to send for him first thing in the morning."

Her fate now clear to her—for there was no misconstruing the white knight's dark meaning—Pamela grabbed a handful of the thick, curly hair she had admired so often in the past and yanked it with all her force.

"No, Rodney," she cried out loudly, "you will fetch him *now,* or not at all. I refuse to be treated like some of your Haymarket ware. Release me at once, or I shall call the host."

"You will have me bald before my time, m'love," he mumbled, showing not the least sign of relenting. "And save your breath, Pamela. That old codger is not going to come bursting in to rescue you, love. I told him we are newly riveted."

His obvious amusement at having outwitted her caused Pamela to give way to outrage rather than hysteria. "Villain!" she exclaimed, catching him a slap on the ear. "I demand you unhand me instantly!" she screamed, hoping that the innkeeper would realize that this was no lover's romp.

Help came sooner than she expected, but when the door burst open, it was not the innkeeper's unctuous tones that assaulted Pamela's overwrought sensibilities.

"It pains me to discover you embroiled in yet another compromising rendezvous, my dear Lady Pamela," a bored voice drawled from the doorway.

Pamela turned to find the Marquess of Monroyal regarding her through his jewel-handled quizzing-glass, a censorial expression on his aristocratic face.

"I say, old chap, I really do not care to meet my Maker on the King's highway, which is what I fear will happen if you do not put a damper on it."

Mr. Hampton, clinging precariously to the handrail of the racing curricle, sounded sorely aggrieved, and with good reason the marquess admitted. After a brief stop at Adelaide Crescent, where Lord Melrose had handed him a hastily scribbled missive from his daughter, the marquess had given his cattle their heads, and the Welsh-bred team had responded gamely, eating up the miles as only sixteen-mile-an-hour tits could.

"I daresay the knot will be tied by the time we catch them, anyway," Hampton said cheerfully, "which is all for the best, of course. So unless you are set on besting Prinny's record from London to Brighton, I recommend we give the happy couple plenty of time to get riveted." When his companion made no response, Hampton glanced at him anxiously. "I gather that *is* your intention, is it not, Robert? You do wish to allow this Morton fellow to beat you to the altar, I presume?"

The marquess did not answer, merely flicking his gloved hand in a gesture that might be taken for yes or no. In truth, he was ambiguous about the whole affair. He knew Hampton was right. This mad start of Lady Pamela's had provided him with a heaven-sent excuse to hedge off his promise to Lord Melrose. The earl could hardly expect him to honor his obligation to a female who had disgraced herself so shamelessly. On the other hand, Robert felt strangely reluctant to let the silly chit get away with this insult. What advantages did she see in Morton, he asked himself for the umpteenth time since reading the lady's insulting missive, that the Marquess of Monroyal could not offer tenfold? Robert could come up with no rational answer to this enigma, and he did not like riddles.

Twilight was settling down in earnest when they made a brief stop at Redhill, where they discovered that Morton had changed horses.

"From what the stable-lads tell me," Hampton remarked as they entered the inn for a flagon of local ale, "Morton and his lady are less than an hour ahead of us."

This assessment was confirmed by the innkeeper as he hurried forward to serve his noble guests. "Why, yes, m'lord. The gentleman ordered a glass of lemonade for the lady not much above an hour ago, and then made the oddest request I've 'eard in a long time." He glanced from one to the other of his guests to make sure they would appreciate the oddity he was about to recount. "As I said, m'lords, this 'ere gentleman 'ad windmills in 'is 'ead to be sure. If ye know what I mean." He favored them with a broad wink.

"No, but I expect we will as soon as you tell us, my good man," Hampton said encouragingly.

The innkeeper took the hint and grinned slyly. "I can see ye're already onto his rig, gentlemen," he chortled.

"More than likely, we are," Hampton agreed patiently. "But do finish your story, man."

"Well, it appears this gentleman gave the ostler a shilling to make sure he poled up the slowest nags in the stable." He gave them a lewd wink, which caused the marquess to think that whatever sins Lady Pamela may have committed, she did not deserve to be the butt of jests in the taprooms along the Brighton Road. "Seems as though the young gent was in no tearing 'urry to get to Lunnon," the man concluded with another suggestive wink.

"Sounds like a dashed rum touch if you want my opinion, Robert," Hampton remarked as they swept out of the inn yard into the approaching dusk. "What the lass saw in that rackety sprig I cannot say, but one would think that any chit with half her wits about her must recognize a shabster when she sees one. Morton's grandfather was in Trade, and according to old Melrose, the family has squandered every last groat the first baronet made in India. Not a feather to fly with, I take it. Of course the lady is full of juice, which may account for young Morton's willingness to take on a female with a cloud hanging over her—"

"Lady Pamela does *not* have a cloud hanging over her," Robert surprised himself by protesting sharply.

His friend stared at him, his mouth acock. "Of course, she has, old man," he insisted vigorously. "She was discovered alone with *you* in a deserted cottage, was she not? Do not, I beg of you, Robert, try to convince me she was not compromised. Her father certainly seemed to think so," he added as if to cinch the argument.

"Of course he did, you sapskull," the marquess responded rudely. "His daughter is at her last prayers, as every half-wit can see, and a bluestocking to boot. What father would not seize the opportunity to thrust her into one of the first families of the land?" He paused, then added half under his breath, "Particular *my* family."

"Oh, you mean because of that old scandal?" Hampton inquired cautiously as they threaded their way past two empty farm wagons on their way home. "I wondered if that had anything to do with it. But you cannot mean that Melrose is still harboring a grudge against your father. All that rivalry happened over thirty years ago, and Melrose went on to wed some other female—I forget her name—after he inherited the title, and apparently was happy with her."

Hampton fell silent as they left the last cottages of Redhill behind them and pushed on through the dusk. The marquess made no reply to his friend's remarks. He was not in the habit of discussing his private affairs, even with intimates like Willy Hampton; and that long-ago scandal was one of the most private memories in his life. He normally did not dwell on his father's duel and the uneasy reconciliation between his parents that followed the late marquess's severe injuries at the hands of Lord Melrose—there was little point in pretending that the mysterious Mr. Brown was a mystery any longer, he thought cynically. He was in a fair way to becoming related to the old devil.

This reminder of his runaway betrothed caused him to push his team recklessly on through the darkness. Purley lay a scant seven miles from Redhill, and Robert was confident that the job horses at Morton's disposal would not get him much farther that night.

"With any luck we shall overtake Morton at Purley," he said when the lights of the village came into view as they crested a hill. When they pulled into the yard of the Two-Headed Boar, this prediction proved to be correct, and Robert felt a strange exhilaration as they made their way into the noisy taproom.

"Aye, m'lord," the host replied to the marquess's query about a gentleman acquaintance traveling to London with a lady, "came in nearly an hour ago they did, and I put 'em in the back parlor. 'Appy as a pair of turtle doves they be, too, m'lord. Just got 'emselves buckled the gentleman told me, confidential like, and not wishing to be disturbed. Took in a plate of Mrs. Todd's tartlets for the lady myself, I did, not ten minutes ago. Complimented me on me brandy, the young gent did. Very civil of 'im I thought to meself."

During this lengthy recital, the marquess felt his exhilaration at catching his quarry drain away, replaced by a cold fury. Could it be that the chit had bested him after all? Had she indeed thrown herself away on a fortune hunter just to spite him? Uttering a low growl of frustration, the marquess glowered at the startled host.

"Where are they?" he demanded harshly.

"Nothing wrong, I 'ope, m'lord," Mr. Todd stammered, and then, apparently thinking better of interrogating this large, irate patron, he pointed to a room at the end of the hall. "The gent did ask not to be disturbed, m'lord," he began, but Robert turned away abruptly.

He stroke purposefully down the narrow hall, Hampton trailing behind him. "I say, old man," the latter protested ineffectually, "do you suppose we ought to burst in on the newlyweds without some warning. Assuming they are wed—"

"Precisely," muttered the marquess between clenched teeth, "assuming they are wed."

As they approached the parlor, Robert clearly heard a woman's voice raised in protest. He needed no further incentive, but grasped the glass handle firmly, prepared to shatter the door if necessary. Surprised to find the door unlocked, he pushed it open and stepped inside.

The scene that met his eyes was so similar to another he had lived through himself two days ago that he was hard put not to laugh. For a well-bred female, Lady Pamela seemed to have an alarming propensity for getting herself into scrapes of the worst kind. He raised his quizzing-glass and took in the scene calmly, overwhelmed by a sense of déjà vu.

Morton was obviously in his cups and had the luckless damsel tightly trapped in his arms. Robert could not see the man's face, which was busy nuzzling the lady's throat and bosom as the marquess had done himself not so long ago, he recalled. To do so himself was one thing, of course, but to watch another man mauling his betrothed was intolerable. And what lack of finesse the baronet displayed, Robert thought disgustedly, noting that the lady was making valiant attempts to free herself. He himself had little experience kissing unwilling females, always having considered there to be little pleasure to be gained from it. In point of fact, he could recall only one in recent history, and that was the lady before him now, struggling once again to preserve her virginity, no doubt, he thought cynically.

The noise of the door opening must have distracted her, for she turned a pale face in his direction. He focused his quizzing-glass upon her.

"It pains me to discover you embroiled in yet another compromising rendezvous, my dear Lady Pamela," he remarked coolly, observing with some satisfaction the blush that rushed into her cheeks.

"God, Robert," Hampton hissed at his elbow, "ain't you going to *do* something?"

The marquess had never been one to avoid a dust-up, and quite suddenly he felt the need to rearrange this uncouth brute's nose. He grasped Morton by the collar, lifted him effortlessly away from his victim, and threw him across the room. The baronet landed heavily on a spindle-backed chair, which cracked under his weight, depositing him on the parlor floor.

The marquess heard Lady Pamela gasp, but paid her no heed, his attention set on Morton, who did not look like a man to take such punishment lying down. He shakily clambered to his feet and stood, one hand on the table for support, his face mottled with rage.

"You will regret this, you arrogant bastard," he snarled, visibly shaken. "Who do you think you are, coming between a man and his wife like this?"

Robert heard another gasp from his runaway lady and guessed Morton was bluffing.

"You are lying, of course," he snapped.

The baronet laughed, but his eyes were hard and dangerous. "That is what you would like to believe, no doubt; but no, my lord, I am not lying. The lady preferred me, you see." He sneered, obviously enjoying taunting his rival. "I know that is a hard pill to swallow for the likes of you, but you have come too late, my lord. She is mine. The knot is tied, and no amount of blustering will undo what is done." He laughed suggestively.

"I still say you are lying." But a suspicion of doubt raised its ugly head, and Robert could not understand why it irked him that there might be any truth to the baronet's claim. Had he not wished to escape this unwelcome entanglement with Lady Pamela? he mused. The intervention of this encroaching mushroom had provided him with the excuse he needed to wash his hands of her.

The marquess turned to the lady and for the first time noticed her disarray and realized that she was close to tears. He raised one eyebrow questioningly, "Is this true, madam?"

"A-absolutely n-not," she stammered. Her slender fingers, clasping the gaping front of her gown, trembled visibly.

It point of fact, the lady looked oddly endearing, the marquess noticed. Her rich chestnut hair—all too well Robert remembered its softness—fell around her pale face in a riot of curls, giving her an air of vulnerability that penetrated his habitual cynicism and made him want to slay dragons on her behalf. A foolish notion admittedly, he thought, since dragons had been extinct for centuries. And was that not admiration he glimpsed in her hazel eyes?

Abruptly this illusion was broken when Hampton let out a warning shout. Robert whirled around in time to take a jarring right to the jaw that sent him reeling against the table, rocking it violently and sending several dishes crashing to the floor.

He heard Lady Pamela utter a squeal of terror, but Robert did not make the same mistake twice. He kept his eyes on Morton, who advanced on him, a grin of unholy anticipation on his lean face. This time, however, the marquess was ready for him, having slipped off his coat and handed it to Hampton.

"Fancy yourself a pugilist, do you, m'lord?" the baronet said scornfully. "Well, let me show you some real fisticuffs, not that elegant flailing around you fancy bucks do in Jackson's Saloon and call it boxing. Here, take this." He feinted to the left and drove his right fist into Robert's middle, bending him over and leaving him gasping for breath.

Thoroughly incensed at being tipped a settler by one he considered an inferior fighter, Robert brushed everything from his mind except the sneering face of the baronet, who needled him at every opportunity. It soon became apparent that the marquess would not draw his opponent's cork as quickly as he expected. Morton was untrained, but he made up for his lack of science with a viciousness that soon jolted Robert out of his complacency. Hampered by notions of fair play and the rules of the game, he suffered in very short order a gash to his cheek that dribbled blood down into the folds of his cravat.

Tugging the offending garment off, he planted a punishing facer to his rival that left the baronet's nose bleeding copiously. With a howl of rage, Morton attempted a home stall, which the marquess barely had time to deflect before he was barraged by all manner of punches, some of which he was quite sure did not come out of the book of rules followed by the habitués of Jackson's sporting parlor.

It did not take Robert more than a minute or two to realize that sportsmanship was not in the baronet's vocabulary. After receiving several vicious and quite illegal hits from an opponent who appeared to have learned his pugilistic skills in taproom brawls or on the London docks, the marquess shed his own inhibitions and got down to some serious fighting.

During this rumpus, the host appeared at the door, followed by what appeared to be the entire drinking contingent from the taproom. Much to Robert's chagrin, most of them chose to root for his opponent, still under the illusion, no doubt, that the younger man was being castigated by an irate relative of the bride.

The outcome of the fight was still uncertain when the marquess took advantage of a reckless opening to mill his rival down with a facer to the baronet's jaw that snapped his head back with a sickening crack and knocked him flying onto the table, now completely destitute of crockery.

Robert paused, swaying slightly, in the midst of broken dishes, spilled wine, a duck's carcass, splintered glass, and ruined table linen, waiting for the baronet to show signs of life. When he made no move to do so, the marquess glared challengingly round the room, feeling more alive than he had in many a day. He met Lady Pamela's wide stare and grinned foolishly.

Upon noticing the host, he waved at the devastation around him. "Put this on my reckoning," he managed to say through puffy, bleeding lips. "And get that rogue out of here." He pointed to Morton. "Throw him in his carriage and send him back to Brighton. I do not wish to see him again."

"And bring me some warm water," Lady Pamela added, recovering from her fright. "We must see to his lordship's injuries."

She made her way across the room through the wreckage. "And send someone to sweep this up," she said in a stronger voice. "And you, my lord," she continued, eyeing his bloodstained person with distaste, "sit down over here." She took his arm gingerly and led him to a damask-covered settle by the hearth. "And drink this." She pressed a brandy glass gently to his lips until he took several large gulps.

For once in his life, the Marquess of Monroyal did what he was bid without a murmur of protest. The truth was he felt much more than exhausted. Every bone in his body ached, one eye was closing up, his lips felt like putty, and his blood was still dripping onto his shirt. He closed his good eye and felt himself drift off into a rosy haze. He would have something to teach those amateurs of the Fancy next time he went to Jackson's Saloon, he thought, amused at the notion of introducing Morton's brand of fighting into that select club.

The soft touch of cool water on his face recalled him to the present. Opening his one eye, Robert stared into Lady Pamela's worried hazel gaze. He tried to remember the question that had been simmering in his mind since he had stretched Morton out like a slab of bacon, but the lady's soft murmurings distracted him as she gently cleaned his face. Suddenly, it came back to him.

"Did you wed him?" he demanded bluntly through split lips.

She looked at him, and Robert could have sworn she was amused. "No, my lord," she said hesitantly. "Your timely intervention removed any thought of marriage from poor Rodney's mind."

For reasons quite beyond his comprehension, this answer pleased him, and he would have grinned had his battered mouth been less painful.

"Tell the host I want the vicar here tomorrow morning at first light," he mumbled incoherently.

The lady stared at him in surprise. "I believe Rodney may already have done so, my lord. At least he said he would." She rinsed out the handkerchief and applied it to his brow, which was throbbing painfully. "But I should warn you it is too late to fob me off on Sir Rodney. You sent him back home, remember. Probably to lick his wounds," she added with some relish. "Here, drink some more brandy." She brought the glass to his mouth again.

"Morton is not the man I had in mind," he mumbled through swollen lips.

After a slight pause, during which he saw the warm amusement fade from Lady Pamela's eyes, Robert received the set-down of his life.

"Then you are either monstrously stupid or unbearably vain and stubborn," she said without mincing words. "Any gentleman with half his wits about him would wash his hands of the whole affair."

"I am not *any* gentleman," he pointed out facetiously, feeling the warmth of the brandy soak into his battered body.

"No, you are more odious than most," she retorted. "I shall not have anything to do with you."

"You really have no choice this time, my dear," he countered, basking in the certainty that, in spite of her resistance, she would not escape again.

"Then I shall wear mourning for the rest of my life," she snapped, going off on a tangent as females were wont to do in his experience when faced by the inevitability of masculine logic.

"Glad to hear it," he murmured, quite enjoying his victory. "I shall save on dressmakers' bills."

"You cannot prevent me from making your life as miserable as you have made mine, sirrah." She glared at him for a second or two, then threw the damp cloth at him and stormed out of the room.

Robert grinned painfully at his friend.

"That was not well done of you, Robert," Hampton said reprovingly. "Cannot you find it in you to feel compassion for the girl?"

"I leave that to you, Sweet Willy," Robert muttered, a wicked light in his one good eye.

"I tremble to think what Lady Pamela will say," Hampton continued, "when she learns she is not to set foot at Stilton Grange."

"I cannot wait to hear it."

CHAPTER ELEVEN

Stranger From the Sea

Holly Lodge, Dorset, September, 1817

The sound of the sea woke her again.

Pamela lay warm and snug in her feather bed, wondering how she had ever lived without the intoxicating rhythms of the waves crashing against the steep Dorset cliffs. They had not always been as soothing as they were this morning, she thought, listening drowsily to the slow rushing movement—regular as a Bach fugue—of sea against sand, punctuated by the occasional crescendo of waves reaching up to envelop the rocks, then falling back in a staccato of silvery spray.

Suddenly wide awake, Pamela threw back the covers and slipped out of bed. In slippered feet she stood by the window, drinking in the sounds of nature's music, which never failed to move and inspire her. Impatient to start the day with her walk along the cliffs, she rang for her morning chocolate, then sat down before the beveled mirror on the antique dresser to brush out her tangled curls.

"Good morning, Betsy," she greeted the shy little maid who brought up her chocolate every morning. "I see we are in for another fine day."

"Aye, milady," the maid replied, her small face lighting up. "Joey says the storm is gone for the rest of the week, milady. And old Scamp is waiting for you by the front door, milady. Fair tickled that dog be to have his run on the cliffs."

An hour later, after a brisk, invigorating hike along the cliff tops with Lady Honoria's spaniel Scamp at her heels, Pamela turned back towards the house. Holly Lodge sat on an incline rising a half mile from the cliff edge and surrounded by a small park. When she arrived three months ago, she had entered from the front, facing away from the sea. In her innocence she had imagined she was arriving at her new husband's principal estate,

Stilton Grange, but her first glimpse of the modest, unpretentious manor house in stone and gray slate had disabused her.

So this must be yet another of Lord Monroyal's minor estates, she had surmised, unwilling to demand an explanation from the marquess as he handed her down from the traveling chaise. They had spoken little during the two-day journey from Brighton along the coast into Dorset. Mr. Hampton had been his cheerful self and had nattered on, mainly about his horses—of which it seemed to Pamela he owned more than he could ever need—when they stopped at various inns along the way.

The thought of her absent husband always evoked mixed emotions in Pamela's breast. More often than not, she felt the whole episode of her flight with Sir Rodney Morton, their discovery by Lord Monroyal, and the subsequent ceremony performed by the starched-up, prune-faced vicar of Purley had been some wild figment of her imagination. How she wished it had been so! But the Reverend Mr. Arthur Cowley had assured her that the special license presented by the marquess was beyond a doubt legal and that she could rest assured that she was bound by all the combined authority of Church and state to Robert Neville Alexander Stilton, sixth Marquess of Monroyal.

For better or for worse, she had added under her breath, convinced that the worst part of this havey-cavey arrangement would be inflicted upon her by her new husband at the first opportunity. When that had not happened, Pamela had at first felt relief. Perhaps the marquess was reluctant to begin their married life in a lumpy bed at some anonymous inn. This unexpected consideration on his part softened her dislike of him a fraction. It was only after he deposited her at Holly Lodge—like a stranger to be tolerated out of courtesy—and continued his journey without her, did the awful truth dawn upon her. Her husband wanted nothing to do with her at all. Not even those intimacies she had fully expected him to claim merely because they were his for the taking. The mortification of his disdain still made her blush.

"Come along, Scamp, you old devil," she called to the spaniel who was sniffing around one of the newly planted rose-trees preparatory to digging up an imaginary bone there. Recognizing these signs of incipient destruction, Pamela ran up the low steps onto the wide, trellised terrace at the back of the house, which served as a haven for leisurely teas on summer afternoons. The old dog followed her at a more sedate pace.

It had been here on the terrace that she had been introduced to Lady Honoria Stilton, younger sister of the late marquess. The poor lady had not been notified of their arrival—which was consistent with the marquess's high-handed methods, Pamela thought privately—but was truly delighted at the sight of her eldest nephew. Her tone changed noticeably, however, when Pamela was introduced as the new marchioness.

"Surely you are bamming me, Robert?" she cried out in astonishment, her sharp gray eyes, so like her nephew's, fastening upon Pamela as if the latter had appeared at the dinner table in her shift. "I will not believe a word of it. You cannot be wed, I insist upon it." Her gaze roved over Pamela's slight form with obvious disapproval, causing her to blush painfully.

Disregarding this rudeness, Lady Pamela said nothing, choosing instead to stare intently at her ladyship's substantial chin. After a moment's impasse, Pamela was gratified to see the chin quiver indignantly.

"Your face is familiar, child," her ladyship said abruptly. "Are you related to the Hancocks?" she snapped. "No," she continued, muttering to herself, "that cannot be. No nephew of mine would . . ." Her voice trailed off, and her eyes swiveled back to Lord Monroyal.

"Tell me this is all a hoax, Robert."

Pamela regarded the scene with no little amusement. She enjoyed seeing the autocratic marquess get the dressing down he deserved. Her eyes met Mr. Hampton's bland gaze, and she was startled when he winked at her. She was tempted to wink back.

After an awkward pause, the marquess cleared his throat. "I fear it is so, Aunt," he acknowledged briefly.

"And when did these clandestine nuptials take place, Robert?" she demanded shrilly, favoring Pamela with a stare calculated to reduce her to *blancmange*. "Come now, I know you must be gammoning me, nephew. Why, I know very well that you are the least likely man in England to take a wife. You have trumpeted that fact yourself these fifteen years or more. Have you gone soft in the head, boy?"

Lady Pamela could not help smiling at her ladyship's bluntness. "My experience—limited though it is—suggests that his lordship suffers rather from hard-headedness, my lady," she remarked, thinking it high time she entered this absurd argument. "I warned him that he was making a terrible mistake in this match, but do you think he would listen?"

Another silence, as if her ladyship did not quite know what to do with this startling piece of information.

"Never say the lad is in love?" Lady Honoria whispered at last in a hushed voice, as if the mere notion were a heresy.

"Not at all," Pamela responded calmly. "I doubt he knows the meaning of the word. It is mere stubbornness on his part, my lady, believe me. His lordship is odiously set in his ways, as you must know. I warned him we would both be miserable. In fact, I promised to do my best to see that he was. But I might have saved my breath."

Lady Honoria was staring at her as though she had suddenly sprouted two heads. "I have never heard of such a thing," she gasped, her chin trembling in dire agitation. "Are you daring to suggest that my nephew is not acceptable to you, young lady? If you did not wish to wed him, why in heaven's name did you accept his offer?"

"Oh, but I did, you see. Refuse him, that is. Several times. But it was like talking to a horse," Pamela explained, reminded suddenly of her father's irascible Satan and the wild ride he had given her out of pure perversity. "Have you not noticed, my lady, that horses never want to do what one tells them? They are naturally cantankerous."

"Are you telling me my nephew is a horse?"

Lady Pamela had to smile at this amusing choice of words. "Oh, no, my lady. Lord Monroyal is much worse than any horse I ever knew. Horses may be put down when they become unmanageable; but I very much doubt his lordship would allow me to get away with such extreme measures."

This concept had been so far outside the bounds of her ladyship's imagination that it was not until after the marquess had left, with Mr. Hampton in tow, that she recovered her serenity enough to acknowledge her nephew's new bride as a legitimate member of the family.

The sound of her chamber door opening brought Pamela out of deep sleep. In that first instant of consciousness, she told herself she had dreamed that someone stood on the threshold, breathing heavily. The next second she heard the tattoo of Scamp's claws in the hall and wondered why the dog had left his warm basket in the kitchen. It was not like him. In his declining years, the aging spaniel had avoided the long climb up the stairs, preferring to rest his old bones beside the kitchen stove.

What was he doing up on the second floor at this time of night? she wondered. A prickle of fear brought her fully awake. She heard the dog's feet making a happy tattoo in the hall, just as he did when she came downstairs to take him for his morning walk. Whoever was out there was definitely not a stranger.

A shadow detached itself from the darkness of the hallway, and Pamela's blood froze, a scream trapped in her throat. A figure stumbled into the room and stood swaying, arms outstretched, feeling around in the darkness. Scamp let out a *woof-woof* of encouragement, and Pamela could hear the dog's tail sweeping excitedly against her bed.

She smelled damp clothes. Whoever the intruder was, he had been out in the storm that had raged for two days along the coast. He was obviously exhausted, and Pamela's fear evaporated when the figure took a tottering step forward and fell prone on the carpet.

Without giving a thought to her own safety, she slid out of bed and lit a candle with steady hands. Whoever the stranger was, he could do her little harm in his present state, she told herself.

When she knelt beside the figure on the floor, Pamela saw it was a young man, dressed in soaking coat and breeches. His top boots were waterlogged, as if he had waded through the breakers, and his cravat hung like a limp rag around his neck. He was shivering violently, and his teeth chattered. He needed immediate assistance, she saw, or he would catch a deadly chill.

It took her only a moment to stoke the dying embers of the fire and drag the half-conscious man closer to the hearth. She pulled the soggy coat from his back and removed his plain buff waistcoat. In the flickering light of the solitary candle, Pamela saw immediately that the fine linen shirt showed several large bloodstains. She hesitated, then carefully removed the soaking garment, revealing an ugly gash in the young man's shoulder. He groaned when she pulled the cloth away from his skin, and mumbled something in French.

Her gaze was drawn to his tightly-fitted breeches, but she balked at the idea of divesting a gentleman of his smallclothes. But they, and his ruined boots, must come off if she were to get him into her warm bed. She must rouse the household, should have done so sooner, she realized.

Scamp had curled up beside the unconscious man by the fire, and Pamela had donned her warm robe and placed a blanket on the shivering stranger by the time the housekeeper and Firth, Lady Honoria's butler, appeared at her door.

"You called, milady?" the butler said mechanically, his eyes starting from his head as he examined the figure beside the hearth.

"Master Geoffrey?" the housekeeper exclaimed, rushing forward to kneel beside the young man. "Oh, my sainted aunt, Mr. Firth," she cried in great agitation, " 'tis young Master Geoffrey come to us from the sea again."

These strange words prompted Pamela to inquire as to the identity of Master Geoffrey.

" 'Tis his lordship's brother, milady," Mr. Firth explained, his voice quavering with distress. "Looks as if those Frenchies got him this time."

"Many's the time I warned him, I did," Mrs. Firth wailed, running a hand over the unruly damp curls. "Oh, Mr. Firth, whatever shall we do?"

"We must get him into bed without further delay," Pamela ordered when neither of the old retainers showed signs of action. "Call one of the footmen to help you remove his breeches, Firth. And you, Mrs. Firth, set some water to boil, for we shall need to clean out the wound, and make some hot broth. He is chilled to the bone and probably starved, too."

Overcoming the servant's resistance to placing the wounded man into her warm bed, Pamela settled the patient comfortably and dressed his wound. He did not regain consciousness, but did mumble several more phrases in a garbled French she did not understand.

At long last the house was quiet again, and Lady Pamela sat at the young man's bedside, sipping a cup of tea, having assured a solicitous Mrs. Firth that they would send for the doctor first thing in the morning.

Privately, Pamela spent the rest of what remained of the night wondering whether Lord Monroyal knew his younger brother was either a smuggler or a spy.

Dr. Henderson straightened up his lanky frame and wiped his bloody hands. His brushy eyebrows obscured so much of his twinkling blue eyes that Lady Pamela wondered how he managed to see what he was doing. He smiled briefly at her. "You would make a fine nurse, my lady," he remarked, gathering his instruments and replacing them in his bag. "It takes a special kind of courage to stand firm when a man is being cut open and the blood is flowing. Congratulations, my dear."

"He will be all right, then?" Pamela asked, trying to hide that she was a good deal more affected by the removal of the ball from Geoffrey's shoulder than she appeared.

"When the fever goes down," Henderson replied laconically. "I shall give him a few drops of laudanum to keep him quiet for a while. After that you may feed him some of Mrs. Firth's gruel and bathe him with cool water. And no getting out of bed, mind you."

Pamela stared at the pale figure of her new-found brother-in-law. "How could he possibly get out of bed, Doctor?" she asked in surprise. "Lord Geoffrey is as weak as a cat."

"Ah, I have treated this young rascal before, you see," the doctor replied with a chuckle. "He spends a good deal of his time here with his aunt. Owns a neat little sloop he uses to go up and down the coast, and over to France for all we know. Master Geoffrey is full of wanderlust, never could stay in the same place for more than a few weeks."

"How do you suppose he got shot?" she demanded, wishing she knew more about firearms.

The doctor glanced at her keenly, then shrugged. "Mistaken for someone else, no doubt," he said calmly, but Pamela knew he was not telling her the truth.

"Yes, naturally," she said with some asperity. "And if you think I believe that Banbury tale, you mistake the mark, Doctor."

Henderson merely chuckled, but would say no more, so Pamela went in search of her hostess, whom she discovered in her favorite morning room, indulging in a cup of tea and freshly made pear tartlets. Scamp rose from the hearth and greeted her with his usual enthusiasm.

"You will not get your walk this morning, Scamp," she told the dog, ruffling his golden coat affectionately.

"Come and have some tea, Pamela," Lady Honoria barked in her strident voice, gesturing to a wing chair beside the brocade settee. It had not taken Pamela long to discover that her ladyship's bark was far worse than her bite. Her normal tone of voice ranged between boisterous and earsplitting, and did not mean her ladyship was either angry or ready to chew her guest up and spit her out.

"How is my dear Geoffrey doing?" she asked as soon as Pamela was seated. "And what did that old sawbones say about the ball in the boy's shoulder?"

"Lord Geoffrey is resting under Mrs. Firth's care," Pamela replied, accepting the fragile Limoges cup from her hostess. "And as for the ball, the doctor wants me to believe that Geoffrey was mistaken for someone else. He must think me a regular gapeseed to be gammoned with such a whisker."

Lady Honoria glanced at her sharply, then let out her bark of a laugh. "I see you are wide awake on all counts, my girl. That is what I like to see in a female. Far too many ninnyhammers in this world for my taste. Perhaps Robert knew what he was about after all."

Disregarding this last comment, which she considered dangerous ground, Pamela steered the old lady's attention back to her other nephew. "Then I gather you do not believe the good doctor either, my lady?"

"Phew! Of course not, child. Everyone around here knows that Geoffrey is hand-in-glove with the smugglers who use the cliffs to hide barrels of French brandy brought in under the very noses of the excise men in Osmington. Or it might have been a French patrol off the coast of France. The boy has been known to bring over a Frenchie or two working for our government. It fair gives me the fidgets to think on it."

This startling information gave Pamela the fidgets, too, and when she took her turn in the sickroom, she examined her patient closely for any sign of depravity. There was none. Lord Geoffrey Stilton looked younger than his years, and his face had more of the finely molded features of a poet than the demeanor of a criminal. In repose he looked no more than twenty, although she knew him to be ten years older. Pamela looked in vain for a resemblance to his elder brother; but there was none. Geoffrey had none of his brother's imposing features and dark coloring. His face had an almost feminine softness to it, and his chestnut curls, worn longer than was fashionable, matched her own almost exactly.

Perhaps because Lord Geoffrey was so unlike his brother, Pamela felt an immediate affinity with him. So when, on the third day after his arrival, his fever subsided and he opened his eyes, Pamela greeted him with a brilliant smile. He immediately returned the smile, and Pamela noted that his eyes were the clearest cornflower blue she had ever seen on a gentleman.

"I presume you are my fairy godmother, madam." His voice, like his demeanor, was warm and friendly, and he sounded amused.

"Well, I do not object to the godmother part," Pamela replied, responding instinctively to his easy charm, "but I have never been mistaken for a fairy before. Perhaps you are still feverish, my lord."

He laughed and glanced around the room. "It is good to be back in my own room again," he murmured.

"Actually it is my room, my lord," she corrected him, wondering how he would receive the news of his brother's sudden nuptials.

He shook his head. "How can it be your room, my dear, when I am installed in it? Quite comfortably, too, I might add."

"I chose not to use the master suite when I arrived, so Lady Honoria put me in here. She said nothing of it being your room, my lord."

"Please do not lord me to death, lady," he insisted. "The name is Geoffrey. And you have not told me who you are, and how you came to be here at all."

Pamela smiled to soften the blow. "I am Lady Pamela, and you may be quite surprised to learn, Lord Geoffrey, that you are addressing your brother's wife."

He stared at her for a full minute, his face blank. "His w-wife?" he stammered. "You?" Then he grinned widely. "You are teasing me, of course. Robert would never take a wife. Not the marrying kind at all, especially . . ." His voice tapered off, and he flushed a bright red.

"Especially to a female so unremarkable as myself, I suppose you mean," she completed the sentence for him. Pamela was getting accustomed to being judged not up to the marquess's usual standards. She rose to her feet and moved to the door. It had been more disheartening than usual to hear her shortcomings noted by a gentleman as handsome and friendly as Lord Geoffrey. She felt the need for privacy to restore her spirits.

"Please do not go," Geoffrey exclaimed. "I did not mean that, truly I did not."

"It does not signify," she replied calmly. "Robert has told me the same thing himself upon occasion. All of London is probably thinking he has lost his senses, as I do. So you are not alone, my lord."

Without any warning and for reasons she did not stop to ponder, Pamela felt tears gather in her eyes, and rather than make a cake of herself, she whisked out of the room and ran down the hall to the master suite, which she had occupied since Lord Geoffrey's arrival.

An hour later, she had recovered sufficiently to respond to an urgent message from the sickroom, summoning her to his bedside. Not long afterwards, having adamantly refused her patient leave to abandon his bed and ride over to Stilton Grange, Pamela had become privy to part of Lord Geoffrey's secret. He admitted that he had acted as courier for a friend and carried important information that must be placed in Lord Monroyal's hands without delay.

Pamela was skeptical of this story and insisted upon knowing the whole. What she did manage to wring out of a reluctant Geof-

frey was that a man they had all thought dead at Waterloo two
years ago was very much alive. Furthermore, this lieutenant had
been secretly betrothed to the Earl of Uxbridge's daughter, who
had joined her father in Brussels. Soon after the lieutenant had
been declared lost in battle, this young lady had hastily married
her ex-lover's commanding officer and immediately returned to
England.

"How incredibly romantic!" Pamela exclaimed breathlessly. "It
seems obvious that the girl had a secret *tendre* for the commanding officer. I do envy her."

Lord Geoffrey looked at her askance. "You will not think it so
romantic when I tell you that the lieutenant has threatened to return to England to confront the pair. He is claiming that Lord—
that the commanding officer, who is a cousin of ours by the way,
in collusion with Lord Uxbridge, forced the lady to wed him."

Lady Pamela digested this for a moment. How well she knew
that such arrangements between gentlemen could seal a lady's future. Had it not happened to her? Geoffrey was right; there was
nothing remotely romantic about that prospect.

"And exactly what do you expect your brother to do?" she
cried, suddenly angry at all these men who seemed to have manipulated the poor lady's life to suit their own selfish ends. "Side
with his cousin to make sure his wife does not run back to her
lieutenant?"

Geoffrey stared at her in shocked silence. "You would condone
such behavior?" he asked in a strange voice. "You would support
a woman who leaves her husband for another man?"

Pamela blinked rapidly. The discussion was getting a little too
close to home for comfort. "If she were forced to marry a man she
despised—"

"Marriages of convenience are contracted every day," he interrupted impatiently. "You must know this, Pamela."

Pamela smiled sadly. "Oh, yes, I know that only too well, my
lord," she said bitterly. "And the convenience is usually for the
gentlemen involved. Fortunes and rank seem to be all that matters
in such events. But what about love and happiness?" she blurted
out impulsively. "Would you care to wed a female who actively
disliked you? One whom you could not bear to set eyes on?"
Your precious brother did so, she wanted to add, but did not dare
to expose her own unhappiness so blatantly.

Lord Geoffrey looked heartily uncomfortable. "You are being a
little melodramatic, Pamela," he protested. "I can name any num-

ber of marriages that started out as a convenience and developed into a tolerable arrangement."

"A tolerable arrangement," she repeated scathingly. "How very delightful, to be sure." His words had fallen far short of describing her own match with his brother, but there was no use repining on that now.

"How do you propose to let your brother know of this?" she inquired, abruptly changing the subject.

"I had hoped to ride over to Stilton Grange myself, but I think you are right. I am still too weak. So I would be much obliged if you would send a groom with this letter. There are several good horses in the stables here, so Robert should receive it tonight."

Pamela twitched the missive out of his fingers and turned towards the door. She was stopped by Geoffrey's voice.

"Perhaps you might not think so harshly of our cousin if you knew that the lieutenant claims the lady's child is his."

CHAPTER TWELVE

A Turbulent Past

A hint of approaching autumn chilled the morning air, and the birds in the hedgerows seemed less boisterous than usual as Lord Monroyal turned his horse off the lane and set out across fields of recently harvested barley towards the River Tone to the south. He had left Stilton Grange before dawn that morning in response to a disturbing missive received from his brother Geoffrey the previous evening. He should be accustomed to Geoffrey's urgent summonses by now, he thought wryly, steadying the big horse as they approached one of the ancient dry walls that crisscrossed the countryside. Robert had chosen his best hunter in lieu of his curricle for the journey to Osmington because he knew that Perseus could make better time than the bays. The horse had more than demonstrated the staying power his friend Hampton had claimed when he sold the six-year-old Irish hunter to the marquess a year ago. Willy might have his quirks, Robert admitted, but he knew his cattle.

When he had shown his brother's note to his stepmother, Sophy, who was the only mother Geoffrey could remember, the dowager marchioness, as she now styled herself, had wanted to accompany him to Holly Lodge.

"I must make certain that the dear boy is properly cared for," she protested when he had flatly refused. "And I am anxious to meet your new bride, Robbie," she added innocently. "I am still at a loss to comprehend why the poor girl must be ostracized in this manner. It is positively medieval of you. As the new Marchioness of Monroyal, Pamela belongs here, my dear. Your poor father must be turning in his grave."

The marquess wondered, not for the first time, why females so often failed to grasp the irrefutability of male logic. He had explained his decision with regard to his inconvenient wife several times, and reminded Sophy, as gently as possible, that his decision was final. But here she was again, pleading a cause that he had settled three months ago by delivering Lady Pamela to his aunt at Holly Lodge.

"My poor father, as you chose to call him, would turn in his grave if I installed the daughter of his archenemy on his ancestral estate," he said patiently. "Is it not mortifying enough to his memory that I was forced to wed the chit? You should have seen Melrose smirk when we signed the settlements; it was all I could do not to draw his cork. The least I can do now is ensure that no Hancock will be the mother of his grandchildren."

He realized that he had said more than he intended when he saw Sophy's beautiful face grow pinched. "Are you telling me that you have not consummated the marriage, Robbie?" she asked in a choked voice.

"No, I have not," he responded harshly. "Nor do I intend to."

Lady Monroyal stared at him as if he had grown warts and lost all his hair. "That is all the more reason why I must go to the poor child at once," she said with more force than was her wont. "You have done the girl a great disservice, Robert. Not only have you deprived her of her rightful place in this family, but also denied her the joys of motherhood."

The marquess cracked a laugh. He knew she was truly angry with him; she had called him Robert. But he refused to relent.

"I was under the distinct impression that I had done the lady a service in repairing her tattered reputation," he drawled. "At great inconvenience to myself, I might add."

The dowager bristled. "You truly are a heartless creature, Robert. What kind of life is the poor girl to lead alone in that old house with only Honoria for company?"

At least he could be sure that his sons are not bastards as Blandford's may well be, he thought cynically. He had never been able to forgive his mother for loving another man, Robert saw with sudden clarity. The whole sordid episode had made him physically sick, and his boyhood dreams had become nightmares of despair.

Convinced that his mother's betrayal had been the cause of his intense unhappiness, Robert remembered begging his father to send her away. He would never forget the shock of his father's response. "I could never do that, Robbie," the marquess had said, his handsome face ravaged with grief. "You see, lad, I love your mother. Always will. You will understand when you are older."

But Robert had never understood what he saw as his father's weakness. He still did not wish to admit that his own father had been so besotted that he would take his mother back after all the world learned she was the cause of that near-fatal duel. Not even the birth of his brother, which his father had tried to convince him would make them a family again, had tempered Robert's mistrust of females. No female, he had decided long ago, much less a Hancock, would ever hold that power over his heart.

"You know nothing of the matter, my dear," he said harshly, the past weighing heavily upon him. "Lady Pamela and I share a mutual dislike that would make her presence at the Grange intolerable, had I thought so little of my father's memory as to bring her here. So let me hear no more on the subject, madam. My mind is made up."

Pushing his stepmother's argument to the back of his mind, Lord Monroyal forded the Tone outside Wellington, then struck out across the Blackdown Hills. Two hours later, he reached the midway point of Axminster, where he stopped for ale and sandwiches. He followed the toll road for twelve miles to Bridgeport, then turned due south to take the coastal road as far as Abbotsbury, where he again cut across open country towards Osmington.

The marquess's reception at Holly Lodge was mixed. Aunt Honoria was, as always, glad to see him. He found her on the terrace at the back of the house, enjoying her afternoon tea with Mrs. Firth's famous pound cake, and soaking up the rays of the late summer sunshine.

"My dear boy," his aunt greeted him effusively. "What a delight to see you. I must say I like your wife, Robert," she remarked, getting straight to the point as usual. "A very prettily mannered chit, in spite of this havey-cavey marriage of yours. I have written to Sophy about it, you may be sure. She is in complete accord with me that this nonsense must cease immediately. How on earth do you expect to start your nursery if you are at the Grange and Pamela closeted here with me?"

The marquess suppressed the urge to inform his meddlesome aunt that the notion of starting his nursery was abhorrent to him, but thought better of it. No sense getting the old girl's back up. Her temper was unpredictable enough as it was.

"If you are looking for Pamela, she is sitting with that rapscallion brother of yours. Geoffrey seems to be in another of his scrapes, but there was no need to ride *vent-à-terre* to the rescue, dear boy. Pamela and I have managed quite nicely, thank you."

Without clarifying that it was his brother he sought, not his wife, Robert made his way upstairs. As he approached the sickroom, he heard Geoffrey let out a crack of laughter, accompanied by female giggles. It occurred to him that he had never heard his wife laugh before, much less giggle. For no apparent reason the sound irked him, and he threw open the chamber door without bothering to knock.

The domesticity of the scene that met his gaze irked the marquess even more acutely. Geoffrey was lounging in bed in a bright green dressing gown, his chestnut hair in lamentable disarray. Remains of a substantial meal were piled on a tray sitting precariously on the dresser, while a bottle of claret and two glasses betrayed the patient's disregard for the doctor's orders. Late afternoon sunlight streamed in through the open window, and he distinctly heard the song of a meadow lark rise above the busy twittering of the swallows in the eaves. An idyllic scene indeed, he thought cynically.

His wife, who had been seated near the bed, turned her head at the interruption. Her face was more animated than Robert had ever seen it, and her hazel eyes danced with amusement. As he watched, he saw the laughter fade and her expression become guarded. She rose, looked at him expectantly for a moment, then threw an apologetic smile at Geoffrey.

"We will finish the game this evening after dinner," she told him. "And I hope I do not catch you cheating again, sir. It is a scurvy trick, you know." Without another word, or a glance in his direction, Pamela picked up the tray of dishes and whisked out of the room, leaving behind an uncomfortable silence.

The two brothers gazed at each other for a long moment, and Robert noted that Geoffrey's expression was faintly hostile.

"That was mighty uncivil of you, Robert," the younger man said at last. "You might have greeted her at the very least. The devil take it, man, Pamela is your wife."

The marquess strolled across the room and took up a stand by the window, which gave a magnificent view of the ocean. Above all things he hated to be chastised when he knew himself at fault. "If I ever feel the need of advice on managing my affairs, Geoffrey," he remarked coolly, "I shall certainly consult you. Until then, I must ask you to concern yourself with other matters." He turned and met his brother's gaze. "Now, tell me all you know about the Blandford case, Geoffrey," he continued in a pleasanter tone. "Anthony is the last man upon whom I would wish an unfaithful wife."

His brother gave a distinctly cynical laugh. "You are a fine one to be censuring unfaithful wives, Robbie. After all, you have contributed to the cuckolding of half the husbands in England at last count. Why are you suddenly so squeamish about Blandford getting himself a pair of horns?"

The marquess felt himself go rigid. This was blunt speaking for his normally easygoing brother. "We are not here to discuss my youthful peccadilloes," he remarked, keeping his temper in check. "What is this letter from Brussels you mentioned in your message? Who exactly is this mysterious lieutenant who has risen from the dead to compromise Lady Blandford's reputation?"

His brother opened an inlaid box on the table beside the bed, withdrawing a sheet of hot-pressed paper covered with spidery writing. "This Lieutenant Parker appears to be a gazetted Bedlamite," Robert remarked after perusing the letter. "And his claim that the countess's child is his should be easily disproved. I fail to see that Anthony has anything to worry about. After all, the man was reported missing a month before Anthony took Uxbridge's daughter to wife."

"Unless it is true, as the man claims, that Lady Blandford was carrying his child when she wed the earl," Geoffrey pointed out. "The cloak of matrimony covers a multitude of sins, or so I have heard tell."

The hint of cynicism in his brother's tone caused Robert to wonder whether Geoffrey's remark was directed at him. He brushed the thought aside as unworthy. Crossing the room, he sat in the chair recently vacated by Lady Pamela. "Be that as it may, it concerns neither of us at present, so there is no point in pulling caps over it. I shall ride up to Blandford tomorrow and break the news to Anthony. Perhaps this Parker fellow is a madman after all."

"I hope so," Geoffrey said, "for Lady Blandford's sake. It cannot be much fun for a female to be seduced and abandoned by some heartless bounder."

The marquess had nothing to contribute to this odd remark, but once again it struck him that it might be aimed at him. It described his own recent dealings with Miss Erksin-Jones rather too accurately. "How is your shoulder, lad?" he said, changing the subject abruptly. At this distance, his brother's face looked paler than usual, and Robert saw the boy grimace as he adjusted his position on the bed.

"Better than I had expected," Geoffrey replied with a crooked grin. "Pamela is a top-of-the-trees nurse." He paused, then continued in a serious voice. "What inspired you to wed her, Robbie? I hear there is no love lost between you."

The marquess smiled grimly as he thought back on that utterly appalling scene at Willy's seaside cottage. To be caught red-handed with a female whose innocence was still intact had galled him. Her disparaging remarks and flat rejection of his offer had been downright mortifying, but the crowning impertinence had been her impulsive flight with a man so far beneath her in rank and fortune as to be a deliberate insult to a man of Robert's position. Perhaps if his naive brother knew the lady's true nature, he might not champion her cause so ardently.

"Actually, it is a very amusing story," he began, his sense of humor beginning to see that this was true. He glanced at the clock. "It all began with an exceedingly stupid wager on my part concerning a tasty bit of muslin called Prudence," he began, settling himself more comfortably in the chair.

Plagued by insomnia and lurid dreams of young females confined to towers with barred windows, Pamela slept little the night following her husband's return. After recognizing herself as the pathetic creature in one of these unhappy dreams, and Geoffrey as the bedraggled knight sitting on a dispirited-looking horse on the far side of the moat in the pouring rain, Pamela gave up any further attempt to sleep. She was in no mood to endure her husband's making an appearance in her dreams. Furthermore, she was vaguely uneasy that if the marquess did enter her dreams, he might indulge that side of himself she had experienced so briefly at the cottage in Brighton. The notion both frightened and fascinated her.

As the insidious memory of that scandalous encounter filtered back into her drowsy mind, Pamela felt herself slipping into the rogue's arms again. Her eyes drifted shut, and she again knew the intoxicating warmth of his highly improper embrace, the hard planes of his body against hers, the forbidden delight of his lips trailing their delicious heat over her face and neck, the wild longing in her own heart to taste, if only for a brief moment, the ecstasy his hands seemed to promise.

Shaken by the force of these clandestine longings, Pamela sat up abruptly, shattering the illusion of harmony with the man who was now her husband. These were the romantical moonings of a schoolroom chit, she chided herself, sliding resolutely out of bed. She was now—thanks to forces beyond her control—a respectable married matron, although the married part of it was merely a courtesy title. She did not feel the least bit married. When Monroyal had appeared so unexpected in Geoffrey's room yesterday, for a wild, giddy moment her heart had betrayed her. Had the marquess relented towards her? she thought, her pulse racing madly. Had he come to bridge the unnatural gap between them? Was she to be a real wife after all?

One look at his cold face had dispatched these fanciful hopes to the realm of impossible dreams, and Pamela had escaped as soon as she could, determined to return his aloofness with cool disdain. She had avoided him for the rest of the afternoon, but when it came time to dress for dinner, Pamela found herself taking extra care with her appearance. She might have saved herself the trouble, for the marquess ignored her throughout dinner, addressing himself almost exclusively to his brother, who had obtained the good doctor's permission to come downstairs that evening.

When the gentlemen joined the ladies in the drawing room, the marquess had let his brother bear the brunt of the conversation and had sat staring at her as Pamela played the pianoforte. After a half hour of such rudeness, Pamela had convinced herself that her husband was looking *through* her, not at her, and promptly lost herself in a new composition she had recently completed. After the tea-tray had been brought in, the marquess carried his brother off to the billiard room, and that was the last Pamela saw of him that evening.

Much later, as she accompanied Lady Honoria up to bed, they heard loud voices coming from the billiard room. Although she could not hear everything that was said, Pamela did hear the marquess's angry voice mention her father's name. She paused in the hallway outside the room and distinctly heard Geoffrey say that someone—she did not catch the name—should not be punished for the sins of the father.

She glanced uneasily at Lady Honoria and saw that this lady was following her usual practice of not hearing anything she found disagreeable. Suddenly, Pamela recalled that the old lady, sister to the late marquess, must have known the marquess's first wife intimately. She recalled Geoffrey saying as much. Why had it not occurred to her before to ask her hostess about the mystery of her father's connection with the Stiltons?

Determined to get to the truth of the matter without further roundaboutation, Pamela accompanied the good lady to her chamber—as she often did when Lady Honoria wished to continue a particularly interesting book they were reading together. After helping her ladyship's ancient abigail prepare her mistress for bed—a task that required considerable time since Lady Honoria was addicted to ribbons and bows and sashes and laces, besides voluminous underskirts and petticoats and stays to hold her ample person together—Pamela sat down on a pretty blue brocade settee and watched with no little amusement the bed sway alarmingly as her ladyship clambered into it.

Lady Honoria settled herself amongst the mountain of pillows and smiled at Pamela from beneath her flamboyant, lacy nightcap. "I gather you have something you want to tell me, child," she boomed in what was, for her, a tone approaching normal volume. "Out with it, then, my dear, although I think I can hazard a guess at what is fretting you. It is Robert, is it not? The lad is behaving very shabbily. I confess I never thought to see the day when a man of his address and experience would turn into a buffle-headed clodpole. It is most annoying, and I was of half a mind to tell him so during dinner, I can tell you."

"I am grateful that you did not, madam," Pamela said, imagining the disastrous effect such admonishment might have had on the marquess. "I suspect that his lordship is regretting his hasty marriage even more than I do. I tried to warn him how it would be, but do you think he would listen?"

"Of course he did not," interjected Lady Honoria loudly. "He is a gentleman, and gentlemen have this addle-patted notion that we females have no brains to speak of. The way they see the world is the way it must be, and woe betide us if we suggest otherwise. They are tiresome creatures, I have always maintained. And so I told my poor father when he insisted that I accept an offer from the Duke of Nottingham's heir. I would be a duchess he claimed, and live in grand style. Grand style, indeed! As it turned out, the Nottinghams have nary a farthing to spend between them, and poor Arthur succumbed to smallpox before he got himself an heir on that pasty-faced wife of his." She paused to draw a breath after this barrage of words. "So you see, aversion to matrimony runs in the family, that and choosing the wrong female as Robert's father did."

"That is precisely what I wished to ask you, Lady Honoria," Pamela cut in before the lady could smother her with another blanket of words. "I have known for years that there had once been bad blood between the Stiltons and my father on account of that duel. My father never spoke of it, but when . . ." Pamela hesitated and felt the color stain her cheeks. She had never told her hostess how she came to be wed to the marquess, but she imagined the old lady, who was as sharp as she could hold together, had long ago guessed the truth.

"When Robert decided he was duty bound to repair your reputation, I presume," her ladyship offered, confirming Pamela's suspicions.

"Precisely," Pamela acknowledged quickly. "When he was forced to offer for me, I could see that my father was in high gig. It was as if he got a great deal of satisfaction in seeing the marquess brought to that pass. I understand he was notorious for his aversion to matrimony, and it must have galled him to find himself obliged to offer for the daughter of his father's old enemy. I refused him, of course, but—"

"I still find it difficult to believe that you refused the Marquess of Monroyal," Lady Honoria repeated in stentorious tones, her eyes twinkling with amusement. "Refused him, indeed! That must have been a severe blow to his self-consequence. Robert is so stiff-necked about his own importance, you understand. Always has been, particularly where the fairer sex is concerned. Refused him, did you?" She chuckled loudly. "I wish I had been there to see it, my dear. It is not every day that Robert gets a set-down, you know." She chortled again, her chin trembling rhythmically.

Encouraged by Lady Honoria's charitable reception of her story, Pamela continued. "After my father insisted that I accept the marquess, I did something far worse, I am afraid."

"What could be worse than telling the lad you would not have him?" demanded her ladyship.

"I eloped with an old beau of mine who had offered for me several times in the past," Pamela confessed in a rush, uncertain of Lady Honoria's reaction to this reprehensible action. She should not have worried, however, for her ladyship let out a gargantuan peal of laughter that must have been heard all the way down to the kitchens, Pamela thought.

"Never say, Monroyal went after you, dear?" she demanded in what was for her ladyship a whisper.

"Oh, but he did," Pamela responded, beginning to enjoy herself. "And not only that. When he caught up with us, the marquess came to fisticuffs with poor Sir Rodney, which left them both torn and bleeding. I never suspected he had it in him, I must confess. It was an edifying experience, let me tell you. And I have to admit now that it was a relief, for I do believe Rodney would have suited me even less than your nephew."

Lady Honoria, who had laughed so much during Pamela's recital that the tears ran down her cheeks, regarded her guest with new respect. "I see there is more to you than meets the eye, my dear Pamela," she said unsteadily. "And perhaps you and my nephew are more suited than you think. It is high time that toplofty coxcomb met a female who is not afraid to thwart him. He has been so spoiled ever since he came down from Oxford by silly creatures who swoon when he looks at them, that he has come to believe himself beyond criticism."

Pamela shook her head. "All I did was inform his lordship that we would make each other miserable, my lady, which was nothing but the truth, plain and simple. I think he is finding out that there are moral and ethical responsibilities to the act of taking a wife far beyond the mere physical ones. And to make matters worse, he seems to associate me in his mind with whatever sin my father committed against the late marquess, your brother."

"So you want me to tell you what that sin is, I presume," Lady Honoria said after a lengthy pause, her former amusement quite dissipated.

"I gather you are not in love with this Sir Rodney you mentioned," she said unexpectedly. When Pamela shook her head, her ladyship smiled grimly. "Then history is not repeating itself as closely as my nephew appears to imagine," she said. "You see, years ago, before any of you were born, my dear, Robert's mother was in love with your father, and he with her. Quite immoderately, I can assure you. The kind of grand passion that is so unfashionable today. Quite impossible, of course, since your father was a younger son at the time with little to offer except love."

"How romantic," Pamela breathed, her heart touched by the plight of this lady she would never know. "They sound like characters in one of Mrs. Radcliffe's romantical novels."

"Perhaps," Lady Honoria said dryly, "but such unbridled passion is highly unsuitable in real life. Lady Pamela Whitlock was quite my dearest friend, and my most ardent wish was that she would get over her infatuation with Hancock and wed my brother, who had his heart set on her, too. I wanted her to become my real sister, you see."

Lady Honoria paused, her gray eyes taking on a dreamy aspect. Pamela guessed the old lady was reliving that turbulent past she had shared with two of the principal actors of that unhappy love triangle. By comparison, she thought, her own experience was rather drab and uninteresting. She had certainly been forced into matrimony, but she had not been loved by two gentlemen. She never had been loved by *any* gentlemen, she corrected herself with painful honesty. Nor was she likely to be. Sir Rodney's offers had been motivated by necessity; she had never doubted it. Neither had she experienced the pangs of that tender passion—as Mrs. Radcliffe described it so vividly. Life was not at all fair.

* * *

Short, muffled barks coming from the far side of a clump of gorse bushes jerked Pamela's thoughts back from her enlightening conversation with Lady Honoria the night before. Perhaps it had been these confidences and her new understanding of the former Lady Pamela's unhappy marriage that had provoked the odd dreams that kept her from her rest last night, she mused, as she hurried forward to find the cause of Scamp's excitement.

The dog had an uncanny knack of getting himself into trouble. At his advanced age, Pamela thought, he should know better than to get himself wedged into a rabbit hole. How much intelligence did it take to sense when a hole was too narrow to accommodate the considerable girth the spaniel had accumulated over the years? Cats did it all the time, using their whiskers as yardsticks. But, unfortunately, Scamp lacked this innate discretion. As she watched the dog's rump wriggling wildly at the bottom of a deep pit, head and shoulders wedged firmly into a hole too small for him, Pamela realized that she would be required to rescue him once again.

"Scamp," she called out, hoping that the dog would get himself loose. "Come here, boy."

When nothing happened except a low, pitiful whine from deep inside the rabbit hole, Pamela sighed. Lifting her skirts, she edged down the steep slope, her half-boots, sinking ankle deep in the soft earth. Halfway down she slipped and fell, completing the rest of the descent in a most undignified manner.

It took her several minutes of digging and pulling to free the dog, who promptly jumped all over her, leaving muddy imprints on her skirt and warm, wet tongue marks on her face.

"Stop it, you silly dog," she cried, laughing at Scamp's boisterous expressions of gratitude. Still kneeling in the dirt, she grasped the squirming little body in her arms and held the dog firmly against her. "Stop it, I say," she chided, nuzzling the dog's silky ears with her chin. Ever a fool for affection, Scamp relaxed and limited himself to licking whatever part of her face he could reach.

At least this old dog loves me, Pamela thought wryly, resigned to changing her gown when she returned to the house.

At that moment Scamp pricked his ears and put his head to one side, as he did every morning when she came down for their walk. Then he let out a sharp bark of warning, and Pamela raised her eyes above the rim of the pit.

She saw his boots first—gleaming Hessians with silver tassels. Her heart skipped a beat, for she recognized them. Her eyes traveled up, past the buckskin breeches molded to strong thighs, past the conservative moleskin waistcoat and bottle-green hunting jacket, resting briefly on the Belcher kerchief at his throat.

"What might I ask are you doing groveling in the mud, my dear?"

Her eyes flew to meet his, finding them filled with amusement. Taken by surprise, Pamela released the dog, who promptly abandoned her and scampered up the slope to fawn over the marquess. She struggled to get to her feet, uncomfortably conscious of her soiled appearance.

"I was *not* groveling, my lord," she said stiffly. "Scamp got stuck in a rabbit hole again, and it is one of my duties to pull him out." She scrambled up the slope, ignoring the hand he was extending to her. Once on level ground, Pamela brushed ineffectually at the earth stains on the plain blue round gown she had put on fresh that morning. She noticed with no little disgust that the dog had deserted her and now sat on his fat haunches, staring adoringly up at the marquess, who ignored him.

"Ungrateful beast," she muttered under her breath.

"I beg your pardon?" The marquess had obviously thought she was addressing him and had every right to be startled, she thought.

Pamela cursed her thoughtless tongue. "I was talking to the dog," she stammered, wishing she had worn a bonnet with a larger brim to hide her confusion.

"I looked for you in your chamber this morning," he said in a tone so cordial that Pamela dared to glance up. "But your abigail informed me you might be found on the cliffs with Scamp." The thought of her husband entering her chamber uninvited shook Pamela's composure and she looked away. "There are certain, ah . . . certain arrangements I need to discuss with you, Pamela," he added, and she felt her heart stand still with apprehension.

"I must go up to Blandford today, but I should be back in a day or two and will talk to you then."

Oh you will, will you? Pamela thought to herself after the marquess had taken his leave and ridden away towards the north. Perhaps so, but then again, perhaps she would not be there, she reflected, more disturbed by her husband's sudden amiability than by his disaffection. Perhaps she would drown in the sea, or fall off a cliff, or be taken deathly ill. Or disappear into a rabbit hole with Scamp. Or run away with a knight in shining armor, she fantasized, allowing her imagination free rein.

Would the elusive marquess follow her, *vent-à-terre*, pennants flying, armor clanking, breathing fire?

Or would he let her go this time, content to be rid of a wife he must find very inconvenient indeed?

As she made her way slowly homewards, Scamp following at her heels, tongue lolling and tail drooping, Pamela was startled by the discovery that she would not change her destiny even if she could. Without quite knowing how such a change of heart had occurred, Pamela acknowledged that the prospect of a lifetime as the Marchioness of Monroyal had become oddly appealing.

It remained to be seen if his lordship was of a similar mind.

CHAPTER THIRTEEN

A Family Reunion

As the marquess rode northwards, he spent little time in admiring the early morning dew on the tall grasses beside the path and the late-blooming gorse bushes alive with bees gathering the last of the nectar for their winter hoard of honey. His thoughts turned inwards, seeing once again the figure of his wife as he had left her, standing with Scamp on the cliff path. The pale sun, rising into the cloudless summer sky, tinted her cheeks with color, and glittered on the stray chestnut curl that escaped her bonnet.

For some odd reason Robert was at a loss to explain, the picture triggered memories in his heart of happier times. And there had been happy times in his turbulent childhood, he remembered. Afternoons when the beautiful, temperamental creature who was his mother came up to the nursery to play with him. Other times—less frequent and infinitely more precious—when his father would join them, and they appeared to be a family again. If he banished the recriminations, the cold silences, his father's absences, his mother's tears, from his memory, he might say with some truth that there had been happy times in his childhood.

But how was he supposed to forget that dreadful day when they brought his father back to the house, pale and bleeding? he wondered, turning his horse's head towards the Dorchester Road. How was he to forget that his own mother had been the cause of the late marquess's near-fatal injury? The joy of Geoffrey's birth soon after had been tempered by the deep resentment he had felt then—and still did if his brother's accusation had any validity—against his mother for her betrayal.

And now his own cousin Blandford—son of his mother's sister—was to face a similar betrayal by his wife of two years, if Geoffrey's correspondent in Brussels could be believed. Robert recalled Anthony's letter announcing his return to England with a bride. Colonel Anthony Whitlock, fifth Earl of Blandford, was not given to boyish exuberance, but Robert had detected the joy shining through his cousin's brief notice that he had married the

woman he had secretly admired for years. Robert had been happy
for him, but now he was not so sure.

He urged his horse into a canter, his thoughts divided between
his cousin's dilemma with his first child, if indeed it was his, and
his own confused reactions towards his wife. Pamela was so un-
demanding and reticent that Robert did not quite know what to do
with her. She was not like any of the women he usually frequented, and he had known hundreds, Robert thought wryly.

But Pamela was as unlike those lovely, bored creatures who
had filled his nights with ephemeral passion as this pleasant
Dorset meadow beyond the hedgerow was to the stinking streets
of London during the summer. The analogy amused him. His wife
still had the simplicity of a country flower about her, a freshness
and innocence that defied description. Perhaps that was the cause
of her strange effect on him, he mused. His wife was still virginal,
and innocence had always made him uneasy.

One day he would have to settle that question with her, of
course. He had known it from the moment in that dingy parlor at
the Two-Headed Boar in Purley three months ago when they had
made their vows together. The actual words had meant less than
nothing to him at the time, a mere formality softening the sting of
lost freedom. But as he rode onwards in the warming sunshine,
the marquess began to recall some of those vows he had made so
casually.

> *Wilt thou have this Woman to thy wedded wife, to live together*
> *after God's ordinance in the holy estate of Matrimony? Wilt*
> *thou love her, comfort her, honor, and keep her in sickness and*
> *in health; and, forsaking all other . . .*

The marquess's memory faltered. Had he really promised all
these impossible things? *Love?* He had never loved her, or any
other female. How could he love his wife? He hardly knew her.
He was prepared to comfort and honor her, of course, if the need
should arise, and if she were to fall sick, but he had been prepared—indeed had actively planned—to forsake her for any number of other women when he returned to Town after the hunting
season was over.

As he had always done. It was what all his friends expected of
him. Or would they, now that he was a married man? So many of
his intimates, members of that select group known as the
Corinthians, had also married in the last year or so that London
ton was in danger of becoming respectable. Even Robert Heather-

cott, the Marquess of Gresham, the most cold-hearted rake of his entire acquaintance, had recently lost his heart to an obscure widow from north Devon who was as far removed from his friend's usual *amourettes* as Pamela was from his own previous *chers amies.*

He was suddenly unsure about his own feelings in the matter.

For the first time in his life, the notion of infidelity took on a new meaning for Monroyal. This time it was not the infidelity of other men's wives, from which he had benefitted without a qualm. It was not even his mother's infidelity, which had destroyed his childhood innocence. Or the unconfirmed infidelity of Blandford's wife.

It was his own infidelity.

Unaccustomed to question the motivations or consequences of his own conduct, the marquess dismissed the uneasy sensation in his stomach as the result of those coddled eggs he had consumed at breakfast that morning. He would make a short stop at Puddletown, he decided on the spur of the moment. A glass of local ale at the Four-In-Hand would go a long way towards curing those morbid thoughts that plagued him.

Convinced that he had hit upon the right solution, the marquess turned his thoughts to what he would say to Colonel Anthony Whitlock about a far more serious kind of infidelity.

Pamela spent the morning of her husband's departure in the music room, working on a new *étude* she had started upon learning of the disputed paternity of Lady Blandford's child. She began the piece with a lively *allegro* movement signaling the joy of finding one's self in that happy condition. Then she introduced the first somber note, an *allegro ma non troppo* section that progressed at a more measured pace for several bars before descending abruptly into a funereal *largo,* which suggested the possibility of disaster and shame. But somehow Pamela was reluctant to end the piece on that unhappy note. The deathlike cadence of that last passage did not satisfy her either aesthetically or emotionally. Her woman's intuition convinced her that there must be, deep down in a man's heart, the possibility of reconciliation, of rapprochement, of forgiveness for a woman's sins.

And there was always—she firmly believed this—the miracle of love.

Pamela wondered if Lord Blandford loved his young wife enough to weather the storm that appeared to be brewing for them. From the little Geoffrey had told her, the earl was no young buck under the influence of his first infatuation. He had been one of Monroyal's circle at Oxford, so they must be of an age—the age of responsibility, of duty, perhaps even of love.

The intrusion of her husband into her thoughts brought Pamela back to her present task, and on sudden impulse she decided to conclude the *étude* on an optimistic note. The alternative did not bear thinking on.

Her encounter with the marquess that morning on the cliff had left her pensive. He wished to talk to her, he had said. There was so little between them that warranted serious discussion. She could think of only two possible topics: her continued residence at Holly Lodge, or her removal to Stilton Grange. Since the latter seemed highly improbable, even to her optimistic nature, her husband must have plans to settle a reasonable allowance on her so that she could support herself without applying to him for every expense. In effect, he would be washing his hands of her.

The notion of removing to the marquess's family seat was daunting, and Pamela wondered if perhaps she was not better off where she was. The Stilton family was large. Besides the two elder brothers from the late marquess's first marriage, Geoffrey had informed her that he had two sisters and four younger brothers from a second marriage. The prospect of taking her place as the mistress of such an establishment filled her with trepidation. As an only child, Pamela had always longed for a houseful of brothers and sisters, but now that the opportunity might conceivably present itself, her emotions were mixed.

Still, she told herself as she went downstairs when the nuncheon bell sounded, there was no sense worrying about something that might never happen, and she felt more than comfortable running an establishment like Holly Lodge, with no pretensions at grandeur and pomp.

Pamela's afternoon was spent with Geoffrey, who insisted upon driving over to Weymouth to inspect his yacht, which was undergoing repairs there. After some argument about whether or not his shoulder was mended enough to allow him to drive, Pamela managed to convince him that she would not land them both in the ditch and took over the ribbons of his curricle.

"You are a first-rate fiddler," he acknowledged reluctantly after she had maneuvered the vehicle without incident through a gaggle of angry geese and a flock of nervous sheep in the narrow country lane. "For a female, that is," he added with enough condescension to cause Pamela to bristle.

"I am no mere whipster, sir, if that is what you are implying," she protested, flicking the tip of her whip over the ears of her left horse that appeared sluggish. "I am used to handle my father's four-in-hand rather than drive with a pair under the pole, I would have you know, but I must admit a pair is easier to handle on these lanes."

"Robert would not be caught dead up behind a team of two," Geoffrey remarked. "He drives his bays everywhere. I'm surprised he rode over from Milverton yesterday."

"Perhaps he wished to keep his precious horses out of your way, Geoffrey," she responded with a warm smile. "If what Mrs. Firth has told me about your penchant for accidents is true, I would have done the same."

"These two are a pair of commoners compared to Robert's Welsh-bred bays," her companion answered disgustedly. "But they are good enough if you are looking for endurance and not to prance around on Rotton Row during the Season, or to race the London–Brighton Road on a bet." He paused while Pamela gave the go-by to a cumbersome landau pulled by two ewe-necked job horses of uncertain parentage.

"That was old Mrs. Stonesworth," Geoffrey remarked as the curricle shot away from the lumbering vehicle. "She fancied herself a first-rate whip before she married Stonesworth, they say. People around here are still talking about the number of horses she ran into the ditch, or overturned, or lamed in one way or another. Luckily, Stonesworth put a stop to that soon enough. Confined her to that old landau and a traveling coach that dates from the days of my grandfather."

"How arbitrary of him to deprive his wife of one of life's little pleasures," Pamela protested. "But how like a man to do so, after all."

Geoffrey threw back his head and laughed. "I gather that my brother has not allowed you to drive his bays, so you are naturally peeved at men in general."

Pamela stared at him pityingly. "Drive his bays? Have you lost your senses, Geoffrey? I have yet to be invited to *ride* in your brother's curricle, much less drive it." She regretted the words as soon as they were spoken; they had revealed too much of the bitterness in her heart.

Her companion was silent for several miles, but when he spoke, his voice was gentle. "I know things are not as they should be between you and Robert, my dear. But I know my brother, Pamela. He is no monster, believe me. He has rescued me from more scrapes than I care to recall, and you should see him with our four young brothers; he dotes on them."

"I am sure he does," Pamela interrupted sharply. "But it is highly unlikely that I shall see it." She stopped speaking abruptly, fearful of revealing any more of her despair.

They were silent for the rest of the way home, and Pamela sensed there was much Geoffrey wished to say to her, but, perhaps out of respect for his brother, chose not to. She herself had many unanswered questions that her husband's brother would doubtless have answers for, but for some stubborn reason, she was reluctant to reveal the depth of the chasm in her marriage.

All thoughts on the subject were abruptly banished from her mind as the curricle turned south off the Weymouth road into the gently sloping driveway that led up to the house overlooking the cliff that was now her home. The circle before the manor appeared to their startled gazes to be teaming with activity, as though one of Wellington's divisions had bivouacked in the park.

"God save us all!" Geoffrey exclaimed as they drew closer. "The devil take it if that ain't Sophy arrived in her usual grand style trailing the whole household in her wake." He glanced at Pamela with a merry light in his eyes. "Prepare yourself for an experience of a lifetime, my dear. Sophy under full sail is enough to make a bishop quail. That is sort of a family motto," he added with a grin.

"And who is this Sophy?" Pamela demanded, more than a little daunted by her companion's words.

"Are you telling me that clodpole of a brother of mine has not warned you about our Sophy?" Geoffrey stared at her in mock horror. "My sweet innocent, our dear Sophy is the best thing that has happened to the Stiltons in over four hundred years of existence. She is credited with saving us all from chaos after my mother died. Thanks to that incredible female, we are all relatively sane and suffer only an occasional quirk of madness during a full moon. We all love green cheese, too, of course."

Pamela listened in growing trepidation to this recital, but at the mention of madness and full moons, she realized that Geoffrey was jesting with her. "You are a sad tease," she chided as they inched their way past a long line of carriages, wagons, and an elegant traveling chaise clustered before the front door.

A stream of liveried servants worked like ants carrying in a mass of luggage of all shapes and sizes, from six large trunks, sundry valises, pormanteaux, huge baskets of food, crates of vegetables, and innumerable smaller nondescript bundles and packages, blankets, cloaks, cushions, books, parasols, to a covered basket obviously containing a squalling kitten. Other paraphernalia lay higgledy-piggledy all over the shallow front steps, and various maid servants, unknown to Pamela, rooted about industriously among the chaos.

Several liveried outriders labored mightily unloading this endless stream of belongings from the various vehicles, while two grooms led four fat ponies towards the stables. Other grooms stood ready to tend to the coach horses, while two huge dogs, also unknown to a bewildered Pamela, bounded about excitedly, adding to the disorder with excited barks and an occasional whine.

"Relax, my dear," a reassuring voice said at her elbow, as Pamela concentrated on her team, which had grown skittish at the sudden bustle. "I know it looks like the aftermath of a major military skirmish, but Sophy has this whole maneuver down to a fine art. She refuses to travel any other way. Nothing is left to chance, and what is more astonishing, she knows where everything is packed. She even brings the under-cook," Geoffrey added, indicating a rotund female overseeing the disposal of baskets of provisions. "There should be two nurses and the boys' tutor about somewhere." He paused and glanced around. "I wonder what those little beggars are up to," he remarked. "My four brothers," he clarified at Pamela's blank look. "I think you will like them."

By that time two grooms had approached to take Lord Geoffrey's team, both greeted with easy familiarity by the young man.

" 'Morning, Ted," Geoffrey said to one of them. "No trouble along the road, I trust?"

This seemed to be a family joke, for both grooms broke into wide grins. "Not with her ladyship at the helm, so to speak," the older groom responded. " 'Tis good to see ye looking well, Master Geoffrey. We 'eard ye'd been in one of yer little scraps again."

"I ran into a little trouble with the Frenchies, 'tis all," he replied. "Nothing serious," he added with deplorable lack of accuracy, Pamela thought. "I'll leave the team in your hands, Ted, while I make your new mistress known to her ladyship and the hell-hounds."

Upon learning her identity, both men touched their forelocks respectfully.

"Ted and Jacob," Geoffrey introduced them casually. "Taught me how to drive, Ted did, back when I was a wee lad in shortpants." He laughed and turned to lift Pamela down before remembering that his shoulder was still tender.

They learned from Firth, who was looking fit to be tied, that her ladyship and the two young ladies were taking tea with Lady Honoria in the Blue Saloon, usually reserved for honored guests.

"Her ladyship . . . Lady Honoria that is . . ." the old man began, his eyes rolling nervously, "requested me to ask your ladyship which rooms you wish to assign to the dowager? Mrs. Firth has already set the maids to airing all the bedchambers, but . . ." He paused, evidently uneasy.

Pamela saw the butler's dilemma immediately and smiled kindly. "You may instruct Betty to remove my things from the master suite and install her ladyship there, Firth. No doubt she is accustomed to that chamber already. I shall be quite content with one of the chambers on the West Hall."

She was rewarded by a grateful look from the old retainer, who conducted them up to the first floor and flung open the doors to the Blue Saloon, announcing her with her full title in what seemed to Pamela an excessively formal tone. She had never been announced by her new rank before, and it struck her that the moment had finally arrived to step forward to play the role her marriage to the marquess had thrust upon her.

The momentary awkwardness Pamela felt as she was ushered into the Blue Saloon was immediately dispelled—first by Geoffrey, who escorted her across the room, one hand firmly under her elbow, then by the slim, extremely elegant lady who sat on the blue brocade settee with Aunt Honoria, sipping her tea.

This lady, who could be none other than the formidable Dowager Marchioness of Monroyal, rose at Pamela's entrance with the agility of a much younger woman and approached with both hands outstretched in greeting. The welcoming smile of her beautiful face was genuine, and Pamela felt a lump rising in her throat.

"Mama," Geoffrey said in an amused voice, "let me make you known to the latest member of our family. This is Pamela, and—"

"Of course, it is Pamela," her ladyship said in a low, musical voice that touched off resonances in Pamela's mind of another voice stilled five years since. "Honoria has been telling me all about you, dear," the dowager continued, bestowing an affectionate huge on her. "I simply could not wait around any longer for Robert to decide to install you at the Grange. He is being very nonsensical about the whole thing, as I know you will agree, dear."

Pamela wondered how much Lady Honoria had told the dowager about her abrupt marriage to the marquess. She had little pause to ponder the marquess's reaction to the sudden appearance of his family and half his household staff at Holly Lodge, however. The dowager slipped an arm affectionately through hers and turned to the two young ladies seated together on a low settee.

"These are my daughters, Constance and Letitia, who have been all agog to meet you ever since their brother made his startling announcement that he had finally discovered a female who would have him. You must know that Robert is long past what I consider a reasonable age for matrimony. In truth, we had quite given up on him, had we not, girls? And were resigned to see him wither into a gray and gouty old age without the solace of a loving wife to cheer his declining years."

This incongruous—and deliberately amusing, she guessed—picture of the man she had seen in quite a different light momentarily deprived Pamela of speech. She gazed at the dowager with increasing respect and asked herself if this intrepid lady actually addressed the marquess to his face in this frank vein. The suspicion that her ladyship did not scruple to do so made her smile, but most of all she felt an instant surge of gratitude for the deft way in which the dowager had glossed over the more lurid details of her son's marriage. Lady Monroyal must, of all people, be aware of the true nature of Pamela's abrupt and unheralded elevation to her present rank.

Both girls had risen when their mother approached, and Pamela saw that they were as unlike as two sisters could be. The eldest, Lady Constance, smiled shyly as she made her curtsey, her dark hair and soft brown eyes fading into insignificance beside her sister's profusion of pale ringlets and sparkling blue eyes. Predictably, it was the precocious Letitia who responded instantly to Pamela's greeting.

"You have no idea how relieved we are to see our poor Robert leg-shackled at long last," this delicate beauty remarked baldly, with a tinkling laugh that sounded for all the world like bird song to Pamela. "He has sworn off matrimony for as long as I can remember, and we thought to see him enter his dotage—if indeed he is not already halfway there," she added with a charming giggle—"and were living in dread of his grumpy disposition getting worse with age."

Taken aback as she was by this candid, uncomplimentary glimpse of the imposing man she had married, Pamela could not take her gaze from the heart-shaped face where pansy-blue eyes danced mischievously. This child was a stunning Beauty, she thought and felt a pang of compassion for the men who would inevitably fall beneath the spell of those lovely eyes.

"Letty!" her mother interjected sharply, but with obvious affection. "How many times must I beg you not to use those dreadful expressions you pick up in the stables, dear. And it is not fitting that you speak so of your brother. Pamela will think we are all savages. Actually," the dowager added, turning her dazzling smile on Pamela, "Robert dotes on the girls, and he has been a father to his four brothers. He is really quite kindhearted beneath that autocratic exterior."

"He is a bear," Lady Letitia stated firmly, her pretty mouth compressing in a charming pout.

"All gentlemen are bears at one time or another," her ladyship remarked philosophically, "but they can be quite charming and generous when handled with patience and forbearing."

"Well, I trust that Pamela—I may call you Pamela, may I not?—has a limitless fund of patience and forbearing," Letitia remarked in her pert manner, not pausing for her hostess's response. "Because I intend to enlist her aid in convincing Robert that I simply cannot face another assembly without a new gown." She turned her charming smile on Pamela. "So I trust you know exactly how to wheedle your way into my brother's pockets, which are deeper than most, let me tell you."

"Hush, dear," her mother said firmly. "Pamela will think you are a sad rattle, which of course you are, but we do not wish it to be bruited about, do we, love?"

"You sound just like Robert, Mama," Letty pouted. "All I want is a new gown. And perhaps a bonnet to go with it—"

"And then any number of other articles that you cannot live without, Letty. Why, only recently your brother allowed you to have that dreadful kitten. I tremble to think what he will say when he discovers you have brought the naughty creature here." She sighed, then turned to her eldest daughter. "My Constance is a promising musician," she said with evident pride. "Robert tells me you are an excellent pianist yourself, my dear, so I am hoping you will help me encourage her, although I sometimes feel she spends too much time alone in the music room, instead of concerning herself for her future. I fear she has a tendency to be a bluestocking, which we all know is the kind of female gentlemen most abhor."

Quite unprepared to learn that her elusive husband had bothered to mention her love of music or anything else about her to his family, Pamela felt herself blush. "I rather think his lordship must have told you I am a bluestocking myself," she said gently, relishing the gleam of unexpected amusement that flashed in Lady Constance's brown eyes.

"Robert tells me that you compose your own music, too," the girl said in a soft voice. "I do so envy you. I have tried to do so myself, but my music teacher, Signor Montadini, tells me that I have little talent in that direction."

Pamela smiled warmly, more touched than she cared to admit at this further evidence of the marquess's acknowledgment of her musical abilities. "I would not pay much attention to any gentleman's opinion of what you can or cannot do, Constance," she said firmly. "Trust yourself, and follow your own tastes and inclinations. I fear too many gentlemen prefer to think we are brainless, frivolous creatures—in truth they often encourage us to be ignorant. My own father prefers to believe that my love of music, which I shared with my mother, was a passing fancy that might enhance my chances in the Marriage Mart."

"And did it?" Lady Letitia inquired, obviously tired of not being the center of attention. "It does not seem to have helped Constance catch a husband so far," she added with a tinge of spitefulness.

Pamela was saved from finding a suitable reply to this impertinence by Geoffrey, who let out a crack of boisterous laughter. "That should hardly concern you, my dear Letty," he teased. "You cannot carry a tune to save your life. And most gentlemen are tone deaf, if they would only admit it, so save your energy for—"

"That is not fair, Geoffrey," his mother interjected. "Robert plays both the violin and the pianoforte very nicely, if one can only convince him to do so. I saw to it myself that both my elder boys had the best music teachers available, but Geoffrey never showed any aptitude at all. He preferred to be off in that dirty old sailboat of his. But Robert . . ." She paused, glancing at Pamela with an enigmatic little smile on her face. "Well, Robert has many hidden talents, my dear, as I am sure you are finding out for yourself."

Pamela felt herself blush again, and since she was unable to recall any but the one unmentionable talent the notorious libertine she had married flaunted above all others, she racked her mind for a change of subject. This came in the figure of Mrs. Firth, who sent word to her mistress that the rooms were ready for the guests.

CHAPTER FOURTEEN

A Rude Awakening

Two days later, Lord Monroyal rode back to Holly Lodge at a leisurely pace, his mind in a turmoil. He needed time to think although he sincerely doubted whether he would ever reach an understanding of the state of affairs he had encountered at Blandford Manor. To say that he was bewildered and deeply perturbed over what he considered his cousin's dangerous departure from acceptable social attitudes regarding marriage was an understatement. Actually, Robert was shocked beyond anything he had imagined possible.

Accustomed to think of himself as an experienced practitioner of the sensory arts in all their forms, the marquess had dabbled in the delights of debauchery since coming down from Oxford. Together with others of his rank and fortune, intimates like Anthony Whitlock, Robert Heathercott, Willy Hampton, and other scions of noble houses, the marquess had taken that way of life for granted and had excelled at it.

For years he had been a leader in the fine art of hedonism in all its forms. No new form of debauchery had surfaced in the tawdry underworld of London but the young marquess had been ready to endorse it, either as participant or spectator. There was no wager he would not accept, however outrageous. There was no woman among the circle of demi-mondaines and bored matrons whom he could not enjoy. His winnings at Newmarket were legendary, and he was known as an avid follower of the Fancy and a favorite with Gentleman Jackson.

Until his recent visit to Blandford Manor, Robert Stilton had considered himself beyond the scope of shock. One evening's conversation with his cousin had changed all that forever.

Anthony Whitlock and his lady had received him with gratifying cordiality. They appeared, in Robert's amused and somewhat jaded eyes, to be living an idyllic existence that had no basis at all in reality. He had always considered Anthony as one of his more serious-minded cousins, a level-headed fellow, cool and dependable. A good officer, popular with his men. A man who would not scruple to forgo a hunting expedition in Melton Mowbray if summoned to his estate to settle an emergency.

But soon after his arrival, Robert discovered a side of Blandford's personality he had never suspected. A less indulgent man might have called it a flaw, he thought, following his host up to the nursery, where he met the lovely creature Robert had every reason to believe had cuckolded his favorite cousin. And Lady Blandford was indeed a Beauty. Robert could well understand how Anthony had fallen under her spell.

Up there in the sunny nursery at Blandford Manor, under the doting eyes of the besotted parents, Robert had felt obliged to concur—almost ad nauseam, he thought uncomfortably—that baby Alexandra was the most beautiful angel to be born in the length and breadth of England. And indeed, the infant was a pleasant surprise. Robert had been intimately involved in the arrival and nurturing of four lively brothers and had no illusions about the realities of raising small children. He had also experienced the joy of watching the boys develop in a loving family he had missed as a child himself. That part had been understandable, and he had only regretted that the news he brought from Brussels would destroy his cousin's fragile marital harmony as nothing else could.

It was much later, during their first after-dinner tête-à-tête, however, that the earl had delivered the blow that reminded Robert of the first time he had caught a flush hit from Gentleman Jackson during a sparring practice. The venerable master slipped in a wisty caster that had left the marquess sprawled on the canvas, gasping desperately for breath. He had never forgotten that lesson, but he was entirely unprepared for the blow that came from another quarter to shake the foundations of his male existence.

"*What* are you saying, Tony?" he had demanded in a voice that sounded incredulous and deeply outraged, nothing like his own. He had expected anything but bland complacency from a man learning his wife had betrayed him.

Blandford turned from the sideboard, where he was pouring their second brandies and looked straight at him, a wary expression in his blue eyes. "Yes, you heard aright, old chap," he said in a low voice. "I knew Sylvia was with child when I wed her."

The marquess paused to absorb this startling admission, his mind wrestling to understand its significance. His initial reaction was relief. "So you are sure the child is yours?" he asked gently, more than willing to overlook a man's eagerness to anticipate the wedding vows.

Blandford's smile might have held a glimmer of self-reproach, Robert could not be certain. "No," he said without hesitation, "I know for certain the child is *not* mine."

They had talked long into the night, and although Robert had recognized his cousin's obsession with and need to protect the woman he loved, he cringed at the risk the earl had run in acknowledging a possible son and heir who was not of his blood. There were several rumored cases of such occurrences among the *ton,* of course, including—and here Robert gingerly glanced into a compartment of his mind that he had locked and bolted years ago—the case of his own brother. But Geoffrey was a younger son, he reminded himself, and the question of his own mortality had never concerned him. Confident in his own standing as a true Stilton in every ounce of his being, Robert was suddenly forced to recognize that arrogance had blinded him to the pitfalls in the succession should he die.

It sobered the marquess to think that over four hundred years of family heritage and traditions of blood might, if those old rumors concerning Geoffrey's legitimacy held any truth at all, devolve upon the line of his father's rival. Anthony Whitlock had not scrupled to remind him that the hated Hancock blood would be irrevocably mixed with his when the marquess started his own nursery. Was not his wife Melrose's daughter?

"I vow to die celibate before I give that rogue Melrose the satisfaction of seeing any grandson of his as master of the Grange," he replied tersely, wondering why this threat—one he had made with such relish as recently as three months ago—seemed to have lost its bite.

His cousin laughed. "More fool you, Robert. At the very least you can ensure that your heir is a legitimate Stilton, old man," he said with gentle irony. "From what you have told me, Lady Monroyal is a far better wife than you deserve, and starting your nursery would solve any question of the succession—"

"There *is* no question with the succession," the marquess interrupted harshly, knowing he was being petulant. He wondered how the conversation on adultery had veered from Blandford's wife to focus on his own family. On his *wife,* for God's sake! "And I do not *deserve* a wife, Tony, as you choose to call it. Pamela is a bluestocking and a dashed strong-minded female into the bargain. Not exactly my style."

"And what does style have to do with anything if I might ask?"

Blandford cut in with a touch of derision. "The deed is done, is it not? You insisted upon it, I believe. There is little to be gained in blaming the lady for her father's sins—if indeed he committed any of real significance."

The marquess paused in his restless pacing up and down before the library fire. "What exactly are you suggesting, Tony?"

"Has it ever occurred to you that your mother was innocent?"

Robert gaped at Blandford for several seconds before replying.

"No," he said slowly, weighing his words carefully. The excuses he had tried so hard as a child to find for his mother rushed back in a tangled web of painful memories. He refused to go through that agony again. "No," he said firmly. "I was there, you see. That . . . that Mr. Brown, as he called himself, was hanging around all the time. And my father was away so often." He stopped, suppressing the flood of recriminations that threatened to explode from the secret core of his heart. There was so much more that he could say. So much more the child he had been had seen and suffered.

The marquess was two miles out of Dorchester before he noticed that he had not stopped at the Four-in-Hand for the tankard of ale he had promised himself. It was well past the noon hour, for he had not left Blandford Manor as early as planned, but he had no appetite. Anthony had urged him to stay another day or two for some pigeon shooting in the woods along the banks of the Stour, which ran through his estate, but Robert had felt an odd urgency to get back to . . . Get back to what? he asked himself a dozen times as his horse ambled leisurely southwards towards Holly Lodge. A wife he had not wanted? A woman who had— flying in the face of everything that Robert knew about females— not wanted him?

The image of his wife as he had last seen her became sharper as Robert cut across the fields above Osmington and heeled Perseus into a canter. The irrational urge came upon him to approach the house by the cliff path, a whim he suppressed immediately, for it would take him out of his way. He understood his uncharacteristic desire to follow his instincts, however, and the knowledge rattled his habitual calm.

Pamela might be out on the cliff at this hour. *Pamela.* His wife . . . his mother. The latter image intruded itself incongruously into the picture, and Robert grimaced. His mother had been a great Beauty, a celebrated, pampered girl who had had the execrable taste to favor a second son over the heir to a marquess—to put love before duty to her father. Fortunately, his own father had saved her from what had been rumored as an imminent elopement with Hancock. Who could have foreseen the misery that arrangement had wrought in so many lives?

And had he not saved *his* Pamela from just such an act of folly? he wondered, turning his horse's head into the entrance of the Lodge and cantering up the driveway. *His* Pamela? The phrasing amused him, but the uncomfortable notion that perhaps *his* Pamela might have preferred that gapeseed Morton after all caused a knot to form in his stomach. While never the Beauty his mother had been, his wife was a female, a highly imaginative one he had discovered. She undoubtedly believed in all that romantical nonsense about undying love. Passion Robert understood. But love? Until recently he had scoffed at such effeminate affectations. After his visit to Blandford Manor he was not sure of anything anymore.

He threw himself off Perseus and tossed the reins to a young groom he had seen somewhere before. Brushing this idle thought aside, the marquess strode into the house, determined to set his world in order again by the simple expedient of reasserting his God-given authority over a female who should know her place and accept it.

Lady Pamela listened with unexpected pleasure to the sonata her sister-in-law was executing on the old rosewood pianoforte. She had been slightly apprehensive about the dowager's insistence that she judge Lady Constance's musical abilities for herself. In her experience, doting mothers rarely had accurate notions of their daughters' skills. But in this case, she was not disappointed.

They had escaped up to the music room shortly after tea-time that afternoon, leaving the two elder ladies in the midst of a comfortable coze on the terrace overlooking the cliffs. Pamela had obliged her guest by performing some of her own compositions, but for the past twenty minutes, Constance had gained enough confidence to demonstrate her own skill. What the girl lacked in forceful execution, she more than made up in expressive interpretation of the various pieces she selected. Her skill at composition was less developed, but Pamela was able to reassure her on that score, offering to pass on some of the many techniques she had learned from her mother.

They were interrupted in the midst of this delightful exchange by a hullabaloo of boyish shouts and laughter rising from the front hall, punctuated by Scamp's excited barks.

"That cannot be yet another neighbor calling on Mama, thank goodness," Constance remarked in her low voice, referring to the influx of local gentry who had caught wind of the arrival of the Dowager Marchioness of Monroyal at Holly Lodge. "The boys are terribly noisy," she added apologetically, "but I am glad to say they reserve their most rambunctious behavior for their brother. One can always tell when Robert enters the house, for he is welcomed like Wellington returning to London after Waterloo."

The mention of her husband's return chased any thought of music from Pamela's mind. "We had better see if his lordship has had his tea," she said prosaically, marveling at how calm she sounded. "I do hope he will not be too put out to find your mama here. Her ladyship told me that he expressly refused to bring her to attend Geoffrey on his sickbed."

Constance smiled as the two ladies made their way towards the staircase. "Do not alarm yourself over that, Pamela," she said. "Robert can be terribly stuffy at times, as I am sure you have discovered. But he dotes on all of us, particularly Mama, although their affection for each other is not always apparent. You should know that Mama defies him at every turn and does what she pleases. He will be annoyed, but not surprised to find us all here."

Annoyed the marquess certainly was, Pamela saw at once as they descended into the hall to find him struggling to remove his greatcoat with the assistance of four eager but unofficial footmen, each pulling in opposite directions. His tall beaver had fallen to the tiled floor and was in serious danger of being shredded by a wildly excited Scamp.

He glanced up at that moment, and Pamela was unprepared for the intensity in his eyes as they seemed to pierce her very garments. She felt her feet waver on the stair and reached a hand for the oak banister. But it was to his sister he spoke, and Pamela sensed his withdrawal as if he had snubbed her.

"Get these wretched boys off me, Constance," he grunted between gritted teeth. "And remind me to arrange to send the whole pack of them back to the Grange tomorrow."

This pronouncement, hardly received as a dire threat by the brothers, caused a noticeable increase in the volume of noise.

"You would not be such an old rumstick, Robbie," cried William, the youngest, with an informality that spoke volumes on the closely knit relationship that existed between the austere marquess and his four young brothers.

In the past two days Pamela had grown accustomed to the rowdy banter from the boys, but the ease with which they included their imposing brother in their horseplay revealed an endearing aspect of her husband's character she had not suspected. The eldest two, George and Gerald, were closer to being young men than their mother appeared willing to acknowledge. Pamela could not find it in her heart to fault her, although she had caught George only yesterday evening ogling one of the pretty housemaids in the kitchen. He already displayed an alarming resemblance to his eldest brother, and it was evident from the clothes he affected and the style of his cravat that young George was a genuine Stilton in disposition as well as in breeding.

At that moment the marquess glanced at her again as the two ladies reached the bottom of the stair. Some of the intensity had faded from his eyes, but he looked troubled. Recalling one of her mother's favorite explanations for Lord Melrose's frequent testiness, Pamela fell back on that cure-all of masculine irritability.

"Have you had your tea, my lord?" she ventured, feeling virtuous and relatively safe in her wifely concern.

Had Pamela imagined the marquess capable of amusement at that moment, she might have read something other than disdain in the curl of his lip. "I have eaten nothing since this morning," he replied crushingly.

"Well, that comes from being such a slow-top, Robbie," Constance cut in mildly. "And you need not snap at Pamela in that rude manner," she added, leaving no doubt as to her feelings on the matter. "She is not to blame if you failed to stop in Dorchester for refreshments."

The marquess appeared nonplussed by this reproof. "I did not snap at her," he began, taking a good-natured slap at Scamp, who seemed determined to leave his paw prints on his pristine buff breeches.

"You did, too," muttered young William, tugging ineffectually at his coat sleeves, which appeared to be too short for his arms, "'cause I heard you, Robbie. You used that tone you use to squelch old Mr. Goodwin when he goes on and on about his goats."

The marquess appeared to be torn between annoyance and amusement at this attack from the flank. Pamela wanted to laugh, and to hide her smile, she turned to Firth, who had retrieved his master's beaver from the floor and was brushing it industriously.

"Firth," she said calmly, "ask Cook to send up a tray of something more substantial than tea and scones for his lordship. Perhaps some of that excellent chicken we had at nuncheon today would be acceptable."

Any response from the marquess was cut short by the appearance of Lord Geoffrey, who had pronounced himself well enough to quit the sickroom for good the day before. He greeted his brother with unself-conscious affection, and Pamela was once more startled at the subtle differences she detected between the two gentlemen, based entirely—she was sure of it—on her hazy recollection of those long-ago scandalous rumors concerning their mother.

These and other uneasy thoughts followed her as she ushered the young Stiltons out onto the terrace, very conscious of her husband's voice behind her, deep in conversation with a man who might well be related to her more closely than she cared to imagine.

The next day began with relative quiet.

Pamela stood in the front hall, listening to the sounds of the house around her. After several days of chaos, the unfamiliar routines of the marquess's family had settled into comfortable patterns. Although it was not yet nine o'clock, she knew that her husband and Geoffrey had risen betimes and gone out for a tramp along the cliffs. The younger Stilton brothers could be heard in the breakfast parlor, arguing hotly about a promised outing in Geoffrey's boat that afternoon and consuming alarming portions of any sustenance Cook cared to set before them.

Pamela made a quick mental note to speak to Mrs. Firth about sending the wagon over to Osmington that morning. Since the estate had only a small home farm, the weekly market was their chief source of supplies. Perhaps she would go herself, she thought, amused at her sudden interest in domestic affairs. The well-run establishment at Melrose Park had required little supervision, but at Holly Lodge Pamela had found herself drawn into lengthy discussions with Cook, a local woman of great girth and a tendency to overcook the lamb. She also knew her way about the kitchen and scullery as well as she did about her own bedchamber. Perhaps better, she thought wryly, since she had changed chambers twice in the past two weeks—once for Geoffrey and now for the dowager.

These complacent musings were interrupted by a shriek from the lower regions, followed by the sound of heated female voices and breaking crockery.

"Oh, milady, do come quickly. That *woman* is making trouble for Cook again." In her agitation Mrs. Firth forgot her dignity long enough to run up the back stairs, her gray crimped curls escaping in all directions from her lace cap.

"Calm yourself, Mrs. Firth," Pamela warned her. "I cannot afford to have you confined to your bed with spasms today." She placed a comforting hand on the other woman's arm, realizing that the elderly housekeeper was close to tears. Nothing in her service with Lady Honoria had prepared her to deal with stiff-necked upper domestics of the sort employed by the best families. Nothing had prepared Pamela to deal with such prima-donna dependents either, but she was far better equipped to do so.

"I understand, milady," the housekeeper whimpered, "but t-that witch is on the rampage again. And all because Molly forgot to warm the extra water she asked for—"

"Well, you must tell Molly not to forget her duties in the future," Pamela said. "And leave Mrs. Hinds to me. I shall speak to her myself."

After this unpleasant task had been completed, and a flustered Mrs. Hinds—the dowager's starched-up abigail and self-appointed guardian and defender—had been smoothly convinced that her valued experience and indisputable dedication to the dowager's well-being were urgently required for the smooth running of the household, Pamela decided that she deserved a reviving cup of tea.

"Excuse me, milady."

She turned to find Firth at her elbow, an anxious crease on his homely face. Pamela wondered idly if the butler at Stilton Grange—there were probably two under-butlers as well, she thought fleetingly—would be as easy to deal with as poor old Firth.

"What is it, Firth?"

The butler cleared his throat awkwardly. "His lordship requests that you step into the library at your first convenience, milady."

Pamela smiled inwardly at this mild rendering of what she knew to be his lordship's dictatorial manner of speech. With a nod she allowed the butler to lead the way towards one of the less frequented rooms in the house.

The library was one of Pamela's favorite hideaways from Lady Honoria's strident, ever-present commentaries on anything she considered herself qualified to speak upon, and many she did not. It was a small, cozy room, rather sparsely filled with books, but providing the solitude she so often missed. As she stepped across the threshold, Pamela felt herself enveloped by the stifling masculine presence of the two gentlemen present. Lord Geoffrey was lounging on the faded brocade sofa, while the marquess stood at the window, his back to the room.

Geoffrey grinned at her and rose languidly to his feet. But when the marquess turned, his face was unsmiling, intense, and showed recent signs of anger.

"You wished to see me, my lord?"

"Aye, and that he does, my dear," Geoffrey drawled, and Pamela got the impression that he was also keeping his anger in check. "I trust you have your armor on and your sword at the ready, Pamela, because his bloody lordship here is spoiling for a fight."

Shocked to be thrust into what appeared to be a nasty altercation between the brothers, Pamela fell back on rigid politeness. "In that case," she said with all the calm she could muster, "perhaps I should sit down." Suiting action to words, she selected a wing chair in faded green leather and sank into it, her knees trembling.

"There," she added encouragingly, aware of Geoffrey's approving grin from the sofa, "that is much better. Now," she forced herself to continue in exactly the same tone of voice she had used yesterday to discover the reason for an incipient bout of fisticuffs between two of the younger Stiltons, "tell me all about it, my lord."

There followed a long moment of silence, during which Pamela had the distinct impression she had taken the wind out of his lordship's sails. He relaxed fractionally, and she caught a quick exchange of glances between the brothers. Whatever it was they were about, she guessed, she had not reacted predictably.

When he spoke, it was Pamela's turn to be surprised. "I merely wished to ask why you have allowed our mother to roust you out of your rooms."

Prepared for something much more deadly, Pamela took a moment to recover. "The dowager did no such thing," she said. "I made that decision myself. Had you seen the quantity of luggage, you would have agreed that there was no way her ladyship could have been comfortable in one of the smaller chambers. I fear she finds even that master suite rather cramped."

"Why was I not informed where I might find you?"

Pamela felt herself blush. The implications of such a question did not bear thinking on. But he could not mean *that*, could he? she asked herself wildly. *That* was not an issue between them. He had made that quite clear from the start of this awkward marriage. Keeping her expression deliberately blank and ignoring the ribald chuckle from the sofa, Pamela returned her husband's gray stare without blinking.

"You had only to send a message, my lord," she said gently.

"As he might have guessed, had he given it any thought," Geoffrey cut in brusquely. "And now that we have dispensed with these embarrassing domestic arrangements, Robbie, I suggest you get down to the meat of the issue here." Ignoring his brother's scowl, Geoffrey turned to Pamela, and she saw that his anger had returned.

"The truth of the matter, my dear, is that my esteemed brother has had me on the carpet for the past hour, raking me over the coals for revealing what he considers matters highly unfitting for your gentle ears. And God knows, there is enough scandal in this family to keep the *ton* buzzing with crim-con. stories for generations to come."

Pamela stared at him in astonishment. Where was this conversation leading? she wondered. Surely, the marquess did not wish to dig up that old scandal concerning his mother? And her own father? Particularly with Lord Geoffrey—the chief victim of those long-ago events if there was any truth in them—standing here listening, a defiant sneer on his handsome face?

Fragmented pieces of wisdom about sleeping dogs and allowing them to lie undisturbed flashed through her mind, but Pamela saw at once that the two men had long passed that stage of prudence.

CHAPTER FIFTEEN

Tradition Totters

Lord Monroyal stared at his brother as if he had never seen the broad-shouldered, angry-eyed young man before. The unsettling thought occurred to him that perhaps he never had known Geoffrey as well as he imagined. Robert absorbed the novel idea reluctantly. They had been as close as two siblings could be, and the six years between them had given Robert the added weight of responsibility for the motherless babe that had, he suddenly realized, stayed with him ever since.

It was for Geoffrey's sake, as well as his own, that Robert had buried all the ugly, confusing memories of those early days of his childhood. In an effort to follow his father's lead, as a young boy he had maintained a rigid silence about that early scandal and perpetuated the legend of Lady Pamela's incomparable beauty, wit, and charm. And then barely a year after his mother's death, the late marquess had brought Lady Sophia to Stilton Grange, and the sunshine of love and laughter had filled those austere halls again.

His brother had taken to the new marchioness instantly. As happy and uncomplicated as a baby as he now appeared as a young man, Geoffrey had never hesitated to call Lady Sophia Mama, and seeing them together, Robert had never doubted the love between them. For himself, the process of letting go of the nightmares had taken longer, but under the gentle guidance of this charming creature, life had returned to normal, and as the house began to fill up with little Stiltons, Robert had been able to forgive his father for past weaknesses.

He had never forgiven his mother.

But now, gazing in rising dismay at the fury and bitterness on his brother's face, Robert wondered if those family ghosts were not closer to the surface than he had realized.

"I rather think, Geoffrey," he said, tight-lipped but calm, "that you are exaggerating the matter. The incidents you speak of lie in the past, and are best left there. What concerns me—will ultimately concern us all—is the threat of scandal that may burst over

Blandford's head at any time. And when it does, I wish to avoid any unfortunate comparisons being drawn to our own . . . our own less than spotless history."

Geoffrey let out a crack of cynical laughter. "Well, if that don't beat the Dutch," he growled. "History, indeed? You speak as if all this happened in the dark days of the Crusades, Robert. This is our *mother* you are talking about, old chap—"

"That is quite enough, Geoffrey!" The marquess's voice cut across the room like a whiplash. "May I remind you that we are not alone." He glanced at his wife, sitting demurely in the green chair, and wondered what was going through that clear-eyed head of hers. Perhaps it had been a mistake to include a female in this delicate conversation, but if there was to be a scandal over Lady Bland-ford's bastard child—and he saw little way of avoiding it—then Pamela must know the basic facts, however unsavory, and follow his lead in squashing any rumors that might be bruited about.

He cleared his throat. "Since my brother has been so unwise as to burden you with the unpalatable details of this matter," he began cautiously, "I have been persuaded—against my better judgment I might add—to confirm the unsettling truth that—"

"What a mealy-mouthed windbag you are, to be sure, Robbie," his brother burst out impatiently. "The truth of the matter," he said with repressed savagery, turning to Pamela, "is that Lady Blandford was secretly betrothed to some dashing commoner who came up through the ranks. It appears this fire-breathing mush-room bedazzled General Wellington's staff with his utter disre-gard for life and limb, and became a full-blown legend in his company. From there, it was but a short step to bedazzling the ladies with his heroics."

He paused and glanced at the marquess, his smile cynical. "Have I got the gist of it correct, Robert?"

The marquess nodded. From what his cousin Blandford had told him, the fellow had been a natural leader and intrepid soldier, worshipped by his men and capable of incredible feats of courage. Anthony had confessed that, as his commanding officer, he had developed a strong bond of friendship with the man, in spite of the differences in their stations.

"It appears that Lord Uxbridge's daughter took one look at this prime piece of manhood and threw herself at him," Geoffrey con-tinued with a gusto that grated on Robert's ears. "Poor old Bland-ford, who is a bit of a duffer, of course, and a slow-top when it comes to the petticoat company," he added with a grin, "was left to eat this young buck's dust."

"We can do without this vulgar embellishment," the marquess remarked coldly. "The trouble arose," he added, taking up the narrative, "when this jackstraw lieutenant, instead of formalizing the relationship instantly, as a gentleman would have done, of course, chose to go into a major battle and get himself killed, leaving matters unsettled."

Geoffrey's grin turned sour. "This small matter my brother refers to is the unborn child the bounder left behind. Now known, poor little mite, as Lady Alexandra Whitlock."

In the pause that followed this remark, Robert watched his wife's eyes grow round and soft with emotions at the mention of the child. It *had* been a mistake to include her in this discussion, and he regretted listening to his brother's assurances that Pamela was not one of those fuddle-brained females who swooned at the least provocation. Perhaps not, he thought, but the expressions that chased one another across his wife's face warned him that Pamela, like other females of her delicate upbringing, could not be expected to take a practical, much less a rational stand on matters of the heart. And the Blandford affair—much as Robert hated to admit it—had all the makings of a lurid romantic melodrama popularized by the Minerva Press.

"But the lieutenant was not killed in this major battle," she murmured into the silent room. "And now he is to return to England to claim his daughter?"

"Aye," Geoffrey responded dryly, "although according to my informant, the man believes he has a son. The wretch is obviously intent on extorting a pretty penny out of a poor old Blandford. But if the earl stands firm, as Robert says he plans to, the whole nasty mess may blow over."

"Lord Blandford will claim the child as his own?" Pamela asked, and the suppressed excitement in her voice alarmed the marquess. "How very noble of him, to be sure."

"Noble? Supreme foolhardiness is what I call it," Robert snapped impatiently. "That a level-headed man like Blandford could be so taken in by a pretty face is one thing, but to accept responsibility for another man's child is beyond the pale."

He stopped abruptly, brought up by the uncomfortable realization that he might well be describing his own father. The same thought must have occurred to Geoffrey, for the younger man's upper lip curled derisively, his eyes flat and cold.

"Of course, the true perversion lies with the lady," he added quickly, shifting away from memories of his mother that seemed to swirl about beneath the surface of his mind, and disconcerted by the hard expression on his brother's face. "I shall never comprehend how a female with all the advantages and privilege of rank and fortune could so far forget both duty and decency as to throw herself away on a braggart commoner."

"No, I would not expect you to understand that at all," Pamela surprised him by agreeing. "Lady Blandford must have enjoyed one of those rare, paralyzing experiences that transcend duty and even decency."

The marquess stared at his wife as he had earlier studied his brother, as if she were an unwelcome stranger appearing uninvited in his drawing room, speaking gibberish.

Ignoring the shadow of a smile that flickered on Geoffrey's lean face, Robert retaliated instantly against such dangerous notions coming from the mouth of a female.

"I beg your pardon?" he said quellingly. "Are you telling us, Pamela, that you actually condone Lady Blandford's aberrant taste and utter lack of morals?"

He was mortified at his wife's almost pitying smile. "Oh, no, my lord," she replied with the gentleness of a mother reprimanding a contentious child. "I said nothing of condoning her ladyship's actions; but I do understand why she may have chosen to . . . to t-throw herself off the cliff, so to speak."

From the light blush that mantled her cheeks, Robert could not misunderstand what Pamela was telling him. He wanted most urgently to misunderstand her. He did not wish to hear his own wife admitting to understanding the unbridled passion—he could find no other expression for it—that had thrust an otherwise respectable female into the depths of what must be recognized as nothing less than carnal sin.

There was another lengthy pause. Robert perceived on the periphery of his mind that Geoffrey was taking perverse pleasure at his discomfiture. His brother was regarding Pamela with something akin to reverence.

Robert spoke around the awkward constriction in his throat. "Perhaps you would care to enlighten us, my dear," he said, trying hard to keep in mind his father's dictum that females should be reprimanded firmly but with every courtesy. How would the late marquess have handled this brazen admission of sympathy for moral turpitude and depraved inclinations? he wondered, not yet sure how he would deal with it himself.

Incredibly, Pamela smiled at him. "Of course, my lord. I understand what must have happened to Lady Blandford," she explained brightly, "because a similar incident happened to me when I was very young. I found myself, quite out of the blue, standing on the edge of—"

Robert did not recognize the roar that came out of his mouth as his own. "You did *what*?" he shouted, the blood surging into his face with the force of his fury.

The tension in the room was abruptly broken by a crack of delighted laughter. The marquess, distracted from the object of his wrath, whirled on his brother, who was doubled up with mirth.

"This is no laughing matter, Geoffrey."

For some reason Robert could not immediately identify, this remark increased his brother's mirth until the tears ran down his face.

Her husband's outraged exclamation alerted Pamela that she had trespassed beyond the boundaries of good taste. Or at least beyond those considered acceptable by the tradition-bound gentleman who had unexpectedly emerged from behind the facade of rake and libertine. The heretical notion flashed through her mind that the latter might have proved a more desirable life companion than the former, but she could understand why the marquess would insist upon playing the former role with his wife.

She smiled at the incongruity of masculine intellect.

"I believe you misunderstand me, my lord," she hastened to explain, fearing another explosion from that quarter. "One may understand the temptations of this world without actually . . ." She hesitated, searching for the right words. "Without actually—"

"Jumping off the cliff?" Geoffrey offered helpfully, his tone light and amused.

She glanced at him gratefully. "Precisely, Geoffrey. I am glad you seem to understand."

"And I do not?" the marquess cut in sharply. "Is that what you mean, Pamela? If you would cease speaking in metaphors, perhaps we might get to the bottom of this matter."

"I think this particular metaphor is exceptionally appropriate, Robert," his brother remarked. "After all, I imagine that for a female, such an action must take considerable courage and a sense of adventure."

Pamela's smile broadened. "You are right again, Geoffrey. Females are bound by so many traditional restrictions and conventions that it takes an enormous amount of fortitude to break away"—she paused fractionally—"and fly."

"Courage? Fortitude?" The outrage was back in his voice, coupled with contempt. "Have you both run mad? Do you wish me to accept that illicit activity in unmarried women is to be commended? Balderdash! I will not listen to this heresy any longer, Pamela. I warn you. It is not becoming in a lady who is my wife."

Pamela no longer felt like smiling. Such pomposity depressed her, reminding her of her father. If the marquess turned into a stiff-rumped autocrat like Lord Melrose, she must instantly look around for an appropriate cliff to jump off. The thought was so unexpectedly titillating and scandalous that she yearned to share it with Geoffrey. Her husband's formidable presence deterred her.

"I am very well aware of what is becoming and what is not in a lady of my station," she said tartly. "Besides, we were not talking about me, but about Lady Blandford and her particular conundrum."

"I had hoped you were about to share with us this particular flying adventure you mentioned, Pamela. I am all agog to hear it."

Pamela threw Geoffrey a grateful look. Her husband's brother was turning out to be unusually perceptive—for a gentleman—and she wondered how different her childhood might have been had she had a real brother like Lord Geoffrey. She felt a deep sadness at what she had missed.

Her eyes slid back to the marquess, who regarded her stonily from beneath lowered brows. Taking this silence as tacit approval, she clasped her hands in her lap and sent her mind back to that first ball she had attended as a chit of eighteen.

"It was all very innocent," she began tentatively, "and at eighteen I knew nothing of the world. But I had eyes, and a vivid imagination." She paused self-consciously. "I suppose you would have called me a schoolroom romantic, and no doubt I was that."

"A common female ailment by all accounts," her husband muttered under his breath.

"I was standing with some other ladies watching the dancing," she continued, ignoring this interruption, "when across the room I noticed a strange gentleman staring straight at me—"

"I am surprised that you were not warned against encouraging the attention of strangers."

"Oh, but I was, of course." She waved the marquess's reproof away impatiently. "As all females are, I imagine. But his gaze was so compelling, I could not stop . . . I forgot what I should do, what my mother had expressly told me not an hour since."

"And what *did* you do?" Pamela sensed that her husband was deeply disturbed, perhaps disgusted by her innocent revelations.

"Nothing at all," she replied promptly, intent on removing any doubt in his mind. "But in that instant I saw a whole world open up before my eyes. And I knew in my heart—do not ask me how for I could not tell you—that if that stranger had crossed the room and asked me to run off to China with him, I would not have hesitated."

"You would have jumped off the cliff, in other words," Geoffrey said quietly.

"I would have jumped, yes. And never looked back. So I can say with some certainty that Lady Blandford must have felt something similar for her gallant lieutenant."

"And who was this paragon of depravity?" the marquess said, an edge of derision in his cold voice.

"I never knew the gentleman's name," she responded. "I never spoke to him or saw him again. And in any case, it did not signify in the least. You see"—and here she smiled disparagingly—"he was not looking at me at all, as it turned out, but at that stunning Beauty of the Season, I forget her name. The one who wed the heir to the Earl of Hargrove within the year."

After a brief pause, during which neither man spoke, Pamela continued in a pensive tone. "I have often wondered whether the lady regretted her lack of courage."

"That is the most cockle-headed piece of farradiddle I have ever heard," the marquess retorted acidly. "Regret her courage, indeed? The chit is to be commended for her proper behavior in repulsing the encroaching coxcomb."

"Oh, but she did not repulse him exactly," Pamela corrected him. "She danced with him. I have often wondered about that, too," she said, her voice tinged with regret.

"I know exactly what you mean, my dear," Geoffrey exclaimed impetuously. "Remember that summer when Mama took us both over to Bath to visit that quite dreadful second or third cousin or some distant relative of hers, who had broken her leg falling out of a carriage? She had this chit from Yorkshire—a godchild, I believe—staying with her. I distinctly remember this provocative little minx had us both mesmerized with those violet eyes of hers. Remember, Robbie? You swore you would—"

"That is quite enough, thank you," the marquess cut in coldly. "We do not need to hear a recital of your lurid tales of youthful debauchery. Besides, such boyish adventures are traditionally accepted expressions of a young man's wild oats. He is expected to . . ." His voice died away as he caught Pamela's eye.

She could not repress a small smile. "I think I see what you mean," she said with gentle sarcasm. "Young gentlemen are encouraged to try their wings, while young ladies must stand on the edge of the cliff, wondering what lies out there beyond their reach."

Geoffrey laughed. "I doubt Robert would have put it quite that way, Pamela," he said, "but essentially you are right. The notion of a lady of our class wishing to fly is beyond a gentleman's powers of comprehension. Why should she, when we are here to provide for her every desire?" The sarcasm in this remark was unmistakable.

"So you cannot forgive Lady Blandford for following her heart?"

"No, I cannot," the marquess snapped. He was beginning to lose his temper, she noted, taking a certain perverse joy in his discomfiture. "And I do not wish to hear any more on the subject of cliffs and flying and such nonsense. Is that understood?"

Pamela rose to her feet and brushed out her skirts. "Perfectly, my lord," she said demurely. "And now if you will excuse me, I have to speak to Cook about a blood pudding."

She had seized upon the first excuse that entered her head, but it seemed to work, for neither gentleman attempted to detain her as she left the room.

"Blood pudding!"

Geoffrey echoed Pamela's parting shot with a raucous guffaw, no sooner had the door closed behind the whisper of that lady's skirt. "If that don't take the cake, old man." He wiped a large hand across his face and threw himself back onto the settee. "Your wife, in case you had not noticed, Robbie, is an original. How did you happen to find such a treasure? I cannot say she is anything like your usual style, but then your taste in females has always run to the flamboyant hussies who are doubtless abominable wives."

"I did not *find* her," the marquess replied. "She was thrust upon me, as well you know. And now I discover that she is a dashed free-thinker like that immoral Wollstonecraft woman. I will not stand for it, Geoffrey. What rights could any self-respecting female possible want that my wife does not already enjoy as the Marchioness of Monroyal?"

Robert saw his brother's amusement fade abruptly. His blue eyes became wary. "If you have to ask that question, Robert," he said softly, "I fear you will miss all the delight of sharing your life with a female of rare wit and understanding. To say nothing of courage and imagination."

The marquess felt himself tense. "I can do without wit and

imagination in a female," he said harshly. "And the one I have been saddled with appears to have a dangerously independent and mutinous streak in her character. I would prefer to see obedience and modesty, and if necessary, I shall insist upon it."

His brother shrugged. "I daresay you are refining too much on the matter, Robert. From where I stand, Pamela does not seem like one of your fribble-headed widgeons with more hair than wit."

"Blandford assures me that his lady appeared equally tractable and well bred. He was practically assured of his success with her, and was ready to approach her father, when this upstart lieutenant stole her from under his very nose."

"I always told you the man was a slow-top," Geoffrey remarked callously. "How he ever made a career as a cavalry officer is beyond me. Apparently, the lady thought so, too. And if that braggart lieutenant had not been reported dead at Waterloo, she would be wed to him by now and all would have been well."

"But he *was* reported dead," Robert snapped, impatient with this line of reasoning. "And it is a lucky thing for everyone involved that Blandford was standing by to cover up the lady's indiscretion. More fool he," he muttered under his breath.

The notion of unbridled female passion, like that displayed by Lady Blandford, made the marquess uncomfortable. It was a flaw that reminded him too closely of his mother. And anything that came close to that aberration of motherhood was to be condemned without recourse. Every male instinct demanded it.

Geoffrey rose to his feet and stretched languorously. "I have promised to take the boys to Weymouth this afternoon to look at the *Seagull*." He walked to the door and paused, one hand on the knob. "If you value my advice at all, Robert, I suggest you remember that Pamela is not Lady Blandford. Nor is she . . ." he hesitated a fraction of a second, then continued in a level voice, his clear blue eyes fixed on the marquess, "nor is she anything like our mother."

They stared at each other for a long moment. Robert felt his face freeze into harsh lines of disbelief. How could his brother brazenly bring up the family scandal he had tried so hard for years to suppress? How dare he link his wife, even by disassociation, with that past shame? Geoffrey of all people, the man who had the most to lose if such rumors that had set the *ton* on its ears years ago were ever confirmed. The very idea gave him goose bumps.

Geoffrey opened the door, but he was not yet finished.

"One last piece of advice, Robert," he said with a tentative smile. "If I were you, I would pay off that damned ridiculous wager on White's Betting Book and let things take their natural course." His grin widened. "You might find that there is something special about a virgin bride, after all."

Without waiting for a reply, he stepped out and shut the door. He was gone before Robert could confess that he had discharged that offensive wager less than a month after bringing his bride to Holly Lodge.

For the rest of the day, and for several days thereafter, Pamela went about her household tasks in a pensive mood. That odd conversation in the library with her husband and Geoffrey had revealed a side to Lord Monroyal that had not been apparent before. Or even suspected, she mused, running a finger absentmindedly along the back of a spindle-legged chair standing on the first landing and detecting, with a certain amount of satisfaction, that it had been recently and thoroughly dusted.

The staff had pulled together much better than expected, she thought, continuing her way downstairs to the kitchens, where Mrs. Firth had promised to make up a batch of blackberry jam from the season's last fruit, gathered enthusiastically by the boys yesterday. After thrusting six extra maidservants into the house, the dowager had left their supervision entirely in Pamela's hands. The prospect of assuming this responsibility had daunted her, but she soon discovered that she actually enjoyed the challenge, and—aside from the prickly Mrs. Hinds, the dowager's abigail—had even become receptive to Cook's plan for installing a new stove.

The question of Lady Blandford's fall from grace returned to nag her often, however, particularly since her own response to that lady's dilemma differed so diametrically from that of the marquess. More frequently than ever did Pamela wish for the comforting presence of her mother, with whom she could have expressed her true feelings. She was therefore surprised and pleased to discover in the dowager a sympathetic confidant, one who not only knew all the parties involved, but had no scruples about sharing her views on the matter.

"Robert has hinted to me that you are a devotee of Mary Wollstonecraft's rather extraordinary views on women, my dear," the dowager remarked quite out of the blue one afternoon as the ladies sat on the beach, watching the younger boys romp barefooted in the waves. "I fear you gave the poor boy rather a shock," she added with a smile.

Pamela gave the older woman a scrutinizing glance. "I am quite sure I never admitted to such a thing, my lady," she protested. "For one thing, I would not dare. There is nothing so calculated to send a gentleman into the boughs as to mention that name. Something about a woman speaking her mind on certain topics appears to deprive gentlemen of all rational understanding."

"All of which does not tell me you deny having read the work," the dowager insisted with a twinkle in her eyes.

Pamela had to laugh. "I confess I am guilty," she said. "My father nearly had an apoplexy when he discovered me reading it and actually burned my copy. Luckily, I was able to read my mother's. She obtained an autographed copy from the author soon after the book was published in 1792." She paused for a second. "I still have it. But I would not wish his lordship to know, if you please."

"Oh, it is no secret to Robert that I have my own copy of *Vindication*," the dowager responded briskly. "I often wish I had insisted he read it years ago, as Geoffrey did. The poor boy might have been able to understand, if not precisely accept, his mother's defiance of all social taboos when Robert was so very young and impressionable. I fear Robert's lifelong aversion to matrimony stems directly from that unfortunate affair."

This was exactly what Pamela had feared herself, and she was dismayed at the prospect of living in the shadow of another woman's scandal for the rest of her life.

"I can assure you, my lady," she said earnestly, "that rebellion and disobedience are the last things on my mind. I have not Lady Blandford's temerity, although his lordship appears to think I am poised on the brink of some foolish escapade. I am not surprised that he is annoyed with me."

"Not so much annoyed, my dear," the dowager said, "as perplexed to find that he is wed to a female of complexity and intellect rather than to some pretty ninny who would bore him silly with her eternal simperings. Give him time, Pamela. The whole experience of marriage must be rather shattering to a man who has vowed for years to remain unattached."

"I did try to warn him," Pamela began, but was interrupted by a loud shriek from the youngest Stilton, who had been knocked over by a large wave and now lay wallowing in the swirling water.

"Mama, Gerald pushed me," William screamed at the top of his lungs. "He tried to drown me. Mama, save me!" Scrambling to his feet and dripping seawater as he ran, William made a beeline for his mother, who had risen abruptly at the disturbance. With sublime disregard for her elegant French cambric afternoon gown, Lady Sophy opened her arms and took her youngest son to her bosom, lavishing upon him the comfort he so craved.

This altercation put an end to the afternoon's activities, and to the enlightening coze Pamela had enjoyed with the dowager. But from Lady Sophy's remarks, added to those Pamela had accumulated over the past week from both the marquess and his brother, there began to emerge a man as enigmatic as his past.

Eager to pursue these confidences further with the dowager, Pamela encouraged family excursions to the beach, one of the dowager's favorite outings, every afternoon as long as the weather held. All too often, however, they were accompanied by the marquess himself, which precluded the confidences she sought. This assiduous attendance by the master of the house upon the ladies on their varied drives around the neighborhood and informal gatherings on the beach gave rise to another kind of intimacy that Pamela had not expected.

"I am beginning to suspect that you have a civilizing influence on Robert, my dear girl," the dowager remarked one afternoon as they strolled together towards the cliff. "Not once have I heard him mention our return to the Grange or complain about the meager entertainment in this rural area. And I was positively astounded yesterday at his forbearance when the Grimshaw sisters insisted upon reliving their first Season in London fifty years ago. I thought I would split my sides when Miss Agatha described how she had danced the gavotte with Robert's grandfather."

"Yes," Pamela agreed, "the dear old lady has a vivid memory. I got the impression that the dance was a triumph of a sort."

"Oh, indeed it was. To hear her tell the story, one might imagine she had that old rogue sitting in her pocket," the dowager remarked, "which I can assure you is a piece of nonsense. The old marquess was a delightful flirt, I am told, but not one to be caught in parson's mousetrap. He was nearly forty when he finally succumbed to family pressure and took a wife."

"His grandson appears to have taken his example to heart," Pamela said dryly, her gaze flowing out across the slate-colored expanse of sea to the horizon, where a thin dark line of clouds marred the beauty of the scene. "I wonder if he will always resent being forced into a inconvenient match," she continued pensively. "Perhaps I should have tried harder to bring Sir Rodney before the vicar in Purley that night—"

"Fiddlesticks!" the dowager burst out indignantly. "Never say that you would have preferred Morton to my Robert?"

Pamela had to laugh at her ladyship's outrage. "It was never a question of preference, my lady," she replied, shaking her head. "To tell the truth, I wanted neither of them. But faced with a choice, and his lordship's ill-concealed disgust at the notion of a union between our families, I thought to relieve him of the duty—"

"Ah, I thought as much," the dowager interrupted. "And therein lies the rub, my dear. One does not interfere with a Stilton's idea of duty. I learned that a long time ago with Robert's father." She paused, a smile playing around her expressive mouth. "I only regret not being there to see Robert trounce this unfortunate Sir Rodney for daring to get in the way."

"It was not a pretty sight," Pamela admitted ruefully.

"And you may undeceive yourself about Robert harboring any resentment, my dear," Lady Sophy said. "He may be rather set in his ways—he is not far short of forty himself, you know—but I have been asking myself for the past few days why we are still here, and not back at the Grange, where I know Robert must have a dozen things to take care of."

Pamela laughed at this naive remark. "It is clear to me, my lady, that your son is reluctant to cut short your holiday by the seaside, which you so obviously enjoy."

Lady Sophy nodded her agreement. "That is part of it, of course. The boys also love being with Geoffrey and his sailboat. But there is more to it than that. Robert must be wrestling with a momentous decision that will affect us all . . ."

Pamela never did find out what that decision might be, for at that moment the subject of their conversation came striding up the cliff path to assist the ladies in their descent. Her hand tucked companionably in the crook of her husband's arm, Pamela listened to the shouts of the four younger Stiltons on the beach below, punctuated by an occasional shriek from Lady Letitia, who had shed some of her ladylike airs and was romping freely on the sand with her brothers. The scene was boisterous but idyllic in a way her own solitary childhood had never been.

The play of muscles beneath her fingers reminded her vividly that this man, still too much the stranger to her, was the key to it all. Her acceptance into this warm and loving family. Her future happiness. Her fulfillment as a woman.

For the first time since that havey-cavey ceremony before the vicar at Purley, Pamela felt that the future held something precious for her.

If only she could find the key.

CHAPTER SIXTEEN

A Gathering Storm

Long after it was all over, Pamela looked back on that last idyllic afternoon in the late summer sunshine and marveled that she had had so little inkling of the storms that gathered over their heads.

The beach activities—boisterous and punctuated by minor quarrels as all Stilton family gatherings invariably were—proceeded without any disaster more serious than Lady Letitia getting her petticoats wet, until it came time for tea. The marquess had long since given up on the informal game of croquet set up on the damp sand, which had quickly deteriorated into a contest of who could smack the ball farthest into the sea, and thrown himself down in one of the wicker chairs clustered in the lee of the outcropping rocks.

"Are we to get no tea and tarts today, Mama?" Lord Geoffrey drawled, sauntering up to drop at the dowager's feet, and smile up at her with an open affection that tugged at Pamela's heart. "We are in for a blow"—he gestured towards the sky, where that earlier dark line of clouds appeared to have taken a sudden leap nearer them across the uneasy water—"and I would hate to see Cook's tarts get soggy."

"No chance of that," the marquess said, his gaze rising to the top of the cliff, where the first of a line of footmen had appeared, heralding the arrival of what the dowager chose to call light afternoon refreshments. In actuality, it required six footmen three trips each to convey the vast assortment of currant buns, damson and blackberry tarts, rhubarb and gooseberry pie, seed cake, freshly baked scones, and huge platters of toast and jelly, and the occasional plum cake that it took to appease the appetites of the younger Stiltons.

As official butler of Holly Lodge, Firth had appropriated the honor of transporting the silver tea-pot, and as the old man trudged across the sand, Pamela noticed the first signs of the blow Geoffrey had mentioned. The white hair that usually lay like solid snow on Firth's head now waved irreverently in the stiff breeze that came directly from the sea.

The change in the weather affected the party's appetites not a whit, and in less than twenty minutes what had been provisions for an army was reduced to a few crumbs that the younger boys delighted in throwing into the air for the seagulls to scramble over. The first large drops of rain put an instant halt to this amusement and sent the servants scurrying up the cliff path with chairs, tables, books, shawls, and china.

But they had tarried too long. Those first innocuous drops were followed by an avalanche of cold, biting rain that cut through the ladies' thin summer garments and left them breathless and chilled.

"Here, put this on." The marquess surprised Pamela by appearing at her side and throwing his coat over her shoulders. "That shawl is no earthly protection in this weather." He kept his arms around her and tucked her close in to his side as they made their way up the slippery path.

"Your mother . . ." Pamela began, glancing back to search for the dowager through the curtain of rain, but he cut her short.

"Geoffrey has her in hand. Watch your step, girl," he added roughly. "I do not wish to—" The rest of his words were lost in a gust of wind that blew her bonnet off and sent it tumbling over the edge of the path and down onto the rocks below. "Forget it," the marquess muttered in her ear, holding her fast as though he feared she might blow away, too. "I shall buy you another."

It occurred to Pamela as they sloshed through the driving rain and puddles to the terrace door, that her husband had yet to buy her anything of a personal nature. How many bonnets must he have purchased for other females over the years? she wondered. Oddly, the thought did not perturb her. Those other women might have the bonnets, the jewels, the expensive gowns, and other fripperies, but she was here with him now. His arm heavy on her shoulders, his hip pressed against her, moving in unison with her own. She must look a fright, her hair undone and plastered against her face, but the warmth of his coat about her gave her a sense of belonging she had never felt before.

Pamela smiled at her own foolishness. This was a fantasy fraught with danger. She would do well to remember that this man had not wanted a wife. He had been quite rude to her, she recalled. Had he not actually accused her of tricking him? That fear at least had been laid to rest with her elopement with Sir Rodney, had it not? Her own motivations were clear enough, but Pamela still wondered about her father's.

She had little time to worry about such things after the whole party had assembled in the hall, dripping, laughing, shouting, lamenting the lost entertainment of relay races planned for later that afternoon. She quickly dispatched the younger boys and the two girls up to their rooms and ordered fires to be lit in all the hearths to ward off the dampness that had followed them into the house.

For the dowager, Pamela ordered hot water for a hip bath and a warming-pan, insisting that the best remedy for such an exposure to the elements was an hour or two in a warm bed, and perhaps even a dinner tray in her chamber.

"Pooh-pooh to that, my dear," the dowager protested. "What do you take me for? Some missish widgeon who succumbs to a few drops of water?"

But by that evening, Lady Sophia had changed her mind. She had taken her hot bath and suffered her abigail to bundle her into a warm bed for a short nap, as she called it. When Pamela slipped into her chamber shortly before the hour the dowager dressed for dinner, however, she found her heavy-eyed and lethargic.

"Perhaps you are right, my dear," she said with a small smile. "All that excitement has quite tired me out. I shall take your advice, Pamela, and have my dinner on a tray. I do believe I am getting a slight megrim, too, which is unusual for me. Hinds," she addressed her abigail, who was hovering anxiously in the background, "mix me one of those possets you are so good at. The hot one for colds. I expect I did take a chill after all this afternoon, but a posset should put all to rights again."

"Yes, milady," the abigail murmured, giving Pamela a withering glare that indicated more clearly than words who was to blame for the dowager's sudden indisposition. "I remember warning your ladyship that the sea air was far too damp for a delicate constitution," she muttered under her breath.

"Fiddle!" the dowager replied, closing her eyes with a sigh. "Pamela, tell Robert not to fly into a pucker about this little indisposition of mine. He does tend to exaggerate so when any of us catches the least little thing . . ." Her voice trailed off, and when Pamela leaned over to tuck the silk sheet under her chin, she saw that her ladyship had dropped off to sleep.

As Pamela was returning to her own chamber, she saw the marquess coming upstairs two at a time and remembered the dowager's request to calm any fears he might have.

"What is this farradiddle I hear about Lady Sophy having her dinner on a tray?" he demanded brusquely, barring her passage along the hall. "She is never sick. *Never.*" He spoke so emphatically that Pamela suspected he wished to remind himself of this basic truth.

"Her ladyship is not sick," she said calmly. "The excitement and sudden change in weather has given her a slight megrim, and of course, she was chilled like everyone else. Her abigail is even now making up a hot posset, and after a good night's rest, her ladyship should be fully recovered."

"I shall send for the local sawbones," he said abruptly, giving no sign that he had heard anything she said. "What is his name? Anderson?"

"Henderson," Pamela corrected automatically. "But I can assure you, my lord, there is no need to disturb the good doctor. A simple chill and a megrim are no cause for alarm. I am well versed in sickroom procedures, and I—"

"I am sure you are," he interrupted absentmindedly, "but I refuse to take any chances." He turned to go back downstairs, but Pamela detained him.

"My lord," she said firmly, "I am as anxious as you are to see her ladyship back in prime twig, but unnecessary fussing will only distress her. At least let us wait until after dinner to send for Dr. Henderson. Osmington is such a short drive, he may be conveyed here immediately if he is required." She hesitated, wondering how best she could allay the fear she saw in his eyes, then added, "I promise to stay with her ladyship myself and report any change in her condition instantly."

He looked at her then, as if he had only just recognized her. Pamela refused to be daunted by this unflattering masculine characteristic. Her father had invariably failed to notice her existence unless he particularly needed her assistance in some task he found little to his liking.

"Thank you," the marquess murmured under his breath, as though he were unwilling to acknowledge her assistance. Without another word, he turned and descended into the hall below.

With mixed emotions, Pamela watched him go. At least he had heeded her advice, which was more than her father often did. A minor victory, perhaps, but one that cheered her heart.

Lord Monroyal glared across the dowager's still, slight form beneath the pink silk eiderdown at the tall, thin gentleman on the other side of the bed. He felt an irrational urge to strangle the man. Why was the worthless wretch standing there chattering with Lady Pamela when his patient was in obvious distress?

Robert asked himself savagely. The sound of each labored breath felt as though it were his own.

"I shall leave you this digestive powder, my lady, in case her ladyship should experience discomfort when she awakens." The marquess listened in quiet fury as the doctor spoke, quite as though he were dosing some horse in the stables for an attack of colic. "But the laudanum I have given her should see her peacefully through the night. The fever is very slight at present, but keep applying the cool compresses, and in the morning, after I have attended Mrs. Cobb's first confinement, which promises to be a difficult one, I might add—"

"You are not thinking of leaving her ladyship to fend for herself, I trust."

At the sound of his voice, harsh even to his own ears, the doctor glanced across at him in surprise.

"There is no need for alarm, my lord," Henderson said smoothly. "Her ladyship is an outstanding nurse," he said and turned towards Lady Pamela with a smile, "and quite capable of following my instructions to the letter. I confess I have yet to see more stalwart courage in a lady when faced with the grisly prospect of removing that ball from Lord Geoffrey's shoulder."

Momentarily distracted, the marquess glanced at his wife. So, this rather insignificant, self-effacing female he had married had yet another surprising facet to her nature, did she? Eloping with fortune hunters, reading seditious tracts, jumping off cliffs. And now it appeared that she did not swoon at the sight of blood and bullets. What other surprises might be in store for him over the coming years? he mused.

"I was speaking of my mother," he said sharply, pulling his mind away from the uncertain future to fix it firmly on the present catastrophe that loomed before him. "I cannot believe you hold her ladyship's health so lightly," he added, a distinct edge to his voice. Robert knew he was being unreasonable, but he derived a certain pleasure when the jovial doctor winced.

As he should have expected, it was Lady Pamela who intervened to diffuse the tension and restore reason to the discussion.

"Her ladyship is asleep now, my lord," she said with that unshakable composure that seemed to be so integral a part of her nature, "and will remain so for the next three or four hours. There is little point in detaining Dr. Henderson kicking his heels here when he might be assisting poor Mrs. Cobb through a very difficult time."

His wife's words sounded far more reasonable than Robert

wanted to hear, and he would have liked to destroy them with the force of his authority. But even as he opened his mouth to order the doctor to remain at Lady Sophy's bedside, a silent message in Pamela's eyes brought him up short. Robert was not accustomed to a female looking at him in just that way, as if she knew exactly what was going through his mind. In truth, he had cared little over the years about the contents of the female mind. Beauty and sensuality and compliance to his desires determined his choice of *amourettes*. Not intellect. And now he was saddled with a bloody bluestocking. One with a clear hazel gaze that offered compassion in place of passion, understanding instead of titillation.

She must have sensed his hesitation, for his wife smiled gently. "The Cobb farm is just over the hill on the Dorcester Road, my lord. Dr. Henderson may be sent for at a moment's notice. I myself will see to it if it becomes necessary."

For the second time that evening, the marquess backed down before his wife's reasoning. "Very well," he said, reluctant to capitulate; equally unwilling to ignore the appeal in her eyes. "But I shall hold you personally responsible, Doctor, if any harm should come to her ladyship." He paused, then added, "And you too, my lady."

Lady Pamela got no more rest that night. She had been both surprised and pleased at the marquess's acceptance of her suggestion and vowed to make sure that she did not forfeit his trust. She spent the time sitting by the dowager's bedside, taking turns with Hinds in bathing the patient's face with cool lavender water.

As the clock in the hall below struck four, the marquess appeared in his mother's chamber, fully clothed, demanding to know whether the doctor had been summoned. He appeared put out when Pamela informed him that the patient had slept, albeit restlessly, through the night, and that rest was more important than dosing at this point.

"But she is burning up with fever," he protested, upon checking the dowager's brow. "There must be something the doctor can do."

"Hinds and I are already doing everything possible," Pamela pointed out. "The fever is mild as yet. And besides, Dr. Henderson promised to stop by on his way back to Osmington this morning." She glanced at the elegant ormolu clock on the mantelpiece. "I expect him by six at the latest."

The marquess appeared unconvinced. "I cannot like it," he said harshly. "What if the fever worsens?"

"Oh, it will," Pamela assured him candidly. "I expect it will get considerably worse before it runs its course. It is in the nature of fevers to do so."

He strode over to the window and twitched at the curtain, but there was only darkness outside. When he turned to face her, Pamela saw at once that her husband was truly worried. Deep furrows creased his brow, marring the rugged beauty of his features and hinting at the weight of years to come. His eyes looked through her, unfocused and bleak. Pamela repressed a sudden urge to enfold him in her arms and comfort him, as she would a frightened child.

"I shall send for Nurse Williams," he said finally. "She has seen the children through every imaginable ailment. She will know what to do."

Pamela caught the flicker of exasperation that crossed the abigail's pinched face and gathered that Hinds would not welcome the interference of yet another interloper at her mistress's bedside.

"That is an excellent idea, my lord," she agreed, ready to countenance any suggestion that would keep the marquess out of the sickroom. She was about to add something to that effect, but a scratching at the door forestalled her. It was an anxious-looking Firth with a pot of freshly-made tea for his mistress.

"I trust you and the staff got plenty of rest last night, Firth," she said briskly, grateful for Cook's thoughtfulness. "Her ladyship will need all of you in the days to come."

"Yes, indeed, milady," the butler responded, "and well we know it. Cook instructed me to inform you that she has the chicken gruel ready, and hot water for her ladyship's posset."

"You may tell Cook from me that I shall make her ladyship's posset myself, Firth," the abigail cut in sharply, her prune features rigid with disapproval.

"I am counting on you to do so, Hinds," Pamela said quickly, breathing a sigh of relief when the abigail bustled out of the room. The last thing she wanted was a tantrum-prone abigail on a rampage in the kitchens. "And Firth, perhaps his lordship would like to have his breakfast served early this morning," she suggested gently. "And when Dr. Henderson arrives, he will need something to sustain him. The poor man has been up all night, too."

Having adroitly cleared the room, Pamela bathed the dowager's face once more, then explored the dresser for a fresh night-rail. When Hinds returned, she would change the bed linens and the diaphanous pink silk garment the dowager had slept in. The dresser-drawer was full of lacy undergarments in a rainbow of soft colors and delicate textures. The sensuousness of them quite took Pamela's breath away.

She had never been given to luxury, and it had not occurred to her to use anything but soft cotton for her own nightwear. But the subtle glow of the dowager's silk garments tempted her, and before she realized what she was about, Pamela held up a pale sea-green confection that fell barely below her knees. She made two discoveries: the dowager's slim figure was very much like her own, and, horror of horrors, the silk night-rail was alarmingly transparent. She gaped at her reflection in the mirror, unable to avoid wondering how one could possibly appear before a gentleman dressed—or rather undressed—in such wanton garments.

"Very, *very* nice, indeed, my dear," a voice behind her murmured admiringly, causing Pamela to jump guiltily.

She whirled to find Lord Geoffrey standing in the doorway, eyeing her with no little amusement. Mortified at the spectacle she had made of herself, she felt a deep blush mantle her cheeks.

"Oh, I did not hear you come in," she muttered, stuffing the offending garment into the drawer willy-nilly. "I need to change your mother's shift, but I do not think that one is suitable."

"No, you are quite right," Geoffrey agreed, as if they were discussing something quite innocuous. "Not for a sickbed, at all events," he added, and Pamela could not mistake the humorous innuendo in his voice.

Flustered beyond anything she had ever experienced, Pamela closed the drawer with more force than necessary. "Your brother has this moment gone down to an early breakfast," she said, keeping her eyes firmly on the cloth she dipped in the lavender water.

"And you are wishing me out of your way, too, I suppose," Geoffrey drawled, amusement still in his voice. "But I have come expressly to visit Mama, and to see for myself that she is getting the proper care."

"You may rest easy on that head," Pamela replied sharply, tired of having her sickroom skills questioned. "And you must take second place behind his lordship, who has already hinted once this morning that my knowledge of patient care is inadequate. I understand that he intends to send for Nurse Williams, who is, it appears, the acknowledged expert."

Geoffrey, who had thrown himself into the chair by the dowager's bedside, grinned up at Pamela. "Predictable, my dear girl," he said. "I am only surprised he did not do so last night. Do not fret yourself into a lather over Robert's starts, Pamela. He invariably reacts like a dashed nodcock whenever any of us gets sick.

Particularly Mama." He paused, as if about to say something else. "But you will like Nanna. She was Robert's wet-nurse; mine, too, when I came along. Between them, she and Mama rescued the whole Stilton clan from extinction."

Pamela wrung out the cloth and applied it to her patient's forehead. "I shall try not to regard his lordship's starts, as you call them," she murmured. "But he appeared so . . . well, actually *frightened* when he was here earlier. Of course, a fever should never be taken lightly, but more often than not, it will run its course—"

"Oh, Robert is frightened, all right," Geoffrey broke in. "You see, for me life was so much simpler as a child. Sophy is the only mother I ever knew. I remember nothing of that awful scandal that Robert lived through. All I know is hearsay and rumor; but Robert lived it, breathed it, failed to understand it in his child's mind, and it scarred him. You saw how he reacted to the Lady Blandford affair. And when it dawned on him that his own wife was a devotee of Wollstonecraft's radical notions, he turned quite blue."

"Not a devotee, exactly," Pamela corrected him. "But I do like to be abreast of new ideas. There are so many things that might be done to improve the lot of women, but I lack the courage—"

"What a plumper!" Geoffrey exclaimed. He took the dowager's hand in his, and his smile faded. "She is so hot," he said, and Pamela caught a hint of the same fear in his voice she had heard earlier in his brother's.

How gratifying, she thought enviously, to be treasured by one's family as Lady Sophy obviously was. Perhaps, one day, if she ever had a family of her own. The thought was a novel one, and it slid unheralded into her mind like an elusive echo of a dream.

The marquess lost count of the days and nights that followed the precipitous arrival of Nurse Williams at Holly Lodge. The house seemed to be in a perpetual turmoil, but at the center of it, deftly holding back the chaos that threatened to engulf them all, he was conscious of the unobtrusive presence of his wife.

By some miraculous combination of patience and quiet authority, Lady Pamela managed to see meals always served on time, the servants steadfast in their appointed tasks, the younger boys out from underfoot, supplies delivered regularly from Osmington, and the sickroom in a state of relative peace and quiet. Perhaps of more significance, a volatile Lay Letitia had been prevailed upon to desist from shedding hysterical tears all over her mother's still form every time she ventured into the dowager's chamber, and assume the responsibility of changing the flowers in the downstairs rooms. Aunt Honoria had been delegated to assist Mrs. Firth in planning daily menus and ordering the crates of supplies, while Lady Constance took regular turns at sitting by her mother's bedside whenever needed.

Everything, as far as Robert could see, was under control. Gradually, he ceased to worry about the rest of the household and concentrated upon attending the patient's bedside. He found it difficult to tear himself away from the slim figure under the covers. The dowager appeared to his distraught imagination to be slipping away before his eyes, growing more and more indistinct beneath the frilly pink eiderdown.

And the nightmares had returned.

He dared not lie down to rest on his own bed in the adjoining chamber, for invariably he would slip back into that desperate world of his childhood. His mother's perfume reached out from the dark past to envelop him in its seductive aroma. Her beautiful face, ravaged by a force she no longer had the will to resist, looked lost and defeated in the massive four-poster that had seen a steady stream of Stiltons burst noisily upon the world.

With the unhappy Lady Pamela the noisy babies had stilled. Robert had been the last noisy Stilton to make his voice heard in that ancestral chamber. The latest Stilton—his baby brother Geoffrey—had been unnaturally silent, and he knew the servants whispered that Death had already set his mark on the marchioness. Perhaps on the new babe as well.

A wave of anguish jerked him upright. He was sitting by the dowager's bedside, but this had not kept the demons at bay. He must have closed his eyes for a moment, Robert thought, and that had been enough to drag him back into the past.

The patient moved restlessly, and instantly his wife appeared beside her, hands gently raising the damp face for a sip of the potion left by the doctor on his latest visit. The dowager moaned fretfully, and Lady Pamela murmured something he could not catch. The patient relaxed and settled back into the pillow with a small sigh.

His heart clamped in his chest at the sound, and he glanced up at his wife. He noticed for the first time that her face showed signs of exhaustion, but her movements were sure as she deftly bathed the dowager's face and arms with cool water. Her hands were small and beautifully shaped; a musician's hands, he remembered.

He moved restlessly in the chair, and Pamela glanced at him. "It is almost dawn, my lord," she said softly, "I am sure that Firth is ready to serve your breakfast whenever you wish." She paused, and a slight smile lightened her face. "You have been up all night."

"I cannot sleep," he answered gruffly. "And what about you? When was the last time you rested?"

She appeared surprised at his question, and it hit Robert forcibly that he had taken his wife's attendance on the dowager very much for granted. He had depended on her without being aware of it. They all had.

"You may not be able to sleep, my lord, but you must eat. I shall instruct Firth to prepare your breakfast."

"And what about you?" he insisted, aware that this female was managing him again. Oddly, he did not mind enough to protest.

"Firth will bring my tea up in a moment, and Dr. Henderson will be here at six. He will wish to hear the latest developments in her ladyship's case."

Suddenly apprehensive, Robert stood up abruptly. "Has something happened I am not aware of?" he growled, scanning the dowager's wan face for the dreaded signs he feared to acknowledge even to himself.

"She is not going to . . . to d-die, is she?"

He wished the words unsaid instantly, but he had to know. He had to prepare himself, as no one had prepared him all those years ago, for a loss that had shattered a small boy's world.

Pamela turned from the bellpull, which she had just rung. Her expression was unreadable, and Robert felt his panic rise. How could a mere female give him the answers he wanted? Needed so desperately?

"I see no reason for undue alarm," she replied with her usual calm.

The marquess felt his fear explode within him. "You sound like that bloody sawbones," he cried, frustrated at the terror of not knowing. "Give me a straight answer, damn you!"

After a slight pause she spoke in a tired voice. "I have had considerable experience with sickness and . . . and death, my lord. I was at my mother's bedside when she died, and there was a moment—and I know you will find this hard to believe—when I felt her let go of her will to live. She died the next morning, but it was at that moment I knew I had lost her. She had fought so hard— mostly for my sake, I know that now—but the fight was desperately unfair. Mama had scarlet fever, you know. It killed twenty-five tenants and villagers." She assayed a small smile. "I have no such feeling here, my lord."

"Are you suggesting she is still fighting? She looks so heart-breakingly fragile."

Her smile quirked up at the corners. "Very definitely so, my lord. But disabuse yourself; Lady Sophia is not fragile. There will be no giving up for her. Unless, of course," she added, and Robert thought he caught a hint of mockery in her voice, "her ladyship were to regain her health only to discover that you have starved yourself to a shadow."

Minutes later—he could not recall how he had allowed himself to be dictated to once again by this unprepossessing female—the marquess found himself descending the stairs to the breakfast room, his thoughts focused on the business of replenishing his energies for what lay ahead, instead of on the darkness of the past.

CHAPTER SEVENTEEN

Virgin Bride

That final day of the dowager's indisposition weighed heavily on the marquess; but he was midway through the tedious afternoon before he recognized the cause of his increased anxiety. A small, unconscious sigh from the unflagging figure by the dowager's bedside opened his eyes to the astonishing fact that there were two females here whose well-being was of paramount importance to him.

"You *must* rest, milady," he heard Nurse Williams whisper to Lady Pamela shortly after Firth had brought up a tray with a cold nuncheon, of which his wife had eaten barely enough for a bird. "And I insist you eat another slice of Cook's excellent chicken. You are worn to a frazzle, my girl, and we cannot have you falling sick at a time like this. Your ladyship heard what Dr. Henderson said not an hour ago. You are not Wellington holding back the Frenchies at Waterloo." This stricture was accompanied by one of those disapproving snorts Robert remembered so well from his childhood. One did not argue with Nurse's snorts, and he glanced at Pamela to see if she was as cowed as he had always been as a boy by the old nurse's plain speaking.

Oddly, his wife was smiling, not cringing. But her mouth drooped, and her eyes had dark circles round them. Her rich chestnut hair was coming undone from the severe chignon she wore during the day, and two large smudges of green stained her sleeve, signs of the dowager's vigorous resistance to being physicked earlier that afternoon.

The notion that Lady Pamela's health might be at risk caused a tremor of alarm to snake its way past his bone-weariness into his lethargic brain. He tried to focus on the dowager, who was—he reminded himself sternly—the true cause of his anxiety, but his eyes remained on his wife's pale face. She appeared about ready to drop from exhaustion. What would happen to all of them if she did? he wondered. The prospect was alarming enough to shake him into action.

"I agree with Nurse," he said. "You are fagged to death, my lady. Go and lie down for an hour or two. I am sure that between them, Nurse and Hinds can watch over the patient."

"Oh, yes, indeed, my lord," Nurse hastened to agree. "That is precisely what I have been begging her ladyship to do. But she is as stubborn as our dear Lady Sophy, let me tell you." She gave another expressive snort to emphasize her disapproval.

Lady Pamela merely gave him a small smile.

Robert was struck by the sweetness of it. Females rarely smiled at him just so. He was far more accustomed to flirtatious smiles, those that tantalized, made seductive promises, raised expectations that were rarely met. His wife's smile was guileless, unconscious of its own untainted charm. It hinted at that paralyzing, hypocritical innocence he had avoided all his life. He had ceased believing in female innocence as the inescapable proof of his own mother's perversity unfolded before his child's eyes. His avoidance of innocence was recorded in White's Betting Book for all the world to see. He had paid off that wager months ago, of course, not because he had suddenly recovered his faith in female morality, but because none of his acquaintances could be expected to believe that he had lived up to his boast of avoiding virgins.

He was married to one. That was abundantly clear in the smile she was giving him from across the bed. Had Geoffrey been right about virgin brides? he wondered idly. Was there truly something special about them that he had yet to discover? Traditionally, men had insisted upon untouched brides, and although the practice had always struck Robert as verging on barbarism, he recognized the need to assure legitimate heirs to the great families of the realm. Although judging from his own family, he thought bitterly, legitimacy was a myth pursued by men vain enough to believe in innocence.

"When was the last time you took Scamp for a walk?" he asked abruptly, uneasy at the direction his thoughts were taking. "You are too pale for my liking. A tramp along the cliffs will set that aright."

Her smile flickered again. "I have delegated young William for that task," she murmured. "Poor old Scamp has had his legs walked off every morning. But today it is raining, my lord," she added, and Robert detected that subtle hint of mockery he had heard before.

"Raining?" He had paid so little attention to the world outside the dowager's room, that the news surprised him. He stood up and went to the window. The sky was overcast, and dark clouds scudded across the horizon in menacing formations. The weather appeared unchanged from the disastrous afternoon when they had all been caught on the beach by the storm. The day the dowager had been taken ill. He wondered if there was any sinister significance to the absence of sunshine.

After dinner that evening, where his presence was required to maintain a semblance of order among his noisy siblings, it became apparent that Lady Pamela was not about to heed his orders to spend at least part of the night in her own bed. Bowing to what he had begun to recognize as an impregnable trait in his wife's quiet demeanor, Robert gave up and retired to his own chamber.

He had not expected to sleep, but eventually he must have dozed off in his chair, for the next thing Robert knew someone was tugging urgently at his sleeve and calling his name.

Instantly awake, he jumped to his feet. His wife stood beside his chair, and in the candle-lit chamber her face appeared pale and drawn. Panic coiled in his stomach and rocketed up to his chest until he could not breathe. He reached out and grasped her shoulders roughly with both hands.

"She is worse?" he croaked, his voice unrecognizable.

Lady Pamela smiled, and the marquess felt his fear recede.

"She is better," his wife said simply, her smile glowing with suppressed joy. "Dr. Henderson has just pronounced her ladyship out of danger."

Before Robert knew what he was doing, his arms encompassed her, and he found himself clutching his wife to his chest as though he would never let her go. "Thank the Lord," he muttered into the curve of her neck. "And thank *you,* Pamela," he added impulsively. "I cannot imagine what we would have done without you."

He heard himself sob, a great gulp of pent-up emotions he had never expected to feel again after his mother's funeral. And then the hot tears were running, silent and uncontrollable, down his cheeks. He cringed at this unprecedented display of mawkishness, and would have flung away in disgust had not a cool hand on his wet cheek stilled him, holding him in her embrace.

"There is no shame in weeping for those we love, Robert," his wife said in that quiet voice that seemed to possess the power to soothe him. She pulled a serviceable square of plain linen from her sleeve and mopped his face. "Lady Sophy is conscious again, and asking for you, my lord."

The marquess felt a sense of loss as Pamela retreated behind the formality of his title. There had been so much unexpected sweetness in hearing his given name on her lips.

"Go," his wife urged gently, "she is waiting for you."

On impulse, Robert grasped his wife's hand and pulled her towards the connecting door.

"Come with me, my dear," he murmured, "she will want to see us together."

From the depth of her subconscious Pamela felt herself being watched.

It was not a threatening sensation, and she had no trouble ignoring it and allowing her exhausted mind and body to sink back into the ecstasy of oblivion that promised blessed relief from the tensions of the past few days. Something else nagged at her intermittently, however, and impressed itself upon her drugged consciousness with annoying persistence.

Gradually, the nagging became so insistent that Pamela knew she must discover its source or she would never rest. Reluctantly, she moved under the bedclothes and discovered that she lay within a soft, warm nest that held no resemblance at all to the Spartan bed she was accustomed to. This was luxury in the ultimate degree, and a sigh of pure pleasure escaped her. She was safe, and warm, and happy. What else mattered at that moment?

But there was a threat here somewhere, if only she could put a name to it. Part of her mind wanted to ignore it and sink back into the enveloping haze of unconsciousness. The other part . . . Impatiently, she snuggled her head around on the pillow, seeking escape. But the sensation of being observed became stronger, accompanied by a scent she did not recognize.

And then something tickled her nose.

Gingerly, she raised her hand to brush whatever it was away, but her fingers encountered what could only be . . . As the reality of it seeped in, Pamela jolted awake, her body rigid, eyes flickering open. She knew exactly where she was, although she remembered nothing of getting there.

She was in her husband's bed—her nose against his chest, his *bare* chest.

The novelty of the situation took a moment to assert itself, because Pamela tried to convince herself she was dreaming again. But the warmth of his skin was too real, and the look in his eyes was nothing like the lascivious, lustful glances she had imagined de rigueur in such intimate encounters.

His eyes held a faintly amused expression, which disconcerted her.

"Where am I?" she heard herself murmur inanely.

He smiled. "I think you know where you are, Pamela."

"I do not remember . . . a-anything," she began, furiously scrambling for the correct way to ask one's husband whether whatever was supposed to happen in his bed had actually happened.

"That should not surprise you; you fell asleep in your chair. Our very much recovered patient insisted that I put you to bed. Mine happened to be the nearest bed, so here you are."

He had answered none of her questions, but Pamela consoled herself; he did not have the air of a gentleman satiated with pleasures of the flesh. Actually, now that she examined him more closely, the marquess looked particularly youthful and vulnerable. And unexpectedly handsome, she saw with surprise. With his sleepy eyes smiling at her, black hair tousled about his ears, and the hard angles of his face softened in the candlelight, her husband came close to being what Pamela imagined must be every young girl's dream.

Naturally, this was an illusion, she reminded herself prosaically. She was no young girl; the marquess was not—never had been, she was certain—a romantic lover of the sort that populated novels from the Minerva Press. Such gentlemen tended to be—at least in the novels she had read—rather cloying, and no doubt would be underfoot all the time just when she needed to decide whether to serve braised duck or chicken fricassée at a particularly important dinner party.

It was a relief to know that she had a husband who would not meddle in her household decisions, or insist upon retiring in the middle of the afternoon—as she had heard some amorous husbands did—to indulge their animal passions on wives who had important culinary decisions to make. This train of thought carried her inevitably to the conclusion that while she was idling here in bed, the dowager might be in need of her services.

She pushed herself into a sitting position. "I am neglecting my duties, my lord," she murmured. "I must see to her ladyship's change of linen and send down instructions for a more sustaining breakfast than gruel and dry toast."

His eyes gleamed with laughter. "It is but two of the clock, my dear," he drawled. "Your patient was sleeping soundly when I left her a bare twenty minutes ago. And Nurse is sitting with her." He paused, then added in an entirely different voice, "But I agree that perhaps you are neglecting your other duties, Pamela." His gaze dropped suggestively, and Pamela suddenly understood the huskiness in his voice. She no longer wore her serviceable gown. Someone had removed it; and in its place she was robed in a soft satin night-rail that rested like thistledown against her skin.

Far more shocking, however, was the inescapable realization that she could see her breasts clearly through the diaphanous material.

So, most certainly, could his lordship.

For a paralyzing second Pamela watched her husband's expression fearfully. Would he change into a ravishing maniac as rumors would have it gentlemen did at times like these? Or would he . . . ?

"Oh, dear." She grasped frantically at the covers, but they appeared to be in a tangle and did not respond to her tugging. She distinctly heard the marquess chuckle and shot him a glance from under her lashes. He appeared to be enjoying himself.

"I do wish you would not regard me as though I were some leathery leviathan about to pounce on poor Andromeda, my dear Pamela," he murmured.

Pamela was startled enough to cease struggling with the covers and cross her arms over her breasts. How did he know she had once considered him a dragon of sorts? she wondered.

"I consider you no such thing, my lord. How very absurd you are."

"And my name is Robert," he said gently. "I am your husband, Pamela, and it is quite fashionable nowadays to use my first name when we are together in bed."

The audacity of this pronouncement took her breath away, though upon further reflection, she could not deny that he was her husband, and that they *were* in bed together. There was something else, however, that was not clear at all.

"This is not mine," she said, gesturing at the scanty satin that made little or no pretense at covering her. "Where did you find it?"

He grinned. "I did not find it anywhere, you silly minx. Our ingenious Sophy, who is, I suspect, playing Cupid, told Nurse to select one of her very own garments." He paused, then added in a carefully neutral voice, "Geoffrey suggested the green."

"Your brother?" Pamela gasped, discovering she could still be shocked. "Whatever has Geoffrey to do with any of this?"

"An interesting question, I must confess," the marquess murmured, and Pamela felt her heart grow still. "One I had hopes you would resolve for me."

Pamela stared at the marquess, forgetting her embarrassment. He was no longer smiling. "I was about to change the dowager's linens and happened to pick up the green silk. It was so very beautiful, I could not resist . . . that is to say, I—"

"You wished to try it on, no doubt?"

She gasped at the implication of what was obviously on his mind. "I did no such thing, of course," she said forcefully. "Geoffrey happened to come into the room while I was holding it. That is all."

"I know," he admitted, his smile returning. "The wretch had the gall to tell me. I shall tear him limb from limb if he does not show my wife a little more respect."

Vivid pictures of the debacle in the parlor at the Two-Headed Boar in Purley flashed through her mind, and she shuddered. The threat held a core of truth to it, although she doubted Geoffrey would make such an easy opponent as poor Sir Rodney. "You are being absurd again, my lord," she said.

"Robert," he reminded her.

"When I am cross with you, I reserve the right to call you—" She stopped abruptly when he put up a hand in protest.

"I do believe we are having our first marital squabble," he remarked, but Pamela knew from the gleam in his eyes that he was teasing.

"Oh, no, my lord," she argued. "I recall several previous occasions when you have come to cuffs with me. If I remember aright, you were none too pleased—"

"I am speaking of after that snivelling curate tied the knot in Purley, my dear. Have we quarreled since then?"

She thought for a moment. "I do recall you objected most strenuously to my ordering shepherd's pie at that little inn at Fareham. You said it was probably made with cat instead of rabbit."

"But you ate it anyway if I remember rightly."

"Yes. Mr. Hampton did, too. It was definitely rabbit."

"Then it was hardly a quarrel." He paused, and his smile became rather more sensuous than Pamela cared for. "On the other hand, you cannot deny that I have yet to kiss you."

She blinked. If there was one incident that remained firmly rooted in her memory, it was that kiss he had given her in the seaside cottage. How could he possibly have forgotten so momentous an encounter?

"You are mistaken again, my lord," she retorted before she lost her nerve. "You most certainly did, and I was never so mortified in my life." She felt the heat rise again to her cheeks as the insidious details of that clandestine embrace came back to her. "You behaved in a highly improper and scandalous manner."

A deep chuckle rumbled in the bare chest sprawled among the covers beside her, and Pamela had the distinct impression that the marquess found her indignation amusing.

"I am delighted to hear I made such a favorable impression upon you, my dear," he drawled.

Pamela glared at him, reluctant to believe her ears. "I beg to differ, my lord," she protested stiffly. "You made an abominable impression upon me." She hoped that she would be forgiven this small untruth, which was no less than any respectable female would use to preserve her dignity.

"That is odd," he murmured, his voice amused. "I seem to remember something quite different." The warmth in his eyes told her all too plainly that he remembered as well as she did the incident at the cottage.

"You must be thinking of someone else, my lord," she said primly, glad to have escaped so lightly. "Now, if you will excuse me, I think I should look in on the dowager—"

"And I think we have more important matters to settle between us, my dear wife." He spoke softly, but Pamela felt her heart flutter wildly. The way he called her *wife,* sounded both faintly ominous and deliciously caressing. She wanted to hide, but another tug on the covers did not work, so she slid down beneath them, relieved to be able to escape the heat of his interested gaze.

She closed her eyes and drew a deep breath. If she willed it hard enough, would this disturbing man disappear? Would she wake up in her own narrow bed with the memory of this interlude lingering in her mind like an impossible dream. But then again, did she really want to throw away this wondrous moment? The answer was suddenly so obvious that she smiled at her own foolish fears.

She opened her eyes and smiled shyly up at him.

The featherlike touch of his fingers on her cheek banished all thoughts of making the marquess disappear. And when she felt them trail sensuously down her neck, slip under the covers, and curl around her breast, Pamela knew, beyond a shadow of a doubt, that she longed to jump off this particular cliff.

The marquess had been the object of many a seductive, inviting, flirtatious smile. The smile his wife gave him that night in the privacy of his own bed, where no *amourette* of his—no matter how charming and accomplished a lover—had ever been allowed to trespass, was none of these things. Robert could not quite put a name to it, but it enveloped him with a magic all its own.

He touched her cheek, then slid his hand under the covers to cup her breast. The firmness of it surprised him. Why had he not noticed before now that his wife's slender figure held a promise of voluptuousness he had never suspected, never associated with this insignificant female he had been obliged to take to wife?

She was a continual surprise to him.

Since the dowager had taken to her bed, Lady Pamela had stepped quietly and unobtrusively into the very hub of the household. She had become, without fanfare or unseemly display, the staff upon which they had all leaned in the past week of uncertainty. He himself had taken her entirely for granted without considering that the management of so large an establishment might be intimidating to a new bride. The dowager had pointed that out to him last night during the quiet hour they had spent together while his wife slept.

"You have the luck of Old Nick, Robbie, I swear you do," she murmured, her voice still showing signs of weakness. When he had raised his brow inquiringly, she laughed with some of her old spirit. "I am speaking of Pamela, you oaf. She is the only female I know who is likely to put up with your overbearing ways."

"Overbearing? Me?" He grinned foolishly, more relieved than he cared to admit to hear her teasing him again. "As a matter of fact, my dear lady, I have a long list of females vying for the privilege of putting up with me and my ways."

The dowager's smile faded, and Robert could have sworn a flash of alarm flickered in her blue eyes.

"I trust we are talking in the past tense here, Robert," she said, so softly he had to lean forward to catch her words. "I know it is not my place to tell you how to run your life—"

"I do not recall that ever stopped you before, my love," the marquess cut in brusquely, uncomfortably aware of the lump in his throat. "You may tell me anything you wish, Sophy, and well you know it." He paused briefly, then added with a rare show of emotion, "You are the only one who may."

Impulsively, the dowager reached out to him. Robert clasped her hand, pressing it to his lips as if he needed to reassure himself that all was right again in his world.

And now, as he looked down into his wife's hazel eyes, Robert understood what his darling Sophy had meant. Yes, he was indeed lucky. And yes, his world was stable again, and not solely because the dowager was restored to him, hale and hearty.

The unconditional surrender in his wife's wide gaze offered another source of comfort and support he rarely if ever admitted to needing. With an odd feeling of vulnerability, Robert admitted that he needed it now. Yet he also feared this intimacy with a female he had sworn never to touch. What if Pamela were to entangle him in a quagmire of emotion as his father had been entangled?

All his life Robert had ruthlessly avoided the weakness that had, in his eyes, ruined his father: intemperate love of a beautiful, willful woman. He had known many women, perhaps too many of them, but he had loved none. His heart was safe. It would be safe with Pamela, he reassured himself. One lost one's heart to beautiful women who had the power to destroy, to betray, to make men suffer as his father had suffered.

Pamela was not beautiful, he reasoned; his heart was safe.

But she was unquestionably sweet, desirable, and his for the taking.

He bent and brushed her lips with his. There was no longer any doubt in his mind that he would consummate the bond between them, and the soft sigh that greeted his first kiss told him that his wife would welcome him.

Robert felt himself stir at the thought. He deepened his kiss, inordinately pleased when Pamela responded instinctively to his questing tongue. He let his hand wander lazily over her body, murmuring soothingly at her startled reaction to his intimate invasion, until there was no part of her he did not know.

He had expected awkwardness, perhaps dreaded it; but there was none. When they came together, she was breathless and eager, and Robert discovered that broaching his virgin bride was an experience he would remember with rare affection. Above all, her surprised gasp of pleasure delighted him, and it gradually dawned upon him, as he lay listening to his wife fall asleep in his arms, that he had embarked on a new stage of his life.

Could he look forward to the reefs of betrayal that had destroyed his father's marriage? Or could he trust Pamela—in spite of her radical defense of Lady Blandford's wayward behavior—to cleave to him only, forsaking all others?

This surge of possessiveness—a weakness he had seen destroy his father's happiness—alarmed him. Had he unwittingly stepped into the same trap as his father?

Long after Pamela's deep breathing told him she slept, Robert lay awake with that old fear gnawing at his heart.

CHAPTER EIGHTEEN

Unexpected Visitor

The sea breeze was gentle against her face. Pamela stood on the cliff, watching the rising sun move up into the cloudless sky like a soft yellow egg on one of her mother's blue Staffordshire plates.

The memory of her mother had been with her ever since she slipped out of her husband's bed before dawn, praying that he would not wake, wishing her mother had lived to share this moment with her daughter.

There were so many things she did not understand about gentlemen, about this gentleman in particular. Perhaps her mother might have been able to explain why the aloof, often overbearing marquess had changed—quite as though fairy-dust had been sprinkled on his dark head—into a man she could truly like. Almost find it in her heart to love, she added with a wry smile, were it not so obvious that he wanted nothing to do with tenderer emotions.

She must remember not to fall in love with him.

After last night it might be all too easy to let herself believe that he cared for her. She felt her cheeks growing hot at the memory of his smile; his hands gently exploring her body, shocking her with intimacies she had never imagined possible; his eyes, full of a tenderness she had never seen in any man's before. Not even in Sir Rodney's.

Especially not in Sir Rodney's, she amended with a grimace. The notion of sharing such intimacies with her childhood admirer—a man she had literally bribed to save her from the marquess—gave Pamela chills. How foolish she had been, she thought, giving silent thanks for odious, autocratic gentlemen who thought nothing of trampling anyone underfoot who stood in the way of duty and honor.

Because that had been the crux of the matter, Pamela reminded herself. The marquess had done his duty to preserve her honor. And foolishly, she had given him a monstrous amount of unnecessary mortification, when she should have known he would prevail. He had prevailed because he knew he was right. Pamela had known it, too, deep in her heart.

Their world was so unforgiving of those who dared to overstep the boundaries of propriety and good taste. The marquess had overstepped that invisible line that afternoon at the seaside cottage. Oh, yes, indeed, she recalled with a shudder of pleasure, he had definitely done so. And so had she, Pamela suddenly saw with new clarity. He might have escaped unscathed, but in the eyes of the *beau monde* she had sinned by driving about alone in an open gig. Her advanced age would not have saved her from the censure of society. Her father's rank and fortune would not have saved her. Even a run-away marriage to Sir Rodney would not have saved her from vicious tongues.

Only the Marquess of Monroyal could have saved her.

She was infinitely glad that he had done so.

Pamela took a deep breath of sea air and let it out slowly, savoring its salty tang. Things had fallen into place; harmony had been restored, the *ton*'s sense of propriety appeased because *Robert*—she whispered the name into the breeze—had done his duty by her. He had made no secret that it was a distasteful duty; but he had not hesitated. Indeed, he had been most odious about the whole affair.

She should love him for that act alone.

But, of course, she must remember not to do so. He would be most uncomfortable if he knew his inconvenient wife entertained such maudlin thoughts.

A protesting whine distracted her, and she glanced down at Scamp, sitting patiently beside her. The old dog had been overjoyed to resume their morning rambles, and Pamela suspected that—much as he loved the boys—his ancient bones had been hard put to keep up with them.

"Time to go home, is it, Scamp?"

The answering yelp was definitely a yes, reinforced by a vigorous tail-thumping.

"Come along, then," she said, turning back towards the house. "I have a suspicion that the recovery of our patient will throw the whole household into another uproar." One that, she added to herself, might perhaps allow her to avoid coming face-to-face with her new husband.

Pamela was only partially successful in her endeavor to play least-in-sight. Her very first visit to the sickroom reminded her that the dowager—weak as she was after days of fever—had very sharp eyes, indeed. She had no difficulty at all in reading the significance of Pamela's covert glance at the adjoining door into the master's suite.

"Robert is still abed, dear," she remarked archly, as though Pamela had asked the question aloud. "I cannot imagine what you did to him last night, my dear"—although she plainly had a very good notion—"but the poor lamb is sleeping like a baby. I have given orders for him not to be disturbed on any account."

Pamela felt her face flame at this blunt reminder of what had happened last night in her husband's bed.

The empty dishes on the dowager's breakfast tray, evidence of her return to health, rattled as Pamela removed it from the bed to the table by the door. No appropriately modest response leapt to mind, so she fussed with the array of vials, powers, and bottles of green tonic on the dresser.

"That was very wicked of me, I know," the dowager confessed instantly, "but please, please forgive a shameless old busybody who cares very much for both of you. Admit that you would not have told me had I asked."

Pamela could not resist the cajoling tone and turned to see if she had heard aright. She had to smile at the gleam of devilry in the dowager's blue eyes. The lady was evidently back in fine fettle.

"I admit I have been very cross with Robert," the dowager continued, quite as though they were discussing inconsequential matters, "he can be so pigheaded and obnoxious, that one tends to forget that he is so often right. Not always, of course," she added hastily at Pamela's startled glance, "and we must not let him think he can always have his own way. But in general, my dear, we may trust him to do what is right for all of us."

"My sentiments exactly, my lady," Pamela admitted. Had she not come to the very same conclusion this morning at the cliff top? "I only wish I had been wise enough to recognize it sooner." She paused, amazed at her new understanding of herself. "Running off with Sir Rodney was not the solution to anything. On the contrary, I see now it inconvenienced his lordship beyond bearing. No wonder he lost his temper with the poor man."

The dowager laughed aloud at that. "Do not repine on it, love. If I know my Robert, he thoroughly enjoyed knocking Sir Rodney's teeth down his throat for him."

"I do not think it was as bad as that," Pamela protested, "but come to think on it, I believe you are right. His lordship did look rather pleased with himself. And paid for all the damages without a whimper, too."

"Which only goes to show," the dowager remarked with a certain amount of satisfaction, "what overgrown boys gentlemen really are. How lucky for them that we love them anyway."

Pamela found herself in total agreement with this sage remark.

Later that afternoon, still intent on keeping out of her husband's way, Pamela went out to the herb garden, trailed by Scamp. The dog appeared thoroughly fatigued by the noisy traffic up and down the stairs to visit the dowager, whose chamber doors now stood wide open, inviting all and sundry to enter at will.

She was joined a few minutes later by Lady Honoria, whose plump cheeks, Pamela noticed, appeared unnaturally rosy.

"Ah, there you are, dear," she gasped breathlessly, as though she had just run upstairs and down again without pausing. "And you, too, Scamp, my lad," she added, addressing the dog who lay sprawled under a flowering sage bush out of the sun. "Where is your bonnet, Pamela?" she demanded, absentmindedly. "You will be burned to a crisp, dear, and you know gentlemen cannot abide *brown* females."

Pamela realized instantly that her ladyship was severely rattled, and straightened from plucking sprigs of mint for a tea the dowager was particularly fond of. What could have caused this agitation in the usually unflappable lady? she wondered, mildly amused.

"Oh, Pamela," Lady Honoria gasped, fanning her warm cheeks with a scrap of lace. "You will never guess who is here to see you."

Pamela sighed. "I do trust it is not the Misses Jenkins come to wish our patient a speedy recovery yet again. I vow I cannot bear to hear another of their dead relative stories this afternoon. And I simply refuse to have that incontinent old pug of theirs in my drawing room."

"Oh, no," Lady Honoria broke in hastily. "It is not those old Tabbies, my dear."

"Then who?" Pamela racked her brain, but could come up with no one likely to seek her out.

"Oh, someone much closer, my love." The old lady sounded positively delirious.

"Closer?" Surely, not Sir Rodney? No, that was ridiculous. Her Cousin Freddy, perhaps? That was not likely, unless he had got himself into another Bumble-broth. She sincerely hoped that was not the case.

"Your father, dear," Lady Honoria exclaimed, evidently unable to bear the suspense any longer. "Lord Melrose is arrived and demanding to see you." When Pamela made no response, stunned by the news, Lady Honoria rattled on. "If you wish, my dear, I can entertain his lordship while you inform Robert of his arrival."

Pamela gaped at the incongruity and unexpectedness of this suggestion. "You know my father, madam?"

Lady Honoria blushed, adding to Pamela's confusion. "Yes, his lordship and I are old friends. In a m-manner of speaking. Of c-course, I have not laid eyes on him in a number of years. For obvious reasons," she added, lowering her eyes. This coyness was so unlike the elder lady's normal demeanor that Pamela heard warning bells in her head.

What fresh calamity lay in store for her? she wondered. And why would her father, of all people, choose to invade a Stilton stronghold when the master was in residence? Such blatant disregard for life and limb had not been his hallmark in the past, she remembered from what little gossip she had heard of her father's illicit connections with the Stiltons.

She instantly reproached herself for this uncharitable thought.

There would be time enough later to get to the bottom of this mystery. At the moment she needed time to collect herself; to decide if she still harbored too much resentment against her father to receive him civilly; to inform the marquess of this extraordinary arrival, and to beg him, either to send the caller to the rightabout, or to receive him.

And if they received him, how much of the past would he bring with him? she wondered. How much would her husband be willing to hear?

"Oh, what a coil," Pamela whispered the words aloud as she gazed at the garden door closing behind Lady Honoria. There had been an unmistakable eagerness about the elder lady's abrupt departure to, as she put it, entertain his lordship until his daughter made herself presentable. Entirely too much eagerness, she mused.

Pamela glanced down at her simple green jaconet muslin morning gown. As far as she could determine, she *was* presentable. She had chosen the gown deliberately; it was one of her newer purchases, and it appealed to her sense of propriety with sleeves tightly buttoned at the wrists and hem modestly embellished with an embroidered flounce. It had the added advantage of setting off her chestnut hair.

It suddenly occurred to her that dear Aunt Honoria had probably not noticed the new gown at all.

"Well, Scamp," she said, addressing the spaniel lolling under the sage bush and fighting to keep her nerves at bay, "his lordship is not going to like hearing that his father's archenemy has come calling at his castle. He will want to fight this old battle all over again." She paused, her heart racing at the prospect of an ugly encounter between the two most important men in her life.

For there was no denying it, she admitted. Her father's sudden arrival had brought home to Pamela most forcefully the truth she had been hiding from herself: she had missed her father dearly. For all his faults—and she had to admit he had many—Lord Melrose was and always had been a central force in her life.

With new insight Pamela realized that her father had—in his own way, and perhaps with less than charitable motives—done for his daughter exactly what the marquess had achieved. He had saved her from her own folly. Any lady less given to radical notions of Mrs. Wollstonecraft's stamp would have recognized this long ago. In Lord Melrose's eyes, and in the eyes of polite society, Lady Pamela Hancock—with no beauty to recommend her and enough years on her plate to place her firmly at her last prayers—had achieved the match of the century.

The thought made her smile. One night of love in her husband's arms—no, not *love,* she amended hastily, she must remember that it was only marital duty—had turned her thoughts from radical theories to practical matters that affected her directly.

That the union had been forced upon them did not seem to matter any longer. It was done; society was appeased; she was saved from disgrace. She clung to this irrefutable fact. And after last night, Pamela knew she would not have it any other way.

Marriage might well be a pit of slavery for many unfortunate females; men made laws for their own convenience—her mother had always said—but her own case was not so desperate. Her husband had turned from monster into lover—surely, she might call him thus in private—and her father was here to see her.

Perhaps he had missed her, too.

Her path was suddenly clear to her. She shook off her lethargy and followed Lady Honoria into the house.

"No," the marquess repeated firmly. "I shall drive Pamela home in that poor excuse for a curricle of yours. I wish to show her the approach to the Grange from an open carriage. You shall ride Perseus back for me. But I warn you, Geoffrey, if that horse comes to any harm, I shall have your hide."

"One of Hampton's stock, is he?"

"Yes, and a prime goer, as Willy promised he would be. You would do well to order one of Hampton's for yourself if you wish to make a showing at Melton Mobrey in November."

His brother, sprawled as was his wont in an easy chair, grunted. "Rather beyond my means, old chap. Besides, if I had a thousand pounds to throw away on a horse, I would rather spend it on the *Seagull.* She needs a new rudder."

Robert regarded his brother speculatively. With difficulty he restrained his urge to offer to pay for both horse and rudder. But he knew better. Unlike many younger sons, Geoffrey was fiercely independent, making do with a small inheritance from their mother, supplemented—Robert had heard from reliable sources—with ventures into the realm of questionable trade and an occasional secret assignment from the War Office that took him across the Channel.

"You might do better to see Pamela well mounted," he said, diverting Robert's thoughts from this old source of contention between them. "I have not seen her on a horse, but I know for a fact she drives to an inch."

The marquess raised an eyebrow. "Indeed?" He suppressed a flash of irritation that his brother knew these details about his wife.

The news surprised him. But then so much about his wife had surprised him over the past few weeks. And last night Pamela had not only surprised him, but delighted him as well. Robert had not counted on delight. Deflowering virgins had never been on the list of things he considered worthy of his attention.

That appeared to have changed. For some odd reason he had found himself listening to her voice at the end of the table during an exceedingly noisy nuncheon, instead of paying attention to the Reverend Mr. James Wakefield, whose discourse on Greek scholarship, on which the vicar was a local authority, had never before failed to intrigue him.

And even now, he found his mind wandering. What was she doing at that very moment? he wondered. Would she continue to avoid him when the family gathered in the drawing room for tea? He was sure that she had ordered his favorite blackberry tarts and William's cherry cake and Letitia's delicate macaroons. His wife knew all their little vices and catered to them shamelessly.

Was she thinking about last night? How could she not? he wondered. It must have been a shock to wake and find him there, waiting to claim what was his.

No, that was not the way it happened. He had been as surprised as she to find himself there, uncertain as a raw youth at his first seduction. Had it not been for that smile, he might not have discovered the delights his wife had offered.

But Pamela had smiled. Tension had unwound inside him, a palpable thing, giving way to a harmony that was entirely new to him. He wished nothing more than to taste that feeling again. And he would, he thought. Tonight . . .

He became aware of his brother's amused glance, and felt himself color. Had his thoughts been that obvious?

A scratching at the door interrupted him, and then the cause of his restlessness stood before him on the threshold.

"Forgive me, my lord," his wife said, her cheeks tinged a delightful pink. "Something of importance has occurred."

She moved gracefully into the library and closed the door.

Geoffrey rose languidly to his feet. "My dear Pamela," he said, his voice exuding charm, "you are a sight for sore eyes, my dear. That gown is particularly fetching on you. Your color exactly."

The marquess glared at his brother, put out that he had not thought to remark on his wife's gown, which was indeed very becoming.

"Well?" he said instead, sounding sharper than he intended. "What has happened to upset you, my lady?"

"An unexpected visitor, my lord," she replied with unnecessary formality. "One I fear will not please you above half."

Robert tried to smile, but a sudden presentiment of disaster turned it into a grimace. "And who is this unwelcome intruder?"

A slight pause before she answered. "My father, Lord Melrose," she said, an audible tremor in her voice.

A longer pause ensued while the marquess recovered his breath. "Your father?" he repeated ominously. "What in blue blazes is he doing here?"

"He wishes to see me."

The marquess exploded. "Well, Firth may tell him that you are not receiving," he growled, his teeth clenched with fury. "How dare he assume that he would be welcome here, on Stilton property?"

In the silence that followed this intemperate speech, Robert noted that his wife's hazel eyes regarded him steadily, filled with compassion. The devil take it, he thought irritably, he did not want her compassion; he wanted her obedience. No bloody bluestocking would dictate to him who was to be received in his own house.

"So, I may not receive my father, my lord? May I know the reason why?" There was no hint of defiance in her voice, but Robert flinched.

He glared at her, willing her to bend to his will, as a decent wife must. "That should be obvious to any ninnyhammer," he said coldly. "Is it not enough that I wish it?"

"Only in your fog-encrusted mind, Robbie," Geoffrey cut in impatiently. "Does it not occur to that benighted brain of yours that Pamela might wish to see her father? And what is so odd about that, after all? Lord Melrose is not here to see *you*."

The marquess reeled under this unexpected attack. He must remember to have a serious talk with his brother about the folly of challenging the traditional authority of the head of the family.

He looked at his wife. "Is this true?" he demanded coldly. "Am I to understand you wish to receive your parent, my lady?" He might just as well have said: *Do you wish to defy me?* for that is what he meant; but Pamela chose to ignore the implied warning.

She actually smiled, reminding Robert forcibly of last night's smile. It transformed her face, softening its rather ordinary features until they glowed with an inner force that baffled him. Its effect was subtle, and it took a moment before Robert experienced the dazzling sensation he had discovered the night before. Enveloping him, weakening his will, subverting his authority . . . turning him into a spineless puppet like his father.

"Oh, yes, Robert," she whispered, demolishing his resistance with the sound of his name. Her smile moved up to overflow from her shining eyes, and the marquess was shocked at the unmistakable tingle of desire that assailed him.

This could not be happening to him, he told himself, torn between outrage and panic. A gentleman did not feel desire for his wife in the middle of the afternoon. And never in public. He was *not* his father.

"But only if it pleases you," she added with the same shyness he remembered from last night. "I need to make my peace with him. I need to know that he truly cares for me."

This revealing confession touched a chord deep in Robert's heart. Over the years he had grown adept at pretending that he did not care whether his mother loved him or not. His father had doted on him; that should have been enough. But of course it never had been. The discovery that his mother had loved another man, a man who was not even his father, had shattered his illusions and turned him into the cynic he was today.

Now this same man had come knocking on his door again, an unpleasant reminder of a painful past. One thing was certain, the marquess vowed silently. If Lord Melrose so much as ruffled one hair on Pamela's innocent head, he would knock the earl's teeth down his throat with the greatest gusto.

"Then by all means receive your father, my dear," he heard himself say mildly. "Geoffrey and I will leave you."

"Oh," Pamela exclaimed, her cheeks pink with embarrassment. "I thought that perhaps . . . p-perhaps Geoffrey . . ."

Robert caught the flash of understanding between them, and he braced for yet another unsettling request.

But it was Geoffrey who spoke. "I believe Pamela is suggesting that we all need to receive Lord Melrose, Robert. Perhaps it is time to learn the truth about the past—particularly *my* past—and lay it to rest."

Whatever the marquess had expected to hear, it was not this preposterous suggestion. He felt himself grow rigid with disapproval.

Before he could speak, however, Pamela seconded his brother's wild proposal. "My father is, after all, the only one who can tell us the truth."

The marquess stared at his brother in disbelief. "And do you honestly wish to know the truth, Geoffrey?" he demanded slowly. "Think carefully before you rush into something from which there will be no turning back."

The library was silent for so long that Robert wondered if he had not perhaps imagined he had actually entertained the notion of discussing his mother's shameless behavior with the instigator of her disgrace.

Eventually, Geoffrey swept away any hope Robert might have had of averting disaster.

"Yes, Pamela is right," his brother agreed, his smile defiant. "It is time to face the truth, Robert. Bring in the trumpets and roll out the red carpet."

His brother's levity grated on his nerves, but Robert reached for the bellpull and jerked it harder than necessary.

When the butler appeared, he gave his order reluctantly.

"Ask Lord Melrose to join us, Firth."

CHAPTER NINETEEN

Past Revisited

The library door clicked shut behind the butler, leaving the room oppressively silent.

Pamela glanced nervously at her husband, mistrusting his granite expression. Had she committed a tactical error in suggesting they receive her father together? she wondered. Was the marquess ready to hear the truth about his mother from the lips of her acknowledged lover? Her own daring at suggesting such a radical notion left her breathless.

Even Lord Geoffrey's smile was slightly forced, but he winked at her, and she recognized his attempt to reassure her. Her heart went out to him.

The noise of the opening door made Pamela jump. Ready or not, she told herself prosaically, the past was about to catch up with them. While her own life had not been irreparably traumatized by the tall gentleman who paused on the threshold to glance around the room, she sensed that there were many corners in her father's past where secrets lurked.

Her eyes flew to Lord Melrose's face, and she was overcome by the need to feel his comforting arms about her again, as she had so often as a little girl. The wave of nostalgia was so palpable that Pamela felt her body sway forward to launch itself onto her father's broad chest.

Then painful reality set in. Her father had given the occupants of the room a perfunctory nod. Then he appeared to freeze, his gaze riveted on Lord Geoffrey, whose face had gone white and still.

Seeing them together for the first time, Pamela's heart constricted. How could anyone doubt that they were father and son? The color of their hair—her father's lightly shot with gray at the temples—was identical, matching her own chestnut curls precisely. The same intense blue eyes—so unlike her own hazel, inherited from her mother, or the traditional Stilton gray—invited the obvious conclusion.

Was this the son her father had always wanted? A son he might have claimed as his own had not fortune, and rank, and a privileged rival suitor stolen it away from him? A son her mother had not been able to give him, whose place Pamela had eventually taken. Or rather never really taken, for she had long been conscious of that empty space in her father's heart, which Freddy, her frivolous cousin, had never been able to fill.

These chaotic thoughts swirled through Pamela's mind as she watched the two men sizing each other up. Had she made a terrible mistake in bringing them together?

She ventured a glance at her husband and was startled to find him regarding her from beneath hooded lids with something oddly akin to compassion. Pamela hoped that her expression had not been too unguarded, revealing too much of her own longing for a father's approval and love.

An involuntary exclamation from Lord Melrose shattered the palpable tension in the room.

"The devil take it, lad," he muttered, his voice hoarse, "you are your mother all over again. I cannot bear it."

He tore his eyes away from Geoffrey and focused them on Pamela—without seeing her, she realized. The pain in them sent a searing jolt through her heart. It was strange to think of her father, that seemingly unassailable tower of strength and authority of her childhood, in the throes of raw emotion. But it was becoming increasingly clear to her that gentlemen, although pretending to deny it, were as capable of deep emotions as any female. Pamela recalled her delighted amazement at her husband's tears of relief at the dowager's recovery.

"That topic is one we try to avoid around here, my lord." The stiffness and patent hostility in the marquess's tone brought Pamela rudely back to the present.

The two men stared at each other for a long moment before she heard her father sigh. "I see no reason for such foolishness. After all, none of this was Pamela's fault."

The shock of hearing her name used for that other woman in her father's life was only exceeded by the blinding certainty— perhaps deliberately suppressed in her mind all these years—that she owed her name to Robert's mother. The connection between them had existed long before she was born. Why had she never acknowledged it before? she wondered. Was it her way of blotting out, much as the marquess had done, an event too soul-wrenching to risk admitting?

The marquess muttered an oath under his breath that caused Pamela to blink and glance apprehensively at her father, who deplored such vulgarities. "A pox on it, man," her husband added viciously. "Do you propose to tell me it was not your fault either, sir? That you were both lily-white?"

"Oh, no, it was my fault, all right," her father responded in a tired voice. "It was *all* my fault. I should have let her go before the whole thing got out of hand."

The marquess snorted in disgust, and Pamela trembled at the rage she saw building in him. "Then why did you not do so?" he demanded harshly. "Thirty years ago you might have saved a woman from sin and disgrace. Only a selfish, depraved coward would not have done so."

A bitter smile flickered across Lord Melrose's still handsome face. "Did it never occur to you, my lord," he responded with a lack of rancor that Pamela had not expected, "that your father might have saved her, too? Had he let her go when she begged him to—she actually got down on her knees, you know—I might have been able to call this lad my son before the world."

For a terrifying instant Pamela thought the marquess would smash his clenched fist into her father's face. With what must have been a superhuman effort, he controlled himself.

"How dare you suggest that my father was anything but the unfortunate victim of a dastardly betrayal?" he snapped. "He was her husband, for God's sake. He had the *right* to expect obedience and loyalty from a wife."

The deep-seated outrage in her husband's voice caused Pamela's heart to shrink. Was he so entrenched in tradition that he could not see, much less admit, how *wrong* some of those so-called rights were?

"Perhaps so," her father continued with a bleak smile. "But did he have the right to break a woman's heart?"

"Poppycock!" the marquess shot back, his tone dripping cynicism. "We are not discussing some maudlin romantical tale from the lending library here, Melrose. The issue is adultery." He pronounced the word as if it were acid on his tongue. "The wanton undermining of an institution upon which the greatness of this country rests."

Pamela sighed. If the marquess insisted upon taking refuge in pomposity and empty platitudes, she might as well wash her hands of him. Where was the tender lover she had discovered last night in her husband's bed? she wondered, averting her eyes from his frozen face. She glanced at Geoffrey and was revived by one of his irrepressible winks. Thank goodness someone besides herself recognized the absurdity of the situation.

"Great Scott, Robert," Geoffrey drawled in a fair imitation of his normal tone, "and here I thought we were talking about our mother's broken heart."

This rampant irreverence appeared to leave the marquess thunderstruck, and it was her father who broke the awkward silence.

"That is the crux of this whole tragedy, lad," he said heavily. "Between them, her father and yours broke the lady's heart by forcing her into a marriage she could not accept. Not that she did not try, of course—"

"A very advantageous marriage, unless memory fails me," the marquess snapped angrily. "What had *you* to offer her? A second son with no prospects whatsoever."

"The lady thought differently."

"You were a fool to trust a female."

The words assaulted Pamela's ears like a clap of thunder, severely shaking all her illusions about her future happiness as this man's wife. She flinched, and her hands fluttered up to her bosom, as if to ward off a physical attack.

"As was my father," the marquess added, as though the admission cost him a great effort. "I shall not fall into the same trap."

Pamela heard herself gasp and felt her eyes prickle with unshed tears. How could he stand there and declare, in front of everyone, that he did not trust her? After last night she had been so full of hopes . . . not that he could ever love her, of course—a man who denied that a woman's heart could break would know nothing of love—but that there might be trust and harmony between them. Now even that small comfort was to be denied her.

The three men stared at her, and Pamela realized that she was on the brink of making a spectacle of herself. Ignoring the two Stiltons, she focused her gaze on her father, straightening her back and willing herself to ignore the pain. She would not embarrass her father, she told herself firmly. She might not be the son he had wished for, but she certainly was a Hancock, a family whose heritage was as ancient and illustrious as any in England. She was every bit a match for any Stilton.

Gamely, she tilted her head, and, repressing the urge to flee in panic from this masculine scrutiny, she assayed a smile. That was a mistake, for her lips trembled uncontrollably.

With a muttered oath quite unlike him, Lord Melrose stepped forward and clasped both her hands, drawing her against his broad chest. The sensation of being rescued from disaster in the nick of time washed over her, and Pamela felt the years drop away as she gave her father a watery smile.

"My dear child," Lord Melrose murmured unsteadily. "I can see I have done you a great wrong." He appeared so upset that Pamela's own grief faded. "How could I not have seen that in forcing you into marriage with this man"—he shot a murderous glance at the marquess—"I have repeated all the mistakes of the past?"

Confused at this sudden turn of events, Pamela stared up at her father blankly, ignoring a muttered imprecation from the marquess.

"Tell me, Pamela, my love, have we broken your heart, too, between the two of us? Did you have it set on that Morton fellow? I should have listened to you, sweetheart. I was a heartless wretch to bully you into a match with a man you despised almost as much as I despised his father."

Pamela was seized with a wild urge to laugh.

There was nothing remotely amusing about the things her father was suggesting. It rather resembled a Canterbury farce, she thought. A droll commedia dell'arte rendition of a stale plot of unrequited love. What maggot had got into her father's mind to trigger such a muddled perception of what had happened? Could he not see that what he had lived thirty years ago with *his* Lady Pamela had little or nothing to do with her own arranged marriage to Lord Monroyal?

There had been love in that unhappy triangle, perhaps too much love, a passionate force that brought disaster to all of them. In both Sir Rodney and the marquess such tender emotion was noticeably absent. And what of herself? A moot question and of little real significance in the scheme of things, Pamela reminded herself. Her father must have windmills in his head to draw the comparison at all. And as for her husband, how could he seriously believe that she was even remotely similar to that unhappy romantic lady who had staked her heart on true love and lost?

Laughter welled up again in her throat, but Pamela knew that if she gave in to it, she would burst into tears. She wished she had listened to her Aunt Rose and learned the art of swooning gracefully at moments of unbearable stress.

"I shall thank you not to fill my wife's head with such maudlin flummery," the marquess snapped impatiently. "That Morton fellow is a Bond Street fribble of the worst kind. And what we did was for the best, as anyone of sense must recognize." He paused, glancing uneasily at Pamela. "And as for bullying you into any-thing, my dear, I have never bullied anyone in my life."

A great hoot of laughter erupted from Geoffrey, who doubled over in a fit of coughing, then flung himself into a chair, his eyes streaming.

Lord Melrose gave an amused grunt and glanced at his host. "I think you have your answer to that bouncer, Monroyal. And need I remind you that Pamela is *my* daughter? My one and only and most cherished child, and I do not need you to tell me . . ."

Pamela did not hear the rest of her father's words. Her mind fastened instinctively on the implications of what he had just ad-mitted.

His *one* and *only* child.

His *only* child.

When the significance sank in, Pamela's gaze flew to Geoffrey, whose sudden hilarity had fled as quickly as it had appeared. He stood up slowly, his face pale, gaze fixed on her father. Fasci-nated, she watched as a confusion of emotions chased one another across his handsome features. His eyes, which she had once thought a replica of her father's, now appeared to have cooled to a blue-gray. Had she been too quick to assume a blood connection? In light of Lord Melrose's startling declaration, they had all been mistaken.

A sudden, uneasy silence settled upon the group gathered in the library, and Pamela knew that the next step might not be taken unless she took a hand in the matter. She looked into her father's eyes.

"What are you telling us, Father?" she murmured, her voice al-most inaudible. She cleared her throat. "Are you saying that Geoffrey is not . . . is n-not . . . ?"

Lord Melrose's brief smile was crooked. "Not my son?" He turned to face the younger Stilton, who had moved over to stand beside his brother.

The silence became oppressive, and Pamela felt perspiration break out on the back of her neck. After what seemed like an eter-nity, he sighed. "If thirty years of wishing might make it so, then I could have said yes, lad," he said, "and God knows I have wished with all my heart that it were so."

He paused to squeeze Pamela's hands absentmindedly, perhaps taking comfort in her presence, she hoped.

"But wishing is never enough, is it? Our past is set in stone. No amount of regret can change that." He paused again, then continued with a touch of bitterness. "So the answer is no, lad. You are not my son."

"How can you be so sure?"

How like her husband to doubt everything and everyone, Pamela thought. Did he trust no one at all?

"Because your mother told me so," Lord Melrose responded, and Pamela knew in her heart that her father had taken a certain perverse pleasure in reminding the marquess that they were talking about his mother.

"And how can you know this to be true?"

Pamela was surprised at her father's grin. "A woman's word is good enough for me," he said softly. "If a man is wise, he learns which females to trust. Besides, I have her last letter, in which she confirms it. Knowing how much I had hoped otherwise, she took the time, during that last week of her life, to set the record straight."

"That letter belongs to her family," Pamela heard the marquess say, but there was an unmistakable tremor in his voice. "I demand—"

"That is one thing you will not take away from me, Monroyal," Lord Melrose cut in sharply. "I was forbidden to attend her funeral, you know. Your father made quite sure of that. But her letter you will not have, take my word for it."

"I would take it as a great kindness were you to allow me to read it, my lord. I have lived in the shadow of scandal for too long."

Pamela looked at the brother she might have claimed as her own had things been different and smiled.

"I am sure that you, of all people, are entitled to know the truth, Geoffrey," she said. "Would you not agree, Father?"

"I have just told him the truth, my dear."

"She was his mother," Pamela insisted gently.

"Very well," Lord Melrose agreed reluctantly. "But Honoria has a copy of it. She could have shared it thirty years ago."

"Lady Honoria?" Pamela gasped, startled at this bizarre news. She stared at her father. "How . . . ?"

But it was Geoffrey who answered, his ready laugh dispelling some of the tension in the room. "I thought you knew, my dear Pamela," he drawled, his blue eyes sparkling with amusement. "Our darling aunt was banished to Holly Lodge thirty years ago when my father discovered she had played a vital role as confidant and instigator in the family scandal. She was bosom-bows with our mother, you know."

Before Pamela could digest this startling piece of news, the library door burst open, and Lady Honoria, her face flushed but determined, stood on the threshold.

"What are you doing to the poor man?" she demanded, indignation ringing in her voice. "I swear you have been locked up here for over an hour. I will not stand by and let you badger poor James to death. Besides, tea is being served, and I have ordered your favorite apricot tarts, James," she added, casting him a look that belied her abrupt tone. "Come with me, at once."

Before Pamela could react, Lady Honoria gestured imperiously, and her father, a bemused look on his face, was whisked out of the room without a backward glance.

"Well, well," Geoffrey said as they listened to Lady Honoria's chatter growing fainter down the hall, "it seems that our dear aunt has not lost her taste for intrigue in the past thirty years."

The marquess stood rooted before the library window, listening to his aunt's excited chatter interspersed by the regular tattoo of Lord Melrose's heels as he accompanied Lady Honoria upstairs to the drawing room.

The earl's startling denial of Geoffrey's paternity had left him feeling drained of emotion. So many years of fearing the worst; of pretending that his brother was not tainted by his mother's shame; that the family honor was miraculously intact in spite of what seemed incontrovertible evidence to the contrary.

Geoffrey was a Stilton after all, as much a legitimate member of their line as he was himself. The relief was slow in coming. The rigid mask he had maintained for so long had cracked, but Robert knew it would take a long time to dissolve. It had become a part of who he was, at least that part of himself he displayed to the *ton*. That bulwark he had thrown up in defense against those vicious rumors.

And it had been his Pamela, his mother's namesake—he saw it clearly now—who had dared to ask that terrifying question.

Could he have asked it himself? he wondered. Could he have endured hearing from the lips of his mother's paramour that her child was a love child. That his beloved brother was—as he had secretly feared all these years—a cuckoo on the illustrious Stilton nest?

The thought troubled him. Had Geoffrey ever guessed at his doubts? Perhaps he should have talked openly with his brother about it, brought it out of the shadows into the light. Perhaps—and the very idea left him suddenly breathless—perhaps he should have trusted their mother.

He shied away from this notion, so contrary to all his male instincts.

His gaze had been fixed on his brother's face, but a gurgle of laughter drew his eyes to his wife.

"Oh, Geoffrey!" she exclaimed, stepping forward impulsively, both arms outstretched. "I know I should be ecstatic for you, and of course I am. You must *know* I am." Her voice wavered. "But I so wanted to have a brother when I was little . . . I know that sounds foolish, but . . ."

She was smiling that special smile, Robert noticed, his heart clenching in his chest. Her hazel eyes glowed with that innocent joy he had discovered in them last night. *His* smile, he thought, conscious of a sneaking loss that she could squander it on another. He brushed the maudlin thought away impatiently.

"Not foolish at all, love," his brother was saying, his voice unsteady, hands grasping Pamela's arms. "I confess the same thought crossed my mind when old Henderson told me what a trouper you are, Pamela. Never so much as turned a hair when he dug that ball out of my shoulder, he said. Steady as a rock. I knew right away you were the kind of female we need in this family. Mama has been carrying the burden for too long."

His voice faltered, and Robert heard his brother swallow hard. Then his arms were about her, and he was clutching Pamela to his chest as if he would never let her go. "And you have that brother you always wanted, love. After what you did for me today, you can count on it. And four more lads out there who will slay dragons for you."

The marquess cleared his throat.

The sight of his wife in another man's arms caused a knot of emotion in his stomach that he could not identify. Jealousy? That was patently absurd. Why would he feel jealousy over Pamela? She meant nothing to him, after all. Well, he corrected himself, not exactly nothing. Actually, she had come to mean a lot of things to him—things he had never looked for in a female before, things he had not expected to find.

The knife seemed to twist more deeply inside him.

If his brother did not take his hands off Pamela this instant, Robert would not answer for his actions. His fists balled at his sides. He could feel himself scowling.

And then it was over, and both of them were regarding him; Geoffrey's clear blue eyes looking right into his soul and seeing the confusion there; Pamela's full of delight and laughter and a tenderness Robert felt the urge to reach out and capture for himself.

As usual it was Geoffrey who broke the tension with his infectious laughter. "It seems we have shocked old sober-sides Robbie again, my dear," he drawled, his slow smile taking the sting out of the words. "But you will have to learn to live with him if you are to gain five real brothers. He's not too impossible once you get used to his overbearing ways."

Pamela's smile wavered, and Robert felt his scowl deepen at his brother's unflattering words.

"Of course, that scowl is enough to drive the most sainted female to run for her life," his irreverent brother added nonchalantly. "But I for one am counting on you staying the course, my dear. It is as plain as a pikestaff that your father is looking for any excuse to carry you off home again, Pamela, but please take pity on us, my dear. We do not wish to lose you, do we, Robbie?"

The notion was so preposterous that Robert answered without thinking. "Pamela's home is here," he said coldly. "She is not going anywhere with her father."

"I presume you mean the Grange, old man," Geoffrey remarked, a faint warning in his voice. "I cannot see a female of Pamela's talents kicking her heels at Holly Lodge for the rest of her life."

And that was the crux of the matter, of course. Robert stared into his wife's eyes, searching for the words he wanted to say but could not find. He saw the eagerness slowly fade, replaced by the cool poise she invariably adopted to mask the hurt he knew he was inflicting upon her.

"There will be time enough for that later," she remarked, flashing a small smile at his brother. "And unless you wish to miss all those apricot tarts your aunt has so obligingly ordered, I suggest we go upstairs to tea immediately."

She slipped a small hand into the crook of Geoffrey's proffered arm; but suddenly Robert had had quite enough of his brother's encroaching ways. He stepped forward and took her other hand, tucking it firmly under his arm.

"You are quite right, my dear," he murmured, deliberately dropping his voice to a seductive level. "Our future together is something you and I must discuss at a more appropriate time."

Her eyes opened wide, as he had known they would, delighting him again with all the things he saw lurking there.

"Later tonight," he could not resist adding, just to show this impudent puppy who was in charge here.

The instant flush that stained his wife's cheeks and the tightening of her fingers on his arm told Robert all he wanted to know.

CHAPTER TWENTY

Vindicated

The marquess was in a pensive mood that evening. He stood by the small fire crackling in the drawing-room hearth, one elbow on the marble mantel, his eyes taking in the lively scene playing out around him.

Dinner in the formal dining room had proceeded without any noticeable awkwardness. He had dreaded, although he had refused to admit it, sitting down to dine with his father's rival. The notion of introducing his mother's paramour into the heart of his family had violated his deep-seated sense of propriety and good taste. But oddly enough, he had not experienced a recurrence of that blinding outrage the memory of Lord Melrose's iniquity was wont to provoke.

Perhaps those terrible memories from the past had softened, become nebulous and confused in his mind as a result of all that had transpired in the last few days. Perhaps the relief that his brother was not the black sheep they had always thought him had lowered his guard, leaving him vulnerable to this odd restlessness he felt. For the first time since he could remember, the future seemed to hold out a promise of something beyond the endless round of gentlemanly pursuits that had formed the center of his existence up to the moment of his unheralded marriage.

It was that inconvenient marriage to the most inconvenient female he could have hoped to encounter that had sent his life reeling off in its present rudderless direction. Robert was unused to feeling out of control. He had been the head of his family for so long that he had fallen into the habit of taking for granted the rightness of his decisions. Perhaps he had grown a trifle arbitrary, he mused, watching his wife's face glow with happiness as she sat at the pianoforte, rendering a medley of jigs that Geoffrey and Letty executed with growing abandon. Had not his brother accused him of pompousness any number of times?

Perhaps Geoffrey was right, as he had been about other things recently. Notably about Pamela. Perhaps this odd restlessness he felt was a logical outcome of the ennui he had experienced in Brighton at the prospect of wasting his time with a contentious little tart instead of enjoying the summer playing cricket with his younger brothers. Perhaps he was entering his dotage after all if playing cricket held more appeal than adding another conquest to a list too numerous to recall.

If that were true—and Robert had to admit the alarming possibility that it was—then he could hardly blame Pamela for upsetting the calm and orderly pattern of his life, could he? She had certainly upset it, in no small measure, but she had also provided a welcome variety. That dust-up with Morton had been satisfying, as had the wild chase up the Brighton Road after the runaways. He smiled at the memory.

But what of the more serious changes his wife had wrought? The vows he had broken on her behalf? Like getting himself well and truly riveted. Or the ten thousand guineas he had paid out long before he had taken her to his bed. And now he was seriously considering installing his wife, the daughter of his father's nemesis, as mistress of Stilton Grange, a move he had sworn most vehemently to avoid.

No, he corrected himself wryly; he was passed the stage of considering it. Pamela's position at the Grange was a foregone conclusion. Why not admit it?

He *wanted* her there. He *wanted* her as his wife, in his bed, in his life. Worse yet, Robert had the sneaking suspicion that he *needed* this unassuming, quietly efficient, sensible female as he had never needed any other woman. It was his wife's sweet smile that had bedazzled him; it so obviously came from her heart and held no guile.

This revelation did not startle him as much as it might have done a few weeks earlier. Watching the deft way she had handled the recent emergency of the dowager's indisposition, how effortlessly she had played hostess at an awkward dinner table, Robert had to admit that she was right for the role.

He suddenly knew in his bones that Pamela was the right wife for him. The only wife. Everybody had told him so. Watching her across the room, Robert wondered why he had not seen it before.

Without warning, Lady Pamela caught his gaze and a faint blush touched her cheeks. The silent message that passed between them pleased him immeasurably, and he suddenly understood something of what Pamela had tried to tell him about that stranger across the room. The sensation was indeed a little like jumping off a cliff, he thought wryly, although he might not have described it thus had she not done so first.

Then she smiled at him. The smile made the now familiar trajectory from her lips to her eyes, dazzling him with its sweetness.

Quite irrationally, Robert felt the urge to ring for Firth to bring in the tea-tray. Once that formality was over with, the party might start to disperse. The dowager would wish to retire early, and Pamela would accompany her.

And shortly thereafter, Robert told himself, conscious of his own growing excitement, he would be able to visit his wife again.

There were certain things he needed to tell her.

The disturbing events of the day had left Pamela with little desire to sleep. The smoldering look the marquess had given her across the room just before Firth brought in the tea-tray had not helped, of course. It had set her blood racing and her imagination bouncing around into all sorts of unlikely fantasies. It had taken every ounce of her rapidly dwindling self-control to tackle the heavy silver tea-pot and pass the delicate porcelain cups around as though this were another ordinary evening *en famille*.

It was no such thing, of course.

Not with her father and husband in the same drawing room together. Dinner had passed off relatively smoothly, but Pamela had dreaded the chances of conflict between the two men in the informal setting of an after-dinner gathering.

"You worry too much, love," Geoffrey had said with his engaging smile during a lull in the jig dancing that Letty had insisted upon. "If Robbie did not draw your father's cork in the library—and I confess that for a moment I was afraid he would—then he will not do so in the drawing room. He is a stickler for propriety, as I think you may have guessed by now. But at the moment, I suspect he is reeling under the shock of seeing your father in his drawing room at all."

"I trust your brother will not hold me responsible for enticing my father to visit me," Pamela murmured with a worried frown. "I would not wish him to imagine I am about to run away again."

Geoffrey appeared to find this notion amusing. "It might not be a bad idea if he did," he said callously. "Something that shattering might well jolt him out of his complacency. Remind him that faint heart never won fair lady."

"Now you are being absurd, Geoffrey," she replied, startled and not a little amused herself at the picture of the marquess being faint of heart.

Letty appeared at that moment to drag her brother back onto the floor for another jig, but Pamela spent the rest of the evening wondering how she might convince her husband that she had no intention of running away from him again. Ever.

Her heart had made it abundantly clear that afternoon in the library that her happiness lay here with him. He could be overbearing at times, and often pompous when he felt threatened; but her husband had shown her that beneath his harsh exterior there was a man she could love. She *did* love. And somehow, as yet Pamela was not quite sure how, she would make Robert see that he needed, perhaps even loved, her, too.

But hours later, as the clock downstairs struck two loud chimes that rang through the silent house, Pamela wondered if perhaps her own enthusiasm had betrayed her. Perhaps she had misread her husband's interest.

She glanced down at the open diary in her lap, her eyes skimming the entry for the day before. As yet she had lacked the daring to record the magical moments of last night. They were still too incredibly real, too intimate, too precious; but she remembered every single word he had spoken, every move the marquess had made. Every touch. Every kiss. Every . . .

Resolutely, she took up her quill and dipped it in the inkwell on the rosewood table beside her. She shook off the excess ink and placed the tip of the quill on the pristine white page. It seemed fitting to start a fresh page to record her initiation into womanhood, into the mysteries of becoming a wife and perhaps a mother.

The idea of motherhood took hold of her imagination, and Pamela smiled. She had never given it much thought before, but now she realized that after last night, she had taken a very real step in that direction. Surprised at the glow of contentment that spread through her whole body, Pamela forced herself to be practical. She had no very exact notion of how such miracles worked, but she did know that some women—her own mother was one of them—spent years praying for a child who did not come. Others, like the dowager, seemed to be as fertile as the fragrant meadows in springtime.

Pamela felt her smile soften. She leaned her head back against the cushions, closing her eyes. She would pray that the Stilton line held strong, and that she would follow in the dowager's footsteps, producing not only the heir required of her, but a troop of little black-haired, gray-eyed cupids who would proclaim to all the world—in that aspect at least—Robert was all hers.

She felt her cheeks grow warm at the thought.

"What naughty thoughts are you thinking, my dear, to bring that color to your face?"

Pamela jerked upright. She had been so engrossed in day-dreaming that she had not heard the door open.

The marquess stood beside her elegant brocade chaise longue, looking down at her with an enigmatic smile on his lean face. The firelight glittered in his eyes, giving them a devilish cast.

Her blush deepened. She would die rather than admit that she had been dreaming of children. His children.

She glanced around nervously before her eyes settled on the blank page of her diary. "I was merely putting my diary up to date, my lord," she murmured.

"You appear to have a difficult time remembering anything," he remarked gently. "What is your last entry?"

Wondering where this was leading, Pamela answered truthfully. "Lady Sophia's recovery, I believe."

A slow smile moved from his lips up into his eyes, reminding Pamela that this man had been a charming rake long before she was out of the schoolroom. Even now he was charming her, mesmerizing her with his warm voice, his speaking glance. It was then she noticed that the marquess was wearing neither coat nor cravat. His disheveled appearance reminded her forcefully of that afternoon in the seaside cottage where their destinies had become irrevocably intertwined.

"Ah, then you still have some important entries to make, my dear," he said, his voice teasing. "Or can it be that you do not re-call the precise sequence of events?"

Astounded that he could imagine she would ever forget, Pamela groped for words. None came, of course, and even if they had, how could she bring herself to speak of such things?

His smile became positively wicked. "I see that I have hit on the mark. Perhaps I can help to jog your memory, my dear." Without further ado, he sat down on the edge of the chaise longue, his hip pressing against her. Casually, he rested a hand on her knee and gazed innocently down at her. The intimate gesture reminded Pamela that she was dressed for bed in her own cotton night-rail and robe. Unlike the transparent gossamer confection of the night before, it covered her from throat to ankle.

"Tell me, Pamela, what is it exactly you cannot recall about last night?"

Pamela swallowed hard and lowered her gaze. "I c-can remember everything q-quite well, thank you, my lord," she said, hating the telltale quaver in her voice.

"Then what were you thinking about sitting here with that sphinxy smile on your face?" He paused, and Pamela saw his smile fade. "Not contemplating running off again, are you, my dear? Your father has not been filling your head with that nonsense, has he?"

Alarmed at the edge in his tone, Pamela sat up and closed her diary. She set it, together with the now dry quill, on the table.

"Not at all," she said calmly. "I have convinced my father that all is well with me. He had heard that I was here alone, you see, abandoned, if you will—"

"You were," the marquess interrupted brusquely. "I have made a lot of mistakes in my time, but Geoffrey tells me that was the most cow-handed to date." He paused, as though disconcerted to find himself admitting that the Marquess of Monroyal had committed an error of judgment. Pamela wondered if she would have to be content with this indirect apology, but he surprised her.

"Your father was right, Pamela. I had vowed to exclude you from my life. Punish you for sins you had not committed." He stopped abruptly, and Pamela could only guess at the effort this confession had cost him.

He reached for her hand and carried it to his lips. "But when I take you home to the Grange, I will make it up to you, Pamela, I swear it." He pressed a kiss to her palm, causing the most delightful sensation to tingle up and down her spine. "Now, let us get back to your diary, love. I propose to add another page to it, with variations, of course."

So saying he put his hands around her waist and picked her up, swinging her onto the floor. Before she knew what he was about, Pamela felt her robe slither off her shoulders and drop in a pool at her feet.

"Well," he murmured, raking her with amused eyes. "What have we here?"

Pamela looked down at herself, vaguely dissatisfied with the spinsterish cotton gown with its unpretentious ruff around the hem, embellished with tiny pink rosebuds.

"This is *mine*," she said, rather defensively, as if daring him to find fault with her modesty.

"So I see, my love," he said, his voice dropping into a throaty growl that made Pamela's heart flip violently in her breast. "And very delightful it is, too. But you cannot hide from me, my dear." Before she realized what the rogue was about to do, he reached out to encircle her breast in a warm palm. The other hand slipped around her waist and drew her against him.

With a small sigh Pamela allowed herself to sink against his chest. He cradled her there, resting his chin briefly on the top of her head. When nothing else happened, she grew wary, braced for disappointment. Where was the passion she had dreamed of in such moments as these? Had she dampened his ardor with this very proper night-rail?

But no, she told herself firmly, his heart was racing; she could hear it plainly. Then his hand began to caress her back, and Pamela imagined she heard the angels sing.

"So," he murmured against her ear, "you told your father you are happy here?" His fingers cupped her chin and turned her face up until their eyes met.

"I do not believe I used those precise words," she replied honestly.

For the space of a heartbeat he stared at her, and Pamela was startled to see a flicker of fear in his eyes.

"You are *not* happy? Is that it?"

With sudden clarity Pamela sensed the uncertainty behind these words. For reasons not immediately clear to her, her happiness had become important to this enigmatic gentleman she had married. A cheering thought, although she had dreamed of so much more.

"I am sure I never said so," she assured him, giving him her tenderest, most revealing smile that must surely lay bare the secret of her heart for even a slow-top like the Marquess of Monroyal to see.

He must have detected something, for Pamela saw the fire return to his eyes. She smiled again, willing him to kiss her. When he did, brushing her lips lightly before taking full and enthusiastic possession of them, she was delighted. How easy this was, she marveled, snuggling up against him until he groaned.

"What can I do to make you truly happy, my love?"

The question was so unexpected that Pamela caught her breath, glancing up at him to make sure he was serious.

A dozen impulsive answers trembled on her lips, but Pamela resisted the urge to blurt them all out. How could she tell this husband of hers that she loved him? That she wanted his love in return? Wanted him to tell her so a hundred times a day. And tell her so again at night? To tell her *now*?

She could not say any of these things, of course. Not yet, in any case. After all, love was not a treat one handed out like raspberry tarts at a tea-party. It had to spring up on its own, as hers had done for this man she had thought she would despise forever.

Speaking of it might inhibit the growth of the undeniable affection she could see in his eyes.

Long ago her mother had impressed upon her that gentlemen shied away from such emotional truths. They preferred to believe they were unaffected by matters of the heart. Among themselves they probably scoffed at any mention of love; Pamela had been convinced of it.

But now she knew differently.

Her husband's eyes were telling her so. It would only be a matter of time, she knew it instinctively, before he learned to put a name to his feelings for her.

"I think," she said slowly, making a show of answering his question honestly if not fully, "that I could be happy if you trusted me, Robert."

He looked nonplussed, and Pamela wondered if her husband was remembering the cruel cut he had thrown at her that very afternoon in the library. Had he meant that no women were to be trusted? She hoped not, for his trust was so much of what she craved. "I had expected you to ask for—"

"I can well imagine what you expected, my lord," she interrupted with a small smile. "You expected me to demand expensive jewels, satin gowns, visits to the opera, a carriage of my very own—"

"You shall have them all," he murmured, a suspiciously besotted look on his face.

"—when actually," Pamela continued as though he had not interrupted, "I was wondering about the nursery at the Grange."

That caught his attention, for he released her a fraction. "What about the nursery at the Grange?" he repeated, although Pamela saw from his grin that he had understood her perfectly. Perhaps her husband was not such a slow-top as Geoffrey had claimed.

"I was just wondering," she murmured, suddenly losing her nerve. "I am sure it will be adequate," she added lamely, wishing she had not ventured into such suggestive ground.

She felt his rumble of amusement against her breast as he pulled her hard against him. "I am sure it will be, love. And we can always add another wing if we get carried away."

It was Pamela's turn to be amused. "You are being absurd, my lord," she protested, secretly delighted to discover this streak of whimsy.

"Not a bit of it," he whispered into her ear. "Merely practical, my dear. And speaking of practical, I seem to remember promising to help you write your diary, Pamela." He picked her up and cradled her in his arms. "I think that calls for some immediate action of a quite specific nature, would you not agree?"

This, Pamela admitted shamelessly, was what she had been waiting for all day. "Yes, indeed you did, Robert," she said with no hesitation whatsoever. "Make that promise, I mean. And yes, I do agree that those blank pages need to be filled—"

His crack of delighted laughter caused her to blush as the implications of her naive remark sank in. He laid her on the turned-down bed and with the practiced ease of an experienced lover—a point that was not lost on Pamela—stripped off his clothes and joined her.

He leaned over her, gray eyes tender in the candlelight. "You are a delight, my love," he murmured unevenly as she reached up to draw him down into her eager arms.

In the long, languorous hours of that second night together, Pamela discovered just how delightful she was to her husband. And by the time the dawn began to filter through the curtains, and the martins launched their twittering in the eaves outside their window, Pamela knew that the Marquess of Monroyal, contrary to every wager in the book, had given her much more of himself than he was yet ready to admit.

She held the certainty of that love deep in her heart.

DANGEROUS DESIRE

☐ **DIAMOND IN THE ROUGH by Suzanne Simmons.** Juliet Jones, New York's richest heiress, could have her pick of suitors. But she was holding out for a treasure of a different kind: a husband who would love her for more than just her money. Lawrence, the eighth Duke of Deakin, needed to wed a wealthy American to save his ancestral estate. Now these two warring opposites are bound together in a marriage of convenience.

(403843—$4.99)

☐ **FALLING STARS by Anita Mills.** In a game of danger and desire where the stakes are shockingly high, the key cards are hidden, and love holds the final startling trump, Kate Winstead must choose between a husband she does not trust and a libertine lord who makes her doubt herself.

(403657—$4.99)

☐ **SWEET AWAKENING by Marjorie Farrell.** Lord Justin Rainsborough dazzled lovely Lady Clare Dysart with his charm and intoxicated her with his passion. Only when she was bound to him in wedlock did she discover his violent side . . . the side of him that led to his violent demise. Lord Giles Whitton, Clare's childhood friend, was the complete opposite of Justin. But it would take a miracle to make her feel anew the sweet heat of desire—a miracle called love.

(404920—$4.99)

Prices slightly higher in Canada

Buy them at your local bookstore or use this convenient coupon for ordering.

PENGUIN USA
P.O. Box 999 — Dept. #17109
Bergenfield, New Jersey 07621

Please send me the books I have checked above.
I am enclosing $_____ (please add $2.00 to cover postage and handling). Send check or money order (no cash or C.O.D.'s) or charge by Mastercard or VISA (with a $15.00 minimum). Prices and numbers are subject to change without notice.

Card #_____ Exp. Date _____
Signature_____
Name_____
Address_____
City _____ State _____ Zip Code _____

For faster service when ordering by credit card call **1-800-253-6476**

Allow a minimum of 4-6 weeks for delivery. This offer is subject to change without notice.